SHADOWS OF AVARICE

SHADOWS OF AVARICE

Ron Goodman

HALLMARK PRESS

Published by Hallmark Press International Ltd
34 Lambton Court,
Peterlee,
County Durham
SR8 1NG

Typeset by TW Typesetting, Plymouth, Devon

Printed by Antony Rowe, Eastbourne

ISBN 978 1 906459 09 3

To Eileen

If life were a wall, she would be its foundation.

(Anon)

ACKNOWLEDGEMENTS

Criticism corrects the paths of writers so it is proper to thank those who make valid criticisms as well as those who praise.

In which case, I thank my friend George Bailey who had the courage to struggle through the first draft, to Davinda Sharma who corrected my Indian mistakes, to John King who queries everything he reads, and does so to good effect, and to Vic Lowman who had no doubt there was some talent somewhere. I hope he is right.

To Vic

with Best wishes

and thanks

Ron G.

DISCLAIMER

I'm sure there are characters like some of these in the world, I am equally sure there are similar places and organisations that care for kids as these fictional people do. If any are the same, it is an amazing coincidence. So far as I am concerned those in the novel do not exist and although similar characteristics are present in many people, these are all figments of my imagination.

I did visit places in India that resembled the setting but India is a beautiful country and places described in the novel are representative of parts that I may have seen and not one particular place. To my knowledge there is no such town as Amitar nor an organisation called Orphindi.

Ron Goodman.

LIST OF CHARACTERS

John Prichard	Founder of a charity for boys in India
Sanjay Parmar	Manager of the boys' camp and Prichard's former lover
Kumar	Camp inmate and Prichard's current lover
Dhankar Mitra	Millionaire businessman, money lender and political candidate
Shankar Joshi	Local police chief
Shamin Jha	Camp secretary
Harbens Mahmood	Local businessman and hotel owner
Tony and Samantha Baker Andrew and Hillary	British tourists
Ashook Grewall	Former manager of the boys' camp
Kenneth, Anil and Samuel	Camp inmates and schoolchildren
Kashi Sharma	Local Council's chief construction engineer
Rasa Punja	Headmaster
Ahmed Jaitley	Ex-jailbird and clothing factory manager
Vijay and Sunil	Former inmates and tour guides
Graham Prichard and Nadeen	Prichard's brother and his partner

ONE

Tamil Nadu province, Southern India

Crouched low over the handlebars the Tamil opened the throttle fully in his effort to reach the camp on time. Five hundred cc of power thrust him forward into cold, chilling air leaving behind a whirlwind of dust and rubbish as he raced past peanut bushes and banana plants edging the roadside, where the uneven tarmac merged with the dusty shoulder.

A swift look at his watch showed three thirty; half an hour, would he make it, would he be waiting? The arrangements could not have been simpler, four, four, four, the fourth of the fourth at four AM – would he be there? They'd had little contact, letters were intercepted and there were no telephones, leaving no other way to communicate except visit, and that jeopardised security.

'Security?' he sneered at the thought, he'd be better off anywhere but there and free from abuse!

Gripping the throttle one handed, he struggled to pull up the zip of his billowing jacket and hit a pothole. He yelled, snatched at the bars to control a violent wobble and settled the bike again before flipping the throttle. He gripped firmly, driving the bike forward at eighty, sweeping past tilled fields and tea plantations until forced to slow by a bank of low mist that spilled worryingly from a lake.

He cursed and switched on the main beam; it reflected back.

'For the sake of Krishna!' he swore and switched off.

At reduced speed now, he strained half-closed eyes in the chilly air, gambling in the blanket of fog. The mist thinned, he upped his speed again and glimpsed the taller structures of Amitar straight ahead, disorderly and squalid, silhouetted against the beginnings of a brightening sky and just visible above the low lying heat haze that covered the open plain before him.

In minutes he entered the town shaking, after scraping the side of an unlit, oncoming truck.

Amitar, as ever, looked dilapidated; dirty streets, vagrants on temple steps and empty stalls. The signs of daytime trading had gone

1

and rats scavenged the square. Nothing was clean or smart with the exception of Linkers Bank, a building of colonial appearance sporting a sign that said, 'The Bank That Cares'. Looking around he shook his head in dismay, for whom did it care he wondered, certainly not his boys, who were taught never to encourage vermin with litter.

Passing the hotel brought unpleasant memories of the owner, Mahmood, he should have reported his suspicions to the police but would the new inspector, Joshi, have believed him after the manner of his departure, he would have been too busy settling in to deal with the trauma of one individual – especially one due for release. No, this option was chancier – but better than risking a suicide.

Leaving the town behind, he zipped along a newly laid stretch of black tarmac shining like a silver ribbon under a brilliant moon, slowing where rice, spread for de-husking by trucks, made the surface treacherous.

Once past, on buzzing tyres, he urged the machine to its limit, forcing a strangled shriek from the exhaust. He saw the bell-mouth of the slip road, slowed and swung right. Ten yards in the tarmac ended and, in stingy light, he passed under silent, motionless palms, dodging fallen coconuts littering the familiar path, pulling constantly at the clutch.

In miserly light he was able to see larger obstacles now and, knowing he was near his objective he slowed further and checked his watch again. Three minutes to go, would he be there?

He peered along the grassy track, and, keeping right at the fork he shut the power down. The engine grumbled and then burbled quietly as if aware of the need for silence, he switched off the beam and searched ahead. The broken perimeter fence came slowly into view and a figure, keeping low, crept cautiously from concealment.

Smiling with relief the Tamil slowed to a crawl, but before he stopped the machine completely, the anxious youth leapt on the pillion, balanced precariously while he turned the Honda and grinned broadly as they raced back to Amitar.

Not a word had passed between them.

TWO

In the foothills of the Western Gnats, bordering Kerala and Tamil Nadu in Southern India, an elevated, double fronted bungalow stood, isolated, two hundred yards from a placid lake that shimmered in scorching heat. To the east, south, and west, high mountains protected residents from the searing sun part of the day and a trellised central pergola covered in leafy plants and an abundance of flowers provided much needed shade for the remainder.

Six mesh-covered doors and windows were shut firmly against animals, snakes and intruding insects, three each side, where wide steps to the front met the single path leading to a lake. Over the steps hung a sign and letters, crudely burned into an unpolished, angled slice, cut from an acacia stump, declared the house name, 'Paradise Lake', the home of John Prichard.

A second track from the other side of the building rambled north, through steep, rocky hillocks over red, dusty earth covered with a mixture of paw prints, foot prints, tyre tracks and slithery lines, indicating use by vehicles, animals, reptiles and humans. Used as the principal entrance it began and ended the single route towards a new tarmac road two miles away, the only vehicular route to the busy agricultural town of Amitar.

Beneath the pergola, three men and two women chatted over gins and tonics around a low, unsteady rattan table, not noticing the twilight shadows beyond the lake that climbed the eastern mountains and turned the foothills a smoky blue, a daily ritual and nature's conjuring act that made mountains disappear nightly until the appearance of the moon.

Four of the five were tourists, on their first trip to India, perspiring on the hottest day they had ever experienced. The other, seated at the head, was John Prichard, a large, solid man of sixty odd, dressed casually in shorts, a damp-in-places tee shirt and sandals. His hair was thick iron grey and bushy eyebrows appeared glued to a fleshy face. His lips hardly moved when he spoke but his mouth lifted at the corners, giving the impression of a permanent smile, and when he laughed, a rare occurrence, his jowls wobbled. The smile, an action of utter insincerity noticed only by the observant, never quite reached his eyes and veiled his habit of summing up the nuisance potential of guests. Under that he concealed displeasure for the loss of privacy and anxiety over the doubtful rewards of his new venture into tourism.

The privacy and nuisance issues vexed him, but he was prepared to put up with that provided the final reward was worth the last eighteen months of effort; he'd find out this Friday at a meeting with his accountants, then, perhaps, his uneasiness would disappear, although that, and his temper, usually worsened after meeting them.

At his elbow Kumar, a handsome, bare-chested teenager, unaffected by the sweltering, sweaty heat, stood passive and watchful in his skirt-like dhoti. He responded deferentially to John's silent eye contact with obedient glides to replenish glasses from a large white jug. John watched him, envious that age had diminished most of the intimate, personal, benefits he'd enjoyed as a younger man. Although Kumar helped fill that gap – to a point.

He watched the youth carefully who, not surprisingly to him, paid little attention to Samantha, a black haired beauty clearly intent on attracting his interest. Instead, and to her apparent chagrin, he stared indiscreetly at Hillary, a petite, sandy haired woman of about thirty with strawberry blonde locks that reached her shoulders. She appeared to John somewhat haughty with, it appeared, an avid interest in gardening.

His guess was confirmed when she looked up at the canopy. 'Bougainvillea and oleander simply will not grow in Richmond,' she said. 'Are you the gardener here, Mr Prichard?'

'No, it's the boys' doing,' he said with practised modesty, prepared for inevitable questions. After all, looking after two hundred boys was unique and begged enquiry. He was usually able to satisfy the intrusively inquisitive, with a brief description of his arrival in the sixties when, he said, saddened by the deprivation, he sold his UK home and set up a camp on scrounged land and encouraged the lads to built their own shacks of mud and rush matting. It became their camp, they called it Orphindi and they all lived on the proceeds of the sale of his house.

What he told the visitors was not necessarily the truth but a calculated romantic version, coloured specifically for tourists. 'We are two hundred strong now,' he said with a touch of pride. Yes, they were educated until fourteen, yes he'd built a school, yes, he tried to make them self sufficient, yes life was raw but they survived and yes, they were always short of money. 'In fact, I have just returned after a begging expedition to schools in Europe,' he said. 'It's the main source of our income at present and my hope is that tourism will help.'

Andrew, a tall, inquisitive Scotsman with hair the colour of cinnamon probed about costs, expenses and other income – a little too much for John's liking – but aware of the implications of divulging too much information, John asked casually, 'Are you an accountant Andrew?'

'Aye,' he said.

John nodded wisely. He disliked accountants; they were all the same. His own were fastidious and inquisitive, they were like butchers summing up a cow for slaughter or undertakers measuring a corpse, only with cash, devious bastards all of them, so he used diversion.

'Our farm supports us, we have become partly self sufficient, chickens, ducks, goats that sort of thing, we stick to livestock. If we are ever caught short we can eat our stock,' he said, to laughter.

'We also make . . .' he was going to say 'tripper trash' but changed his mind, '. . . trinkets in the camp workshop. I'll show you some later.'

Hillary thought him, 'terribly brave' to undertake such a 'daunting task' and in turn he amused them with embroidered tales of his mugging on arrival in Maroutai, how he followed the gang of scavengers, led by Sanjay, now his senior man, to a rat infested shelter and befriended them. 'The boys,' he said with a grin, 'not the rats; the poverty was awful.' He brought tears to the women's eyes recounting the moment an emaciated little mite stared with lifeless eyes at him before she died in his arms.

They had no way of knowing he was telling the truth but that story was fact and truer than his claim to have been a lay preacher. A godly background, he felt, drew respect, and people rarely probed the past of men of the cloth. Anyway, respectability added to his ring of protection.

His generosity and care was such that when the local authority found he was doing their work, they stayed away, to his annoyance, and left the responsibility entirely to him. They contributed little, refusing help to extend the path beyond the camp to the bungalow, leaving the very track he needed to carry tourists, hazardous.

Any contribution from the council carried a penalty. It was only when he embarrassed them, through the local press, claiming that Europeans did more for his children than they did, that he received a grant to build the camp workshops. It was a war, but he won that battle, the surplus cash was not enough to extend the road but it doubled the size of his bungalow, though even that was at a cost. They imposed a committee to monitor his progress; he cheated a bit and recruited friends and acquaintances. That thwarted them for a while, but they retaliated and imposed a hostile sneak.

John spoke in Tamil to Kumar; the lights came on.

He held in reserve scathing thoughts about the church when Hillary asked if his church helped; she found it 'such a comfort'. She seemed to grimace at the lack of divine intervention, when he told her it refused help, despite awareness of the kid's rat-bitten bodies.

Conversation ceased for a moment as the surroundings darkened, and only the sound of chirring crickets broke the silence. He wondered for a moment if he had upset Hillary's obvious faith and diplomatically pacified her saying that it was not always expedient to follow church doctrine, in extreme circumstances, 'justified dishonesty was acceptable!' At times even he was forced to use other means.

'Other means?' said Samantha, raising a single, inquisitive eyebrow attractively and lifting her sunglasses to rest them on her hair in a new, rather pretentious, fashion.

'Yes,' he said, 'we ... sort of ... er ... purloined things,' he stammered with apparent embarrassment.

'And ... er ... what sort of ... er ... things did you ... er ... purloin John?' she said teasing, with a passable impersonation and an impertinent laugh.

'Well,' he said, 'Sanjay pinched stuff from market stalls, trinkets and so on and sold it to tourists and ... well ... you know how things develop. We, sort of, "acquired" chickens, goats or anything that we could eat or sell. Once he came back with a water buffalo!'

'A what!' she said with an understanding grin. 'I bet he didn't tuck that under his arm!'

He looked at her for a moment, noting how remarkably attractive she was. 'No,' he said and paused reflectively, 'we bred from her. Got a herd now,' he mused.

He looked down at his drink, sensing their sympathy and admiration. 'However,' he said looking up, 'enough about us, you will want to know what to expect in India ...'

They listened intently to his descriptions of temples, forts, architecture; hills of saffron-bearing crocuses, abject poverty and lavish riches. He warned of curry. 'Garam masala tends to be warm,' he said, and corrected himself. 'No, I tell a lie,' he said in a practised ritual, drawing expected laughter, 'it will blow your head off!'

He warned of traffic pollution, river pollution, upsetting poverty, grime, heat, dust and breathtaking beauty. 'Take plenty of water, wear hats and ... watch that table!' he warned, as a leg knocked it, sending gin and tonic slopping over rims of glasses.

The bulb's glow had started to attract midges and moths that flitted towards the brightness only to be swooped on by resident bats.

'Hungry?' he said.

'Very appropriate,' laughed Samantha.

John smiled, stood, turned and muttered something in Tamil to Kumar, sending him swiftly towards the steps leading to the roof, watched by Samantha who studied him closely, admiringly, as he passed, clearly unaware that Kumar was ... well it's best to keep one's personal preferences aside, some people would not be happy ...

He liked this group, they seemed amused by him, found pleasure in simplicity, were tolerant in the absence of sophistication, but most of all they brought in cash – and he was always desperate for that.

* * *

Seated at the elegantly laid table on the flat roof and lit only by moonlight, the cutlery and glasses sparkled with tiny lightning-like flashes as they ate. John watched Tony, Samantha's husband, watch her watching Kumar. She seemed unable to take her eyes off him, switching her gaze from his head to his feet.

'He's very handsome,' she whispered.

John smiled. 'He is, Samantha.'

'Please don't call me that, it sounds like a reprimand – at least, it does when he says it,' she nodded scornfully towards Tony, 'the name's Sam. By the way, what does "Namaste" mean? I heard it on our way down ... from ... Cochin ...' she said, punctuating the sentence with pauses while her eyes followed Kumar.

'Well,' started John, 'it's bad manners to ...' and stopped to observe while her attention centred on Kumar again.

She'd not heard; her dark glasses concealed her eyes but not her admiration as she feasted on Kumar's movements. Her looks swept from his head and naked upper half, down his dhoti to his naked feet.

Tony fixed John with amused, twinkling eyes. 'You were saying,' he prompted loudly, 'something about bad manners ...'

She threw him a disdainful look, and swivelled her head towards John. 'What's that skirt thing he wears?' she asked, unaffected.

'A dhoti, sometimes a lunghi, Sam. That's the one tucked between their knees.'

'Mmm – sexy aren't they?'

7

'You would think of something like that Samantha!'

'There you are!' she said triumphantly – smirking, 'Samantha! See what I mean John, a rebuke?'

John smiled and Tony raised tolerant eyes heavenwards.

Kumar lingered at Hillary's side. 'No thank you ... I ... er ... thank you ... er ... um ...' she stammered.

'Kumar, his name is Kumar,' Sam whispered, as Kumar's eyes again fixed on the sandy hair that curled loosely to Hillary's shoulders.

John turned his attention back to Sam, running his eyes over her discreetly.

Buxom? No that would be unfair, voluptuous and sensuously attractive, indeed! About five feet six tall with strong bone structure, her long shapely legs, topped by curves and dark good looks would turn men's heads. Good teeth gleamed when she smiled, which was often and, melon shaped eyebrows, over caramel coloured eyes set into a broad face surrounded by curly hair that stopped short of her shoulders accentuated a longish neck. She was extremely attractive and would have no trouble magnetising males even without the short skirt and tops that ended a less than discreet distance below her ample bust.

John suspected that she liked showing off, reciprocated admiration and hated contempt. She was frivolous and likeable – if you like that sort of thing – in an unusual combination of brashness and sensitivity. He felt justified in his analysis when she looked up at Kumar and subtly drew her shoulders back to enhance the prominence of her bust.

Her sense of humour too was refreshing, cutting, perhaps, with Tony, but amusing. It surfaced when Tony said, as predicted by her earlier, that he would eventually mention his dad's stint in India during the war. With a giggle, she called him Britain's last hope. 'Without him,' she said, 'the war would have been over in two years.'

Tony's reaction was to close his eyes in what looked like a prayer for help, and slowly shake his head.

They seemed well matched and John gleaned that what Tony had learned in the way of speech and manners, he'd learned from Sam. His circumstances and education had not been the best and although his cockney accent was not polished it excluded the coarse, 'wiv and bowf' so common in Londoners, although slang, inbred from youth, still crept into his sentences.

He seemed tolerant and forthright and, from the earlier conversation, John gathered that he was a city dealer. He was not sure what that meant but from his memory of the London stock market, there was a lot of uncouth shouting. That suited too, as did the impression of covert shrewdness and intelligence. He needed that to cope with Sam, who was as sharp as a tack.

Tony's legs were quite short for a six-footer, 'footballers legs' the kids at his old school in Wiltshire would have called them, and out of proportion with his long body. Athletic, with sparkling grey eyes and a fresh, healthy pink glow on his round face combined to make him good looking, despite a tonsure-like baldness. John concluded that he was about thirty and, from his complexion, he would need warning about the sun again.

People were not always comfortable with John's preferences, his father wasn't, and he met Sam's question about his family with another prepared sympathy card.

'Sadly none Sam,' he said softly, 'my wife and son died in childbirth.'

She seemed to cringe and received a disapproving scowl from Tony, who swiftly asked about retirement.

John chuckled that he would be happy to join the ranks of the great rocking chair proletariat, but, with plughole economics like his, and no immediate deputy, he had no chance of living in Switzerland, his land of dreams.

'Why Switzerland?'

'It's cool, snowy and dust free, Sam.'

'So is the Arctic, but I wouldn't want to live *there*,' retorted Sam.

He smiled and sneaked a sideways glance at Hillary who was quietly reprimanding Andrew for patting his brow with a handkerchief. She rummaged in her bag.

'Here darling, use this tissue,' she said in a harsh whisper, 'I bought them when we touched down in Goa.'

Andrew swiftly hid the handkerchief and took the tissue, passed along by Sam who, with a giggle and a conspiratorial smile, said it was like finessing the queen in a game of bridge.

'How old is he?' she whispered nodding towards Kumar.

'No need to whisper Sam, he speaks only Tamil. He's nineteen we believe, not sure really, his parents were killed in a car crash and his only relative is an old aunt whom he sees weekly and . . .'

He stopped speaking, amused again at her body language that sought hope for contact as Kumar moved to her side. She leaned forward this time and folded her arms to expose more of her cleavage while the eager look of hope never left her face. With chin lifted, she stared, eyes wide open, lips parted in an enticing smile.

'Thank – you Kumar,' she beaming at him.

Tony shook his head indulgently and grinned, 'Hot here ain'it John?'

He returned a knowing smile, saying diplomatically, 'Yes, make sure you wear your hat tomorrow.'

'We always take precautions,' said Hillary self-righteously.

'John didn't mean that!' said Sam, chuckling loudly.

THREE

Sam had seen no evidence of his sixty years as she followed the six feet two figure to the roof. There was still a youthful mobility in the flexed muscles of John's sturdy legs and she couldn't help thinking how attractive he must have been when he was young. She liked him and was especially flattered on those occasions when she caught him looking at her. He might be over sixty but he had the demeanour of a forty-year-old and, studying him discreetly, she noticed that his small, uniform, teeth rarely showed, even if he did smile, and wondered if it contributed to the slight lisp. There was something sensual about the way he could not quite manage an 'S', sounding like 'th', comic to some but enticing to her and when she had grasped the offered hand at the top of the steps, she was surprised at its softness.

He seemed reservedly cheerful but with two hundred kids he must face worrying times, especially after losing a wife and child. Had their loss propelled him into his vocation, did he miss the company of women? She was dying to know but even she was too sensitive to ask. Surely though, he occasionally craved for . . . well . . .? Perhaps not, especially at his age and in all-male company.

She envied his closeness to Kumar, he was gorgeous. Six feet tall and built beautifully and yet he, disappointingly, failed to respond to her. She understood why he favoured Hillary – neat, petite and fresh she looked like a young, diminutive model, with creamy skin and freckles, who advertised children's toys in flowered dresses on television. Old fashioned and pretty . . .

Her thoughts came to an abrupt halt. Kumar stood by her with the wine. She noticed his feet, unshod, clean and beautifully shaped sliding from beneath the white dhoti. Cautiously she turned her head as he leaned forward to serve, his rich chestnut body shone in the moonlight as though oiled, his hair black, wavy, shiny and faultlessly tidy.

Arm and chest muscles rippled with every gentle movement, his abdomen flat and fat-less. She rested her arms on the table and drew the glass closer to her chest noticing the way his fingers curled round the stem when he grasped it as though in a caress. The action was sensuous and for one inexplicable moment, she felt his hands touching her. The motion, aided by the delicate scent of jasmine, pervaded her senses, bringing a tingle to her skin, enhancing the sexual sensation she was experiencing.

He was close, so close she could see a bead of perspiration on the moustache beginning to form on his upper lip. He leaned over, his face only inches from hers, his eyes unable to miss her deep cleavage and partly exposed breasts. It was all she could do to stop herself running her hands over him, his presence so provocative that her eyes fastened on him ...

'Cradle snatcher!'

She looked up sharply. Tony was smiling his, 'leave the kid alone?' smile. She recovered quickly and grinned. 'I'd rock his cradle in preference to yours mate!' she retorted, her face red in flustered embarrassment.

'Don't let her near him John,' snapped Tony, 'she'll ruin him with her tricks.'

She poked out her tongue and nodded in the direction of the empty seat. 'Expecting a visitor, John?'

'Possibly. Sanjay, my assistant.'

He said it casually with an uncertain shrug like a note of dissent. Was it because he had *not* turned up or that he *might*? She couldn't wait to see if he was a younger version of John or an older version of Kumar – either would do ... her attention returned to John who was cautioning them against beggars.

'... young women with babies whose bum they pinch,' he said, 'usually employed by pimps. 'The baby cries and you give ... you'll see.'

Sam whined and Hillary frowned.

'It brings in the cash, Sanjay will tell you, he knows all the tricks and ...'

He stopped abruptly looking towards the stairs, 'Talk of the devil!'

She turned to look, her hopes shattered. The newcomer sauntered towards them, grabbed a chair and dragged it with a terrible grating noise in an action of arrogance. Is this the resourceful man mentioned in John's stories? He was a terrible disappointment and not in keeping with her impression at all.

'This is Sanjay, everyone,' said John, introducing them all to a curt grunt and an unconcerned nod, between his attempts to attract Kumar who performed a game of nonchalant avoidance, earnestly inspecting cutlery at a side table.

Sanjay was stocky and disappointingly unattractive. A good inch shorter than her with powerful arms and broad shoulders, his squat face was immediately noticeable for its coarse skin. The corners of his mouth turned down rather sourly as though permanently angry. Muscled arms ending in calloused hands emerged from under the short sleeves of his floral shirt. Legs that looked enormous protruded beneath shorts that were due for a wash. She thought he looked grubby, very tough and guessed that he had come directly from work.

'Excuse Sanjay's appearance, he has been building our new bungalow,' said John. 'We were talking about begging, Sanjay.'

He grunted, 'You'd know all about that.'

'You were the master.'

'I was; any chance of a drink?' he said waving at Kumar again with no response.

'How's the new place coming?' John asked, and waited while Sanjay tried to attract Kumar – this time with hypnosis.

'Well?' John asked irritably, knifing the question with a reinforcing stare.

'I told you, get some sand or I stop,' he retorted.

Kumar sauntered towards him, brought by John's assenting nod. Tight lipped, he placed the bottle down with a thump and waited, petulantly refusing to pour, not caring that his action was noticeable. Sam thought there was trouble in camp.

'Is that it!' John said, embarrassed.

'Come and see,' he replied impudently, 'it's not far to walk.'

Impatience alongside restraint took residence in John's eyes now; he stared while Sanjay drained the glass and plonked it down. Kumar stepped forward and filled the glass to the brim. He smirked as he watched a red stain appear on the cloth when it was raised.

Sam could hardly suppress her laughter.

With a censured look, John ordered him away. Sanjay took a long draught and Sam's suspicions that he'd just finished work were confirmed when she saw his armpits.

Andrew tried to engage him. 'Is the bungalow the same as this one Sanjay?' he asked politely.

'Bigger.'

'Are they expensive?'

'Why, you a builder?' he said bluntly.

'Andrew is an accountant,' interjected John.

'Huh,' he said between chews, 'accountants? John says they make figures mean what they want them to mean . . . don't they, John?' he said.

If it was a joke it had fallen flat, the hush told him it was a mistake. John's eyes hardened, his mouth set and Sam gained the impression that in their absence there would have been a row. Hillary broke the awkwardness.

'Will it have spectacular views like this, John?'

John, happy with the intervention, nodded. 'Just the same,' he said, 'until the monsoons, then the view is obscured ... like drawing blinds. The rains are so heavy that we have two months of total idleness,' he said looking hard at Sanjay, 'especially builders! Those streams,' he pointed to silver snakes on the mountainside, 'turn into raging torrents washing grit down that forms beaches. Contractors clear it annually.'

'You shouldn't go short of sand then Sanjay,' said Tony, 'go and nick some.'

John actually laughed. It appeared to break the impasse caused by Sanjay's boorish behaviour and laughter broke out again with John's account of Indian driving tests.

'Two hundred yards in a straight line ... is that all?' said Tony. 'Even she could do that,' he said pointing at Sam.

She didn't retaliate; her attention was with Kumar again. He was haunting Sanjay, who ate ravenously, as though the plate was about to be removed.

Sam noticed that throughout the evening Sanjay continued to look disdainful, as though he felt these transient whites had no right to be in his country let alone sit at the same table. Prejudice, he seemed to have plenty and it appeared to Sam that not only was he at war with John and Kumar, but with the world at large. His animosity changed Kumar's customary pliancy to antagonistic petulance, while John kept up the appearance of affability, although Sam had a premonition that if he continued to be upset an eruption, presently dormant, would surface very quickly.

For the remainder of the evening Sanjay sat in sour silence, sipping brandy from a balloon glass, disinterested and ignored, locked in reticent gloom, which deepened as the evening wore on. His frequent visits to the bottle appeared to inflict its damaging effect more on him in melancholy, than on others in enjoyment. His seclusion became exclusion and, ignored completely, he contributed nothing.

Kumar, silent and watchful, hovered at John's right shoulder, alerted to any move by Sanjay. Sam only saw him smile once.

John stood. 'Have a brandy with me downstairs, lads,' he said, 'if I can rescue the bottle!' He took it from Sanjay and strolled towards the stairs, leading the group.

Sam took a last backward glance; Sanjay leaned heavily on the table, sullen and droopy eyed, gripping a half-filled brandy glass, nodding absently in response to their 'Goodnights'.

Kumar, who had started to clear away the debris, wore a grin and a mischievous look of victory, as he emptied the table around the lonely, morose figure.

FOUR

Vapour trails, touched with pink in the morning sunshine, hung like silken scarves in the azure sky. Below them, mountains seemed to sit majestically above blue-grey mist that layered the surface of the lake and crept insidiously among palms edging the children's school route.

The line of boys, so familiar with the beauty, ignored it and stepped out smartly, barefoot and bare-headed, to walk two miles, intent on reaching school on time and avoiding Mrs Burhama's acrimonious reprimands.

Dressed in a crisp white shirts and blue knee-length trousers, their leader, Kenneth, a bright twelve-year-old, strode in front of the orderly line with his best friend Anil, the school craftsman, their bare feet unaffected by the uneven, stony surface.

They were arguing as usual with Kenneth occasionally breaking off to warn of bicycles with impish, envious riders who rang bells at the last moment scattering these privileged kids like skittles.

He returned to his argument, almost having won it. 'He did not, Anil!'

'Yes he did! I heard him tell you.'

'You couldn't have you were yards away, and Old Digits speaks softly when he wants a favour. He asked, he actually asked me Anil, *if* we would clean the workshop before we go swimming, and when he *asks* he's worried . . .,' he looked around furtively, grabbed Anil's arm and pulled him hurriedly ahead.

'You haven't told anyone?' he demanded, aware of Anil's roving attention.

'No.'

'Make sure you don't, *just make sure you don't*, or it'll be Mata and others at the end of his spite. I'm going home to see her this weekend, so while you are in charge, give him a head count every day or I will be for it on Monday!'

'Alright,' said Anil, irritated, 'I know! You're the one who needs to be careful, he expects gratitude because he gives your mother work!'

'That's why I keep out of his way ...' he stopped abruptly as another cycle rider swerved between them, cursing and ringing his bell, forcing them apart.

'... forget Sanjay now – what you are making in the workshop Anil?'

'Snakes,' he enthused, 'it's easier than carving animals. I cut wood into pieces like corks, drill them, make a head and thread some string through; it looks like a cobra when you wriggle it. Digits said he sells a lot. I don't think Mr John knows and wonder sometimes where the money goes.'

'So do I. Just imagine though Anil, some of your things could be in America or England,' he looked up at streaks in the sky, 'or even on that plane up there, presents from tourists ...' He stopped suddenly. 'Oh! Where's Mr John's present?'

'Who's stupid now?' said Anil, sneering and shoving Kenneth.'I gave it to Mr Rasa yesterday. Digits told me to make another, by the way.'

'And did you?'

'Would you refuse? It's not as good as Mr John's though ...'

They chatted until reaching the school gates where Kenneth counted the one hundred and ninety eight children passing through to form crocodile lines in the playground. He ran his eyes over the assembled group and, satisfied, took his place at the head of his own column.

Looking at the walls of red volcanic rock reminded him of when he took food to his father at the quarry. His dad's grin of welcome concealed the strain of twelve-hour shifts in stifling heat for a pittance. Kenneth filled water bottles from the pump and chatted to the children working there. His father had made the arch over the gate and chipped 'SCHOOL' into it just before he died. Kenneth visualised him now, sitting on his haunches under the shade of a reed roof, smiling, joking, talking and chipping with hammer and chisel until his already calloused hands blistered. He never complained – unless his mother rubbed oil into the skin. He said it was unmanly and gave dire warnings against telling any of their friends. The family laughed and threatened to do so, but nobody did. Kenneth hated snakes and the agony and misery they had brought to his family.

Meeting Vijay, while scavenging in the market, turned out to be an immense piece of luck. The six-year-old put his skinny shoulder to the handcart and heaved, Vijay grinned, took to him, discovered his circumstances and John took him in. Sanjay, as with others, found his mother work and now Mata livened up his occasional visits home with stories, which ridiculed her manager, Mr Ahmed. She too, was grateful to Mr John, had it not been for him Kenneth might be working alongside the other unlucky kids in the quarry.

A whistle blew, the lines straightened and quietened, and Mrs Burhama counted the boys who filed silently into the building to stand in disciplined silence in the tiny central hall. Kenneth waited until last and walked to the front of the assembly, sensing the pleasure of bare feet on a new smooth, grit free, polished surface and the smell of new cedar-wood.

Two hundred voices sang 'Good morning, Namaste' to their headmaster, Rasa Punja, who appeared from a side room to mount the podium. He waited for the mumbling to stop, read morning prayers and turned to Kenneth. 'Is everything arranged Kenneth?'

'Yes sir, Mr John will be here at eleven, sir.'

* * *

John's single cylinder, Royal Enfield stopped with a thump that reverberated around the walls leaving only hollow sounds of teacher's voices floating through window openings, blending in one continuous, confusing echo. It reminded him of his own childhood in Wiltshire and his tiny village school, a mile from his father's chicken farm. It struck him that all his life he never seemed to escape the acrid smell of chickens.

He lifted the machine on to its stand, moving away quickly to avoid the combined heat of the engine and the sun's blistering, perspiring rays. He disliked entering buildings soaked and really needed a car, air-conditioned preferably.

How solid the building looked, he couldn't help smiling when he remembered seven years back, the way he had cajoled the local council into paying for it. It was another victory and deeply satisfying for him to stand and admire his achievement.

Rasa ducked beneath the doorframe of his office as John approached, looking cool and handsome in a white shirt and black trousers. His moustached face and bright eyes beamed a welcome behind gold-framed glasses.

'I know. This machine gives me away,' said John shaking the offered hand.

'Indeed John, I trust you are in the best of good health and I would like to ask, first of all, before we come to today's business, have you any further news?' he said in his rather laboured, formal way.

'News?' said John, confused.

'Yes, anything at all, as you can imagine we are all quite anxious . . .' replied Rasa, strolling through the empty hall towards his office.

'No,' said John, torn between an inspection of the new floor that he'd arranged and striving to remember what it was he was suppose to have heard. 'It's early days yet,' he said guardedly, 'have *you* heard anything?'

'No. I am making full enquiries. It is my intention to see Mrs Jha in the camp office when I get a moment and any . . .'

'I think,' said John, aware of the need to stall until he discovered what he was talking about, 'she has told us all she knows. What exactly have you heard?'

'Nothing different from you I expect, only that Samuel is missing.'

Alerted but unaware which one Samuel was, he asked, 'When . . . er . . . *exactly* did you hear?'

'Wednesday. He was absent Monday, the boys knew nothing. I sent a message to Sanjay and as yet he has not replied.'

'Keeping mum until he has made enquiries I expect,' John said showing support he didn't feel.

'Indeed, I have no doubt that my visit to Mrs Jha will . . .'

'I doubt that she can help,' John interrupted, recognising that prudence would keep the lid on. A boy missing from camp leads to enquiries and he didn't want that, it meant interference. 'Shamin only administrates and I intend to look closer into the matter today.'

'Of course, and as you are back, I'll leave the matter entirely to you.' He paused for a moment. 'Now, about your trip, was it successful and how is the tourist effort?'

'The trip went quite well. As for tourism, I'm meeting my friendly accountants today they'll let me know.'

'You are always sounding sceptical when you mention accountants, John.'

'Rasa my friend, I put up with accountants. We managed for thirty years until the Council stuck in the oar of guilty conscience, before that I had never heard the expressions "child welfare", "at risk" and "accountability".'

'Then it is indeed fortuitous that most of the committee are with you, except our doubtful friend Mr Bhopali. He is not what I would call, "a guiding light", as you Christians say.'

John smiled. He was right, Bhopali was the bullock who pulled the council cart. 'What we need,' John replied, 'are friends like you, Rasa, occasional cash from the council, and no interference.'

'Then we must press harder and win through, John. Now, let us see what is happening.'

They walked back into the hall from Rasa's office, where, to John's astonishment, his boys packed the hall, empty only a few minutes before.

'Good morning. Namaste Mr John,' they chorused.

Perplexed he mumbled, 'Namaste . . . er, good morning . . .'

'Kenneth . . .' called Rasa and waved him forward . . .

The presentation was short; Kenneth struggled through a speech in English thanking John for the new cedar floor that replaced the old dirt one and presented him with a hand-crafted chess set. An Indian adaptation with dancers in traditional dress and holy men in orange robes, who looked remarkably like John, set in a hinged case. It was a masterpiece of precision in old ivory and ebony.

Mumbling embarrassed thanks and jokingly reprimanding them for depicting him as a holy man – although saying he liked the saintly comparison – he raised a great cheer when he finished with, 'If this is an example of the talent we have here then between us we will build an even greater India.'

On the way back to the bike Rasa confided that they might have misappropriated some of the materials, 'But we have a wealth of abilities, John.'

They said goodbye, John stowed the gift in his panniers and kicked the starter, and the engine responded with a thunderous roar inside the walls, the sound dying as he eased his way through the gates.

Rasa's words came back to him, 'A wealth of abilities eh?' He wondered if Sanjay was aware of all that money-making talent?

FIVE

John thought about brother Graham and his devious cow of a smirking girlfriend, Nadeen, on his way to the meeting in Djharli, crooked, corrupt and arrogant. She was too clever for words and he could see her now, leaning back in a chair, arms folded, head to one side with disbelieving eyes fixed annoyingly on him, 'Why didn't you do this, you didn't exactly say that, we need precision John,' demanding and dictating and snapping even before he had time to think! She believed he still needed guidance after thirty years in the driving seat and retaliated in derision if he disagreed with her view.

He arrived hot, flustered and irritated at the market place, empty except for a group of women gossiping on a corner and a single idle owner who stood outside his grocery store, with arms folded, yearning, probably, for streets crowded with people and the chance to haggle.

Unknown here, it made a change for John not to be accosted at every step in this depleted village, nobody waved and smiled in the hope of making a good impression in case they were ever in need of his services.

He parked in the empty square where an old village mother, with bare hands, patted cow dung into wheels like large chapattis and laid them alongside a hut to dry in the stifling heat. He sniffed in the fetid smell of wood smoke and dung and grimaced at the thought of those hands preparing the evening meal – if she had one – and hoped the village pump, nearby, came into use.

Looking around, the sad sight of fading posters of protest still displayed behind dusty windows reflected the loss of hope since the sugar conglomerate moved in and took the factory out, leaving a once prosperous village starved of everything, work, shops, food, inhabitants and livings. Corporate finance cares little for communities and leaves them poverty stricken even here. Was it surprising that women used dung for fuel?

He glanced at the dilapidated hotel, isolated and grubby. His spirit sank. It was bad enough meeting those two but worse in this sad,

---

depressing place where he could just make out the words, 'Taj Mahal Hotel' above an entrance. He grinned in derision, having never seen anything less like the Taj Mahal in his life, and entered 'Reception', marked in worn and faded letters, through a rickety, saloon-type swing door to an inside as grim as the outside. The reception desk was empty, the area unkempt and an off centre fan clanked. Damaged cane chairs sat each side of a large pot containing a dead palm and, perspiring heavily, he pushed open the lounge door.

After the brightness outside the interior was gloomy and dismal. He peered, screwed up his forehead and muttered, 'Scruffy bloody place,' then spotted Graham's self-conscious wave. He reached them soaked in perspiration.

'You ordered?' he said to wooden smiles, pulling out a chair to inspect and brush it.

'And good morning, to you too John,' said the woman. He ignored her.

'Coffee?' Graham asked.

He nodded, and watched the waiter saunter over from the bar and stand casually beside him, weary and disinterested.

'Coffee for three please old chap,' said Graham.

'Lazy bugger,' John complained, and glared at the waiter as he strolled away. 'Can't you find somewhere better?'

She smiled sweetly. 'Of course. Paradise Lake would suit but we are never encouraged there.'

He ignored her taunt. 'Accounts,' he countered impatiently, holding out his hand.

'My goodness, we are in a bad mood today Mr Prichard, perhaps a touch of coffee will dissipate your aggression ... and it's preliminary accounts! Before we finalise for presentation to the committee we need to discuss the cost of services provided by Orphindi to your tourist business. We have seen none and they are not free of charge. I don't suppose you thought to bring details of your workshop income either?'

Nadeen's beautifully pronounced English lulled people into the belief that she was sincere; she was not. She was a picky, prickly woman whose velvet tones disguised subtle complaints. Added to that, her single-minded determination and patrimonial stubbornness made her formidable – even John had difficulty handling her – and she was clever, too bloody clever sometimes. In the hope of countering that, he treated her with disdain to frustrate and defeat her. It was a vain hope with a skin as thick as hers.

On the wrong side of forty, her face showed little trace of age.

Crease free, round and firm with silky dark skin and a discreet touch of makeup, she would pass as someone in her early thirties. Long black hair pulled tightly back in a bun seemed to stretch and narrow her eyes, adding an unfortunate touch of cunning belied by the lift at the corners of her mouth that gave a deceiving hint of a smile, similar in some ways to himself. Lower down, large breasts, the beginnings of a protruding stomach and an expanding rear, disguised beneath the swathes of her royal blue sari, fooled any observer.

John looked towards the ceiling, blinked slowly as though bored and held out his hand. 'Figures – if you don't mind?'

'Service charges, farm and workshop sales, if *you* don't mind,' she said curtly copying his gesture.

'What? Every egg my chickens lay, every pint of milk my goats produce, every trinket and every can of petrol? Talk sense, I can't check that. Nobody can.'

'Cash or kind it is all income and expenditure! You forget, your throughput is sizeable and commercial now, *you* cannot treat it casually and *we* are accountable.'

'Sizeable and commercial.' He'd not heard that before, he stored it. 'Speak to him,' he said pointing at Graham, 'he told me that ambiguous transactions are not easily traced – and they saved the pennies.'

Graham was all for saving a few pennies – for himself usually – but he had made the valid point. Nobody could tell whether the minibus was used to carry tourists or to collect goods, and as for consumables, nobody could separate inmates' meals from guests'! Get out of that, he thought smugly, having put one over on her.

Graham ran his fingers through thinning grey hair and said, sheepishly, 'I'm sorry, Nadeen. I had no idea of the amounts we were dealing with.'

John tucked that to the back of his mind alongside 'sizeable and commercial'.

While the waiter served coffee he scanned Graham. He was much like their father, tall, gaunt and erect, a younger version of the miserable old bugger who had sat upright in his Admiral's chair in their farmhouse kitchen, listening to the radio and drumming the arms with his fingers. In his early fifties, Graham bore a resemblance, except that his voice displayed a public school education in contrast to his father's Wiltshire drawl. Suave and deliberate, full of self confidence, his responses were usually cool – drunk or sober. A smart pale grey suit with putty coloured shoes, a tie and even a Panama hat on the chair beside him, showed the very inch of the old fashioned

23

Englishness abroad. Father's favourite, a golf and bridge club member, an allowance, indulged and adored by mother and by women generally and an unmarried itinerant, always making, 'a few pennies', often on the verge of illegal.

But, he was an accountant, and for that reason John had allowed him to stay, hoping he would help exploit loopholes, as in 'ambiguous allocations'. It was a decision he regretted. It happens sometimes, on the spur of the moment sympathy induces compassion – and then regret!

'Accounts,' John said sharply, anxious now to see them and pretending not to notice Graham's 'we have no alternative,' shrug as he took the offered Orphindi papers.

'The cash,' she warned, 'will not be cleared until October.'

'I saw Colin in London last week,' John said, 'and he seemed to think we did well.'

'I'm surprised,' said Graham, sniping, with a sly grin at Nadeen, 'that you got round to accounts with him.'

John looked up, 'What Colin and I got round to when I was in England is none of your bloody business. As my agent his job is to keep the clients coming, and that's what he does. If you've done your job properly we will see just how good Colin is,' he growled and returned his attention to the papers.

After a few minutes he grudgingly said, 'Mmm, not bad – five grand up on last year . . .'

'Less your service payments,' Nadeen added churlishly.

Ignoring her again he stuck out his hand, 'Tourism,' he said, 'you know, the private venture that I put all my money into?'

'Yes,' she said, casting a swift look at Graham, 'we wanted a word.'

'Why,' he asked, 'sizeable and commercial is it?'

Graham started to mutter something about, 'advice and guidance'.

John groaned, shook his head, looked away disinterestedly and pushed out his hand out again. 'For Christ's sake, accounts.'

She passed them over.

He flicked through to 'Profit and Loss,' it was the only section that he understood and while he perused he missed their furtive looks.

'Jesus,' he said suddenly, 'Jesus Christ!'

He puffed out his cheeks, 'Phew . . . is this right?' He stared with mouth open and eyes popping as the papers shook in his hands.

'Unbelievable,' he breathed, and lifted his head to stare into space, dazed. His mouth felt quite dry, 'That's about twenty thousand . . .'

'More coffee?' said Graham.

'No bloody fear, brandy,' he whispered looking again at the figures, 'a large one! Hold on! This is last year that was only a half year, where's this season's?'

'Well,' she started, with her hand inside the briefcase, 'they are not quite completed, the season's not finished,' and tentatively held out more sheets.

He snatched at them and flicked through frantically to Profit and Loss. 'God almighty,' he said, 'is this rupees?'

'If you look carefully,' she said dogmatically, with a touch of sarcasm, 'you will see it is sterling!'

He blinked, 'Forty grand for a full year?'

'Less expenses,' she corrected.

'That's only eight months work?' he said ignoring her again.

'We thought you would be surpr . . .'

But deaf to Graham's words, the enormity of the figures sent his mind racing into orbit; results were ten times greater than expected, four rooms, ten thousand pounds per room; it was astonishing, such enormous profit from so little work. He calculated, four bungalows each with six rooms; four by six is twenty four by ten thousand pounds is two hundred and forty thousand pounds a year. Untold wealth!

He tried to compare that with the pittance they managed on now but his mind raced into fast forward . . . a new complex with pool, restaurants, a fleet of buses, and money, big, big money, the beginning of a dream, and an end to his struggles. Then a Swiss chalet, air conditioned car with cool air, he could almost smell it, then, with the right deputy he could retire . . . an occasional visit to oversee the work building any number of bungalows . . .

Ah . . . wait! Money! October she said . . . monsoons that would sweep Southern India arrive in two or three months . . . no building then . . . sod! His hopes slumped, the ground would be knee deep in water in a couple of months and roads impassable . . . roads . . . that's another problem, the road, that bloody road! In its present state he could kiss his income goodbye. He needed a road built now – right now, three bungalows at least before the monsoons. But where could he lay his hands on twenty grand before October?

And insurance? If he was to grow he would need that and no insurance company would take it on, the road was too dangerous – unless the council, he mused. No! No fear! They'd meddle, definitely not.

He stared into space; his brain dead, in a mass of endless enquiry there were too many snags, mostly money ones. He rubbed his chin; he had something unique here and had to capitalise, it was now or never.

He heard Graham say, '. . . and with expansion, who knows,' he paused, '. . . are you with me?'

'Umm,' he said having not heard a word but well ahead of them on an imaginative expedition.

'That money,' he said softly, 'did you say no chance before October?'

'Yes old boy,' said Graham.

'Who else knows about this?'

'Only us,' she said, leaning back in the chair smugly with arms folded and her head to one side in her familiar confrontational pose. Her supercilious smile tended to deflate his euphoria and her words dissipated it finally. 'If I remember correctly, you bragged, rather indiscreetly if I may say, about your expectations in front of Bhopali. He is bound to ask.'

'It's none of his bloody business, this is a private venture – mine – and so is the profit,' he said petulantly. 'If I make donations to Orphindi it's me who decides how much comes out of my pocket.'

'Your pocket!' she said. 'Orphindi has subsidised your venture to the hilt. Labour is free, guests are fed on Orphindi provisions and taken around in Orphindi transport driven by Orphindi staff and that's why it is so profitable! Anyway what you propose to do is illegal. This whole venture should be scrutinised, modified and developed to run properly, practically and financially. You will need our help to do that. '

'Yes,' he said, 'I've already thought of that.'

'Really John? How very clever of you to think of us,' she said impudently turning to smile at Graham.

'I meant developing the business,' he growled, curious how two hard up accountants could offer finance. 'Anyway,' he said hoping to glean a source, 'what can two hard up accountants afford?'

'Don't sound so sceptical,' said Graham, 'Nadeen's family is not exactly poor. Anyway you have nothing tangible, not even a house.' He sniggered, looking at Nadeen and gaining courage through her, 'although perhaps I'd better not mention that!'

John restrained a temptation to retaliate. It was clear Graham had not lost his vindictive streak, but how interesting it would be to discover where his cash came from, since the good life usually landed him in debt. He'd claimed poverty on arrival and had lived off Orphindi for months, 'Just until I get some funds transferred old boy.' Perhaps he'd found a sideline . . . swindling Orphindi maybe?

Prichard listened carefully seeking a clue to their cash source, while she lectured on what she saw as *'their'* future and how they could make a million in five years with, 'our financial help and guidance ...'

'How much?' he interrupted tersely.

She lifted her head; the look down her nose was condescending and self-satisfied. 'Five thousand pounds – a quarter of a million rupees.'

He again restrained the impulse to ask where it came from, but found himself nodding while stunned sounds of approval escaped from his lips, 'Mmm, OK ... mmm ...' he murmured again.

He stood, suddenly keen to make for the land office.

'Right,' he snapped, 'just get the Orphindi statement ready and keep the other papers out of sight. Ignore tourism at the meeting, I'll deal with that, it's a private matter.'

He rose from the chair and strode towards the door.

* * *

They looked at each other in silent puzzlement; Graham shook his head, 'God almighty!' he said with a deep sigh, 'who does he think he is?'

'God Almighty,' she laughed and nodded towards the departing figure. 'Commanding isn't he? He thinks he has everything under control.'

'Yes old girl, do you think he suspects?'

'Is there proof? I think not, he is glowing with success and has no current resources. If he thinks others will help he is in for a surprise. Who would back his charity, nobody but we are aware of the potential. No,' she said confidently, 'only a fool would lend him money with his credentials – that's why he accepted our offer.'

'Indeed my dear, we have more than sufficient in the "Irrigation Fund" gleaned over the last year, and when we loan it to him we will control the business, then he'll soon know who is in the driving seat.'

'We will make full use of it, but you Graham,' she reproached, 'must learn to curb your sarcasm. I know he is an irritating bully and his male relationships have been the cause of much friction in your family, but we have more to gain with his co-operation than his antipathy. It is not diplomatic to ridicule him about Colin, lover or no lover, nor the problem with his home, or to mention my family. He knows my father's views on us.'

'Yes my dear, I'm sorry, I got carried away. I know how difficult ignorance and prejudice is to overcome, our father was the same.'

'Then be very careful, John is cunning and doesn't only bark.'

'I know. But he is undermined by his conceit and doesn't realise how much he needs us. He'll come round when he is desperate. He is no accountant either, in financial terms he is used to small change not large notes.' He looked down at John's unpaid ten-rupee bill.

'Look at that. Do you see what I mean?'

* * *

'Five grand,' fumed John, swinging his leg over the saddle and kicking the starter viciously, 'he could never hang on to money, so where the hell did they get that?'

It showed when he'd stayed at the lake, periodically drunk and running the boys ragged. He was an indolent, crafty, layabout looking for an easy life. A spineless liar, though not stupid, he usually got what he wanted by charm, unless drink, women or sticky fingers got in the way.

Her family, rich or not, would never help. Her father was as prejudiced and intolerant of mixing races as his own was of un-mixed sexes and she was ostracised for living with white Graham. John smiled to himself, white Graham a red rag to a bull of a black father.

His old bastard of a father died seven years ago, but had made it perfectly clear that because of what he termed, 'John's revolting preferences', he could expect nothing in his will. During the bad times, he wished he hadn't been quite so honest, and when Graham wrote that John had been excluded from the will it was no surprise. He'd never checked, but the old bugger usually meant what he said.

Their offer of cash, like their conniving and her brow beating, disturbed him. They were clearly angling for part of his business but he viewed an association with them much like a prisoner would when given a life sentence. All the same, it made the sudden appearance of five grand more mysterious and he could think of only two sources, Orphindi and Graham's inheritance. He'd searched Graham's room once while he stayed at the lake and found nothing, but then Graham was too crafty to leave anything lying about.

Who else could he turn to? Mahmood? He was wealthy but he'd be in like a rat up a drainpipe and pinch the whole bloody business if he learned just how lucrative it was! No, not him, anyway there was something sleazy and untrustworthy about him, apart from being unsavoury and looking like a sumo wrestler.

He couldn't use Orphindi money, they only just managed on what they got, it came in dribs and drabs anyway, what he needed was a lump sum, ten grand, for the houses and more for the track.

Wait a minute, he had a sudden brainwave: could Sanjay work one of his miracles with Nadu, the council engineer, drop him a few rupees maybe. As things stood all he had was castles in the air, what he needed were foundations!

Opening the throttle he sped back to Amitar and the land office.

* * *

'Yes, it is sudden,' he told Mr Malik. He'd been planning to improve the boys' accommodation for some time and he would look foolish if his plan failed so he would be grateful for his confidence.

'Consider the plots reserved and,' said Malik confidentially, 'you may rely on my discretion Mr John.'

From the Land Office, he went to the 'Facility Centre' and saw the manager who explained the new Fax system. 'An electronic device Mr John, confidential, quicker than telex and less cumbersome.'

He knew of it, Colin had the system, and unknown to Graham and Nadeen he arranged to send a first Fax advising Colin of the situation and asking him to make enquiries. Next he saw his banker at Linkers and cancelled all cash movements in and out of Orphindi Accounts, and within the hour he was on the bucking Enfield climbing and descending the countless rises on the track to Paradise Lake, grimacing and cursing.

'Bloody road, bloody council, bloody insurance.'

* * *

He turned off the path and drifted the bike fifty yards to the new bungalow under construction, hidden behind mounds and a copse, dismounted, and scrutinised Sanjay and his labourer from the shade of a large acacia.

Covered in dust and streaming in sweat they were heaving a new beam into position. The ground floor and walls looked complete and a week or two would see it finished. One down, three to go he thought.

He walked over. 'Making progress I see. When will you finish?'

'I told you, when I get some sand,' grumbled Sanjay, grunting the beam into place.

'Don't be so bloody disagreeable, if you want sand get your mate to pick it up, you heard what that "pain in the arse" westerner, as you called him, said.' He pointed to the end of the lake. 'Down there! Now then, drag yourself away from your work and get yourself over here. I want a word.'

'I'm busy.'

'Tonight then.'

Sanjay pulled a face, 'I am going out tonight.'

'Not before you see me . . . if you don't mind that is.'

'I might as well stay to dinner,' he said, disgruntled.

'Please yourself but if you do, be tidy, I don't want a repetition of last night with you antagonising guests because you've had a bad bloody day.'

'We never have good ones lately – I'm an outcast and my room . . .'

'Stop moaning for Christ's sake Sanjay. Renting your room is temporary, it makes money – anyway you have your privacy . . .'

'What, a hut?' he shouted. 'I built a bungalow for us and now I stay in a hut! Why can't I use the spare room, or are you saving it for . . .'

'Give it a rest,' shouted John. 'Jump on that bike and see your pal, organise that bloody sand for God's sake and see me later; and don't antagonise Kumar if you turn up for dinner!'

'Why not, he antagonises me, he's taking my place and . . .'

'Oh for Christ's sake . . .'

John turned and walked away.

*　*　*

Frustrated with his constant whinging he was glad to be out of earshot and strolled back to the bungalow. It had not been the right time to ask about Samuel with a big eared labourer in the vicinity, but that would come. It had been five days now and Sanjay had said nothing – it was not forgetfulness, concealment and reluctance perhaps but since negligence was Sanjay's norm lately, it would be more likely that or guilt, and it left John wondering if he had been up to his old tricks again. In a few days he'd find out.

It was not uncommon for boys to go walkabout, often curiosity would entice them to attempt to find a parent. Occasionally they found work and were never heard of again. John and the police treated their absence seriously during the first week, casually after two and forgot it after three. Absconders seldom returned and if found, their preference was often to stay put. There was also the new police inspector – if he was as lax as the last one, nothing would change. That remained to be seen.

Nevertheless, this particular situation disturbed him. He wasn't sure but Sanjay's reluctance to comment pointed to his involvement. If he was, the last thing John wanted was the police putting their bloody oar in.

Two gardeners waved to him as they left for camp. His eyes left the path for a minute to wave, he stepped into a straggling bush and a thorn tore his leg, causing blood to run from his ankle into his shoe. He swore and rubbed his leg unconsciously, his mind locked in a search for alternative funds. Mahmood came to mind again and again John dismissed the wheeler dealer, he might be a committee associate but he's as tight as a duck's arse and dealing with him could cost everything. He could think of no one else.

He put his thoughts in abeyance on reaching the bungalow, where Kumar smiled down at him from the top of the steps. 'Hungry Mr John?'

'Starving,' he said, and followed the pointing finger to the coffee table laid with a snack. 'Clever old son,' he said.

'I thought you had left, I heard your machine.'

'That was Sanjay on an errand, my son.'

'I usually do that, Mr John.'

'Not on the bike you don't. Anyway it's nothing important, so wipe that look off your face.'

Kumar dropped his head in dissatisfaction and saw John's leg, 'What has happened, Mr John?'

John looked down at his dust and blood covered foot, 'Just a scratch, son.'

'Sit down Mr John, I will get something.' He hurried inside.

John reached the rattan table at the end of the veranda, poured a cold limejuice from the jug and took a long draught. He gave a lengthy sigh, removed his shirt and threw himself into a chair. With eyes closed he lay back, the tiniest of breezes caught and cooled him. He exhaled again, long and slow, feeling blood course through his veins to liberate the morning's tension.

Soft hands gently removed his sandals, Kumar placed his feet in a bowl and water lapped and cooled him. Pleasant sensations ran through his loins as supple hands sensuously massaged his feet and caressed his calves. He sighed again as the massage and cool liquid soothed him further, evacuating the remaining stress.

'You can do that all day my son,' he said, cooler physically yet stimulated by Kumar's tender touch.

'Better, Mr John?'

John opened his eyes, looked down, stretched out his hand and gently ran it through Kumar's hair.

'I saw the boys – has everybody gone?'

'Yes, Mr John.'

'Good, when I've eaten you can give me a shower.'

SIX

Sunil saw an overloaded lorry sway dangerously in front of them on a bend and calmly hung back.

'Nice one Sunil,' Andrew heard Tony say, as he yawned and repositioned his bony six-feet-two frame in an octopus-like sprawl, crumpling what had been meticulously pressed shorts and shirt. He didn't care; the day had been fascinating and that would override even Hillary's disapproval.

He couldn't count the number of times Sunil had narrowly missed cows lying unconcerned in the road, their brightly painted horns a topic of conversation as he drove round each solid, sacred beast. Which festival – Pongal Harvest, Maroutai Dance? Who knows, festivals are so frequent down here in Tamil Nadu. It was not unusual to be held up for an hour watching a procession of brightly decorated elephants and their mahouts amble along main streets in a splendid parade of colour.

They entered Amitar. Andrew looked around the main square bordered by untidy, dilapidated, buildings as they slowed in traffic. Dust on flat surfaces, congealed by monsoon rains, consolidated in its boundaries rubbish thrown from windows, opened in the relentless heat by persistent optimists hoping to encourage a non-existent breeze. Pavements, broken and cracked, fused with the dirt filled roadway and shops, paintwork shabby with the ravages of heat and monsoon displayed faded coloured packets now blue with age and well past their sell by date.

Beggars lay on temple steps in practised comfort, oblivious to the squalor, taking solace it seemed, from effigies of their Hindu Gods, Vishnu, Shiva, Ganesh, but with no such sanctimonious thoughts, some stall owners slept in the shade on run-down carts, aware but unconcerned with scavenging rats. A sneak thief helped himself from a stall and Andrew saw Sunil smile and shut down the throttle to a purr so as not to wake the owner.

Others peddled lacquered bangles and beads and he could smell the aroma of hot samosas and honeyed bananas mixed with dried, salted fish and spices, sold by squatting traders arguing under a blazing sun, while Dhalea Wallas, in white Neru caps, nipped about on bikes to deliver meals.

They passed the taxi rank, filled with yellow and black cabs and idle drivers, drumming roofs and swearing at rickshaw owners who jockeyed for fares.

'How long to the Lake, Vijay?' Andrew asked, and watched the back of his rocking head.

'Ten minnit.'

Tony grinned. 'Always is mate.' He leaned across the gangway. 'What do you reckon Andy, conflict or peace pie for dinner?'

Andrew gave a snort recalling last night's embarrassing performance, curious as to what was behind it. 'Conflict' was right, sparked off by Sanjay's imprudence, but there are two sides to every story. The animosity, and John's controlled retaliation, reflected lurking malice. Away from company, he imagined John would have leapt at Sanjay and throttled him.

'No idea. Wouldn't you think that some of John's charm would rub off?'

'Yes,' giggled Sam, 'it's like having Frankenstein at one end of the table and Jesus at the other, but I feel sorry for John. He's so patient. Ten years younger and I could fancy him.'

'You,' said Tony, digging her in the back with his finger, 'fancy anyone over ten, Samantha.'

She swivelled round fully to face him. 'Yes, because he has charm and charisma! Can you say that?'

'Yes, charm and charisma!'

'Silly sod,' she scolded, laughing.

Andrew smiled, used to their playful combat, but doubts lingered. Had they really seen all of John? The girls seemed to think so, but was his cherished seclusion, that he called 'privacy,' deliberate isolation? With what he had achieved, one would think him gregarious with nothing to shy away from, yet that's exactly what he seemed to be doing. Perhaps he disliked the changed behaviour of modern society and preferred remoteness. Andrew was as unsure of that and where exactly Kumar fitted. Tony and Hillary seemed to feel the same but Sam was too captivated by his appeal to notice.

He sat up, stretched and leaned across the gangway to reach for a tissue in Hillary's bag. She pulled it away, muttering about rummaging and privacy. 'I want a tissue darling.'

'All you have to do is ask,' she said crossly.

Tony pulled a pack from his shirt pocket. 'Get shrewd,' he whispered, grinning.

The bus lurched, having reached the track and, intent on survival, they gripped the seats in an effort to steady themselves in the pitching, tossing bus.

Ahead of them Andrew could make out a group of boys, some in white dhotis that brushed the path and others in lunghis pulled tightly between their thighs. He gauged they were all between seven and thirteen, from the camp he assumed, and in answer to his thoughts the bus stopped alongside them.

Without reference to the passengers, Vijay threw open the sliding door and called. The group clambered in, their faces wreathed in smiles and wide toothy grins, greeting the occupants with a salute and 'Good evnin' suh.'

Andrew counted them, twenty-two seated into spaces normally occupied by ten, crammed in every corner, on seats, wheel arches and floor, filling the bus with a buzz of conversation without shoving, pushing or arguing.

Vijay looked at Sam. 'OK?'

'Of course Vijay,' she said, putting her arm around the little boy next to her as the bus started to pitch again. The boy looked up and grinned, she gave him a squeeze.

Mumbled words caused ripples of suppressed, confidential laughter as the bus pulled away towards the Lake. Shy and hesitant at first the boys soon relaxed and the lad next to Andrew surprised him.

'Are you have a good day suh?'

Andrew looked down into Kenneth's lively face, his white teeth starkly contrasting with beautiful ebony skin. 'Ah, you speak English! Yes, we have had a good day, and you?'

'I am too having good day suh.'

'Have you finished school for today?'

'We are stopping at three and half past suh, now we are for swim.'

'You are very lucky. What did you do at school today?'

'Today suh, we have gived Mr John a price.'

'A price?' Andrew looked puzzled, Kenneth tapped Vijay on the shoulder and said something in Tamil.

'No suh,' he said turning back, 'his present.'

'A surprise, I see and what was that?'

The other boys had turned to listen over the noise of a straining engine and rattling windows, intrigued by a conversation in which Kenneth clearly stretched his knowledge of English to the limit. He leaned forward to confer with Vijay again, 'Chess game . . . we maked for him.'

'You made a chess set, that was clever of you, and did he like it?'

'Yes suh.'

The halting conversation continued. Andrew found that Kenneth had been at Orphindi for six years and his face lit when asked his age. He knew the answer to that.

'I am twelve years suh,' he replied smiling broadly. The bus heaved suddenly, and, with a jarring impact, threw the occupants in all directions.

'A little bump sir,' he said pulling a face.

They laughed at the understatement.

'What will you do when you leave school?'

'I will be,' his brow creased in an effort to search his memory and leaned forward to speak to Vijay again, 'accountant. I am liking very much sums suh.'

'And what don't you like?' Andrew asked.

Kenneth looked round at the other boys and said something that resulted in a peal of laughter. Vijay turned, glared and spoke sharply, bringing immediate silence and sneaked grins from one boy to another.

'I am an accountant,' said Andrew quickly.

'And what country are you coming from suh, England?' Kenneth asked, his bright smile returning.

'No Kenneth, I am Scottish, that is far better than being English,' he whispered. 'Will you remember that?'

'I am Indian Mr Scottish suh, that is best,' he said, laughing as the bus drew up outside the bungalow. 'Thank you suh, goodbye.'

Andrew smiled back at him and waved. 'Bye son,' he said and watched them troop from the bus.

The boys started to race off but Vijay grabbed Kenneth, and, with an arm that held him firmly around the shoulders, he appeared to be speaking sternly. Kenneth looked solemn as he raced off to catch the others, who had grabbed rubber inner tubes from the storeroom and left their clothes behind.

'OK Vijay?' he asked.

His head rocked from side to side and his lips parted in a brief, embarrassed, smile before walking quickly away.

John grimaced a greeting and Andrew saw that Sam had been right, his teeth rarely showed. He also noticed with a new awareness, that although his face displayed pleasure, his eyes did not. His benign expression became chilly and commanding with the boys, and their carefree attitude disappeared in his presence, but when Sam said, 'Look at their little bums John, aren't they beautiful?' he reverted.

Smiling broadly he chuckled, 'That makes your holiday, doesn't it Sam?'

Andrew supposed that disciplinarians were never popular, however, a look that threatened might encourage obedience but not always affection and, with the boys, John showed little of the love and humour projected in his stories. Added to the dissension he had witnessed last night Andrew detected an undercurrent of unease, reflected, perhaps, in whatever Kenneth had said to make the boys laugh.

It had seemed derogatory. He found himself wishing he spoke Tamil.

* * *

Tony surveyed the front of the building while he waited for the others at the base of the broad front steps; it was well designed, although somewhat crudely finished. The covering of jasmine and honeysuckle in pink, white and yellow reminded him of a picture on a birthday card with vines and flowers softening every line; he bet that Hillary knew every plant.

Sam looked stunning in a white bikini and retorted, 'I wish,' when he suggested she might need protection from the boys.

'Trust you,' he said, 'they are not showing half as much flesh and they're nude.'

'Think yourself lucky mate, it's all yours!' she snapped as John emerged from the building without a shirt, his stomach prominent. Tony felt quite elated.

Hillary 'shushed,' them on the way to the lake to point out a humming bird that dipped its beak into a hibiscus flower. They stared in silence until the tiny creature darted off into the brush as quickly as it came.

'All part of the package,' said John, and jumped into the lake with a tremendous splash.

As Tony removed his shirt the heat hit his body like a blast from a furnace, sweat immediately ran from every pore and trickled over his skin. His feet felt as though they would blister on the burning ground when he removed his shoes, and he quickly put them on again to protect against the stabbing rock. The boys had no such protection and dived from the flesh piercing, volcanic surface without a second thought, followed gingerly by Andrew and Tony.

Tony rose to the surface and lay motionless on his back, lifted by the tepid water to unimaginable serenity. The stickiness dissipated, his blood cooled and a new energy ran through him as the water, made choppy by crashing bodies, chilled and refreshed.

Tony picked up Sam's sentence half way, '... it's the only admiration we get,' and opened his eyes to see a group of boys hanging on to the rock staring blatantly at Sam and Hillary. Two others approached from behind to offer inflated car inner tubes.

One tapped Hillary's arm. She turned. 'Well I never,' she said and shied away quickly.

'For crying out loud Hilly,' laughed Sam, cuddling one, 'they are only kids. Shame they're not ten years older,' she said turning towards Tony and raising her voice as the boys led them to a sandy area.

Tony looked about him. John swam peacefully on his own, Andrew trod water chatting to Kenneth until a water fight developed. In minutes, to an enormous cheer, the two exhausted men raised their arms in surrender. The boys pursued them to the shore and allowed them to flop fatigued on to their towels.

In minutes, they slipped back into the water, 'Having a heart to heart there Andy?'

'Aye, tell you later.'

Tony closed his eyes and lay on his back drifting; his mind a void and him torpid, in an aqua heaven. He had no idea how long he'd been like it until he heard Sam call, 'Come in number five your time is up!'

In euphoric calm with eyes still closed, he replied idly, 'Aye, aye, sir.'

'Come on, tea's ready,' she called irritably, 'it's on the table.'

'Bloody hell woman, don't nag!' he said, 'it's like being at home!'

He clambered out, 'Come on then Sammy, drag yourself away from their little bums,' he mocked, and looked about him. 'Where's John?'

'He went back ten minutes ago,' she replied turning towards him, 'he had visitors. Soldiers.'

'Soldiers?'

'Ye-ees!' she said with heavy sarcasm. 'Khaki uniforms, peaked caps and guns. I'd say they were soldiers Anthony dear.'

'Alright, alright, I only wondered what soldiers want at Paradise Lake?'

'God knows – perhaps they are looking for your dad!'

* * *

Kumar left John's side, 'Tea?' he smiled at Hillary, his white teeth contrasting starkly with his dark skin.

'Thank-you ... um ...'

He moved on and reached Sam, her reactions were, as ever, predictable. Her eyes widened, softened and locked on his, 'Thank you Kumar.'

It was a game, Hillary was aware that Sam used her looks to tease. It was her conceit and her amusement and males, idiots that they were, fell for it. She seemed to be having no success this time. Kumar seemed not to recognise enticement despite her audacity and Hillary felt that despite her experience Sam could be remarkably naive.

'It's a bit hot for tea, Kumar? Got any beer . . .?'

It was typical of Tony to prefer alcohol; he encouraged Andrew. 'Keep up the alcohol content of the body mate,' he said often.

'Contamination by association,' she had sniffed on the last occasion, but intervened here.

'Tea,' she said, 'makes you perspire and cools the blood – and therefore body.'

'OK,' he chirped, 'you talked me into it, Hill.'

She disliked abbreviated names. Sam was acceptable but Andy and Hill sounded lazy and common. Still there was no way she was going to argue with Tony – like Samantha, he had a sarcastic streak and arguments upset the equanimity of a trip. A rather unusual trip actually, she had expected an hotel, not that there was anything wrong with the bungalow, it was a little . . . well . . . basic . . . and one must make the best of it, even if there was an undercurrent of disagreement between the residents.

'I'm for another great British discovery,' said Sam, 'cool hill stations and gin with tonic. The old Brits did get something right, not the clothes and not the nudity, that was a no-no!'

'Bit different now, eh Sammy with your three handkerchiefs – and that's too much. You'd walk about in the nude to attract fellas!'

'Yep,' she said lightly, 'so, here's to bare chests and bikinis. Right Hillary?'

She didn't think she should answer. Sam's libertine jokes were not always in the best taste and although John smiled, she thought he too had reservations. Fortunately he had charm, good manners and a pleasant sense of humour, although sometimes self-effacing and amusing when he compared himself to the old crowd in India. 'They took advantage and pinched what they could lay their hands on. A bit like me really,' he said, but she didn't see it that way.

They laughed again when Tony said, 'My dad reckoned, if the British were so unpopular in India, why did most of them follow him back to England?

Sam stood, 'If we are going to have a conversation about Mr Baker senior and his Indian exploits, I'm off for a shower.'

'Yes, I think I will join you,' said Hillary, 'I need refreshing, otherwise my husband will not speak to me.'

'I'll have to try that, then perhaps he won't talk to me about football and West Ham!'

'Football,' said John, 'is not as popular as cricket here, and Indians are the masters. Do you know in the last series . . .?'

'God Almighty! What have I done?' she groaned and left.

Hillary checked the shower room floor for 'crawlies' and in the silent coolness removed her swimsuit. Testing the initial spurt, she stepped under the tepid stream from the shower to experience the same feeling of mental and physical nourishment as at church.

Closing her eyes, the lukewarm liquid ran down the length of her body to her feet. She revelled and relaxed and, with the exotic smell of jasmine in her nostrils, sighed, placed her hands at the back of her head stretched and luxuriated, her mind discharged of all thought except the sensation of freshness and, what seemed like, a complete change of skin.

With only the sound of water tinkling spasmodically into the drain, she stood there quietly, allowing the water to caress and cool her. It was as though her fatigue was being washed away.

In the distance, she vaguely heard the muted thump of an engine as it stopped, followed by a whirring sound and tyres on gravel.

It wasn't John. She could just hear him talking, it must be Sanjay and for a moment she wondered what he was doing arriving at six thirty in the evening, but that was none of her business.

* * *

An hour later, Hillary joined the others on the patio. She seated herself next to Sam who, as usual, was half-exposed in a white cotton skirt, slit to the thigh, and a sleeveless deep-cut black top with most of her cleavage on display. Why Sam needed to dress like that was beyond her, after all, she was married. She looked vampish and didn't seem to attract John, although Andrew's eyes locked on occasionally . . .

It was past seven and the sun had dipped behind the Western Gnats, casting longer and longer shadows across the plain, changing the landscape yet again. Glaring brightness and harsh colours were replaced by agreeable pastel tones and rearranged outlines. Magical silhouettes appeared as though watching a creative artist at work on his canvas, and quiet replaced the harsh daytime sounds. Even the crickets seemed to provide a muted, whirring background.

The air had cooled, yet it remained unbearably hot, and although she criticised Sam for her indelicacy at times, she had to agree that underclothing became embarrassingly stuck. To prove her point, Tony leaned to one side and pulled at his shorts while Andrew tugged his shirt.

'I hear you were caught unawares today John,' offered Andrew.

She saw John's face stiffen. He reacted as though challenged. 'No,' he said snappily, 'they're regulars ... er ... friends ...'

Andrew looked nonplussed, 'No,' he said, 'not the soldiers, the present ... the one from the boys.'

'Ah,' he said, 'yes, yes,' as though relieved, 'here,' he said taking a parcel from under the table, 'it's a one off.'

Hillary thought the chess set a 'priceless gift,' Andrew complimented and Tony thought it was worth a 'few bob at home,' to a long disapproving glare from Sam before passing it back.

'Is there a barracks round here then John? We see a lot of them soldiers about.'

She saw John hesitate, 'Er, no, they're just ... sort of friends. Did you enjoy the day?' he said quickly in a manner that showed he wanted to avoid the subject. She wondered why but forgot about it when Tony joked that they baked in the market and froze in the temples and, 'the bus was like a fan oven inside, circulating hot air.'

'There was certainly a lot of that about,' sniggered Sam.

She was amusing despite her ribald comments and caused another ripple of laughter when she said they had seen an elephant on town on a roundabout. 'Not many of those in Richmond ... and Sunil took us to a wedding, we just walked in and were welcomed, it was amazing and ... Oh, I forgot, we met a friend of yours at the hotel, a real charmer.'

'Who was that?' he asked casually.

'Mr ... er ... um ... Mitera?'

'Mitera?' he said looking up instantly, 'really?' Suddenly interested, he said, 'Dapper, slicked down black hair, about forty five, charming and,' he made a face, 'a mouth that would curdle milk?'

'Yep, that's him,' said Tony smiling, 'mate of yours is he?'

'His name is Mitra!' John replied, avoiding the question.

'He invited us to his home, but ...'

Hillary caught John's look of interest and although he leaned forward casually she thought his intrigue quite apparent.

'Well he was a bit ...' Tony stopped, short of adequate words.

'Intimidating, Tony?'

Hillary stepped in, 'Perhaps overwhelming, John. He was rather rude to Vijay and ...'

'... he practically threw Vijay out of the hotel! Vijay was well upset,' said Tony finishing her sentence.

John chuckled, 'He'll get over it Tony! Old habits die hard with Mitra. His family was one of the wealthiest in the area and of a high caste, rich with airs and graces to match. He's a millionaire, hotels, big money-lending operation, pompous, overbearing, boorish and spiteful but can be, conversely, the essence of charm. He's a confirmed bachelor and speaks English to show off, although,' he said frowning a little as though puzzled, 'he must have a reason to invite you to his home, did he say anything more?'

'Only that you were included – he spoke very highly of you.'

'Did he now?' he said lifting his eyebrows and pulling a face of disbelief.

'He was a bit too slick for me John but I had to behave, my missus is looking forward to seeing his drum. Upset her and I'm in for a right rollicking.'

Some of Tony's expressions were hateful too, but John seemed intrigued. 'I can imagine,' he said. 'Mitra lives in the past, never the twain, as we say.'

'He said that often, "as we say", and treated us like mates and . . .'

'. . . And,' snapped Sam interrupting Tony, 'had you encouraged him, we could go to his home . . . couldn't we Hillary? I'm dying to see it.'

Hillary recognised Sam's confrontational voice and, not wanting to be involved, she made an assenting nod. John absently run his finger along the edge of the table, still, it seemed, intrigued with the prospect.

She rose, with the others when Kumar announced dinner and watched John's face; it looked as though he had completed a puzzle. He strode resolutely towards the stairs, leaving the group behind in his wake.

How terrible disappointing, she thought – he had forgotten his manners.

SEVEN

The footlights along the edges of the roof helpfully drew an array of miniature creatures towards them and away from the seated five. Although it was sticky and hot, Sam found herself idly thinking that sleeping here would be preferable to sleeping in their room with that clattering fan.

The view, transformed with the disappearance of the sun, had become to her part of the magic of India, scenery changed before their eyes, and tonight music accompanied the transformation.

Foreign to Sam, strings twanged and a repetitive, rapping kettle-drum accompanied melodies from a flute and ravanhetta. Carried by the breeze from Amitar it drifted in undulating waves. Up close, as they experienced at the wedding, the instruments could wreak vengeance on eardrums, but here distance modulated the assault into romantic composition.

She looked across the roof where skewered kebabs hung over a glowing fire in heat so intense that she'd felt it when she'd passed. To her surprise the chef sat close, squatting, crossed legged before the grill, his lunghi tucked between his knees and his face lit by flickering flames.

'He'd better watch himself or he'll burn something,' she whispered across the table with a giggle. Hillary's eyes closed and her head turned away in disapproval, the men sniggered, Andrew briefly, self-consciously and John indulgently.

'He's getting married soon; status counts even here so I gave him the title of 'Chef'. Her parents are less likely to turn him down now.'

'It won't be her parents who turn him down,' laughed Sam to snorts from Tony and Andrew and another frown from Hillary.

Sam found conversation effortless with John; his easy manner helped the flow and it was her intention to mention Mr Mitra again, determined to see his home, and while Hillary was on her favourite subject, plants, and Andrew, as usual, talked about accounts, she studied Kumar.

'Darling,' said Hillary disapprovingly when Andrew asked John about earnings.

'Just curious darling.'

'No idea. Sanjay is our paymaster, I raise it, he pays it. Try him again – if he arrives.'

Sam imagined Andrew's inward groan at the prospect of another staggered conversation. John seemed aware of the aversion and, apologetically, she thought, took a moment to explain that self-taught Sanjay was invaluable. He'd built everything, the bungalow, the camp and his own quarters next to it. He was responsible for it and the boys and, being Indian by birth was an advantage. He was able to negotiate on the same level locally where a white face raised prices. He was rightly proud of himself having started life on a rubbish tip and had difficulty coming to terms with tourism. He would come round, said John. 'In the meantime, you must forgive his lack of diplomacy.'

Sam thought it was tolerant of John but it would be in his generous nature to be so. Andrew must have felt the same and supported John with a nod.

'I might influence the man in the street, but my deputy can influence local authority,' said John. 'He has connections and we have to use every means at our disposal, as you can imagi . . .'

From where she sat, Sam saw a movement on the stairs, Sanjay's head appeared above the parapet. He approached with a subdued, 'Good evening,' and sat next to Andrew waiting, patiently this time, for Kumar to fill his glass.

It was a restrained performance, she guessed John had said something; he did not seem to be a man who would suddenly become conscious of his own boorish behaviour. His clean shirt was a small mercy and Kumar filled his glass, without display. She gleaned they'd both been spoken to, and although Sanjay still carried an aura of arrogance, he seemed reconciled to good behaviour.

Tony eyed him. Andrew could hold his tongue but she was never sure about Tony and the thought kept her on tenterhooks. Fortunately the early conversation was light and excluded Sanjay until John, clearly not wanting him to be left aside, said that Andrew had asked about earnings. 'He is an accountant.'

'I know, you told us last night,' he replied with a foxy smile, and turning towards Andrew, 'John has particular views on accountants,' he whispered.

'Most people have, Sanjay.'

'He says they make figures mean what they want them to.'

'Yes, you joked about that last night, if you remember, but who am I to disagree? We have to probe and that is not popular.'

'We didn't have any trouble before. On our own we didn't need accountants.'

John's silent reproach seemed to say behave or else . . .

'Ach no,' said Andrew, 'but times change and so do rules. But I am intrigued about earnings over here. What does a man earn on average per day?'

'Forty rupees a day . . . although I often work for nothing . . .' Sanjay responded, with a self-conscious snigger and a smile.

It transformed his face and, for the first time, Sam saw his beautiful teeth. Even and white, they helped improve his appearance to a point where he seemed pleasant. It was the first time she had heard him actually converse – other than making a series of grunts. His English was good and his voice pleasantly lilting, as Indian voices tend to be, falling on her Western ear attractively. It needed attention to understand the inflections but she found it engaging. When a joke fell flat Sam felt his embarrassment, the poor man was simply devoid of tact.

'. . . and,' he went on, now on his third glass of wine, generously poured by Kumar, 'I deal with friends, they help us and we help them. We have our ways, haven't we John? I got that sand, by the way,' he said smiling at Tony with a sense of achievement.

She thought the remark sounded damaging, it diminished the air of respectability that John had created; the casual acceptance of illegality seemed more corrupt coming from Sanjay than Tony's idea of 'pulling a few strokes', and being next to John she heard his sharp intake of breath. His eyes widened, his lips tightened and he looked barely in restraint. Although she had never seen him angry she thought he was about to detonate as his threatening glare bored into the Tamil.

Sanjay appeared quite insensitive to it. He put the wineglass to his lips and stared straight back at John, despite the censure and cobra like scrutiny, in the silent battle. Sanjay seemed defiant.

'What Sanjay means, Andrew,' John said stiffly, 'is that, conforming to commercial restraints takes some getting used to, and you are right, things are different, we try to abide by business rules and he finds that difficult after thirty years of freedom. We have to answer to authority and . . .

'. . . and people who interfere,' Sanjay snapped. 'We do as we are told.'

It could have been supportive but it sounded contemptuous.

'The Council make the rules, Sanjay, not accountants, so don't take it out on them.'

'We had no trouble before though, did we?' he answered stubbornly. 'If it wasn't for my friends . . .'

'That has nothing to do with accountants, Sanjay,' John snapped, 'anyway how did we get on to this subject? Eat your dinner,' he spoke with a menace that dared Sanjay to continue, 'or you'll get a sore throat.'

Sam thought the real Sanjay had emerged again, a tactless, insensitive man whose street education excluded social grace and diplomacy. Tony had been something like it once but he'd changed, Sanjay never would. He seemed cocky and oblivious of offence. She gritted her teeth when Tony, clearly intent on ridicule, said with a laugh, 'John told us you got up to a few tricks, I did the same meself when I was a kid. Nothing makes the wheels work like a bit of grease though, does it Sanjay. I 'spect you've tried that.'

Andrew raised his napkin to his mouth and John's lips spread in a smile. Hillary looked confused and Sam threw Tony a devastating scowl. The last thing she wanted was his involvement.

'You British have some strange expressions?'

'I ain't British.'

Sanjay stopped drinking and looked puzzled, 'Not British! Of course you are British! You have a British passport,' he said, expecting that to be the winning line.

'So have the Welsh and Irish,' he taunted. 'I'm English.'

'But if your passport is British so are you.'

He looked Sanjay full in the eyes, grinned cheekily and leaned closer. 'Not me mate, nor him. He's a Scot and don't ever call a Scot British or you'll get a Glasgow kiss.'

Sanjay's face was a picture of confusion, 'A Glasgow kiss . . .?'

'Yeah,' he said seriously, 'funny people them Scots, it's the porridge you know.'

John laughed loudly, partly, Sam suspected, at the release of tension but mainly because Tony had effectively stopped the flow.

'He is pulling your leg Sanjay, anyway, it is time for me to invite the ladies to round off the evening with a liqueurs downstairs – where it's quiet,' he said pointedly. 'Perhaps a wee drop of the hard stuff will diffuse the temper of even the most offended Scotsman? Stay here Sanjay and finish your meal, I'll be up shortly.'

It sounded like a command and the mournful face of last night returned. He reached for his glass and nodded at Kumar who brought another full bottle and, with a grin, placed it cockily, in front of him, in an act, she thought, of unison with John.

Sanjay poured as they rose to descend the stairs and with the tension broken amicably, they walked away leaving him clutching his glass, isolated for a second evening.

* * *

John poured the drinks and compared the four guests; they were so different, in appearance and in attitude, and so suited to their mates.

Andrew was tall, rangy, angular, academic and inquisitive, unlike his friend Tony who was candid, cheeky and sometimes loud. A Londoner; basic, forthright and intolerant of pretentiousness.

Hillary, shapely, neat and shorter than Sam with the palest of blue eyes, was reserved and, at times condescending, her small neat teeth, like his, hardly showed and her looks reminded him of a film star from the musical, *Seven Brides for Seven Brothers* – Jane Powell – he remembered. He imagined her to be a nursery teacher, a committee person who never irritated her partner with playful ridicule like Sam, punctilious though and a quiet observer, with Andrew well under control.

Recognising the disturbance, John felt compelled to offer an explanation, pouring large measures hoping it would mitigate any offence.

'You must forgive Sanjay, he works from 6 a.m. until late and is often unaccompanied for hours. He likes to talk when he gets the chance and sometimes gets carries away,' he said, sensing that they knew he was asking for their indulgence.

Tony grinned broadly. 'That's OK. John, Scotsmen get like that after a couple of these,' he said holding up his single malt.

Andrew laughed. 'Listen to him! Cockneys are a race apart, they canna speak their own tongue – even if they do find themselves sober . . .'

The banter told him the incident was forgotten and for a quarter of an hour, he was pleased to hear the good-natured chatter.

Sam looked at her watch, 'What time tomorrow Hillary – and where?'

'We leave at six for the Wilderness Marshes,' she replied, the schedule ever at her fingertips.

'Right,' said Sam, 'I'm weary, even though it's only nine thirty. Goodnight John, Andrew. Don't be too long Tony, although God knows how I'll manage to sleep in this heat.'

'Nor me,' said Andrew

'You will, darling. Whisky acts like a sedative on you. Two minutes after you clean your teeth and brush your hair you will be asleep.'

John smiled at his own accurate summation as the men finished their single malts to the clink of crockery from the kitchen.

They stood finally. 'Goodnight, see you tomorrow John.'

* * *

Sanjay flopped forward on to the table when they'd gone, perplexed, agitated and convinced that the whites had tried, again unfairly, to ridicule him. With elbows on the table and a sour expression on his face he signalled for another bottle, certain that the call would be futile, but to his amazement Kumar brought one over and banged it down hard on the table.

Too inebriated for the thump to surprise him, he lifted disdainful eyes to see Kumar leaning over him, glaring.

'Pig!' he said, his body shaking with contempt.

Sanjay huffed dismissively.

'Pig,' repeated Kumar, 'you harm him and degrade him, stay away, stay in your pigsty.'

Sanjay, casual with inebriation, sat up and looked at him with eyes that could not quite focus. Sober enough to comprehend but too drunk to control his limbs, he slid back into the chair. 'Me? Me? He's the one who needs a rat catcher,' he burbled, trying to gather what he could of his frayed senses.

'Leave him alone, you are an embarrassment to him!' snarled Kumar, pushing himself away from the table, heading for the stairs and leaving the sluggish, lethargic Sanjay unable to retaliate, breathing wine soaked breath as he refilled the glass, most of which he drank in one swallow. He laid his head on his hand to observe the vessel with eyes that slowly closed. Unsteadily he raised the glass to his lips to empty the final drop and, unfocused, reached forward to grope for the bottle . . .

CRASH . . .! He looked up startled as the bottle, snatched from his grasp, smashed down on the table violently. He threw his head back in surprise to find himself looking directly into the furious face of John. Even in his inebriated state he could feel the rage.

Short of breath, having practically run up the stairs, John's face was a picture of crimson wrath, bursting with impatience to give Sanjay a piece of his bad humour. With one hand on the bottle John leaned over him and rammed his face up close enough for Sanjay to smell the whisky. Quivering with rage, he snarled, 'You stupid bastard, when will you learn to control your mouth?'

Uncaring, half-closed eyes met his and with a silly, intoxicated smirk Sanjay, his head again resting unsteadily in his hand said scornfully, 'Huh . . . what? I din' say anything . . . I . . .'

47

'Didn't what? You antagonise them, you intimidate them, you brag about your genius for pulling frigging strings, you stupid, resentful bastard! Don't you think they are clever enough to read between the lines?'

'I din' say anything . . . few days . . . they'll be off.'

'So in the meantime you thought you'd insult them and cast doubts on our honesty and my authority!'

'So . . .' said Sanjay sneering, 'I don't like them!'

'Why, because they are young, bright and sober? Well make no mistake, son, you will not be upsetting them again, from now on stay away from this table! Your runaway tongue practically told them that I thought accountants were crooked and we steal all we can.'

'We do,' he sniggered, unable to control his limbs as his head slipped from his hand. He recovered, 'We always did . . . it was a joke.'

'A joke?' John thundered. 'Funny is it, telling the world we're thieves?' He moved closer still, so close that Sanjay thought he was going to kiss him, he hoped so, he'd missed that. Instead, John, whose eyes never left Sanjay's face said, 'What went on when I was away?'

For a second, Sanjay sobered, recognising the danger. He didn't answer immediately but perceived, even in his befuddled state, that John was preparing to berate him again. He had to find a defence but could only manage to regain enough control of a slack tongue and a spinning head to say, 'Huh, little boy's tales?'

'No! Frigging Joshi's tales, our friendly Police Inspector who paid me a visit today! Now then, what happened to Samuel?'

He cowered down in the chair . . .

'Come on, you frigging moron, what happened to Samuel?' John pressed. 'Rasa knew on Tuesday and Joshi on Wednesday but not a word to me and it's Friday! What's going on?'

Under the blur of alcohol, Sanjay searched his languishing mind for excuses, he couldn't make contact with the words he wanted and said in desperation, 'He . . . he . . . ran off.'

'I know that you idiot, why? Nothing to do with you I suppose?'

Sanjay said nothing.

It's hard to argue with someone who won't talk, so Sanjay waited and in that brief pause John's attitude seemed to change. His glare softened, he moved back and looked down at him kindly, as though in acceptance.

'Run off has he, when? . . . talk to Kenneth did you? I hear he does your checking these days – with you being so busy. What did Kenneth say?'

'Well he . . . er . . . didn't say . . . anything.'

'Ah . . . I see, he didn't know either?' he said, his tone surprised and restrained. 'Strange that . . . you lying bastard! He does a head count every bloody day and when he finds one short he says nothing and has said nothing since?' he roared. 'Do you expect me to believe that the lad who sleeps next to Samuel doesn't know he's missing? That's like saying you didn't notice that the wheels are missing from my frigging bike! Rasa knows, the Police know and they live bloody miles away! Did he tell them before he left and forget to tell you or have you been up to your tricks again? If you have, I'll bloody well murder you!'

'Why don't you?' he cried, his eyes filling. 'You have him now . . . Kumar . . .'

John nodded slowly, 'So that's it – you resentful sod. You forget that it was you found pastures new, not me, he's here to help with the guests . . .'

'. . . and lives with you,' said Sanjay, able at last to retaliate. 'He took my room . . .'

'Because you spent more time in your mate's bedrooms than your own! Come on, when did he leave? Monday, Tuesday?'

In the foggy, cosy euphoria of intoxication he didn't care. John would find out eventually, he might just as well say, then perhaps he could get some sleep. His eyes started to close; he'd had enough and slid further into the chair . . . 'Sunday,' he mumbled.

'Sunday?' exploded John, bringing Sanjay back to consciousness, 'SUNDAY? You stupid sod, no wonder Joshi is asking. How did he leave, sprout frigging wings?'

'Leave me alone . . .' he cried, trying to stop his head spinning and collect his thoughts from inside an empty cavity and failing. He just couldn't think. Befuddled and confused he wanted out of this conversation now, it was John's fault anyway; yes that was it . . . 'It's your fault . . . and that little rat . . . you let me down,' he blurted out.

John moved back closer again, 'My fault is it, I let you down? Am I banned from the huts,' he said quietly, 'is it me who disappears in the evenings to scout the town on my bike? Yes I heard you come back around six, where do you go in town?'

He paused, waiting. Nothing came.

'Wherever it is, don't. People think it's me when they hear that bloody bike and I don't want to be tarred with your frigging brush and . . .'

Sanjay hardly heard him, he felt gloomy, sorry for himself, he'd lost the respect of the very man he'd loved to that cunning kid. Disconsolate and totally depressed, his depression was fleetingly harmonised by the hollow, haunting music floating on the airwaves from town.

The sounds stopped abruptly and in that poignant moment, choking with anger and misery, tears welled in his eyes, he could not help himself, the tears overflowed and he began to sob.

* * *

John looked down at the pathetic figure, whimpering, in drunken collapse. He shook his head. For thirty years they were close, sharing lives and bodies in exciting and precarious times. He remembered Sanjay's virility and unshakable loyalty. But he'd changed. The loyal, lovable innovator was a suspicious associate who regarded whites as a detriment to his country and his status, and it left him seething like a hissing snake. He blamed Kumar for that and took no responsibility for his own attitude or the fact that he had found new friends and neglected his duties to indulge in the town's pleasures.

John supposed that the age gap may have prompted Sanjay to find new excitements and, being in the prime of life, he'd taken advantage, but the route he had chosen was distasteful. Self indulgent and weak now, he was negligent, took unpalatable advantages and, too feeble to go it alone, he was content to snuggle into the cocoon of John's protection but unable to hide the fits of pique that rose with his objections to Kumar. They caused separation from John and the camp and John subsequently cancelled his concession to equality.

Saddened as he was to see Sanjay like this John was aware just how critical he was to Orphindi's development, particularly now when expansion was possible. He couldn't afford to lose him – not that he would go, he was far too dependent on Orphindi and knew on which side his bread was buttered.

John looked down at the sobbing figure; the sight filled him with a fusion of guilt and compassion, as though he had taken advantage of a defenceless child. He shook his head again. 'Silly bastard,' he muttered, 'come on, let's get you to bed.'

He walked over to the stairs, listened for a moment and returned to half-carry the distraught Tamil down to the spare room to lay him on the bed.

Sanjay opened red, bleary eyes, 'Stay with me . . .' he whispered from unruly lips.

'No, get to sleep,' John said gruffly.

'Stay . . . I miss you . . . I din' mean any harm.'

'Didn't you, now?' growled John. 'Get some sleep.' He left the room, closing the door quietly to make for his own room and the ever attendant Kumar.

EIGHT

The stifling heat and a whirring, clanking fan, that intermittently lost power and subsided into silence, initially had no effect on Sam. The moment she lay down she fell into a deep slumber – and woke, it seemed to her, ten minutes later, hot and uncomfortable.

The fan had stopped. She turned over hoping to regain the wonderful oblivion she had just left, 'Paradise parking,' Tony called it but she now turned restlessly trying to settle into a cooler position. Her nightdress wound irritatingly around her and she found herself sitting up untangling folds, thankful that they were in twin beds.

She lay down again, the fan restarted as did the intermittent clanking every few revolution, adding nuisance to discomfort, compounded by Tony snoring. In minutes she was sitting up again, wide-awake.

Throwing aside the sheet she glimpsed the outline of someone passing the mesh window. Curious, she picked up the portable alarm. Five a.m. 'Bloody hell, must be the nightshift,' she muttered as she flicked the sheet aside. 'God it's hot,' she breathed and swung her feet from the bed.

In the strange, surreal glow, she could see the outline of the rug, and, spotting her slippers, she picked them up remembering what Tony's dad had said about scorpions climbing inside. She tapped them on the floor, heel first and slid her feet in, noticing, for the first time, that the eerie glow was the result of the moon's reflection from the lake, reversing the daylight effect, brightening shadowy places.

She stood, walked to the door and gingerly pulled it open.

Faint streaks of scarlet sneaked across the sky; she watched, fascinated to actually see them creep forward then, stepping up to the veranda rail, she took in the whole scene. In a few minutes the heavens changed intriguingly from black to purple to orange, red and deep pink until a few feathery clouds lay undisturbed and isolated in the azure sky before the landscape opened up. Slowly indistinct shapes assembled into known forms, colours appeared from blackness, green fields, silver streams and multicoloured crops emerged as the daily visitor in the east uncovered concealed splendour. She stood transfixed, content and silent in the cool air.

She had no idea how long she had been there, when she heard the fan start up again. 'Bloody fan,' she said hoarsely.

'Can't you sleep either?'

'Oh!' her hand went to her chest, and she spun round. 'You frightened me, Hilly.'

'Sorry,' Hillary whispered ruefully. 'Can't you sleep?'

'No,' Sam responded, shaking her head, 'and neither can others. Did you see anyone?'

'No' she said, 'and if it was a "he" I hope he didn't see you.' She pointed to Sam's night-dress, 'You can see through that.'

'Let's hope Kumar comes by then, perhaps it'll switch on his motor. I'd like to see him when he's running hot.'

'Samantha!' scolded Hillary.

A Minah bird screamed and they jumped together and sniggered in embarrassment before returning their gaze to the exceptional view, watching the sun slowly light the valley. Then, within minutes, the same unbearable, exhausting heat was back.

'Tea?'

They whirled round at the sound of Kumar's voice.

He stood passively behind them holding a tray and, suddenly conscious of her nakedness under the gauzy cloth, Sam, despite her bravado, moved modestly behind Hillary, covertly hoping that Kumar had made the most of his opportunity.

He gave no indication but placed the tray on the table, turned and left.

Hillary smiled and sang softly, 'You – are – blush – ing – Sam – an – tha!'

Sam flicked at her hair, 'Well ... he surprised me! Is it very transparent?'

'As transparent as you, with more effect on you than you on him!'

'Cor' thanks a lot,' Sam replied, faking damaged pride. 'With Wee Willie Winkie snoring in there and Kumar disinterested out here, it'll do my street cred no good at all!'

'Never mind, I'm sure the marshes will take your mind off that sort of thing – for today at least.'

They giggled and sipped their tea, content to watch the brightening sun cast its astonishing light over the hills, as exotic sounds and gruelling heat began to wake Southern India.

* * *

They finished breakfast as John joined them. He warned them again, 'Take plenty of water, it'll be at least thirty five degrees today, so take your hats and don't forget your long distance lenses, you may see some muggers.'

'Where we going,' said Tony, 'London?'

John chortled, 'No Tony, it'll be a privilege, muggers are a type of crocodile, rare and fish eaters mainly.'

He described the attractive waterways where, untouched by time, old Indian culture survives in basic but gentle conditions. There are no mod cons but an abundance of bird life and best seen from a boat. 'So – if you want primitive – that's the place . . . ah!' he said, 'here are the boys.'

He spoke quickly to Vijay, who did not look too happy. As they set off, his head rocked from sided to side as usual but with a look of disgruntlement, and he only smiled after they'd been travelling a few minutes when Tony asked how long to the Marshes.

'One Indin hour,' said the rocking head . . . and within the hour, they parked in a coconut grove alongside a stretch of water, one of several channels that ran between clusters of palm-covered islands.

Moored next to a collection of palm dwellings were boats; occasional figures emerged from the peculiar cone shaped huts and vanished among the dense palms. Others untied their craft and paddled away with leisurely plops. More still sat beside smoking pits where fish hung from crude stick frames. Two attractive young girls in colourful floor length saris walked past with flowing elegance. Bangles reached half way up their arms and tinkled prettily while clay vessels balanced, unaided, on their heads. They stared curiously at the group of white faces, giggled, laughed and turned away when Andrew pointed his camera.

Vijay returned accompanied by an extraordinarily wizened, bearded and turbaned old man, who seated them in a craft that looked as old as him, and for two hours they flowed along in gentle tranquillity among palms, reed beds and ancient villages to the sound of a popping engine and Vijay's comments on the local bird life.

'Kinfisser,' he said to Tony's question about black and white birds that dived into the water, 'they are not living in England.'

'And that one Vijay?'

'Fish Eagle. Fishmen not like.'

'I'm not surprised,' said Tony, 'looks like he's got someone's dinner.'

They passed through rural villages of huts and a primitive lifestyle untouched by time. River life surrounded them, boys with sisal lines fished and waved or raced along the bank calling, 'pen, pen,' and emerging from the water holding up the thrown ballpoint in triumph.

Sam quipped that it was like *The African Queen* and stifled a scream as a snake slid by, to assurances from Vijay that it was harmless.

'How do the snake charmers do it, Vijay?' asked Andrew.

He rocked his head and wriggled his fingers as though playing an instrument. 'A bin.'

'Ah, a flute.'

'Aam,' he nodded, 'movement, not music.'

They chugged in sheer bliss, witnessing a life of simplicity surrounded for once by unpolluted beauty where people survived on fish and fishing alone.

'Time for a drink yet, Vijay?'

'Ten minnit,' he said, and Tony saw his earlier tension return as the huge temple of Maroutai came into view where Sunil waited on the bank.

'Oh, how kind,' said Hillary five minutes later, when the doorman of the Holiday Inn recognised them with a salute and helped them from the bus.

'John's idea I bet,' said Sam, 'typical . . .'

* * *

The same waiter seated them at a smart table by the window overlooking the harbour cluttered with boxes, trolleys and scurrying porters. He brought two cold beers and two glasses of lime-juice, unasked. Lemon fragrance filled the air-conditioned restaurant while soft percussion beat out an attractive rhythm to sitars twanging melodiously from background speakers as they relaxed in a tranquil environment.

'Is culture infectious, Andy?'

'Pardon?'

'I'm beginning to like Indian music – hear that?'

'Aye, very restful. I suppose even an ignoramus from West Ham must gain in culture if he is exposed to it often enough! While we are about it let's go all the way and eat Indian. That's what they do in West Ham on a Friday night, isn't it?'

'Oi, careful Jock, it beats bloody haggis,' he joked.

Between sips of beer, the waiter's advice guided them through the menu. 'That is masala dosa sir – curried vegetables, idli – you call dumplings, malai kofta – a ball of cheese and vegetables in sauce . . . May I suggest sir that we provide a selection that will suit your palate?'

'Aye. Ma friend only knows poppadoms and chicken masala.'

The waiter smiled and left them to watch the porters handling the fish in the harbour.

'What are they?' Asked Tony.

'Those? Red Snapper, a kind of whiting – and calamari.'

'What's that?'

'Octopus.'

'I only know haddock and cod when it's covered in batter and wrapped in paper.'

'Ye' really are ignorant Tony.'

'Like Sammy and her elephants, mate, we don't see many trawlers in Richmond. Here, look at them soldiers and the old Lee Enfields, is that an officer? Sam said one dressed like that came to see John.'

'Aye could be. What's a Lee Enfield?'

'Now who's ignorant? It's a rifle mate, army issue, three oh three ... wonder if one of them's my dad's ...'

'Discussing Mr Baker again are we?' said Sam, arriving from behind them. 'Do you know Hillary, his dad was a detriment to the army, he never fired his gun in anger and he was here for three years. The only reason we came to India was so that Tony can go home and swap experiences.'

Tony smiled pleasantly, 'Loos nice dear?' he said contemptuously.

'Yep,' she said, 'with proper seats and not those awful foot pads. I got soaked yesterday when I flushed one.'

'Very interesting love, 'he said testily. 'Drink your drink and relax, we are going Indian today.'

* * *

Tony looked round for the waiter to pay the bill, 'Oh Christ, no!'

'What's the matter?'

'Don't look now, it's Mitra.'

On impulse Sam turned. A well-dressed, dapper Indian approached them smiling. She automatically returned his smile.

'Good afternoon my friends,' he said breezily in a manner that indicated long term acquaintance, 'what a coincidence to meet so soon, we must be fated, as we say. I take it you will have no objections if I join you?' He turned and looked at the waiter who hurried to bring another chair.

'How charming you look ladies, I do hope that you have had a good morning under Vijay's guidance.'

Sam saw Tony stiffen but with an objective in mind, she took the initiative as well, as the opportunity to study him. 'We have Mr Mitra, thank you, it's nice to see you again,' she said, noting the white silk shirt and royal blue tie and, turned to glare at Tony, 'isn't it?' she added. His cream suit, which must have cost a fortune, was obviously hand crafted to fit his neat figure and as he moved, she saw the shoes, quality, black, shiny and expensive – but then he was a millionaire.

John's description came to her, 'A face that would curdle milk,' Yes, she could see that. The lips turned down at the corners as though he was grimacing, she supposed it represented a smile and tried to think of a word ... supercilious? Probably but even that would not deter her from her course.

He smiled; his brows rose in a permanent expression of surprise that pulled his eyelids up. 'Please do not think it rude of me,' he said addressing the males, 'I rarely get the chance to speak to English people so I must take every opportunity presented. One is often so isolated from the English in this part of rural India, you know, but there is no need to tell you, situated as you are in your present accommodation ...'

Tony bristled. Sam threw him a visual warning again and Mitra smiled without parting his lips.

'... and how clever of your dear lady to remember my name, I am indeed complimented, but you must call me Dhankar, as my friend John does. I trust he is well and that you passed on my compliments?'

'Certainly did,' said Tony with a straight face, 'he was well surprised.'

Sam gripped her glass. There was a kind of unctuousness about Mitra and she fleetingly imagined that he was trying to ingratiate himself. He would be wasting his time with Tony who would have already summed him up for either ridicule or contempt – but not her – she wanted to see that house.

'I see your glasses are nearly empty, do let me re-order,' he said raising his arm.

Despite their protests, he insisted, saying that had they not eaten they could have enjoyed a convivial lunch together in these modern, pleasant surroundings after the rawness of Paradise Lake.

'We enjoy it,' said Tony in what Sam saw as rising hostility, 'it's what we came for. We're too well fed at home. We will have to make it quick, Vijay is waiting.'

'I will send your boy a message.'

From the corner of her eye, she saw Tony about to retort and jumped in quickly, 'Are you here on business Mr Mitra?'

'No dear lady, I lunch here daily.' He turned to Andrew. 'One of my smaller establishments is situated in the foyer of the Hotel. Perhaps you would like to pay a visit on your departure. Much is hand made and my man will attend to your requirements ...'

Impressed by his command of English and with little trace of an accent, the manner of his delivery and choice of words showed elegance and a good education, but then with his riches ... He also appeared insensitive to sarcasm; he would be of course, businessmen get used to that and even Tony and his East End cheek would be unlikely to penetrate his thick skin. Yet Mitra was no fool, it was his self-importance that would kindle Tony's animosity. She prayed the situation would not arise, particularly since the large table kept her outside kicking range. For all that, Tony would love the key to his particular door and if he ruined her chance of seeing that house, she'd kill him.

She studied Mitra's eyes, 'windows to personality,' according to her 'Personnel Training Manual.' His were small and calculating, crafty, like some of the, 'wide boys' she'd warned Tony about in their early acquaintance. Mitra never actually laughed either, deferential sounds sneaked from behind crimped lips that spread downwards but never fully parted. His voice however, belied his eyes, sonorous, melodious. Yes, melodious, that was the word and she observed that although he was polite to the girls he rarely directed questions at them. At one point she asked him how he'd met John; he directed his reply at Andrew. Our acquaintance has been long lasting so one keeps in touch through friends in the area, "Keeping tabs", as we say, despite the differing directions one takes. I take it he is still very busy, Mr Mackay?'

'He appears to be. Have you known him long?'

'Indeed,' he said, 'a hive of industry who fires his acquaintances with enthusiasm and as industrious as ever. I understand he is now entertaining guests and I imagine that keeps him thoroughly occupied.'

'It seems to,' said Andrew. 'Were you connected through business?'

'One would not say so. Are you the only guests? I hear his establishments are equipped for many.'

'Establishments? We know nothing about those.'

'Indeed, were you not aware there is another a little distance from Paradise Lake?'

'Really? Perhaps that is where Sanjay works.'

'Indeed. How did you get to know of his enterprise?'

'Through his agent in England,' replied Andrew.

'Ah,' he said in recognition, 'that would be his friend Colin? We met when he was in India you know, such a nice fellow, no doubt he will succeed in filling the new constructions . . .?'

'We know nothing of that . . .' replied Andrew and stopped suddenly to look at his watch. 'Goodness, look at the time, we really must be off,' he said, 'Vijay is waiting, I'm sorry Mr Mitra,' he said easing his chair back, 'we must stick to our itinerary.' He pushed out his hand, 'Thank you for your hospitality, perhaps we will meet again.'

'One cannot stop the inevitable march of time I suppose, but be so kind as to take my card and tell my friend that I am insistent. You will visit my humble home, along with him. This weekend will suit, shall we say Sunday at 3 p.m.? He will advise me through Sanjay. Then, perhaps, we will have more time to "chew the fat" as we say.'

Sam, object accomplished, smiled at him, 'Thank you Mr Mitra, we will be there.'

'Dhankar please,' he said with a half bow as they edged their way towards the door. He remained standing with a sardonic smile on his face when they made their exit.

'Smirking sod,' said Tony when they got outside.

'Oi! Keep your opinions to yourself, I want to see that house or you and me will fall out.'

'Alright, alright,' he snapped. 'He sounds like a bad actor with his, "old fellow," and "Ind-yah". Still, enjoy the loos girls,' he called as they disappeared and joined Andrew, who was looking in a shop window.

'Look at this Tony. I thought John said his chess set was a one off?'

Tony looked, 'Yeah, funny that, but it's a replica mate, not as good as John's. Odd though ain't it . . .?' he said as the girls emerged.

Sunil used the main road back to Amitar instead of the country route. The vehicle hummed along steadily, this time dust and noise free. The steady drone, the satisfying meal and the heat combined to make them drowsy until lethargy and eventually sleep took over and, accompanied by the constant resonance from the tyres, they dozed.

Wakened by a group of street vendors yelling beside the halted minibus, Andrew peered into the sunlight, the gleaming brightness forced him to raise his hand and shield his eyes. They waited in traffic while the heat built and an exhaust from a stationary lorry at window level poured choking fumes into the interior. He closed the window.

'Get us out of here Sunil or we'll all die,' called Tony.

'One minnit,' he replied, laughing, 'waiting for pleece.'

'What,' asked Tony, leaning forward and catching a glimpse of more khaki uniforms at the jammed crossroads, 'are they police?'

Sunil's head rocked this time, 'Here for lekshun.'

'Election, why were they at the lake?'

'They are asking for Samuel.'

'Who's Samuel? One of your boys.'

'Aam.'

'When's the election, Vijay?'

'Two, three week . . .'

The minibus moved on haltingly, weaving its way between kerbside stalls. It was odd to see trades carried out on pavements, cobblers, bike menders, barbers and tailors, alongside a mass of traffic and stinking exhausts, all accompanied by the coarse sounds of music, blaring from the crude loudspeakers set up in the square.

'Not as good as the music at the hotel Tony,' he said. 'Do you like it Sam?'

'In the hotel yes, but just think,' she said, 'if that breeze blows in the right direction, we will be treated to it all evening. Still, it might drown out that bloody Sanjay.'

NINE

John left very early and returned to Paradise Lake after a fruitless visit to the Facility Centre, still wrestling with the problem how to obtain half a million rupees. From the look of things now, it was the lover's cash or nothing, but he saw a glimmer of hope in Mitra's friendliness towards his guests. It was so out of character for him to be friendly to strangers that there must be a catch, he was after something. Past differences had kept them apart and, if he did want a favour, John had nothing to give or at least he thought he had nothing. With luck though, the answer might be en-route, via Vijay, today.

He called for Kumar to get some coffee and asked him if Sanjay had left.

Kumar's face clouded, 'Is he here, Mr John?'

'He was last night, go and check there's a good . . .' He saw Kumar's expression, 'hey that's enough of that,' he said harshly, 'go and see him. If he's there get him up . . . and when he's gone you can give me a shower.'

'Yes Mr John,' he grumbled and disappeared along the veranda leaving John smiling in his wake. Causing Sanjay discomfort would make Kumar's day.

Kumar returned smiling and made breakfast. John listened for the shower but heard nothing; ten minutes later Sanjay arrived.

'You took your time – something wrong – got a headache have we?' said John with heavy sarcasm between bites of toast.

Sanjay, pulled at the skin on his face, yawned and crashed into the chair next to John with a long drawn out, 'uuu . . . gh', followed by another deep intake and exhalation of breath.

A look of distaste crossed John's face. 'Don't breathe this way for God's sake,' he complained, turning his head away.

Sanjay shook his head, yawned again and in a voice, rasping with alcohol said, 'Your little boy said you wanted me right away.'

'I did – but not smelling like a bloody carthorse! Go and shower – and clean your teeth while you're at it.'

Sanjay stood wearily and turned towards the bedroom with John following his uncertain progress. His increasing waistline made him appear much stockier than he used to be, ungainly too, reducing his physical attraction while his handsomeness had long diminished. In parallel, his attitude had changed, infusing John with constant mistrust. His indiscreet interference with the boys, minor though it was, had led to his ban from the camp and, so far, John had found no evidence that it had resurfaced. He'd changed though from the person whose incredible streetwise ability and resourceful ideas had saved them frequently, to a bitter, slothful complainer, always hard done by and resentful. His skill in exploiting opportunities which had started many of their enterprises was undermined by a non-existent management ability. He would never advance to leadership in the modern world.

Who else would fill that vacancy though, Vijay, Sunil? No fear, not since they coerced him into sending them to Maroutai College and then insisting that they remain with Orphindi. Even if they had ability there was no way he would offer them the post, after Sunil's stand, especially . . . well, perhaps it was better not to think about that.

'Well think of the devil,' he said pleasantly as Sanjay returned, looking hangdog. 'Feeling better are we?'

Sanjay grunted.

'Sit down, I want a word.' He leaned forward. 'Right,' he said, 'you got the sand then?'

'I told you so, and I ordered a small load too . . .'

'What the bloody hell for?'

'The bill, I need a bill,' he rapped as though hurt, 'just in case.'

'Oh, yes . . .' said John subdued, 'OK, good thinking. Now then, your friend Mitra met your friends the Westerners and gave them a tentative invitation to visit him, which I hope will be confirmed today and . . .'

'I thought you'd fallen out with him?'

'I have – but you have not! So if the invite stands see Mitra and arrange a time. I can't come.'

Sanjay shrugged. 'Why?'

'Never mind why, do as I say. Now we are off to the camp to sort out this Samuel business. Have you spoken to Shamin?'

Sanjay shook his head.

'Haven't done much about it have you?'

* * *

The compound looked as orderly as ever, military in appearance with white painted stones edging the gravel path, surrounding a central rectangle filled with vegetables, no space wasted here. Each side of the rectangle stood five identical, stone based dormitories measuring fifty by twenty feet, with wattle walls and thatched roofs.

Across the top of the rectangle were showers, a toilet block and a new concrete water tank that stood out like chalk from cheese. Next to that was an office and at the lower end were workshops of similar construction to the huts. All were immaculately kept with more neat and tidy vegetable patches using up every available space.

'You haven't painted that tank yet?'

'I haven't had time,' Sanjay answered guardedly.

'Well tell the boys to do it ... today – and I mean today! No swimming till it's finished,' John snapped. 'If anyone sees it they will know we couldn't build that monster. Now then, which is Samuel's hut?'

Sanjay led him to the first dwelling, nearest the entrance, and pushed open the door. John stood looking into institutional orderliness, twenty neatly rolled rush mats placed against oblong green ammunition boxes.

'Tidy,' he complimented. 'Which was his?'

Sanjay pointed to the first, by the door.

'Looked in his box have you?' But before Sanjay could reply, John had lifted the lid. 'Look,' he said holding the lid up, 'what does that tell you?'

Sanjay looked, pulled a face and shook his head.

'It's empty Sanjay, E M P T Y! He cleared it before he left,' he said raising his voice. 'So he didn't just run away, his departure was arranged,' he said, pausing in the hope of drawing something from the blankness facing him. 'Well?'

Sanjay shrugged, 'Kenneth didn't say anything.'

'What?' John lifting his voice an octave, 'Kenneth has been sleeping next to the only empty bed on camp and said nothing? Did you bother to ask or didn't he bother to tell you? Is he taking advantage or don't you care? If he is, don't be so bloody lenient!' he said, slamming the locker lid shut. 'See him today and sort the little tyke out, he's supposed to report to you – and I want chapter and verse. I don't want bloody Joshi turning up and asking questions that I can't answer,' he grumbled.

He stepped out of the hut and turned, about to see the secretary Shamin, then stopped, having second thoughts and turned to face Sanjay.

'Check the store for paint ... then get that tank done ... go on make yourself useful,' and he turned away heading for the office.

Each with a face like a dark cloud they went their separate ways, Sanjay to the workshop and John to the office. A bicycle had been left against the wall and a woman's voice said amicably when he entered, 'I thought I heard an engine.'

'Namaste Shamin, everything in order?' he said to the vivaciously attractive woman sitting behind the desk.

'Yes and such a surprise, you are my second visitor today. You have just missed Sergeant Birkram.'

John stood rooted, 'Birkram?' he said, 'what did he want?'

'He asked about Samuel's friends, the new Inspector sent him. I told him what I knew and showed him the dormitory.'

'I see,' he mumbled, his mind on other things, hoping not to betray his anxiety. 'I'll pop down and see him later. Everything OK?'

She nodded.

'That's fine,' he said, backed out and stalked down the compound opening the workshop door with a crash.

'See what you started, you silly bastard?' he shouted. 'Bloody Joshi sent that nosy sod Birkram here today! I just hope you've told me everything Sanjay.' He paused to study his face, deliberately delaying the next question. 'Have you?' he demanded.

Sanjay twitched and looked at the ground. His effort to control a mouth that quivered failed, he looked about to cry again.

John said nothing for a moment but when he did the lure came softly, no raging voice, no harsh words. 'Look son,' he said, 'we have a lot in common and if you are in trouble you can rely on me, tell me now and then we can prepare for the consequences. We can't help our nature can we, and it's not the first time I've helped, is it?'

Sanjay shook his head.

'Come on then . . .?'

The gentle approach, the soft tones and flowing enticement worked. Encouraged by patience and apparent sympathy, Sanjay seemed powerless to hold back this time. With expected excuses and tumbling justification he mumbled, incoherently at times, while John tried to make sense of it. 'He didn't mean any harm; he didn't know how he would react, he appeared shy but said he was willing, after all he was due to leave this year and there was money in it . . . and . . . well . . .'

John, reading between the lines, nodded patiently, keeping up a friendly profile until the end to place a fatherly hand on his shoulder, 'Alright son, just an induction, a flirtation eh?'

Sanjay nodded enthusiastically, 'Yes . . . that's it . . . a flirtation,' he said, relieved.

'OK son,' said John quietly acquiescing, 'and it all happened when I was away, OK? You made enquiries and did your best before getting me involved. Be warned Sanjay, once more and you are on your own.'

He walked to the door with a frown etched deep into his face and a temper he found difficult to control. 'Don't forget that tank,' he said over his shoulder, 'and see to Mitra, take the bike.'

Sanjay gave a wan smile, unaware that his confession had raised grave new doubts. Behind the big man's soothing words there were more questions, few answers and a deeper mistrust than ever.

He left the Enfield behind and walked to the entrance. Looking left he could see Sanjay's hut opposite the compound, fenced off.

It's not the bloody hut that needs fencing off; he thought vindictively, it's him!

TEN

'You're early, you've caught out the system Sam, we haven't tidied the rooms yet,' John said when he saw her stagger up the steps leading the others.

'Too hot John, give laughing boy here a seat in the shade and a bucket of beer and keep him out of my way while I cool down. If I'm not back in two days I've been washed down the drain.'

Andrew chuckled and Tony winked before they sat with cold beers in front of them at the rattan table. John gave Kumar whispered instructions.

Inside the bedroom Sam shrugged off her damp shorts, peeled off her blouse and stuck-to-skin underclothes and threw them into the wash basket. She made straight for the shower rubbing the weals on her shoulders, thinking how comfortable it would be to live without chaffing clothes or straps in this heat.

She turned on the gentle spray and stood luxuriating under streams of tepid water, resisting an ecstatic squeal of pleasure while the liquid ran over her naked body. In cool rapture, oblivious to sight or sound, she closed her eyes, feeling strangely daring, naked in the unfamiliar room and allowing the intimate water to pet her body. She stretched her arms into the air and parted her thighs enjoying the sensations created by the sprinkled liquid that caressed and massaged like soft, cool hands touching and teasing. The watery fondling seemed to sharpen her senses in one place and then move on to tease another, re-creating the pleasure as she turned. Her skin tightened and tingled while heat and weariness slowly dissipated leaving in its place a new, enhanced sensuousness.

Thought provoking, sexually enhanced and exhilarated, she wished for company. Unwittingly a vision of Kumar naked, facing her, flashed through her mind, before guilt pressed her to shut off the tap and reach for a towel. She gently stroked away the surplus moisture only to become immediately damp again in the humid room, generating a longing to return to the shower. She bent her head towards the floor and wound a towel round her wet hair.

Leaning forward, head down, she stepped quickly out of the shower room into the cooler bedroom, her view restricted to the floor. Using it as a map she made her way towards the dressing table and turned into the narrow space beside her bed.

'Oh!' she gasped and stopped dead. Next to hers was a pair of naked black feet. She looked up into the face of Kumar!

With both hands holding the towel, she stood, statue-like, open-eyed, open-mouthed and immobile, half surprised and half pleased, fully aware, not only of her own exposure, but of his naked chest only inches from her breasts, with him trapped in the narrow passage, his young face only twelve tempting inches away.

His dhoti brush her naked leg. He looked uneasy, she expected that in her fantasy about him and hoped her developing smile would show she was not alarmed. She deliberately clung to the towel with both hands, aware of the enhanced shape of her breasts and stood erect, expectant and playful. Fleetingly she saw the hands that caressed the glass and imagined them touching, stroking, investigating, increasing the sensual experience initiated in the shower. Daring and teasing she tilted her chin upwards.

The draught of his movement kissed her body, heightening her expectancy; her eyes began to close but the delayed touch induced caution. She opened her eyes fully and instead of an eager flush of enthused passion, she saw his stare of astonishment.

Fear, surprise contempt, she was not sure, he backed away vacant, apparently, of any arousal. He didn't examine or assess, look or touch or appear to take pleasure in her nudity; his alarmed, chestnut eyes penetrated hers.

Her smile faded, her confidence drained, she flushed bright red, the shower that had so cooled her skin wasted. Unnerved by his apathy, she felt the need to apologise. Flustered and half choking, she mouthed, 'Sorry Kumar, I . . . er . . . I, didn't know you were here . . .'

It sounded inept, inadequate, she backed away unwinding the towel, covering herself as best she could in retreat and, grabbing clothes from the drawer she exposed her rear as she turned to run to the sanctuary of the shower room.

The encounter had lasted only a moment yet it seemed an age, and mortified with embarrassment she stood in silence on the damp floor, quivering, hurt and angry, pulling on underwear, conscious that her impudent tease, even in accidental circumstances, now seemed so foolish.

She heard the door open and close. Thank goodness, he'd gone. She opened the bathroom door to peek.

''Ello! 'ello! What's all this? My misses alone naked in the bedroom with a male! What's going on?' Tony said, grinning, impishly.

Recovering quickly and retreating further behind the shower room door she answered sharply, 'Damn! You spoiled my chance of an erotic liaison!'

'Oh yeah?' he retorted. 'No chance with the attention he's giving that bed.'

She gave a false laugh and waited for Kumar to depart before leaving the shower to kiss Tony's cheek and seat herself at the dressing table. 'Shame really, he's only a boy, nice looking though,' she complained, 'but he probably lacks the essentials.'

'Does he now?' said Tony approaching her from behind, 'looking for the mature type are we?'

He lowered his head and whispered close to her ear, 'How do I measure up?'

She knew the signs and sat upright smiling at his reflection in the mirror.

'A bit of TLC is called for I think,' he said, placing both hands on her shoulders and massaging them gently, 'how's that?'

'Heaven – don't stop.'

He leaned down and kissed her neck, 'Them straps look a bit tight love, shall I relieve the pressure?'

She rose from the seat and stood facing him, smiling enticingly. 'It's those straps – and you are a bloody pest, Baker, I've just showered . . .!'

* * *

That evening Sam looked out over the moonlit brush at a million shiny leaves that trembled and sparkled like fairy lights in the rare breeze. A nightjar kerred its way across the bushes and bats from hill caves, with wings whirring, swooped to capture moths around the pergola lights. Everything was so pristine and beautiful here, in contrast to the grubby, dilapidated towns they saw on their travels. So caught up with the beauty she forgot to keep a customary eye on the kitchen.

'Pliss,' she heard from behind her and whirled round to see Kumar smiling gently at her, pointing towards the stairway.

She flushed and stammered, 'Er . . . yes . . .' and turned quickly away to hide her discomfort, waiting for the others to take the lead. She rose last but Kumar had waited too and politely moved her chair back. She flushed again sensing that the others were aware of the guilt that saturated her.

'Pliss,' he said again, looking straight at her with a smile.

She sucked in air, lowered her head and followed Hillary upstairs, conscious of her error, evading eye contact.

During the meal, Sam caught Hillary looking at her – curiously. She knew! Sam knew she knew. Shrewd Hillary's eyes questioned her and received condescending smiles in return, Sam's ability to communicate held hostage by her guilt.

She caught Kumar looking at her again, was it self-consciousness, admiration, reconciliation? Whatever, it did nothing to ease the tension knotting her stomach, although it tended, in turn, to intensify her own curiosity. Guilefully she kept an eye on him too.

Tony, seated in the absence of John next to Hillary, seemed aware, he lifted his head suddenly and she caught his quizzical gaze, 'You alright love?' he said.

'Yes' she said offhandedly, 'bit tired that's all.'

'Mmm,' he said grinning mischievously, 'I wonder what caused that?' Her wan smile faded quickly when Kumar approached.

He stood unexpectedly close, looking directly into her face and smiling. She wished he wouldn't, he might give the game away – and so would she unless she faced up to him.

'Wine,' he said and, daring to look unto his face, she saw his acceptance, it lifted her melancholy. Her face lit, she smiled back, 'Yes please Kumar, thank you,' and received an expanded grin before he moved on to Hillary.

'Wine?' he said again, in continuance of a rare interaction.

'Yes Kumar,' said Hillary sweetly, 'thank you.'

Tony leaned towards Andrew. 'Caught her in the bedroom today Andy with Kumar – wearing only her bra and knickers!

'He wasn't,' she retorted instantly, 'I was wearing them.'

It released what remained of her tension, they laughed as John arrived.

His presence generated conversation and she could have kissed him when he said he had arranged the trip to Mitra's hoime on Sunday.

'I can ask him then,' said Andrew, 'where he got the chess set we saw in his shop.'

Sam saw John hesitate; it was momentarily and he replied into his plate, offhandedly, 'Mmm, really? Anything else of interest?'

'Yes,' said Tony, 'You been nicking bullocks again? Amitar was alive with Police. Vijay said they were there for the election?'

'An election, is there an election? I wouldn't know, I rarely go to town.' He offered no more.

Sam turned her attention back to Kumar, intending now to investigate, not attract. Curious and conscious of his change of attitude towards her, she also noted a changed attitude to John. His obedience was, as ever, undiminished yet he appeared to have lost his servility. He worked purposefully, not meekly and his looks did not contain the admiration and obligation she'd seen before. They were, like hers, investigative. It occurred to her that their encounter might actually have pleased and not repulsed him.

He came close to her side again offering a refill, his diffidence and reserve gone and although she could smell the same delicate scent from his body, it failed to excite. His attention, although pleasingly different, kept her curious, was it forgiveness, had she awakened the senses of an adolescent male in a monkish existence that excluded women. It was obvious he had never seen a nude female, could it be that seeing her naked had aroused or confused him in his life of sexual ignorance? Suddenly she felt motherly and sympathetic.

The table talk turned to football. She leaned forward, 'Our cue to move I think,' she said loudly to Hillary and stood.

Kumar passed her against the light as she stood and, in silhouette, she took an unintentional intake of breath. She recognised that silhouette. It had been him passing her window.

* * *

Sam sat in Hillary's room opposite her while Hillary opened a packet of cracker biscuits and cheese. 'The meal not to your taste, Samantha?'

'No – but I'm curious about the use of Samantha! What have I done?'

'We-e-ll,' drawled Hillary, 'ten years working in a library tends to sharpen one's sensitivity, so it's your choice,' she said withholding a cracker and cheese, 'tell me or starve.'

'I see,' she said slowly shaking her head. 'I had the feeling you knew . . . oh what the hell . . .'

Condensing the incident with Kumar and slanting the explanation in her favour with excuses, 'accidental circumstance, so surprised . . . well shocked really,' keeping close to the truth but concealing her deliberate baiting, she related the event but flushed again when she tried to joke that she was 'all talced up, deodorised and virginal, more concerned with the towel slipping . . .'

'You are a fibber Samantha, you teased him but he wouldn't bite would he?'

'No, I did not, I . . .'

'Yes Samantha you did, you always do and to think with your experience you haven't noticed, I am surprised.'

'Noticed what?'

'There,' she said jubilantly and waited, watching Sam's expression. 'He's gay.'

'Gay?' she said, choking on the biscuit. 'Don't be silly ... he's no more gay than ...' Her voice tailed off as she relived the moment. 'No ...' she stopped and searched her mind for any possible other reason. 'Perhaps he ... no, I don't believe it ... although I ...' she didn't finish the sentence, her mind occupied with his uncharacteristic behaviour this evening. 'But Hilly I could swear ...' she stopped again in total confusing as a burst of laughter from the hallway disturbed them.

They hurriedly packed the food away and stepped out on to the veranda to meet the men ambling towards them, visibly under the influence.

'Oh my God, look at the little darlings!' said Sam softly, 'another sleepless night and no chance to use my womanly charms.'

'A contradiction in terms, surely,' whispered Hillary.

'No, his snores will keep me awake just when I'm in the mood to put him through his paces, still I can try! Come on Anthony,' she ordered, 'let's get to bed.'

'But it's early, Sam. ...'

She hooked her arm in his, 'Not for what I have in mind,' she whispered. 'Come on.'

'Certainly my love, no sooner the word than the deed!' replied Tony grinning stupidly and sliding his arm around her waist.

'The little cherub,' she said over her shoulder and led him to the bedroom.

ELEVEN

Sanjay sat at the table in his squalid hut, lit by a single bulb, surrounded by unwashed bowls and sipping whisky. He felt more than one degree under. Self-pitying and resentful at the forced departure from a home that he built for him and John to share, he blamed Kumar.

Something was bound to change when John took the little brat off gardening duties six months ago and charmed and flattered him into bed. Sanjay had watched the process and listened to the excuses: 'I only need him to help with guests Sanjay, you will be comfortable on your own – you can always eat here,' John had said before evicting him from his room, his own room, the room in the house that he had built! Was it surprising that he sought new friends?

Had it not been for that though he would never have thought of the sidelines that brought in a few extra rupees, so it was not all bad. Trouble was, if John knew about the money he would want a share. Sanjay considered it a reward for suffering the embarrassment of being used as the token local, ridiculed by patronising westerners. Not only that but nowadays he was expected to do everything, inside and outside the camp under the thumb of John with no authority and little payment – he deserved his sidelines.

As for that stupid kid Kenneth, he should have said something, not report to that Shamin woman, if he steps out of line again his mother will be in for a shock, she'll be collecting dung for the fire, not buying it! If that idiot Samuel had played ball he too could be enjoying the benefits of . . .

He leapt out of the chair . . . footsteps on the gravel? He'd turned off the engine, the crafty bastard . . . he rushed around clearing up but before he'd hidden the whisky, the door was pushed open and John strolled in with a face like a smacked arse.

Just as a camera pans, his eyes swept the room, a look of distaste spreading across his face and, hoping to modulate his inevitable carping, Sanjay pushed open the front and back windows.

'I should think so, it smells like a zoo in here,' John grumbled.

'I don't have boys to clean up after me,' Sanjay said sullenly, 'What do you want? I got the tank finished,' he said, trying to mitigate an inevitable complaint.

'About time too,' said John as his eyes searched the room again. Spotting the whisky, he took a glass to the sink, washed it in the bowl returned casually to the table and poured a small measure.

'Now then, how did you know Mitra would be at the Holiday Inn?'

Sanjay shook his head and shrugged to gain thinking time ... it came to him, 'He has a shop there.'

'He doesn't run it!' snapped John, 'but I'm told he sells chess sets?'

The remark sent a bead of sweat down Sanjay's forehead. 'I don't know what he sells.'

'Of course not, how silly of me ... but in that case you won't mind me looking over our sales list, because I wonder where he got it?'

'Please yourself. I don't know what you are talking ab ...'

'Stop – you know nothing about my present.'

'What present?'

John gave a series of tiny nods. 'I see. It shows how much attention you pay to the bloody workshop when the lads produced a complete chess set from ivory and ebony and you don't know!' He paused for a moment.

'What else don't you know about ... about Samuel I mean?'

Sanjay gritted his teeth, shook his head and said nothing while John nodded several times openly showing disbelief and eying him suspiciously.

'You did tell me everything didn't you? A flirtation, that's all?'

On the verge of panic Sanjay prayed for John's departure. 'I ... said so didn't I?'

John took a swallow of the whisky and nodded again ... Slowly. 'What you say and what you mean Sanjay ...?' he left the sentence unfinished, sank the rest of the whisky, turned to leave and turned back.

'The less you say at the meeting tomorrow the better, but make sure you see your mate, the construction engineer Nadu, and tap him up about that road – I want something concrete.' He smiled at his joke. 'Be ready for ten and in the meantime, I'll get the figures from the workshop ... if you don't mind that is ...'

Sanjay closed his eyes as the Enfield started and poured a large whisky. Was John aware, was he guessing? He sat holding the glass, staring and swirling the amber liquid around in the tumbler. Damn Samuel and damn those nosy, interfering bloody whites too, he could be in more trouble ...

* * *

It was half past ten when John, having picked up the workshop papers, switched off the engine and listened to the pleasant buzz of the chain on the sprocket and the crunch of tyres on the path as he let the machine drift for the last fifty yards. He braked and parked, tired and uneasy after a particularly long, irritating day.

Being without dinner was bad enough but having to suffer Sanjay's lies – the creeping doubts left him infuriated, it also angered him to have to check up on figures so late at night and he was in a filthy mood when he walked wearily up the steps to the brightly-lit pergola expecting to see Kumar.

To his disappointment Kumar was nowhere to be seen, the door to the boy's quarters was closed and for a minute he stood in front of it perplexed and unsure. Strange, that, Kumar was always there. He didn't bother to check, he would be waiting in the bedroom so he entered the kitchen, made a sandwich and took it to the rattan table.

Anchoring himself to a chair he tried to study the paperwork, plus a fax he'd picked up this evening from the Facility Centre.

It did not relieve his worries, the sales figures confused him and in only minutes, tired and droopy, he gave up trying to understand them and trudged wearily to his, unusually, empty room.

TWELVE

John was awake when the minibus arrived at seven to take the guests off. He'd expected Kumar to wake him – he didn't – so he missed their departure. After a shower he sat down to breakfast served by a distant, almost hostile, Kumar. Temperamental bloody teenagers, he didn't need them to add to his depression, today's meeting would do that.

Colin's fax had cheered and worried him, the goods news was that his latest advertising campaign had attracted many enquiries, the worry that if converted he would have a serious shortage of accommodation. To refuse the bookings would cause Colin to throw a fit and John had enough on his plate without his tantrums. A loan of ten grand would cure the problems but none of these buggers would take a chance.

Despite his reservations, even Mitra's cash would be preferable to Graham's – and there was plenty of it. Given the right incentive he could have business lift off double quick, it might mean giving up some sovereignty but it'll be worth the quick rewards. He'd have to watch though, Mitra was a crafty sod, as crafty as Graham, so where's the difference? There was something curious and intriguing though, about Mitra's offer, he did nothing without good reason.

Finishing his meal John picked up Sanjay and drove to town where traffic jammed the streets. Half the population seemed to head for the square on Saturdays, his progress thwarted by crawling bikes, rickshaws and vans that poured out exhaust fumes. He tried the narrow back roads. 'Sod it,' he shouted in frustration, his progress halted yet again by a parked car blocking the street.

'Mr John,' said an onlooker, 'please, wait – wait.' In seconds a group had gathered, 'Ari baap ri baap,' (Oh my goodness!) they cried and strong arms lifted and bumped the offending car close to a wall allowing him passage to the square.

His reception was, as ever, the same, his very presence drew crowds of people who milled around smiling with hands raised in greeting. His own perfunctory waves and smile did not disclose his awareness that their amiability rested on hope, a mortgage for the future, just in case. He left Sanjay to park the bike, to nod and smile his way to the Land Office and the Telex Centre, from which he emerged smiling and stuffing the latest fax in his pocket.

'Got you, you bastard,' he said vehemently.

* * *

They were the first at the meeting. Sanjay sat at John's side and licked lips, dry with nervous apprehension. This was unnecessary in the old days, a few rupees placed into the right hands and the job was done, often with side benefits; now they were expected to account for everything through this committee.

Members arrived in dribs and drabs: Sharma, the town Construction Engineer was first, small, rounded, western suited and pompous, with a goatee beard, rimless glasses and full of his own superiority. His disdain for the council clerk Bhopali, whose raised hands went unacknowledged, was obvious, Sharma's nose and chin lifted, his mouth hung down disagreeably and the goatee pointed forward like a signpost away from Bhopali. He was a subordinate and, like Nadu his assistant, was treated as such.

Sanjay knew the feeling, as Sharma nodded to him but made directly for John, to apologise that he had family business to attend and that he had instructed Nadu to act on his behalf.

He seemed under the impression that the smile lighting John's face was a greeting, not relief, as he arrogantly excused himself on the grounds that, 'I gather there is little that needs my attention.'

'Nothing Ravi, nothing at all,' answered John, 'Namaste.'

Sharma left, John grinned behind his back at Nadu, unprotected now in Sharma's absence. 'A pleasure to see you Mr Nadu?'

Nadu nodded shyly.

At twenty-four years old he was never comfortable in the limelight and tended to hide behind papers. Bespectacled, softly spoken and clearly ill at ease, John had nicknamed him, 'Brains,' and ridiculed that he was a, 'University educated technician who could mentally work out the square root of an hexagonal jam jar – but couldn't get the bloody lid off.' Nevertheless his weakness served a purpose – Sanjay could bully him.

Nadeen was polite and respectful and smiled sweetly, her hair hung beyond her shoulders today and she was dressed Western style in a long, loose, black skirt and a tight fitting, white cotton blouse that enlarged her bosom to fascination point for unmarried Nadu. Sanjay saw his sneaked glances at breasts that pressed forcefully outwards like orbiting planets.

John's dislike of her didn't surprise Sanjay, he referred to her as a 'cold cow,' and to him that seemed unfair but then, that was John. He also called Graham a cheat who couldn't be trusted and when Graham turned up six months ago, he said that he'd left England just ahead of the police. Although he appeared upper class, he was still a crook – but then John had hardly a good word to say about anyone lately.

Very fat and very short with thin, black, oiled hair, Mahmood arrived, sweating profusely, wearing a quality, but baggy, suit, the smell of cigars clinging to it and wafting in his wake. It was obvious where his interests lay when he sat between the council clerk and Nadu. Contracts! School supplies, consumables and work clothes were his interests, apart from a couple of down-market hotels in town. He nodded discreetly to Sanjay and smiled broadly at John.

Mahmood, picked by John for his wealth, not that he got any of it, reached across and clasped John's hand with a grip that seemed to make him wince. He did the same to the council representative, Mr Bhopali, an unusually small framed, turbaned and bearded man, whom John called 'The Tatler'. Bhopali went out of his way to be polite to all with hollow smiles and raised hands and make copious notes in his pocket book. John said he was an ambitious, contentious spy, despite his benign facade, whom Mahmood intended to cultivate.

Last to arrive was Rasa, tall, popular, polite and useful, even John had to concede that. Educated, honest, modest and dignified, he was a member of the local Education committee and used his influence to pressure the council to improve school finances. He was John's true ally, although behind his back John thought his honesty a weakness and referred, even to him, as 'lily-livered.'

Settled in their places after a few minutes, John tapped the table, 'Secretary, please.'

'The minutes of the last meeting held . . .' announced Nadeen, and in a clear, velvety voice . . . the minutes were read.

Sanjay closed his ears to the waste of words, even John said that that the council needed this committee to ease its conscience over a non-existent child welfare policy, but it was boring and he couldn't wait to leave. Cool Nadeen finished and in no time the minutes were approved in the hot, humid room where everyone, except Nadeen, perspired.

John thanked her curtly. 'Treasurer's report please.'

Sanjay listened to Graham outline the progress and congratulate John on the increased income, before touching on tourism. It had started very slowly and the experiment had only produced a few thousand pounds profit . . .

Sanjay's mouth dropped open. A few thousand pounds, he'd kept that quiet . . .!

Had it lost money,' Graham continued, 'it would have been Mr John's loss, being a private enterprise. He hopes the position improves and . . .'

A few thousand pounds, Sanjay fumed? It was typical of John to pretend he had nothing yet sat on a hundred thousand rupees while he dished out humiliation and restriction! The cunning bastard – and he had the cheek to call Graham a crook! He was so incensed he brooded while John asked Nadu for an update on the road extension mentioned at the last meeting.

Nadu hesitated and stuttered that there were no funds available and . . . 'well I er . . .' He dried up.

John took it up right away saying if that was the case he might be forced to abandon tourism altogether unless he got help with the road. 'How can we hope to get insurance cover? The project was doomed to fail and the prospect for job creation, lost.'

Sanjay knew it was a game, a tease, to frighten them a little, make the council believe they might have to take full responsibility for the children.

John thanked Nadu, saying in gentle sympathy that he understood, '. . . although perhaps you will discuss the matter with Sanjay afterwards and find a compromise.'

Rasa backed him, 'A good road was vital for swift communication and hospital emergencies and it is essential . . .'

Sanjay saw John perk up with a hint of a smile as he leaned back, content to let Rasa fight his battles.

'I am sure,' said Rasa, 'that Mr Bhopali will report Mr Prichard's concerns to his seniors, he has enough worries looking after two hundred children, developing a business and tracing a missing inmate.'

Sanjay felt a ghostly hand tug at his stomach; he felt suddenly sick and caught the astonished look on John's face as the Council clerk scribbled.

John's arms unfolded, 'Thank you Rasa,' he said quickly, 'that matter, as you know, is being dealt with.'

For a moment, Sanjay felt the hand that gripped his stomach release. It tightened again when the little clerk lifted his head, and 'Have you a problem, Mr Prichard?'

'It's nothing.'

'A missing child, nothing?'

'That's right.'

'But the Local Authority needs to know. It has a responsibility.'

'Yes Mr Bhopali, we are aware of that.'

'Then we should be told,' said Bhopali, determinedly.

Sanjay saw John's jaw tighten, the knot in his own stomach remained and in the silence that followed, he heard the tap, tap of John's pencil on the table.

'Mr Bhopali,' John said through tightened lips, 'if the council wants immediate reports, it should work closer with us. I can't run to you with every minor incident.'

'This is hardly minor. You have a duty to report these occurrences.'

'Have I? You ignore us when we need help for essential medical, safety and development purposes, a road for instance, and interfere if it suits your conscience. These things happen. I do not run a prison and short of locking boys in day and night what can I do?'

'But surely Mr Prichard it is your responsibility to tell the council,' he said with quiet, unflappable obstinacy.

Sanjay dropped his head and closed his eyes, he was shaking.

'And what would you do?' snapped John.

'We would investigate the matter.'

'The police are doing that!'

'Then I am duty bound to look into it and report formerly to the council.'

'Are you suggesting the police, will not?' said John raising his voice.

'Well no, but . . .'

'No . . . exactly! I have spent the last thirty years running this charity and after two weeks trying to obtain support in England – which your council is again reluctant to provide – I return to find we are carrying out our own investigation before involving anyone else apart from the police! The headmaster has made enquiries and everything has been done which needs to be done, even you could do no more but clearly, you are not satisfied! If you wish, Mr Bhopali, I will hand over the responsibility for two hundred children to the council. You can fund their schooling, their training, their accommodation and provide work for their families! When you have done that, you can help Mr Punja to educate them and employ my staff of volunteers, it will save the Europeans, and me, a lot of trouble! As an alternative I could always return them to the streets!'

The little clerk looked shaken and winced at the tirade 'Well', he said, 'there is no need . . . I was merely saying . . .'

'... You were saying, Mr Bhopali, that the council has been ignored! If Council members want to monitor everything we do, remind them that my charity is running solely for the benefit of their community. If they wish, they can have it, lock, costs and camps, and I will retire. Now then! Let us come to the next item on the agenda – unless you want to take up my offer!'

Even Sanjay knew that such withering humiliation would never reach the ears of the council and Bhopali sat in mortified silence.

'Now Rasa, your report please.'

'I have nothing adverse to say Mr Chairman. We are happy with our school performance and may I thank you publicly for arranging to install the new floor ... for which we have you, not the council, to thank,' he said looking at Bhopali. 'Sanjay also tells me he that he is, as usual, seeking work for school leavers this August, although our hopes to absorb them into tourism look like being dashed,' he said pointedly again looking at Bhopali. 'It occurred to me John that Mr Grewell, your former manager, might be able to help with the boy problem.'

Sanjay's heart skipped a beat again, he waited in trepidation.

'I don't think so Rasa, he was caught with his hand in the till and dismissed for drunkenness!'

'Ah, I see, I wasn't aware of those circumstances.'

'Now, next item,' said John quickly.

Half an hour later with no further interference, they rose to depart.

Sanjay tailed Nadu but before reaching the door Nadeen caught up with him.

She hoped, she confided, that he would have a successful meeting with Mr Nadu and that if something were resolved, would he be good enough to let her know? 'There are financial considerations,' she whispered.

He returned her friendly smile and told her that he would see what he could do, 'I have my own ways that differ from John's,' he said.

'I see ...' she said slowly, still smiling, 'I shall pretend I did not hear that.'

* * *

'Harbens,' called John to Mahmood who stood in the doorway, 'a word. If I could show you the potential would you be interested in a small investment?'

'What ...?' Said Mahmood bluntly, pulling out a packet of cigars, lighting one and puffing smoke around John's face, 'if you are thinking of tourism forget it, a few thousand pounds in eighteen months, I make that a month. Tourism needs big capital and big

RON GOODMAN

investment, no wonder it is failing. The capital needed is immense and it takes years to make profits,' he said dismissively and walked away.

In those words, John realised that he had something unique and simple and, following Mahmood out he was even more than ever convinced he was on an absolute winner – but where could he get some cash?

* * *

It was cool in the restaurant where Sanjay, with a whisky in front of him, sat opposite Nadu who stirred black tea. The worried frown remained on Nadu's face and deepened when Sanjay asked what was wrong?

'Sharma's in trouble, he spies and checks all the time. I am worried that he will go over the completion notices and find the extras I have done for you, your showers, your pal's factory floor, that tank . . . if he finds out I will be in trouble. He is paying too much attention to my budget and I'm worried Sanjay.'

'I can say we did the tank ourselves and . . .'

'Be sensible,' he interrupted, 'Sharma may be lazy but he is not stupid, he knows a professional job when he sees one. Even he knows that children can't dig a hole thirty feet square and cement it!'

'So how can I get a mechanical hammer and shovel?'

'No idea.'

'I can provide the labour.'

'Don't be ridiculous Sanjay, you can't put kids on a road, it's too dangerous. Anyway I can hardly sneak a mechanical monster from our compound and drive it two miles to your site. Someone might notice.'

'You'll get something out of it.'

'Yes, dismissal! Sharma's been overspending at home and with his position in doubt, he's being careful. There's nothing I can do.'

Sanjay groaned inwardly, when Nadu got difficult there was something seriously wrong, and if Sanjay returned to John without success, it would mean more humiliation and he'd had enough of that. He made one final, desperate attempt.

'Look,' he said, 'let's get off the hook. Talk to Sharma, say John wants to meet him, get them both together and we're out of it.'

Nadu hesitated, he looked uncertain, 'Alright,' he nodded, 'I'll try, but nothing more.'

THIRTEEN

John deviated on his way back to where Sanjay had parked the Enfield and stood on the edge of a market square bustling and alive with colour and weekend people. With the advantage of height, he could see the extraordinary and the bizarre. People kept clear of the snake charmers on footpaths, preferring to gaze at vendors lounging under crude, disorderly awnings or haggling with customers. Prostitutes did likewise, intent on making Saturday a high earner, while colourful gypsy fortune-tellers with hair plaited and ears and noses hung with gold, eyed likely victims for their astrological, anxiety relieving predictions, yet unable to predict arrest as the police eyed them. Husbands wore Neru caps, shaped like upturned boats; while wives and pretty daughters in multi-coloured saris clutched bags tightly, occasionally handing a coin to one of the holy men in orange robes banging collection tins.

Already hands were being raised. 'Namaste,' said the hopefuls.

'Mmm,' John mumbled dismissively, nodding to some virginal looking Jain nuns, in white with mouths sealed to prevent the accidental killing of germs, who incongruously carried shopping in plastic bags. New to him though was the number of young girls who hung around the record and tape stall in jeans, swaying to the music of Elton John. Traditionalists tutted, frowned and pulled their younger children away from the unwanted influence, glaring in disapproval at the culture-less teenagers.

His slow progress, and the constant need to return acknowledgements, began to irritate him. He wished he had a horn as raucous as the one on his bike. 'That would shift a few of the buggers,' he muttered, stepping aside and repeating, 'Namaste,' with lips as tight together as their closed hands.

At one end, next to the temple, construction had begun on a huge stage. Ah, he thought, so that's the cause of the crowd, another festival, and he imagined the choking fumes from lorries driving fairground rides, polluting the pollution. Much of that and he would choke to death.

He neared the stage, where a turbaned, bare-chested old man with boundless energy and ribs like railings, was fixing posters to every available surface. John watched, astonished by the speed with which the things went up. In no time at all, the place was covered and the man moved towards him to plaster a nearby post.

For the first time John saw the detail: a man's head and shoulders stood out starkly against the grimy pillar, bold in black and white. It seemed familiar – older but familiar. He moved closer. It was familiar, the haughty pose, smiling that smug, self satisfied smirk, black hair, white jacket, lips pursed like a canary's bum – it was Mitra!

He hissed in amazement, 'Never!'

'Namaste,' answered a passer by.

Mitra ... an election candidate? 'Never,' he repeated, reading the declaration. How? Why? A cunning, pompous, vengeful crook like him, a candidate for the legislature? Surely, his money lending and debt collection businesses were detriments? Add that to the strength of town communists, weakening it was true, he'd need exceptional luck ... or an exceptional front man to persuade the voting public.

It struck him like a thunderbolt ... public relations ... of course ... an exceptional front man? Wait a moment, does Mitra realise that ... is that why? The cunning bastard ... that invite?

He could not get back fast enough; he raced across the square pushing people roughly aside, ignoring the smiles and raised hands.

'Namaste,' they said, 'Humph', he growled and shoved his way towards the bike.

* * *

A rare, welcoming smile greeted Sanjay when he dragged himself, weary and sweating, up the bungalow steps in the scorching two o'clock heat to the offer of a drink, without the habitual sarcasm.

'Have another,' John offered. 'Hot work cycling from the camp is it?'

'Yes, I could do with proper transport – like yours.'

'You know our funds don't run to that, Sanjay.'

'No, not even the two thousand you made from tourism?'

'No!' he snapped, 'not even that ... that's for the boys.' He paused. 'How did you get on with Brains?'

'He's frightened.'

'He's always bloody frightened.'

'Well ...' In his usual convoluted way Sanjay recounted his conversation. 'Nadu suggests you talk to Sharma!'

John stared for a second, knowing that Sanjay was shifting the responsibility. He said nothing, waiting for him to empty his glass.

The empty glass went down on the table. 'OK,' said John, 'I'll see him. In the meantime did you notice anything unusual in town, my son?'

Sanjay shook his head. 'No.'

'No?' said John, with heavy sarcasm, 'have you been to town lately? His picture is plastered everywhere.'

'Whose?'

John shook his head, 'For Christ's sake, your pal Mitra. You remember,' he said chuckling in good humour, 'the one who doesn't sell chess sets. He is the new Congress Party Candidate.'

Sanjay pulled a face, 'Well?'

'Well, get yourself up there tomorrow and invite him back here.'

'Why me?' he grumbled, 'You go.'

'I don't keep a dog to bark myself, you'll be rewarded. Don't tell him I want to see him, be discreet and indicate . . .'

'Dogs don't make invitations. You do it.'

'Sorry my son, just a manner of speaking. I can't, we had a fall out, but you are in touch, so be a good lad and nip . . .'

'. . . I'm not in touch.'

'Really . . .? I understood you were. Am I wrong?'

'If I see him it's by accident . . .'

'What, like knowing when he is at the Holiday Inn? I see. Nevertheless, you go, and there's a chance of a bike in it for you.'

'A bike? Is that also coming from the few thousand pounds you forgot to mention?'

John looked sharply at him. 'Keep that under your hat my son. Handle this properly and it might come sooner than you think.'

He reached out and refilled Sanjay's glass, took a deep swallow from his own and looked thoughtfully over the rim. 'You see, my son,' he said, 'don't tell him but I have something very valuable to offer Mr Dhankar Mitra and I am relying on you to build a bridge.' He laughed. 'After all you are a construction engineer!'

* * *

The bus with Sanjay driving left Paradise Lake at midday on Sunday and despite the exciting prospect of seeing the home of a millionaire, the occupants were subdued and, in the uncomfortable atmosphere, silence replaced the chatter.

Vijay sensed their disapproval of the gloomy and somewhat incompetent driver and as they turned off to climb the steep inclines of the Lower Gnat mountains.

Andrew asked how far it was.

'One Indin hour!' replied Tony, causing a howl of self-conscious laughter and Sanjay to turn in his seat. The bus veered off line, Vijay grabbed the wheel and then remained stoical watching the road as they climbed the frighteningly steep inclines with unprotected edges and sheer drops. When Sanjay missed a gear-change and stalled the engine, allowing the bus to roll backwards, Vijay heard a stifled scream and yanked at the handbrake. Sanjay re-started, forgetting the clutch to the sound of grinding gears. From then on, he appeared more cautious.

They continued climbing for another thirty minutes, the girls with eyes closed and even occasional gasps of astonishment from the men at the sheer drops and hairpin bends that turned back frighteningly on themselves.

Vijay was vigilant; he had little confidence in Sanjay's ability, being used to Sunil's driving, and nudged Sanjay to keep well to the left and away from the terrifying drops. He turned and smiled reassuringly at them, prematurely, he thought, when the engine began to strain as the slope took its toll. The bus slowed quickly on the steep incline and shuddered but this time Sanjay managed to drop into a lower gear in time, mumbling something about, 'unreliable machines,' while Vijay's hand hovered over the brake.

They rounded the final, perilous hairpin and climbed the steepest of all slopes to sighs of relief from the passengers and descended steeply into the most prosperous and prestigious area they had yet seen in India.

Beautifully kept, colonial type houses with manicured lawns lay behind hedges and ornate railings. Drives, paved or gravel covered, were swept clean of leaves and litter and looked pristine compared to the squalor they knew. In every garden someone seemed to be working.

Passing an unmade track lined with acacia and tamarisk trees, Vijay felt uneasy, a nagging sensation gnawing at his abdomen. It was a long time ago, before John sent him with Sunil to Maroutai College. He was about thirteen and he remembered the woods at the end of the track where John brought them to play before visiting the beautiful house of an English friend, Colin. Blonde and tall he had been very kind and took them inside and played with them. His recollection was vague but he remembered being very annoyed with Sunil for spoiling the day when he quarrelled with John and insisted on going back to camp. They never went again and Sunil refused to talk about it.

The bus swept down the steep hill before stopping inside the iron gates of an imposing, colonial-type villa. Sanjay followed the drive through beautiful gardens to stop in front of a grand, white pillared entrance. 'Wait,' he said, and stepped out.

'Bit steep that climb Vijay?'

'Ver' dangerous.'

'Depends on who is driving.'

Vijay grinned and, ever discreet, rocked his head. He turned and looked at Hillary, who seemed shaken. 'Would you like drink?' he asked.

'How very thoughtful of you Vijay,' she said.

Taking a drink from the cold bag he took the opportunity to look at her closely.

He thought she was quite wonderful, so beautiful and neat, he had never seen hair the colour of straw or skin like goat's cream and her shy smile was so attractive. At times, he just wanted to stare and when she smiled at him, he felt a sense of achievement. He'd never seen such a pretty woman, but then he'd had little chance. The dark one seemed to make them laugh a lot and although pleasant to him she was not as pretty. Kumar though, unusually for him, was very inquisitive about her, he quite liked her but said she made him nervous.

Vijay liked them all for including him in conversations and the way they spoke slowly, for his benefit, unlike some visitors who mumbled, made no allowances and treated him like an imbecile because he didn't understand. Their confidence and jokes with him, gave him a sense of belonging and although he understood their reservations about Sanjay, had they known him in the early days, they might hold a different view.

Uncouth, uneducated, his lack of finesse didn't help his own popularity. He couldn't help what he was – but he was a survivor. In bad times he had held them all together and didn't deserve John's bullying. Sunil said it was his jealousy of Kumar that made him behave stupidly and that his decisions were emotional, not sensible, it was partly John's fault for being so fickle and unfair. Sunil believed he had some responsibility for allowing John to cultivate Kumar when they were at college, and he too had some sympathy with Sanjay.

'Vijay, where's Sunil today?' asked the red haired man with the strange speech.

'Wid family,' he replied.

'I didn't know he was married.'

'Boys, tree an' fibe,' he answered grinning and understanding their amusement. He never could quite get his tongue round English diphthongs.

'Really? And you Vijay?'

He rocked his head from side to side.

'No girlfriend?' said the dark one, his head rocked again as Sanjay reappeared.

'Follow me please,' he said.

Vijay grinned when Tony winked and said, 'Back in one Indin' hour.'

* * *

They stepped from the bus into a manicured garden of stunning beauty. Paths meandered through lawns and the trappings of wealth were evident. Immaculately kept, grasses were ringed with flower-beds and coloured shrubs. In the centre of one manicured lawn a raised rectangular pond with three matching white marble fountains sat under cascading water that fell into gadrooned bowls and tinkled prettily over the edges into the pool beneath. Freshness radiated, together with a sense of calm in contrast to noisy dusty, grubbiness.

'Blimey,' whispered Tony, stopping for a brief look, 'it's Kew Gardens. I wonder who lives in a house like this?'

He could see no boundary to the grounds and the colours astonished him as much as the absence of a sign saying, 'Keep off the grass.'

Sam reached for his hand as they approached the white marble steps where Mitra waited under the glass-covered entrance. 'Is this,' she whispered, 'the Taj Mahal?'

'Good afternoon my friends,' gushed Mitra, in his high-pitched, syrupy voice, leading them into a white walled room, protected and cooled from the sun's glare by the mottled shadows of trees. The inside was no less impressive than the outside and the whole place reeked opulence with red carpets, gilt framed furniture and chairs with matching footstools.

'I am so glad that you have found time to visit me. My man will be along shortly with refreshments, in the meantime, we can have a cosy chat. Your boy has been told to wait.'

Tony bristled but reeled in the impulse to kick the prissy little man up his cast, there are rules after all and looking about him, he saw a manservant by the doorway.

His dad would say he was built like a brick chicken house at well over six feet and dressed as richly as the decor in a short tight-fitting red and gold embroidered waistcoat with billowing white cotton trousers above shoeless feet. Solid, fit and stony faced with arms folded across his chest, the red turban was a work of art, edging a bearded face. His arms looked as large as tree trunks but his movements when he served from a silver tray were surprisingly agile.

Tony surmised he was lightning fast and that Mitra was being well looked after physically. Like some of his mates in the gym, he looked a trained fighter and even they would be well extended to take him on.

Mitra said it was a pity the British left but fortunately they had left behind many fine customs, afternoon tea for instance, to which Andrew replied that he thought most of the ruling British did nothing but bully, cheat and decimate the country.

'No, no, that is simply untrue, they left behind a wonderful political and civil system. My family was never misused, we kept our servants and our possessions and the work they provided was very rewarding. Of course I was only a boy but my parents said they never interfered in their businesses.'

'And what business was that, Mr Mitra?' asked Andrew.

'They were entrepreneurs you know,' he said, as guarded as ever, 'and in my small way I have perpetuated that,' adding that, in a sense, both he and John had the entrepreneurial spirit although their paths had taken very different routes.

'Yes he has mentioned you,' said Tony, remembering his phrase, 'He has a mouth to curdle milk,' and suppressed a snigger when Mitra replied, 'How very kind of him.'

Mitra dominated the conversation with his opinions, vanity and overbearing chatter for the next half-hour, informing, and boring with a forecast of his forthcoming election prospects. Tony detected an element of self-doubt with his prepared excuse for defeat, pointing out, like a politician in need of help, the fickleness of voters.

He noticed too that he never requested but commanded, even the way he said, 'you will have more tea,' was an instruction not an invitation, and Tony's inner sense warned that anyone crossing him would be savagely dealt with. Conversely, and strangely, he seemed to be trying to ingratiate himself. Tony was fascinated.

'Are you being looked after? John's boys are such fine chaps. I spent much time with him you know until business came between us. He is so wrapped up in his remarkable occupation and I in mine, we are like ships that pass in the night, as we say. A likeable and engaging man with such presence, don't you think, with many friends in positions of authority? It is not surprising he is so respected in the district, the makings of a politician one might say and as prospective candidate for the district of Amitar I can think of no better person than him to "carry one's banner". With the absence of such people in this neck of the woods, one must fight tooth and nail for recognition despite one's position in life, and someone with the presence and charisma of . . ., well . . . Mr Prichard, for instance . . .'

'A useful man to know then Mr Mitra,' said Andrew. 'He sends his apologies, by the way.'

'Indeed?'

'You could always chat him up, Mr Mitra,' Tony suggested.

'Dhankar, please . . .' he said and stopped speaking for a moment looking intrigued. 'Do you know,' he said, 'I think you may have hit the nail on the head, as we say, you have given me a jolly good idea. If you will allow me to drive you back I can renew my acquaintance, and take advantage of the opportunity. It will give my man a rest, one doesn't like to work them too hard, I'm sure you understand.'

Tony's his heart sank, 'That'll be nice,' he said.

'Indeed. Now,' said Mitra with shrivelled lips and a prim smile, 'perhaps your dear ladies would wish to view my humble home?'

FOURTEEN

The feel of cold leather on bare legs gave an extra touch of extravagance as they settled back in air-conditioned luxury. Mitra slipped the automatic into drive, the silver Mercedes slid over the ground with more noise from crunching gravel than the engine.

Tony, directed into the front seat as, 'a position of privilege for your inspiration,' relaxed as the machine whispered its way through the gate and effortlessly climbed the steep rise past a tree-lined path where Vijay waited in the parked bus. Tony raised his thumb, Vijay grinned and prepared to follow.

The gleaming Mercedes rolled gracefully over the crest and silently down the steep gradients to the first hairpin and eased effortlessly around it, and although the drop looked steep Tony felt better protected in a quality car. Even the girls dared to look over the edge, secure, no doubt, in the belief that mishaps did not occur to limousines that floated. Such was the effect of absorbent springing that Tony was certain they could have run over a sacred cow and not felt the bump.

In what seemed like minutes, they neared the crowded town, and Tony saw heads turn towards the shining vehicle; walkers stopped to wave. The executive machine attracted attention. Not surprising he thought, most of these poor buggers would be unlikely to ride a Mercedes once in their lifetime, they were staring at a dream.

They entered the town and even the traffic moved aside when observant drivers, who actually used rear view mirrors, spotted the Mercedes and it was clear that Mitra enjoyed recognition.

The increasing traffic, and thickening crowd, slowed the vehicle as they approached the centre of Amitar. Mitra returned a wave, a superior wave, an action more dismissive than acknowledging and his chin rose arrogantly. He looked smug and confident, a smiling icon to them and a self-opinionated windbag to Tony. He was rich, it brought respect and power and gave him options that others would never have.

The crowd became dense, slowing the vehicle as it neared the square. The reception surprised them all and even Tony felt a little like a celebrity as people waved, smiled and shouted. He had an unjustified urge to wave back.

Mitra slowed the car further, the jungle telegraph had signalled ahead and crowds started to throng the streets and spill into the square. Some ran alongside while others rushed towards them from the front, rear and sides and inside a minute, the silver vehicle slowed and crept forward through the mass of bodies.

Tony felt Mitra's apprehension as the crowd pressed in shouting; he saw the smile slowly slip and freeze, Mitra's eyes widened and darted from side to side seeking a way through the mob that began to press against the car. Some looked pleased, some angry, one banged the panels and several copied him. A fist lifted and came down on the window.

Hemmed in now, the vehicle slowed to almost stop, the crowd, dozens deep, crammed in tightly against the car, 'Look what they are doing,' he said, 'they will damage my vehicle.'

It wasn't that which raised Tony's heart rate, it was the ugly, snarling faces that appeared at the windows. 'You all right?' he asked and turned to meet looks of alarm from those in the rear as the car ground to a halt in the very centre of the square and the centre of what was clearly the political opposition. Raised hands, obscenities and faces set in anger threatened them, Mitra, his face grey with concern and clearly terrified could not cope. A fight broke out in front of them and bodies crashed against the bonnet.

Reacting quickly, Tony rammed his hand against the horn, 'Drive,' he yelled as the shock of a raucous horn jerked most of the crowd back a pace. Mitra, quick to see his chance, rolled the car forward and, following Tony's lead, slammed his palm against the horn repeatedly.

In seconds, a policeman carrying a large stick appeared in front of the car and slashed at the combatants, one fell to the ground and was dragged away. A second officer joined his colleague, grabbed another and threw him aside, together they forged ahead of the car lashing out at any human obstruction until slowly the crowd parted and thinned.

The thumping on the bodywork stopped and Tony saw the exit with a sigh of relief. Then, having done their job, the two policemen stepped aside, saluted and waved the car away from the square.

Once clear of Amitar the Mercedes gathered speed and murmured along the newly laid stretch of tarmac while a sense of liberation and relief swept through the group.

Tony sneaked a look at Mitra; his face was the colour of mud, his confidence severely shaken. Signs of alarm registered in his eyes and speaking stiffly he muttered, 'Communists, you know.'

Tony sniggered. 'Bit spiteful though?' he teased.

'They deserve no quarter, Mr Baker.'

'Not the people, the police!' said Tony.

'Indeed,' said Mitra, shooting him a sideways glance.

With collective sighs of relief they sped towards the lake, it was as if they rode over sheet glass until they reached the slip road when Mitra drove cautiously over the uneven track. The swaying and bumping brought his look of concern back and a hundred yards into the rough terrain, the steep inclines caused the body of the car to dip and sway alarmingly as they climbed and dropped over sharp hillocks. Tony heard a grating, abrasive sound from the underside.

'Ari baab ri baab, this is too much,' complained Mitra and stopped the car.

Tony remembered his dad: 'Every man has his weakness,' he would say, 'be patient – you'll find it,' and today he had seen Mitra's. The collapse of confidence in the square and now his flustering antics showed that on his own, in the face of difficulty, he became a piece of jelly.

There was no need to feel subservient in his presence, not that he did, in fact Tony felt cocky to a point of disrespect. Indulged and pampered all his life, without bodyguards or strong-arm persuasion, the man had lost his bottle. He'd need help to stand his ground in an election . . .

Engine noise from the minibus resounded among the hillocks as it headed towards them. Tony waved and Vijay grinned mischievously from behind the wheel.

'Ah!' drawled Mitra, his simpering, confident smile returning, 'Saved by the bell, as we say, perhaps you will permit me to use your transport while your boys attend my vehicle. One never knows, one could be invited to dinner – won't that be nice?'

'Jesus Christ', said Tony under his breath and looked at Vijay. He rocked his head from side to side and showed his white teeth expansively. Then, to Tony's surprise, he winked!

*   *   *

John practically embraced Mitra when he stepped from the bus and Mitra's return reaction was no less than a salutation as he recalled John's 'wonderful work since they had last met. How well you look, it had been far too long,' he said praising, patronising and envying. 'But let's not encumber your guests with our small talk John, I am quite sure they have had enough of me for one day,' he said attempting humorous self-deprecation, 'haven't you my friends?'

Tony's smile broadened, 'We certainly have Mr Mitra,' he said firmly with a laugh.

Sam dug him in the ribs, 'Thank you for your hospitality Mr Mitra,' she said.

He formed another grimacing smile. 'It was absolutely nothing, dear lady.'

She looked at Tony with an expression that dared him to say anything at all. 'Come on you,' she said, 'let's stretch our legs before dinner.'

FIFTEEN

They strolled along the lake's edge, following the path created by wandering goats. The girls shrieked suddenly and then giggled with relief when a flapping bird noisily broke the silence. Tony waved his hat in front of his face and listened to the faint sounds of music carried by the breeze, heralding the election, creating an alien, yet pleasant ambience to remind him he was a foreigner in a remarkable country. He heard other sounds too; faint and foreign, but dismissed them.

He winked and grinned at a young boy of no more than ten who sat in isolation on an elevated rock but, shy or fearful, the boy averted his eyes, studied his stick and self-consciously jabbed it repeatedly at the same spot on the ground.

Further on, Tony heard the sounds again and stopped. 'What's that?' he said turning to look inland where the noises, more distinct now, came from.

'Sounds like metal on metal to me,' said Andrew moving in the direction of the sound and reaching the crest of a bushy hillock.

Tony heard it too, voices laughing, calling and speaking rapidly in the language he had heard but did not understand. He looked over the top to see a part-completed bungalow, a replica of John's, located discreetly behind a group of trees dominated by a large acacia. The others joined him and watched open mouthed.

Fifty or so children, tinged with red ochre and grey dust, using awkward shovels, mixed cement and pushed crude, overloaded barrows in searing heat. Some balanced floppy straw bowls that leaked dusty rubbish on to their heads, smothering them in the process. In a building orgy, children as young as seven or eight laboured and struggled to push and pull weights unsuited to their tiny frames, laughing, as dust rose in clouds from emptied baskets.

One waved in their direction with a cheery smile.

'Isn't he the boy who gave us those rubber tubes, Hillary? Look at the poor little devils, working like slaves, how cruel in this heat,' she said horrified.

'Yea, bit hard . . .'

'Hard? It's brutal!'

'Hold on Sammy,' said Tony gently, 'we don't know the circumstances. They look happy enough; they're not falling over with exhaustion.'

He wished he'd bitten his tongue as she turned on him. 'That's a man's view is it? Six-year-old kids doing men's work at six in the evening and all you can say is, "none of them is falling down"? Have some compassion you stupid sod!'

'All I am saying is you shouldn't judge . . .'

'Shouldn't judge!' she retorted furiously, on the verge of tears, 'for crying out loud, you can see what's going on? They are being used as labourers for the very organisation that is here to protect them! If I were to judge I'd judge they were being ill-treated, I'd judge they were being exploited, I suppose you'd be just as happy if one of them was yours . . .'

'Well . . . no . . . course not.' he said sheepishly.

'I bet that bloody Sanjay is at the bottom of this, I notice he's not here. You wait till I see John!' she bawled and stalked away, her face like thunder, her eyes tear filled.

Tony stood rooted to the spot. 'Jesus, Andrew,' he said shaken by her onslaught, 'she says me brain's not always engaged when I use me mouth. For God's sake don't tell her about that three year old kid we saw tied by her ankle to that lamp-post in Maroutai, or she'll go ballistic.'

* * *

Sam had overcome her anger with Tony by dinner but stubbornly retained her intention to speak to John when they joined Andrew and Hillary on the patio.

'Are Mr John and his friend coming to dinner, Kumar?' he asked.

'No,' he replied briefly and soberly placed drinks on the table to return repeatedly and glance along the track leading to the camp where, an hour earlier, John and Mitra had driven.

Tony gave him a long quizzical look and saw that he hardly gave Sam a second glance, not that it mattered, she seemed to have lost her fascination with him too, but his repeated looks along the track were curious and suspicious, as though he wanted to monitor John's movement.

With Sam having returned to her usual lively self, he joked with her about Mitra and wondered if she had thought about trying her luck with him?

'No,' she replied, 'he couldn't stand the pace, those servants are more my style. Did you see their muscles? Plenty of stamina there.'

'Yea,' said Tony, 'one of 'em might even have a dress to fit you, you're about their size round the chest. By the way, did you get to use the toilet while we were there?'

Sam giggled, Kumar directed them upstairs and, having served dinner, he returned to the side of the roof to look in the direction of the camp.

* * *

Mitra, with John beside him, had turned the car and was driving towards the camp. He had contemplated a political career for five years, but with communism in the ascendancy, the conditions were wrong for a millionaire to entertain the idea. Times had changed; the flaws in communism had begun to show in Russia, India's close neighbour, and its satellites.

Mitra bragged he had 'bitten the bullet,' and, now that capitalism was respectable again, he saw that an association with a respected public figure would enhance his election chances. John Prichard was a benefactor, an icon, a symbol of trust, respected, popular, instantly recognisable and non-controversial and a man able to affect public opinion. To have his support could overcome poor public perception, particularly if he gave the impression that they had been covertly working together.

The incident in the square showed he had a hill to climb, he needed John Prichard; persuasion was his forte and that could get Mitra's foot firmly on the legislatorial ladder.

If unsuccessful, a backstop was available, the other foot in the tourist industry, a second foot on a second ladder. A few thousand pounds profit in eighteen months wasn't much but with good management, and a cash injection, who knows?

* * *

John was having similar thoughts as he sat in the plush passenger seat of the Mercedes. Sanjay had done his job for a change and planted the seed. Mitra appeared receptive to the renewed acquaintance, aware that popularity meant votes while he meant money to John. He had to sell himself as the front man for this prospective candidate, that way he would cover Mitra in glory and himself in cash. It would be worth the loss of some sovereignty over his business to reap rapid benefits and a better alternative that than a stagnating business and the millstone of the conniving lovers.

Having prepared his ground thoroughly, aided by Sanjay's update of the incident in the square, he could see no reason for a refusal and he stepped from the Mercedes with confidence.

Fawned and fussed over, the restaurant owner directed them to the best table; diners raised their hands, respectfully at their appearance and waiters hurried to serve the priority guests. Throughout dinner, John smiled benignly as he listened to Mitra's long-winded approach. Hints and insinuations showed John's prediction had been correct; he needed assistance from a man who had the ear of the public, a man of experience in public protocol, and found himself in something of a quandary with such a personage hard to find. And meeting those delightful guests had reminded him of John's vast experience and, of course, his enviable standing in the community.

'You need a front man, Dhankar, a "warm up man", someone who can take the hostility from the crowd, especially after that incident in the square.'

'Incident,' said Mitra, fabricating surprise, 'are you referring to those communists? It was nothing.'

'They are the opposition, Dhankar and there's a lot of them,' he said hoping to undermine Mitra's self-assurance and show he was an underdog, doubtfully equipped, too distanced and not one of the people. His campaign had started too late and had not won over the press. He was a myth concealed behind a veil of money, and strong-arm tactics do not endear anyone to the public.

'The fact is Dhankar, everyone knows of you but nobody knows about you,' he said to an increasingly anxious face. You must show you have been misrepresented; you are not a rich, uncaring moneylender but a sincere benefactor and your secret cause is Orphindi. That is our way to votes.'

'"Our", John, are you saying you will undertake the task?' he asked, as though he had never thought of it.

'Of course, votes are easier to collect than money Dhankar – if they believe in you. Unfortunately, they don't at the moment, so we have work to do.

'Naturally,' said Mitra, 'I am prepared to pay for any services, subject to appropriate guarantees. What is it you are in need of?'

'Well, first of all . . .'

As they spoke John became aware that for someone who had not visited him in years, Mitra was well informed. He knew about guests, he knew about the new bungalow and did not flinch at the five hundred thousand rupee price tag.

John shrewdly undermined his confidence, he needed to change public misconception, he should not use the Mercedes, he should hide his thugs too and show modesty.

Mitra leaned back in the chair and steepled his fingers, 'I will need guarantees John.'

'I am your guarantee. Place a deposit in Orphindi funds, then I can say you are a secret contributor, and pass the rest to me.'

'Indeed. Now, about your business, let us, as we say get down to the nitty-gritty . . .'

An hour later, they shook hands across the table on a deal that gave Mitra twenty percent of the business and John enough money to build four new bungalows.

They stood to leave, the owner hurried to open the door and stood aside with a slight bow, Mitra walked forward followed by John . . . and Sanjay walked in.

* * *

Returning to Paradise Lake in the Mercedes Mitra reflected on the advantages of becoming a part owner of a new enterprise, a new toy to develop and give him a foothold in the growing holiday industry. He intended to enter a ready-made organisation that would normally take him years to build – if his impetuous informant could be believed?

He felt smug, satisfied that his astute handling had achieved what he wanted, the promised rupees a small price to pay for the support of a prominent benefactor with charisma at voter level to carry him straight to the legislature. With John at his side he could not lose but had to admit that, ironically, his wealth was a detriment. The poor mistrust the rich and the town's best-known patron, with an unsullied reputation, would diffuse the bitterness evident in the square.

Association would bring confidence and tomorrow he would observe John's performance, then, with the preliminary rally over, he could make a more objective assessment before handing over all the cash. 'I see no point in leaping in the dark, as we say.'

* * *

John puzzled too, how Sanjay could afford to eat at the best restaurant in town – regularly according to the waiter. There was something radically wrong when a man who constantly cried 'poverty' ate at the most expensive restaurant.

But why should John care how he spent his money, he had succeeded in opening a road leading to the bridge that would support them for years to come and had helped John achieve all he set out to do. Mitra too was happy.

All the same, it seemed very strange that his helper had turned up at the restaurant where it cost a week's wages for a meal.

Dropped off at the camp, by a Mitra reluctant to drive his vehicle over the terrain, John walked to Sanjay's squalid dwelling and rooted around for the whisky bottle. He cleaned two glasses, made a space on the table and sat down to wait. Two hours later Sanjay came back.

'Sit down my son,' he said, 'I want a word . . .'

SIXTEEN

By 5 a.m., the heat began to mount in the confines of the silent hut. The increasing humidity became so overbearing that claustrophobic stuffiness enveloped the two men slumped at the table, causing them to wake slowly from an evening of excess whisky, during which intentions and drunken conversation had turned from sense into meaningless mouthing.

In the new light, a single bulb still burned above them and on the table, an empty whisky bottle lay on its side next to tumblers, one still a quarter full. On the floor, further confirmation lay with untidy groups of beer cans, further evidence of the previous night's activity.

John's intention to confront Sanjay and discover how he afforded such a posh restaurant failed, the liquor consumed had addled his brain and he lost track. It was also apparent, from their flopped postures, that there was some amiability before they had drifted into unconsciousness.

Now, in the early hours, with dazzling sunshine lighting the room and heating it beyond comfort, Sanjay's eyelids moved. He squinted, yawned, exhaled stinking breath into the numb crook of his arm and sucked in warm, smelly air, the result of a sweat soaked shirt. He slowly opened his eyes and screwed up his face, hating the brightness assaulting him. He twisted his head and wished he hadn't, it hurt. His brain seemed to be half a turn behind the twist.

Across the table John breathed heavily, not snoring, he never snored, that is Sanjay had never heard him when they were together, and he looked peaceful.

Despite an aching head and acid full stomach, he felt happy. It had been a successful day despite the odd looks and curt nods when he entered the restaurant. He'd even covered the questions, 'they are my wages John, I do what I like with them. Anyway we had a good day, didn't we?'

'We did Sanjay my son,' said John, 'things run in cycles. You have bad days and mediocre days but one morning you wake up and it's *your day*. Take advantage my son!'

Well today was Sanjay's day and he would take advantage . . . and talking of cycles?

He walked unsteadily towards the sink, removed his shirt and ducked his head, groping for the water jug to slosh the contents over his head. The tepid water was like a blow, an intense pain, like a sharp object being inserted, shot from one side of his temple to the other. 'Ooh!' he moaned and stood upright so suddenly that water ran down his neck and shoulders, chilling him in the humid room. Gingerly he bent forward again to splash his chubby upper-half, emitting noisy grunts. He rinsed his mouth, gargled, grabbed a towel and, ignoring the wet floor he filled the kettle, placed it with a clatter on the Primus stove and heard guttural sounds from John's tired, waking throat.

John's face, creased like a road map, wrinkled further when he frowned in the glare as he slowly lifted his head. Dark baggy patches swelled under red-rimmed eyes, pallid skin covered fatty flesh that clung to his lower jaw, the first sign of jowls, his hair looked even greyer and matted and his shirt, damp with sweat, stuck to him, the open front exposing an established belly. Sanjay thought he looked quite old.

'Get some tea,' he growled unnecessarily as two steaming mugs materialised unexpectedly, with Sanjay standing over him clean, fresh and superior.

'God I feel terrible,' John moaned, pressing his hands to his face.

'You English tell us never to mix the grape with the grain, so drink your tea,' he said seated on the edge of the table, enjoying his rare moment of control and watching John suck at the surface of the cup, swallowing air and tea in equal quantities. He let out a sigh, burped loudly and said, 'That's better!'

Sanjay scrutinised him, gauging his mood. 'Breakfast?' he asked.

'Juice.'

Sanjay took a can from the fridge and placed it on the table with a glass. 'OK?' he said sitting on the corner of the table.

John picked up the cup and looked over the rim, 'Come on – what is it?' he said in a tone that indicated a negative reply to whatever he was about to ask.

'Transport. You mentioned a motorbike.'

'Why, you going on holiday?'

His sarcasm was always irritating but this morning more so than ever after last night's achievement.

'Don't be sarcastic – a bicycle is slow.'

'Oil it then.'

Sanjay controlled the urge to shout as his temper rose. 'There you go again, I helped you yesterday,' he said, impetuously pointing a finger and feeling the pulses in his temples throbbing, 'can't you show some gratitude?'

'Does defending you count?' John said looking hard into his face. 'Anyway, someone is showing gratitude by the look of the places you can afford to eat at. I'm beginning to wonder where your cash comes from.'

'I told you last night, my wages are mine and I spend them where I want, and I have friends.'

'They must have plenty of money.'

'That's none of your business,' he said, angry and impulsive.

'Oh yes it is Sanjay, I haven't forgotten the trouble you've recently caused. Your friends might be the influence that has changed you from a trustworthy partner to an unreliable associate.'

Sanjay went rigid, 'Are you saying I can't be trusted?' he shouted in a rare show of defiance with a look of fury. 'You ungrateful bloody bastard, I got all you wanted from Mitra yesterday,' he said sliding off the table, his frustration at a peak. 'I've had enough,' he yelled over his shoulder and stormed off into the bedroom.

He took a holdall from the wardrobe and started to pile clothes into it.

The bang of a glass slammed on to the table prepared him for the onslaught. 'What did you call me?' John shouted from the doorway.

'You heard!' yelled Sanjay spinning on bare feet, 'get someone else to do your dirty work.'

'What, another thief and drunk like the one you caught last time, you bloody half wit! You are under an obligation so you are staying, like it or not.'

Sanjay looked as though he would fracture. His eyes and mouth opened, he stood upright, his bare chest huge as he filled his lungs to respond, 'Half wit?' he screamed, 'is that what I am because I pay the back-handers, take all the risks and do all the work while you take a back seat?' he said moving forward to push his face daringly close to John's. 'I am not a jealous old man who keeps a trained monkey at his beck and call, a miserable, spiteful bully who can only take advantage of little boys. You'd better be careful, you forget what I know!' he said, not sure that it made sense but at least it felt good fighting back, even though it meant risking everything.

'And you don't, I suppose,' snapped John, 'not even Samuel?'

'I told you about that, so stop harping on about it, think what you will lose if I go!'

His threat seemed to have an effect, John appeared shaken, and he lost his look of aggression. 'Come on son,' he said rubbing his head with a hand to relieve the ache. 'There's no need for this, we have been part of each other for too long, we go together like a hammer and nails.'

'Yes and you are the bloody hammer,' exploded Sanjay, accepting none of the attempted appeasement. He was in control, it was his day and he was prepared to take risks.

John softened, his look of severity appeared to be replaced by acceptance, he nodded slowly, as though in agreement.

'Alright son,' he said wearily wiping sweat that rolled down his forehead like dew, 'perhaps I have been hasty, I'll see what I can manage.'

'Yes,' he said, losing none of his aggression, 'take it from Mitra's payment or the few thousand pounds you forgot to tell me about.'

John smiled, 'Alright, alright, you've said your piece but don't get cocky; two can play at that game. Remember we are mutually dependent.'

'Then stop bullying,' countered Sanjay, set on having the last word, 'or you'll regret it!'

'OK, OK,' replied John, capitulating and confirming Sanjay's victory. 'You can have your bike – but be careful, I won't always be able to protect you. Just make sure that we don't have any further "mistakes" or liaisons and make sure Kenneth reports to you daily, do you hear, daily. I don't want to hear of another absentee a week late and find Joshi chasing us for an explanation.'

Sanjay turned away, trembling, nervously elated. He'd dared to take John on and won. It really was his day.

He didn't realise though, that he'd inserted a splinter causing a wound that would irritate and fester into a precarious future.

* * *

John's head ached even more when he walked into the sunlight, he rolled it around vigorously making his neck muscles crack and creak. A group of passing kids said dutifully, 'Namaste, Mr John.' An abrasive smile accompanied his grunt.

Companion to his headache and bilious stomach were prowling suspicions, jumbled and intermingled. He could not properly assimilate anything, some things niggled, some were insignificant and dismissed, but one crystallised suddenly. How did Sanjay know that Mitra had coughed up? He wasn't present – and how did he know Mitra would be at that hotel, he'd not really explained? That conniving thick head had a closer association with Mitra than he thought and that threw Mitra's loyalty into doubt! There is a connection.

He set out for the lake riled and tired. What with Graham and Nadeen cruising, Sanjay rebelling and Mitra devious as ever, things were becoming more challenging. The potential of the business had drawn in the vultures and he had to improve his security if he wanted to remain on course. Mitra was the start of progress but he needed watching and John was under no illusion; he was on his own, with the exception of Kumar of course; thank God for his reliability.

In those moments of doubt he couldn't help wondering if it was all worth the trouble? The uncertainty, the conflict, the arguments and the constant inveigling was a trial, and this was only the beginning. Then there was his age, was he too old to cope, and was it worth it?

He turned his thoughts to the money and of the choices he could make with all that wealth 'A million in five years,' he said, savouring the sound, 'a million pounds.'

'Yes,' he said, 'it is bloody worth it!'

SEVENTEEN

The carnival atmosphere of Indian elections is compelling and fascinating to anyone fortunate enough to witness the fever of the ritual. It seems like madness at first but it is the emotional release of a population taking to the streets in the fervent belief that they are about to choose a Messiah. Those not involved would be well advised to stand to one side.

Passion fires frightening mobs which rush screaming through the streets, occasionally controlled by the words of candidates but more often incited by them. Tempers flare, fights are common and dignity is lost when chasing open-backed lorries on which candidates are perched, smiling, waving and delivering orations in one place and then moving to another to cries of, 'chalo, chalo, chalo' (let's go).

At final victory, the winner is doused in vermilion powder, thrown by a succession of supporters who also become blanketed, yet they smile, forgetting that their complete ensemble is ruined and that poverty is an impediment to garment replacement.

The red dye does its work and, like the dye, the smiles are temporary, only to fade when the real worth of the candidate is known after promising promises and failing to keep them. The gullible public falls for it every time and finds out too late.

Two Political parties hold prime positions in India, the Congress Party and the Communist Party, one democratic and socialist, the other communist and socialist. Both claim to be diametrically opposed in their thinking yet are similar in almost every way, including their methods of crowd persuasion.

It was into this situation that John drove on Monday with a diffused headache, after a shower, and a settled stomach after some Rennies, but his relief was only temporary. The stifling heat would bring back the headache as surely as it would stop human movement by midday, offering no sympathy, burning exposed bodies and baking the ground until grasses turned brown and the earth hardened like rock. Every living thing, except humans at election time, sought the shade from the indiscriminate power that could kill the old and feeble, man or beast.

On the way in John saw a cow, having outlived its usefulness, turned loose by the owner to forage. The old, weak and gentle animal, unsuccessful in its search, had laid down at the side of the road in the shade of a tree to rest and die in peace, only to be set upon by a flock of vultures. It lay panting, the scavengers crowded around shoving and threatening, hesitant to approach, at first. Then, with the courage of a cluster of cowards recognising a defenceless victim, they jabbed their huge scimitar like beaks at the helpless animal where it lay, attacking, eventually, in force. They tore at the flesh, at the eyes and legs that kicked weakly in a pathetic attempt to defend and, still alive, the gentle beast was torn to pieces. Afterwards the blood-covered birds preened themselves by the side of the cleanly picked bones in satisfaction of a good meal.

The wretched animal had no chance to die with the dignity it had been expected to exhibit during its sacred life and nobody cared – least of all the owner who had turned it loose. Vultures, John thought, were much like politicians.

It became oppressively hot when he slowed to a crawl in the packed traffic. Heat rose from the engine to flow over him and exhaust gases saturated the air around him. He began to choke and perspire in the congestion, and his trousers and shirt were wet, creased and dusty long before he picked his way through the cars and carts to the polluted town centre.

Entering the square to tinny, rasping music wailing from loud-speakers hurriedly erected each side of the stage, the whining voices, no longer discordant to his Western ear, rose and fell in lengthy, exaggerated sweeps, prompting foreigners to wonder sometimes how the artists managed to draw breath.

Parked in the shade, he kept to the sunless side and wondered if he would find his bike among hundreds of others, while deafening drumming and piercing sitars racked his aching head. He simply had to get to the rear of those speakers and aimed his large frame towards the platform away from the noisy discharge.

Half of the devotees of India appeared to be crushed into the square with him and, as before, many greeted him with raised hands and face-halving smiles. He had almost forgotten what it was like to walk among a crowd with bodies impeding his every stride. Treading carefully to avoid bare feet, he controlled his irritation and side stepped his way across. 'Namaste,' he said repeatedly.

Approached constantly by hopeful parents his popularity was clear. Children tugged at his hands and then hid shyly when acknowledged. He took his time, pressing Mitra's name, doing the job he was paid to do in the holiday atmosphere and, by midday, after hours in the crucifying heat, he pushed his way towards the stage, talking, encouraging, persuading, praising and swaying dissenters.

He could see the temple steps littered with beggars next to the orange garments of holy men; he pulled out his handkerchief to wipe the moisture from his face and, feeling dehydrated, he wished he hadn't drunk so much last night. He needed a drink now – desperately, anything to take away the rasp beginning to irritate his overworked throat.

A vendor with a crude barrow had a pitch near the stage. John made for it, easing bodies aside, his thirst urgent. On reaching the trader, he grabbed a bottle of water, ripped off the cap, reached into his pocket for a coin and closed his eyes as he emptied the contents down his parched throat.

'Illai, Illai,' said the vendor, refusing payment.

'Take it,' he said holding out a coin to a continuously shaking head. 'Give it to him then,' he said pointing to a sad youth with a patch over one eye, leaning heavily on a crutch begging with a single foot protruded from an oversized, grubby dhoti. Poor lad, he thought but looked closer, he grinned when he saw the spotlessly clean hand as the youth grasped the offered coin. John stepped from behind the vendor to face the boy, the lad turned away hurriedly and moved quickly towards the stage.

In his retreat, the head turned again, the one eye looked at John for a split second, the head turned away quickly – but not quickly enough. John had recognised Kenneth.

Shoving bodies aside he pushed his way through the crowd and reached the spot but Kenneth had gone. 'Where is he?' he demanded of a pitiable woman clutching a crying baby in one hand while she held out the other.

'Where is he?' He asked again, this time pulling a one-rupee coin from his pocket. She pointed under the platform and snatched at the coin. He pulled it away hissing, 'Bitch' and moved away followed by a torrent of high-pitched abuse.

Lifting the curtain, he called, 'Out, Kenneth.'

He waited. The command seemed to petrify the twelve-year-old cowering under the hessian curtain. John saw his knees draw up, as though it would aid invisibility.

'Kenneth come out . . . Now!' shouted John, his voice rising above the din around him. He held up the cover and waited, there was no movement.

Softening his tone he said, 'Come out son, I'm not going to bite you,' and bent down low to look under the cover. 'Come on, you won't be punished, out you come.'

He saw Kenneth's feet move and a turban showed as he edged towards the opening. He crept out slowly, dragging the crutch and stood in front of John like a delinquent before a judge, shamefaced, staring at his feet. John lowered himself to meet him at one eye level and looked into his petrified face. It was too much for Kenneth, tears streamed down his cheeks.

Fear, shame, embarrassment, John wasn't sure why the boy cried but trust, it seemed, made him grab John's outstretched hand while trying to stifle his sounds of his anguish that stuttered into a series of short sobs. The reassuring hand pulled the boy close; John slipped his arm around the shaking shoulders easing him to a quiet shady corner.

He kneeled down. 'Take your time son,' he said, 'take your time. What's wrong?'

Slowly, the shoulders stopped shaking, the sobbing subsided into occasional sharp intakes of breath and Kenneth choked out disjointed sentences. He'd arrived home for his three monthly visit on Saturday, his mother had collapsed at work a week earlier. Confined to bed, unable to work and without money the kids were hungry and had been scavenging. He overstayed his visit to help.

'Why not see me?'

'I spent my bus fare on food for Mata,' he sobbed.

'I see, well crying won't help will it? Take this,' he said reaching into his rear pocket and withdrawing a ten rupee note, 'buy what you need. Go home and stay with Mata, I will come later with the doctor.'

He placed his hand on the back of the boy's head and looked into his tear stained face. 'Go on son, away with you.'

He watched the dhoti drag across the ground as both feet moved Kenneth quickly out of the crowd, past the multitude of bodies now beginning to gather near the stage.

Pondering for a moment John recalled the foraging, the stealing and the hunger of his early years. His past flooded back, his original gang thieving indiscriminately until his imposed discipline harnessed their juvenile audacity. With a firm hand and subtle guidance, Sanjay and his gang became deceptive and cleverly self-sufficient – Fagin, he thought, and chuckled. How could he be angry with Kenneth after that? He shook his head forlornly, 'And the meek shall inherit the earth?'

He gave a cynical laugh that harboured resentment of a system where the poor are victims and the corrupt and cunning are wealthy victors – hypocritically forgetting his own credentials.

'Namaste,' he said with a fixed smile for the thousandth time.

* * *

He worked without respite until a clamour behind him announced the arrival of Mitra. He stood on an open backed truck against the forward cabin, garlanded in orange flowers over his white suit and Neru cap, dazzling against the grubbiness of the old vehicle. The noise became a tumult drowning the music as the truck eased its way forward surrounded by impassioned enthusiasts and watched by four goondas (thugs) trotting alongside. The crowd looked up to where he stood, haughty and confident, waving with one hand, while the other gripped the handrail of the rolling truck.

'Namaste,' he mouthed repeatedly, bowing his head humbly and raising his free hand imperiously. Nearing the stage the crowd pressed forward, making it almost impossible to make headway; the nearer he got the slower the progress, the noise deafening with screams and yells as the crowd waved and cheered – apart from one section that jeered loudly.

The vehicle was forced to stop ten yards from its destination, next to John, in the middle of the jeering mob. A young man with a look of fury, and uttering expletives, leapt on to the back of the halted truck. John saw the look of anger on his face and heard his obscenities and threw himself on to the truck, grabbing at the man's feet. He felt an ankle and pulled, the man fell, a foot connected with John's temple and two of Mitra's goondas leapt on the man and threw the assailant roughly from the truck and into the crowd as the police arrived to drive back the crowd in a repeat of Sunday's incident. A minute later the truck drew alongside the stage.

Mitra stepped off, ashen faced, and turned to face the audience.

The event had stimulated the crowd to more excitement; opponents screaming abuse and supporters calling for more police, as confusion followed uproar; the situation looked in danger of becoming out of control. Seeing the pandemonium, John quickly climbed the stage steps as more police arrived to beat back the crowd and form a protective ring around truck and stage.

Casually, with hands on hips, John stood beside Mitra like Goliath next to David, looking silently at the crowd, slowly turning his head, as a camera would pan a scene. With an expression of stunned abhorrence and daring disobedience, he watched for a full minute.

Imperceptibly at first, in twos and threes, the crowd quietened, groups calmed and turned their attention towards the big man. He waited for silence and, squeezing the moment for maximum effect, said nothing for another half minute. Then, the moment he saw their patience and curiosity start to subside he spoke . . .

'My friends, I came to India to join a democracy. You welcomed me, a stranger in your country, and that welcome became help when I needed it and you never let me down. Alongside you, I struggled to live as you live, as the backbone of the nation lives. For years we suffered together, underprivileged citizens paying a heavy price for our freedom, yet to our credit – and I proudly include myself – we built the finest democracy in the world. We did it by being fair, we did it by being tolerant and we did it with understanding. Those qualities, together with your determination, have produced the largest democratic, multi-racial, multi-religious, unbiased society the world has ever seen.'

He paused to observe the reaction. Nodding heads and mumbled approval told him it was the right track.

'If ever there was a time for understanding and tolerance it is now, so show it now, but first let me tell you why I support this man by my side whom you recognise but do not know. For years he has modestly concealed the support given indirectly to you and your children through my organisation, Orphindi. He is a principal contributor who has helped us through our difficulties, a patron and protector, always in the background, always active, yet he receives no credit. He is one of the un-acclaimed; a man helping to provide the care that this community deserves, and his name is Dhankar Mitra.'

He heard murmurs of approval and a smattering of applause.

'With that in mind I ask you to consider your candidates carefully, then in calmness, not frenzy, decide if they are worthy of your support, if they deserve the trust you are about to place in them. But whatever you do, do not allow the democracy you have built under the Congress Party to be ruined,' he said, pointing to a group of youngsters, ringed by police, 'by anarchists thugs. They did nothing to build this country but they are happy to wreck it! Don't let them my friends, they will take us back to the dark, hopeless days. Support my friend Dhankar Mitra and judge him as you would me in our joint aim for a better life in the greatest country in the world, your country, The Republic of India.' He stepped aside.

For a second there was silence and then applause turned into a tumult accompanied by loud cheering, lengthy and deafening. John looked towards Mitra and smiled – a genuine, pleased with the outcome smile. Mitra shook John's hand, before raising it in the air.

It took several minutes to silence the crowd. Patiently Mitra stood at the microphone.

'My friends,' he began, 'you have just heard from a great man, an honest man whom we all know and respect, a man known internationally as a generous benefactor, the protector of children and their families, a humanitarian, and I am proud to say that, as a friend and business partner, he will be at my side throughout this campaign. We have . . .'

While he spoke, the opposition, having re-formed in the very centre, in front of the stage, interrupted in tepid opposition. They shouted and heckled. John took a pace forward, just in case, and noticed Mitra's goondas do the same, then he saw the quality of Mitra in front of an audience with his protection on hand. Confident and self-assured, he broke off what he was saying and, for a moment, shook his head sadly, smiling tolerantly. With hands on hips, he leaned forward.

'My friends,' he said, directing the crowd's attention to the taunting group, 'you will notice that only the unintelligent jeer and ridicule while you listen. What use is that? The good people of Amitar are magnanimous and democratically minded so we tolerate their abuse as one does in a free society – but would they let us in theirs?' Then pointing his finger he said laughing, 'Let them shout and abuse as loudly as they like, the people of Amitar hear only common sense!'

The crowd laughed with him and rose to him, cheering. It took several minutes before they stopped and in the eventual calm, he again taunted the group. 'They have nothing to offer except abuse and, as failures, nothing tangible to say, so let the free people of Amitar take a good look at the unsure, frightened face of communism. It was defeated last time having never kept a promise and having decimated our country and it will do so again unless it is defeated. These thugs are not worthy of being called opposition because they are inspirationally insolvent!'

The crowd began to laugh, his performance convincing, his ridicule potent and, with the audience swayed, he stepped back.

John nodded. Despite all his reservations, he had to admire Mitra. He looked into his face, illuminated by a prissy smile. He had won their support and John was the instigator, but even at that moment of success, he was cautious. Was that the smile on the face of the tiger!'

EIGHTEEN

Ahmed Jaitley peered at Saturday's returns in the dimness of his office, he placed the sheets down and rummaged among the papers scattered on the wooden table, found what he wanted, compared the two, made an entry and tossed one paper aside.

A hand went to his head to remove his damaged glasses and touched the tender spot on his nose where they chaffed. He squinted at the broken pad, whinged that he must get it repaired and wiped his watery eyes with the back of his hand. Laying the spectacles on the table, he rubbed his stiff face and forehead with circular motions, causing wispy grey hairs to stick to his balding pate. He wiped off the sweat with his hand and wiped his hand on his dhoti.

Easing from the chair, slowed by the pain in his back, he crossed the office to a cabinet, unaware of fallen papers, his shuffling steps sending tiny puffs of dust flying that had turned his feet and sandals a powdery white.

Tugging at the drawer he gritted his teeth at the opening screech and rested one elbow on the cabinet to reach inside and withdraw a ledger before shambling back to the table, ignoring the newly soiled patch on the elbow of his black jacket.

His finger explored the columns bringing a creaky grimace to his face that passed for a smile. He nodded and flicked back through the past record. In the six months since his arrival production had increased from four to six hundred pairs of jeans per day. He entered five hundred and eighty.

Snapping the book shut sent dust particles swirling into shafts of evening sunlight seeping through cracks in the door, and he rose to replace the book in the cabinet among another swirl of the white powder. This time he removed a bag of coins and a wad of rupee notes and shuffled to the door to lock it, hating the sound as the key turned and the lock snapped shut.

Pushing papers aside, he counted money into neat piles and checked with a stabbing finger to confirm his count, he then glanced at his battered watch. Time for a check!

He stood slowly switched off the single bulb and made for a second door into the workshop where his lips turned down in distaste at the humid smell of clammy, sweating bodies that greeted him – but that was the price of success.

A bearded cutter glanced quickly at the door and raised his pace, machines responded and a smile ghosted Ahmed's features while his eyes, sharp and cold, darted from person to person, his brain absorbing every movement of the thirty, toiling women on as many sewing machines.

Two tiny boys, no more than ten years old, scurried along the central aisle emptying baskets, while two cutters, bending to their task, never noticeably lifted their heads – yet he was aware that eyes followed his every move as he started his trudge down the aisle.

With hands clasped behind his back and shoulders drooping, his slight frame resembled the shape of a question mark as he slowly moved along, not showing the satisfaction he felt. Mr Mahmood, the owner, had been pleased too that Jaitley's method of placing the fastest girl first in the line forced others to keep up or risk a visible pile up of cloth – and a walk to the exit where other women waited. Willing friends prevented the culprit's exit and Ahmed relied on those friendships.

Stopping occasionally, he would grab a pair of jeans from the basket, look closely and pull at the seam always grimacing with apparent disapproval before throwing them back. Sweating women gave secretive, disparaging smiles behind his back, he knew, but got what he wanted.

The aisle terminated in the warehouse; he glanced in, turned, as quickly as his painful back would allow, hoping to catch any idle watchers, huffed and walked back to the cutters bench where he took a pile of worksheets and snapped something before stepping back into his office, relieved at the drop in humidity.

Leaving the light off he heard the machines run down, he opened the side door and blinked as sunlight flooded the room revealing dusty shelves and lumps of cottony lint congealed in corners. His bedroll and cooking pots lay half-hidden by a filing cabinet and the smell of paraffin pervaded the air. He could well afford a hotel but this was a rent-less, temporary home and much preferable to his recent habitation.

Apart from the occasional whirr of a motor completing a seam and the scrape of metal legs on the newly laid concrete floor, the factory became silent and a line of eager, sari-clad women queued behind the bearded cutter as he handed in today's tally.

The staff filed past, Ahmed ticked names and reached grudgingly towards the piles of notes and coins, handing forty rupees each to two men and thirty to each woman. 'Service,' he said frequently and withheld ten rupees, ticking the book, ignoring their disgruntled looks.

Having finished, he followed the final two boys, closed the outer door, switched on the light, regarded the desk where every coin and note had been accounted for and nodded with satisfaction. Two men, thirty women and two boys paid in a daily ritual with the surplus for, 'service,' residing in his jacket pocket.

He piled everything into the centre of the desk, went to the large metal cupboard and reached to the back to withdraw a worn account book. He shambled back to the desk and meticulously entered a second set of figures before returning the book to its hiding place.

Leaving the office again he made for the far end of the building, collected twenty pairs of jeans, tied them with sisal, struggled back to the office and dumped them by his table on which he leaned heavily – wheezing.

Recovering he removed a half-empty bottle of cheap, Indian whisky from the cupboard and, with a heavy sigh, lowered himself into his chair to pour the spirit into an unwashed mug taken from the same place. He took a mouthful, swished it around as though disinfecting, and exhaled sweet alcoholic fumes, coughing as the fierce spirit burned his throat. With eyes closed, he leaned back in the rickety chair thankful for a moment's respite in a day that had started at 6 a.m. and finished twelve hours later.

The sound of a vehicle reached him and his smile creaked again. Good, he thought, the chair creaked too and he moved to the door, smiling his servile smile at his visitor. The smile remained throughout the transaction until his guest departed with his wares.

'Very satisfactory,' said Ahmed, gently patting his pocket and securing the door for the night, shuddering again at the sound of the key turning in the lock.

NINETEEN

Lances of evening sunlight lit the interior of Kenneth's home as he piled the purchases from plastic bags on the low cane table. Proud to have executed his obligation to his family, he set his two siblings to work preparing a meal.

The house, built by his father, was square, a single room of woven panels under a palm thatch, similar to others set beside an earthen track a few miles north of Amitar, part of a village of piecemeal construction that was fortunate to contain a water pump.

Family possessions were meagre, water pots, cooking pots and mats, rolled and stowed tidily, a rope strung bed and four footstools, essentials of life only. The table was set to one side of an earth floor, brushed as clean as the outside, showing that even in sickness the occupier kept standards, and leaning against outside walls was the usual supply of nature's fuel. The smell of ignited dung hung in the oppressively hot air. Kenneth, sat beside his mother's bed, advantaged compared to the poor souls living in filthy shanty towns amid running sewers.

Hardly believing the change in three months, his pretty, thirty-three year old mother had shrunk, she had become a frail, weak, old woman with huge eyes in a gaunt, expressionless face. Too weak to respond to his words of comfort, she remained motionless, her head to one side staring while he poured water into a bowl and tenderly removed her choli.

Withered breasts and skin stretched taut against ribs that stuck out like bony fingers made him wonder how she had reached that stage in such a short time. She looked old; older than he could ever imagine, her eyes had lost their lustre and skin drawn tight across her face widened her eyes to twice their natural size; her lips drooped at the corners, leaving deep furrows from the sides of her mouth to her chin.

She didn't smile, and that was the saddest difference; her expression reminded him of her sadness when his father died and he stood beside her as the flames consumed his body. He remembered the garlands and the crackle of burning wood as he looked up at the pyre on a huge plinth by the river and smelt the strange, sweet smell of the smoke. She'd held him tightly, but he didn't cry until the night when, woken to the sound of sobbing, he crawled over to lay with mata as his father had, and she held him tightly. From that day he hated snakes and the sorrow and misery they had brought to his family.

Taking responsibility he'd worked in the market, while mata struggled on the pittance he earned, until he met Vijay. He recalled his mother's joy when Sanjay offered her work nearby and John took him on his first ride on a motorcycle; the speed was frightening yet he felt safe jammed between the big man and Sanjay.

He chatted cheerfully while he washed her, hoping his attention and presence would bring life to a lifeless face. 'These are from Mr John, mata, he will be here soon with the doctor,' he said as the smell of a nourishing avial stew drifted in from the fire outside.

Completing her wash, he checked the meal and fed her, gently holding her head in the crook of his arm before laying her down to sleep while his younger brother and sister ate.

Filling a pitcher at the pump, he returned to the rear of the hut and removed the soiled dhoti. He stood naked in the shielding shade of the wattle fence and poured water over his head and lost himself in the dousing, rubbing vigorously to refresh and cleanse.

Clearing the surplus with his hands, he bent to rub his legs, when he sensed he was not alone and, with a quick intake of breath, he spun around. John was standing by the hut, watching with a peculiar strangeness that Kenneth had not seen before. An inexplicable embarrassment swept through him, dismissed only when John's expression changed to a benevolent smile.

'Carry on son,' he said.

I did not hear you Mr John,' he replied, strangely self-conscious under the scrutiny.

'That's alright son,' John said slowly without taking his eyes off him, 'take your time.'

Kenneth stooped quickly and picked up the dhoti.

'Leave that son, put something clean on,' he said, taking the dirty cloth and followed him into the dwelling, scrutinising while he dressed and the doctor examined mata.

When he finished, the doctor asked if Mata had been fasting.

'I do not think so sir.'

'Why, Ranjit?' asked John.

'Malnutrition, John. The mother is clearly emaciated and she has pneumonia. With good food and rest there is no reason why she

115

should not recover in a week or two with proper care. I'll leave some medication – stay with her and see that she gets it Kenneth.'

'Yes sir,' said Kenneth, proud that his status had been recognised by status itself.

John looked hesitant. 'His headmaster is anxious that he should return to school tomorrow Ranjit. I'll see a neighbour, it's surprising what a few rupees will do.'

'As you wish. I'll call in a few days. Namaste,' he said and Kenneth heard his motorcycle start and roar off up the hill. John moved to the side of the bed and knelt beside his mother. 'Mrs Chopra,' he said smiling gently, 'where do you work?'

'Periyar,' she whispered.

'The clothing factory?'

She closed her eyes in assent.

He knew the factory, not that he had been there. 'I see,' he mused, 'I will make sure the owner keeps your job open. Meantime a neighbour will be here to help, Kenneth and I have to go back.' He patted her hand and stood.

'Get your things together son,' he ordered and strode across the track where Kenneth heard him call, 'Vanakkam.' (hello)

Minutes later Kenneth was on the pillion of the Enfield for his second ride on a motor-cycle, clinging to John's ample waist, happy that his mother was in good hands.

*   *   *

It was the freedom of relaxed driving, not forced concentration, that allowed John to think clearly. In the flowing air he was able to dissect the clutter in his mind and focus properly. This afternoon he used the period of moving isolation fruitfully.

It made no sense that Mrs Chopra was starving when she had been working full time in Mahmood's factory. She was starving and yet her income was adequate for her family, either she was no manager, or in debt, and he would bet a thousand rupees on the plague of the poor. Wouldn't it, he smiled, be odd if Mitra was her creditor? He couldn't wait to pay the factory a visit, but that would have to wait.

Arriving at the bungalow, he deposited Kenneth in the boys' quarters with instructions he should be fed. Chef told him that Sergeant Birkram had been there and Inspector Joshi would like to see him at the Police station.

John bit his lip and nodded, acknowledged the seated four briefly as he passed, showered, changed and returned to join the group as evening sounds drifted across the brush in a pink tinged twilight, before blackness enveloped the surroundings.

Sam was unusually quiet, he had a gut feeling that something was wrong, and she didn't react when Hillary made her knowledgeable observation about the speed with which night falls. 'One minute,' she said, 'it is daylight and the next it's inky black. It's being so near to the equator of course.'

Sam seemed to be waiting for the right moment and John realised he'd made an error when he asked about the day.

'Terribly hot and so humid,' Hillary replied, 'we almost melted and . . .'

'. . . and so did the boys,' said Sam sourly.

Her attitude set alarm bells ringing; this was not her usual banter. 'Something wrong, Sam?' he asked, not knowing that Tony's foot was working like a piston.

'I don't suppose, being Westerners,' she started in a bitter tone but regulated it not to cause too much offence, 'that we understand, John, but the boys worked on your building all day – in that heat.'

'Yes,' he said not intimidated at all, 'the sight can be upsetting, seen for the first time.'

'Or even cruel, John, the poor mites were covered in dust and struggling with great blocks. It only needed one to drop and a foot could be crushed.'

The others sat in rigid silence, absorbed yet not daring to intervene. Tony slid back into his chair with his arms on the armrests, not wanting to be part of the skirmish.

John chose his words, careful to avoid open confrontation, hoping to arrest the looming complaint.

It was a question of survival, he said, they lived in a different culture and children had to learn survival. 'You may see it as harsh Sam, but if my kids join the outside world without experience, they will lag behind, what then? They will suffer – so which is better, preparation or starvation?'

She seemed to have no answer and seeing her hesitancy, he pressed home his advantage gently. 'They are volunteers Sam, two hours a month that's all, it would be wrong to deprive them of learning opportunities. You see it as cruel, we see it as cruel not to show them and, to be frank Sam, you must not judge India by the standards of the mollycoddled west, where people live according to style and not income. Here you get nothing for nothing.'

Her saw her uncomfortable recognition and stopped, not wishing to pulverise her.

'It just seems so wrong, John . . .' she said uncertainly, losing the momentum of her argument.

'I agree Sam, but if children are not exposed to some danger, how will they cope when faced with them? It's what is happening in the West, kids can be over-protected?'

'Well . . . yes, I suppose you're right . . .' she said flicking back her hair, unable to find a reasoned argument. 'It was the shock I suppose, they seem so young and . . . and . . . vulnerable,' she ended weakly.

'So what better time to teach them? If you had stayed for the changeover you would have seen their little bums as they dived into the Lake.'

She laughed with the others, pacified, he thought, as Chef arrived in place of Kumar, who had the evening off, to direct them to dinner.

With normality restored, he left for the boy's quarters without joining them for dinner.

* * *

Pulling up a stool John sat down at eye level with Kenneth and with the mantle of a smile, he questioned him gently and kindly, discovering little more than that Mrs Chopra's manager was Mr Ahmed and she earned thirty rupees a day. He asked about debt. Kenneth was horrified. 'No, Mr John!' he said forcefully, 'father forbade her to use those men, they would come and shout at us and the goondas would threaten us.'

'I see,' he said, aware that even Kenneth would not admit to using moneylenders whose reputation for exorbitant repayments and public humiliation brought shame on families. The spectacle of men screaming abuse at defaulters in the street was enough to put anyone off and apart from dragging the poor deeper into debt there was always the possibility of a beating, or worse. In Mrs Chopra's case it was unlikely that any self-respecting moneylender would take a chance on her. Sanjay was the man to ask, he was the procurer, then, perhaps, a visit to Mr Ahmed.

Warning Kenneth not to ignore Sanjay's instructions in future, he led him into his own room. 'Give him the head count every morning. Had you done so last Monday perhaps we might have found Samuel by now.'

'Sanjay was not there, Mr John, so I have to leave the head count with Mrs Jha. She passes it on when he comes in.'

'Do you now?' he said thoughtfully. 'Every day?'

'Yes Mr John.'

'Right, jump in, you can sleep in a real bed tonight and in the morning Vijay will run you to the camp.'

Standing beside the bed, he watched Kenneth remove his clothes.

In the half-light, his dark skin shone with the lustre of youth. His neat body, supple and agile stirred John as the boy climbed naked into the double bed and lay down. John pulled up the single sheet, 'Thank you, Mr John,' he said.

John's mouth had become quite dry and a salacious look slid over his features, he licked his dry lips and tried to swallow but his throat hurt as old sensations returned.

'That's OK,' he croaked and reached down to stroke the boy's thick hair, 'sleep well,' he said hoarsely, his eyes glistening appreciatively.

* * *

Greeted by the peppery, sweet smell of curry as he entered Sanjay's dwelling, normality had returned.

Sanjay was hurrying, shirtless, towards the bedroom with a pile of clothes in his hands. John cursed his engine for the advanced warning and cast his eyes over the half-eaten meal and the empty beer cans on the table.

'Just about finished.'

You will be if you don't learn, he thought spitefully, opening the front and back windows before seating himself on the corner of the table.

'Head aching still?' he asked amiably.

'Tired, that's all.'

'I'm not surprised, he said agreeably, 'all weekend in searing heat, pressing those lads to do that bit extra. It's enough to tire Hercules.'

'Yes,' he said, and added modestly, 'I'll be glad when the monsoons come, I could do with a rest.'

The acceptance and lies incensed John, he held back with difficulty and then, with a mixture of solace and facetiousness that Sanjay did not appear to notice, he said, 'Ye-e-es, I expect you need a break Sanjay, you are entitled to a relaxed evening and a quiet drink after your weekend effort aren't you?'

Sanjay, with his confidence high after this morning's victory, smiled, 'Yes,' he said, 'want to join me?'

'No thanks my son,' he said, 'things to do. Everything under control is it, huts checked, lads checked, all present and correct, no problems?'

'No.'

'No?' chuckled John, 'no problems, or no you haven't checked?'

Sanjay pushed an empty dish away, 'Something wrong?' he ventured looking into John's eyes that twinkled with apparent humour.

'Wrong Sanjay, why should anything be wrong? You are the man with his finger on the pulse.'

'So far as I know it's OK.'

'That's fine then, site closed, camp checked, all the little lads fast asleep on their little mats?' he said, this time with such a deliberate edge of sarcasm that the effect was immediate.

Sanjay sat upright as though keyed for the next question. John could practically see the concern in his eyes mingle with a momentary touch of panic.

'Why?' he asked. 'Has that boy let me down again?'

'Who – Kenneth?' said John with a rare laugh, 'Don't be silly, he wouldn't let you down twice. What did you say to him this morning?'

Sanjay shook his head, 'I can't remember, my head was bad after last night . . .'

'But clear enough,' he yelled, standing upright and banging the table, 'for you to concoct a pack of frigging lies!'

Sanjay's mouth dropped open. 'What?'

'You are a liar! Kenneth is not at the outpost and if you saw him over the weekend it was because you were pissed and had hallucinations!'

'What . . . er . . . what do you mean?'

'What do I mean?' he yelled. 'Check the boys!' he yelled crashing his fist down on the table. 'The last thing I said to you yesterday was check the bloody boys,' he repeated thrusting his jaw to within a foot of Sanjay's face, glowering threateningly and bearing down closer. 'You careless, useless bastard, forget did you?' he blasted, 'I wish I could forget you, you bloody moron! When I went to town, what did I find? What – did – I – find?' he yelled, '. . . well . . .? come on . . .'

But without waiting for an answer he banged his fist on the table in rhythm with his words, 'a one-legged – bang, one-eyed – bang, beggar in Amitar, bang, bang, bang. He wasn't here Saturday, he wasn't here Sunday and he wasn't here today and he is the boy who reports to you daily! You lying bastard.'

Sanjay's face turned to a sickly, dispirited mask. Another boy absconding would heighten Joshi's suspicions. He put his hand to his head, 'I wasn't well, I . . .'

But John would not let up. 'How many others, eh? You make the same bloody mistake over and over again, and then lie! You lied to me about today, you lied to me about yesterday and who knows what other lies you tell? "On site, it's very hot, very tiring",' he mimicked. 'You have not seen the bloody site, the supervisor covered for you!'

Sanjay, with moistened eyes, sank into the chair in cowering silence.

'No reply I see – a different bloody Sanjay from the cocksure little sod arguing this morning,' he yelled, allowing the full force of his temper to crush Sanjay's abating spirit.

'Get a shower and see Rasa – now! Yes now, and don't look at me like that, it's only nine o'clock. Tell the truth for once. The boy's mother is sick and he will be in tomorrow,' he bellowed, his face only an inch away as Sanjay took on a terrified look. 'I want to know what's going on here because I've been summoned to see that nosy bloody copper! Yes you heard, Joshi, and I hope he didn't get to Rasa first because you are next on his check list.'

Feckless Sanjay, whose sweat ran so profusely that it looked like tears where it had reached his cheeks, sat petrified and motionless. John felt no sympathy and neither was he about to give way to the complete liability that sat before him. He turned to leave and on reaching the door, stopped.

'And another thing, seal off the approaches to the new site. I don't want any more awkward questions from curious bloody visitors. Then tomorrow you can tell me where you spend your missing hours and what goes on at Periyar-bloody-fashions, if I don't find out first!

'I'll leave the bike,' he said – and slammed the door.

* * *

With his face contorted in resentment at the unfairness of the attack and terror at the thought of facing Joshi, Sanjay rushed into the bathroom. He seemed unable to get anything right, he'd intended to see Kenneth today but his head had played up. 'Bloody bastard,' he said bitterly.

Depressed and saturated in self-pity he ducked his head into the bowl, splashed his face and rubbed his torso furiously. If only he could find a reason to fight back – he never seemed to have one, John always had the upper hand and never did anything to complain about . . . and then it struck him.

Of course! He gives orders but does no work, he doesn't negotiate, he doesn't look after the camp, he doesn't build, he does do anything at all, he's pampered and only gossips to those westerners! How he wished he had thought of that at the time.

The thought cheered him and, in the mirror, he saw the enmity drain from his face, only to return when he thought about Periyar. What did he know, who told him, one of the boys, not Kenneth again, he'll see that little runt, tomorrow.

In the meantime, if John complained, he would remind him why he came to India, the boys, the lies, the cheating, Colin, the house and the lack of help. Yes, he could make trouble, he was better as a friend than an enemy, there could be consequences if Sanjay chose . . .

'Yes,' he said savouring the phrase, 'there could be consequences.'

Content that his knowledge of the past was his strength, Sanjay mounted the Enfield, opened the throttle and sped off to Amitar.

* * *

John, his hands stuck in his pockets, stared at the ground in a temper born out of suspicion and spite. He walked into to the compound and quietly opened each door checking the occupants. Every mat except two was occupied, the whereabouts of one was known and although he knew why the other left, he hoped to God he would not be found. With luck, the election would place too much of a burden on the new Inspector's stretched force to search effectively and, like other inspectors before him, he would give up.

He heard the Enfield start. 'I wonder,' he mumbled and stepped into the workshop office, waiting until the sound disappeared before turning on the light to rummage among the files for the sales figures. After a brief check he left with papers to compare with workshop output records, questions, some answers and a broad smile on his face wondering idly, if, when confronted with this lot, Mitra's look would match the alarm he had shown at the rally. It would certainly add ammunition to John's armoury and alienate Sanjay.

All in all tomorrow should be an interesting day, visit Mitra, Joshi, Mrs Chopra and Mahmood's factory. Yes, he thought, as his steps took him towards the silent bungalow, tomorrow should be interesting.

He heard a young goat bleat nearby in the head high brush before it rushed away. He stopped suddenly, recognising the eight feet of slithering menace that crossed the path ahead. He stamped his feet noisily before moving on cautiously, hoping the cobra, warned by the vibrations, had moved on too. He watched the front carefully and smiled ruefully – it was his back that needed watching.

Climbing the steps he thought how sustaining it was having someone like Kumar to provide the soothing treatment he needed, tonight in particular. It had been a hell of a day. 'Bugger,' he said aloud, 'it's his night off.'

He headed for the kitchen and switched on the light, poured a large beer and a scotch and made a sandwich. He took them to the rattan table on the veranda and sat studying the papers.

Half an hour later he leaned back, vexed and suspicious, unable to make sense of the inadequate records. They didn't tally with those he remembered, and he grunted his dissatisfaction. He folded the sheets and carried them along the silent veranda to his room.

Isolation, he thought as he stepped inside his door, might have its advantages, but without Kumar to read his mood and provide his intimate remedies it could be so bloody miserable ... he froze in mid-breath listening ... was Kumar back? He could hear breathing and ... no, he'd forgotten ... Kenneth!

In the gloom he could just make out his shape in the centre of his double bed, a small, half covered figure. He recalled the sight of him undressing, his skin dripping and glistening in the sunlight, his slim, young, body, lithe and naked, supple and so beautiful. His head began to pound, his breathing quickened and he shuddered with imagined thrills as he listened to the gentle sounds.

Nervously he tiptoed towards the bed and lifted the sheet, the naked form, black against white, looked angelic, enticing and stimulating.

Impetuously he slipped off his clothes and eased himself on to the bed sliding gently under the cloth so as not to waken the boy. Carefully he lowered himself, brushing the lad's silken torso.

A shiver ran through him as Kenneth, in his slumber, turned towards him and swung an arm across his chest.

With a sharp intake of breath, John closed his eyes tightly and bit his lip in restraint to curb his rising excitement but, unable to suppress his natural desires, he gently pulled the lad closer.

TWENTY

Kumar followed the same path as John on his way back to the bungalow, having walked the four miles from his great aunt's home east of Amitar as usual on Monday evenings.

Now in her late seventies, she had worked for the British as accounts secretary to an army supplies officer before and during the war until Independence in 1947. Then, when the British left, she transferred to a Local Government Department where she continued until retirement, ten years earlier. She remained unmarried.

Her English was perfect and years of experience in accounts gave her the knowledge to enlighten Kumar in the mysteries of figures and the English language. In turn, he helped dig and plant vegetables, fill her pots at the well and undertake heavy tasks. With her encouragement, his education expanded and he imagined John's surprise the day he would unveil his abilities in English and accountancy.

The shared evenings of work and endless fascinating stories of the antics of the English and their progressiveness infected him, firing his imagination to the extent that at times he became restless in the restrictive world of institutionalised repetition. His appetite for knowledge and ambitions grew and had it not been for his adoration of John, he would like to have savoured new experiences and pitted himself against new challenges in the outside world.

In the meantime, he listened, learned and secretly read everything, including John's papers from the Facility Centre, gathering that John was on the verge of something called, 'capitalisation of potential'. His aunt said it meant grasping his chance, he assumed that was why he was dealing with Mr Mitra again.

He told no one of his ability in English, not even Vijay and Sunil, who believed they were the only English speakers, and discovered the advantage of pretended ignorance and willing docility; it aided misconception. People misjudged his intelligence, believing he was not mentally equal, and from that unique position, he became discreetly and thoroughly informed. Anyway, eavesdropping was fun, it amused him to hear John argue with Sanjay and to keep one step ahead. He also understood most of what the visitors said – except for the tall man with red hair, he had a strange way of speaking but the others were usually clear – especially the dark woman – she didn't need to speak.

She intrigued him now. The incident in her bedroom had initially troubled him: her nudity surprised and disturbed him leaving an alien, exotic, sexual uncertainty. He began to think about her, differently and unexpectedly, the vision of her nakedness, from which he derived new, unusual thoughts, came back to him repeatedly. It made him uncomfortable and uncertain, he put it down to ignorance and being distanced from females, yet he re-imagined her shape and form repeatedly, finding it strangely attractive and exciting. He had considered speaking to John but hesitated in unexplained reservation. Perhaps he should speak to Sunil.

Later than usual tonight, having become deeply involved in the use of active and passive voices, 'The bombers destroyed the town – active, the town was destroyed by bombers – passive,' repetition, that was the secret of good language his aunt had said. 'The bombers . . .' he repeated over and over from the moment he started out, going over the lesson on the four-mile stroll back in the breeze-reduced heat.

Within view of the bungalow, he stopped repeating his lesson and slowed to admire the lighted-up building from a mere two hundred yards, hearing nothing but the rustle of dry leaves kissed by a gentle wind. He peered ahead through moonlit brush, one day, perhaps; his knowledge of English would help him secure work like his aunt and a home like Mr John's. Just imagine a replica of Paradise Lake by a . . .

He stopped abruptly, there was a movement, too quick to catch positively but he was certain something raced across the path. Leopard, goat? No it was too upright in the moon's glow, it looked like a person. He bent low; his eyes scoured the sides of the path ahead and focused just above the spot, then shifting his gaze to the bungalow, he saw something else, it looked like Mr John pacing the patio, waiting for him probably. Another movement ahead drew his attention to the original point of concentration and, straining to look into the blackness, he saw something small dash across the path and hide behind a bush.

It could be nobody else but John who paced the veranda but was it his imagination or did his body language show anxiety as he paced, stopped and peered, first from one position and then another, was he there to warn Kumar? Had he seen a leopard, should he shout? No, noise could startle an animal into attack and for no reason in particular Kumar kept low, intrigued, with the possibility of sneaking up on John to surprise him? He did that sometimes, it made him laugh and . . .

There it was again, the movement, ahead, only twenty yards away in the bush, it was no leopard – the shape was wrong, he started forward silently to within a few metres. It was human and stooped in concealment, like he did, watching the bungalow from behind a dense bush.

Kumar cautiously, silently, moved towards the outline, clearer now. It was a boy, naked. Carefully he placed his books on the ground and, with his eyes glued on the shape, he moved forward keeping low, stopping directly in the path of the retreating figure, who, never taking his eyes off the bungalow, backed towards him until he was almost on top of Kumar.

Believing he was clear, he turned slowly, ready to run. Kumar grabbed him!

He let out a strangled howl, 'No, no-o-o,' and fell to the ground with Kumar holding tightly to his wrist, a hand clamped over his mouth.

'Kenneth!' he snapped in a whispered challenge releasing him, 'what are you doing?'

Kenneth tried to back away, 'Don't let him catch me . . .' he whispered, hushed and desperate.

'Who? Mr John? why?' he said, sensing desperation in the frightened boy.

With a staggered intake of breath, he said, 'Don't . . . don't let him . . .'

'Why? What have you done?'

The boy shivered, Kumar pulled him nearer and, in the silvery light, he saw the distress and fear as lips quivered in an effort to control his emotions. He reigned in his aggression, 'What is it Kenneth?' he soothed.

The boy's young face creased as he struggled to speak, words failed and, choked by throaty sobs, he pointed to the house. 'He put me in his bed and came in and . . . and . . .'

The effort was too much and his attempt to explain gave way to a relentless sobbing for a second time that day.

With suspicions deepening, Kumar looked closely at the misery before him. 'Did you stay with Mr John tonight?'

He received a verifying nod.

'Why?'

'Mata . . . is sick . . . he brought me back . . .' he sobbed, 'put me . . . to bed and . . . woke me and . . .'

A suppressed wailing gave the answer that devastated Kumar. His doubts turned to suspicion. 'Did Mr John get into bed with you?'

Kenneth nodded. 'I ran . . . I . . . ran . . .,' he sobbed.

Kumar needed no more, the series of babbling half statements told him of the attempted violation. The distraught boy's words made little sense but Kumar understood precisely how their guardian's soft words and compassion encouraged and ensnared. He understood the persuasiveness and how gentle teachings had worked on him. He had accepted the kindness and returned it with innocent, grateful affection, ignorant of the skilful coercion. Like most boys at Orphindi, he had never known womanly love in youth or maturity and John's beguiling tenderness had cunningly defiled his adolescent purity.

In Kenneth, he saw repetition; it brought back his own conversion and confusion, raising more questions, linking them with the naked woman. Why did she disturb him so? Was there another kind of love? Was it her body, the shape, the texture, the difference? Perplexed and in a dilemma, he looked at Kenneth, half wanting to believe he had made a mistake and yet, standing before him was miserable evidence.

Too young to pretend, Kumar believed him and, as he listened to the choking sobs, his scepticism turned to rage and then disgust. How could John undermine the very protection he offered? He was like a hungry tiger in a herd of sheep!

In those few moments, his trust changed to loathing and, unaccountably, he found himself momentarily in sympathy with Sanjay.

Placing a protective arm around the lad's shoulders, he weighed his options: discretion or disclosure? His aunt would favour discretion, disclosure would bring an investigation and doubtful benefit and he imagined the outcome of a young boy pitted against a respected figure, he would be laughed away. But, as John was so fond of saying, 'Use what you know son – give nothing away'. It would be foolish not to follow his advice.

Kumar checked the veranda, collected his books and cautiously led Kenneth towards the bungalow. When they were near he walked ahead. John was nowhere to be seen. They stole quietly into the boy's quarters.

Instantly responsible and with the kindness of a caring parent Kumar reassured him, 'Forget this Kenneth, it will bring you unhappiness, it is our secret, say nothing and never be alone with him. Say nothing to anyone, we will repay him, trust me, trust me,' he repeated holding him close and keeping up the whispered persuasion long into the night.

The sobbing had stopped, but Kumar knew the hurt would return to be diluted only with the passing of time. Kenneth needed a friend to repair the wound and ease the unearned shame. Compassion and trust would slowly sway him and encouraging words from Kumar would play their part to put the elements of faith and trust back together.

* * *

Kumar rose ahead of everyone else at Paradise Lake, his standard routine. Regardless of the time he went to bed, his infallible in-built clock signalled restlessness at the faintest sign of dawn and compelled him into activity.

Rising at four thirty he rolled and silently stowed his mat and, without waking the others, went to the kitchen, filled the electric kettle and made tea, strong and black. Taking his tea to the end of the pergola with his books, he would sit in one of the cane chairs and study. From that vantage point he could, by leaning a few inches forward, see all the bedroom doors and hear any movement that might disturb his secret learning, without being seen.

Today was the exception; he changed his routine. At five thirty he roused Kenneth, washed him, fed him, used one of his own dhotis and talked incessant, comforting words. Sunil arrived and by six thirty Kenneth was back in camp confirming Kumar's effective persuasion with a smile of confidence when he left.

He watched the cloud of red dust disappear and at once realised the strength of his position. He had something tucked away, as John said, 'for a rainy day.'

In the aftermath of John's treachery he questioned John's teachings as he mechanically prepared for the day. Was it possible that Kenneth was being groomed as he had been? Was he different or had he been made different? Misguidance and misuse began at an early age. Had he tried the same with Samuel? Is that why he ran off?

Could it be that John's kindness led him to mistake kindness for love, and therefore he loved in return? His early reluctance had been overcome, he could have been deceived into believing that love was the appropriate response? Baffled, and struggling to find an answer, he found himself linking those questions with what he knew of the woman.

She had brought new thoughts, new thrills to him again last night and he found himself curiously attracted. She was brash, blatant and conceited but exciting and stimulating and, although at the time he was shocked and somewhat frightened by her display, the vision returned, stirring him to re-imagined appearances. He regretted his reluctance now, especially alone in his bed when he visualised her naked. Since then, when he prudently cast an eye over her, she, disappointingly, never returned his looks. Was it possible she had awakened something that was there all the time?

Uncertain and confused about her, he concentrated on John. There was no confusion there, his intentions with Kenneth were perfectly clear but it would have to remain their secret until needed – alongside the other secret, his English. It was not a waste of time and, used discreetly in the light of John's duplicity, it could prove be a huge advantage.

Placing the knives and forks on the table he pondered John's words again, 'Use what you know son, give nothing away.'

He would. It would be wrong to disobey and spoil John's surprise.

TWENTY-ONE

Excited by the promised ride on an elephant, the visitors had left at seven; Chef and Kumar busied themselves until John appeared at the breakfast table around eight, announced that he would be out all day and casually asked Kumar if he had seen Kenneth?

'Yes Mr John, Sunil took him to the camp,' he replied casually, watching him slyly as he circled the table.

'How was he?'

He waited a moment before replying. 'Frightened Mr John . . .' he hesitated again protracting the agony that he knew John must be feeling. 'But who wouldn't be after an experience like that?' he said.

The fork paused in front of John's mouth.

'Experience, what experience?' he asked with eyes fixed on the plate while Kumar again deliberately delayed his reply in secret glee to heighten the anxiety. He turned as though to walk towards the kitchen.

'Did you hear me, I said what experience?'

He sounded tense and Kumar continued the tease. Slowly he turned, noticing the fork still poised. 'You know what I mean Mr John, the same thing happened to me.'

John appeared paralysed, his jaw locked and veins stood out on his neck and forehead, blue against white. 'He's upset,' he said frostily, 'his mother is sick.'

'No Mr John' said Kumar deferentially, 'it was not that . . .'

'Yes it was,' he interrupted, 'I bloody well know! I went to help her so don't bloody argue. He was upset and slept in my bed. I had to sleep on that bloody couch until he ran off! I don't suppose he said anything about that did he?'

'No,' Mr John,' he said, calmly, 'he was too upset, just as I was when it first happened to me, and I know how he feels.'

John sat bolt upright, 'What do you mean?' he barked.

'I just told you,' he replied impertinently and watched as the knuckles of the fists that gripped the utensils showed white. He moved near to him and whispered in his ear, 'I had the same experience, don't you remember?'

'You have nothing to complain about,' John retorted, his hands shaking. 'I've been good to you!'

'And to him ... apparently,' said Kumar enjoying the tease and seeing John's face turn purple with a mixture of fright and rage. But before he had a chance to speak, Kumar pre-empted him. 'You were the same with me, Mr John.'

'Then spit it out for Christ's sake Kumar,' he hissed.

'When I had nightmares Mr John ... you must remember.'

The relief was so noticeable and so complete that John dropped his fork with a clatter on the floor. His chest and shoulders sank as he exhaled pent-up breath, 'Hmm, yes ...'

'You do remember, Mr John,' he said picking up the utensil with the friendliest of smiles and saying innocuously, 'I was nine when my parents died and you comforted me, it's how I learned to understand you. Had you forgotten my nightmares, Mr John?'

'I can't be expected to remember everybody's circumstances,' said John, working his utensils again as the relief settled him.

'Of course not Mr John, I told him if it happens again he is to tell me, after all, we wouldn't want him to worry and then disappear like Samuel.'

The look of apprehension returned. 'You'd better remind him that I'm looking after his mother then.'

'Yes Mr John,' he replied calmly, noting the threat. 'And if anyone asks I will make sure they know what you have done and that he is not the only one with that experience,' he confirmed with innocent obedience and walked towards the kitchen, aware of the turmoil he was leaving behind.

Halfway there he looked over his shoulder and caught John's perplexed look and, despite his deep mistrust, he gave an anxiety-relieving smile.

How easy, he thought, to open the doors of guilt with innocent remarks, it made him wonder if he was a sole lover or one of many transient victims.

* * *

Elevated at having won a verbal and mental tussle with John, whom he'd always regarded as having a superior intellect, Kumar felt sure of himself; the contretemps gave him confidence, he had unknown ability and there was no need to be subservient, constantly passive and deferential. He had come of age. His mental abilities plus the knowledge he was acquiring were fine assets and his aunt, like John, had always taught him to capitalise on those. He felt capable of matching anyone and equally sure that from now on, he was in a position to change his own circumstances. Why not – and why not now?

The moment he heard John leave on the Enfield to complete his errands and see Inspector Joshi, he called the boys in from the garden.

Taking responsibility he redistributed their tasks, restricted their gardening to the cool hours between 7 and 9 a.m. and 4 and 6 p.m. He directed them how to clean floors and rooms and change bed linen, their new duties starting as of tomorrow, relieving him of such menial tasks. To Chef he said that he was responsible for setting menus and ordering provisions while Kumar, with Vijay, would collect them. Table duty was still to be Kumar's responsibility.

By late morning, he sent the lads back to the workshop, thus ending the first period of a new routine that would change his life.

On his way to the kitchen, he heard a vehicle and walked to the pergola steps; a khaki car drew up, he recognised Inspector Joshi as the same policeman who had visited last week. When he stepped from the car Kumar greeted him and, hoping to be better informed, asked could he help as Mr John was out.

'And you are?' said the officer, to which Kumar frostily replied, in an attempt to assert his new-found authority, that he was in charge while Mr John was away.

'When will he be back?'

'Later.'

'Does that mean his is temporarily out?'

'Yes,' he replied, wondering why the officer smiled.

'Do you know who I am?'

Kumar shrugged and rocked his head. 'No,' he said contentiously.

'No sir!' said Joshi hardening his tone, 'I am Inspector Joshi and, in case it had escaped your notice, I am a policeman.'

Kumar resented his sarcasm as John resented Police, having called them repeatedly, 'crafty coppers', and with that in mind he suspected that this new one was probably the same as the last, ready to take the line of least resistance to an easy life.

'Is this about Samuel – sir?' he asked with the intention of playing with him as he had played with John.

'Did you know Samuel?'

'A little.'

'How little?' asked Joshi looking at the sergeant who took out a notebook.

'A little – sir,' he shrugged

'Were you friends, did he have friends, parents?'

'We are all friends here – sir,' he replied, 'this is an orphanage – sir.'

Joshi's eyes narrowed, his head nodded knowingly. 'Who knew him well?' he asked.

'The camp manager – sir.'

'And he is?'

'He left,' replied Kumar, causing Joshi's eyes to harden at his impertinence, but Kumar, realising he could put Sanjay in the firing line, said, 'Sanjay Parmar may help – sir, he knows all the boys . . . very well.'

'I see,' said Joshi, with an exasperated sigh, 'are records kept here?'

'No sir,' he said keeping up the evasion, hoping to win the cat and mouse game.

'Where are they?' said the inspector wearily.

'At the camp office sir,' he answered briefly.

'And where is the camp?'

'Follow the track sir and turn left at the fork.'

'Well done Kumar,' said Joshi praising, 'you managed three answers without ambiguity. Now, try really hard and think very, very carefully, where can I find Sanjay Parmar?'

Rattled with his patronising sarcasm and determined now to conceal as much as he could, he snapped angrily, 'Working.'

'And Mr John . . .?' Joshi said quickly

'Gone to meet you . . .'

The Inspector smiled, 'Thank-you Kumar,' he said motioning his grinning sergeant to the car and saying over his shoulder as he left, 'Tell Mr John I came to apologise for being away this morning. I will see him later in my office . . . I would not like to miss him for a second time. Namaste – Kumar.'

Kumar bit his tongue.

*　*　*

Joshi hadn't expected much from Kumar from the moment that he saw him. Young, evasive and full of assumed cleverness, he had seen prevarication and protectiveness a thousand times before. Not that he could see any need in Prichard's case. John seemed to know very little about the lads, he was an administrator after all and any answers would be found either at the camp, among the records, or from inmates.

Samuel had probably acted impulsively, thoughtless of the consequences. An argument, a disagreement, an imagined excitement influenced young minds; it was more likely that hard-pressed parents would disappear and they were more difficult to trace.

Joshi recalled an instance from the files he saw on taking over, the heartless parents of an unwanted boy removed themselves while he was out begging. The unfortunate six-year-old, left to fend for himself, was lodged temporarily in one of John's other camps. Joshi's predecessor found his callous parents living in the same village.

Councils, although liking the profile of care, were too hard pressed to take responsibility. They preferred to rely on the likes of John Prichard who cost them little and undertook much, and after only a few weeks of casual acquaintance, Joshi admired him. This was the first incident at the camp since arriving and from what he'd gleaned, there were no suspicious circumstances, the child just left. Nevertheless, a missing child from a charity home ranked higher in priority than other sad cases and so far, his men had made all the basic checks, tourist areas, hotels without success, but it took resources that he didn't have, particularly at election time. Cases like this were difficult to conclude but he felt he should take a final, cursory, look at the camp.

'You know where the camp is sergeant, take me there.'

The sergeant swung the wheel left at the turn. 'We rarely have problems sir,' he said, 'Prichard and Parmar work hard for the boys – have you met Parmar sir?' he said absently, avoiding rocks and wandering goats as they approached the camp.

'No, but working closely with John, some of his qualities would have rubbed off no doubt. Stop here, I'd like to look around,' he said as they reached the entrance to the compound, and stepped out when the car came to a standstill.

He noted the wattle fencing and unlocked gates but as the sergeant said, it's a home not a prison. The sergeant showed him the workshops, 'a handyman's delight', he said seeing the tools, lathes and drills, and continued along the rectangle, opening a door to one of the dormitories.

'Very tidy sergeant, did John build all this?'

'Parmar sir, the water tank is new though,' he said looking over the wall at the newly painted structure, 'and the toilets and showers.'

Joshi looked at the vegetable patches and the orderly neatness of the place, 'Some townsfolk would kill to live like this, look at the orderliness sergeant, every facility. Parmar must be a stickler for tidiness! And what's in here?' he said turning a handle and pushing a door that swung inwards.

'Oh,' a female voice said in surprise, 'can I help you?'

The startled greeting was pleasant and warm and he was not surprised when he looked. With a face like that, he would expect a voice like hers, he stood in the doorway, completely taken aback, his mouth dropped open stupidly and he stared rudely.

'Can I help you?' she said again with a dazzling smile.

'Yes,' he said absently, completely overwhelmed. At a guess, he would say she was about thirty, and although most of her figure was concealed beneath the desk and a royal blue sari, he gained the impression she was tall and slim. Her hair, loosely waved and black, shone as it moved, blown by the draught of a swaying fan. Makeup would have spoiled the translucency of her deep, olive skin around large, dominating dark brown eyes that drew attention away from her slim straight nose.

'Can I help,' she said again with a light laugh.

He gave an embarrassing cough when he realised how he must appear, staring, captivated by a smile that drew attention to a lavish mouth with sensuous lips and white, even teeth . . .

'Ah . . . yes . . . certainly, I . . . er,' he stumbled, suddenly and foolishly, confused to be confronted by such attraction. Bumbling, he could only manage, 'I . . . er, good morning . . . I am looking for . . . er . . . Mr Prichard or Mr Parmar . . .' he faltered, sensing she knew the cause of his distraction.

'I am sorry, neither is here. Mr Prichard is more likely to be at the bungalow and Mr Parmar is probably on site. Have you tried the site?' she asked raising her eyebrows to an attractive, enquiring arch.

Unable to take his eyes from hers and not recovered, his teeth got in the way of his tongue and chaos preceded clarity, 'I, er . . . no, I'm . . . I mean . . . I am not familiar with . . . I am new here!' He reached to remove his cap, fumbled foolishly and grabbed it before it fell to the floor.

She appeared to restrain a giggle, 'I can pass on a message.'

Her directness made a change from the evasiveness of Kumar. The voice enchanted and fascinated him, like the silky, caressing tones of a charming melody. She remained motionless, waiting for his next word and in an effort to re-collect his tangled senses he said, again, feebly, 'I would like to see them.'

'Yes,' she smiled, 'I do understand sir, is there anything else?'

'Well, er . . . yes . . . there is another matter,' he said, just able to detach himself from her stunning looks, vexed to think his embarrassment was so obvious.

'Ah, yes,' she offered, 'that would be Samuel's file?' She raised her brows again encouragingly, creating a peculiar, inexplicable hope.

'Yes Miss . . .?' he stopped not knowing her name.

'Jha.'

'Ah,' he said suddenly aware,' Miss Jha? I should have known!' he said in astonishment, 'how stupid of me not to realise. I am Inspector

Joshi, we have exchanged correspondence.' He stepped inside and put his hand out toward hers.

Her touch sent a wave of excitement surging through him, it abated immediately he saw the ring. Why, he thought, should that disappoint him? Looking the way she did it was inevitable that she was married. 'Mrs Jha I mean.'

'I should have realised too inspector, but you are such a surprise.'

It was her turn to be embarrassed, 'Oh! I am sorry,' she said quickly, 'that must have sounded very rude.'

'Not at all, what did you expect?'

She fumbled, 'Inspectors are well . . . you are not . . . I mean . . .'

'Older?' he volunteered and smiled at her unease, 'I hope my youth will not be an impediment to our relationship.'

'Yes . . . I mean no, I . . .' she faltered again, giving his confidence a lift.

'Please don't explain,' he said laughing, 'the department ran short of old inspectors – I'm all they have.' They laughed together.

He asked about Samuel's background, she indicated a chair, he sat and the sergeant took out his notebook, knowing better than to interfere as Joshi watched her walk – well, glide – towards a cabinet. She was, as he expected, tall and slim and when she turned he felt like a child caught staring admiringly at a teacher. She smiled indulgently and placed the file on the desk.

Nodding his thanks, he said. 'Did you know him Mrs Jha?'

'Not well, Inspector. Samuel was nearly fourteen, innocent, a little immature perhaps, not a good mixer, more likely to be led than to lead, no family. This is the only home he knew from the age of six and he was due to leave this summer if Sanjay finds him work, otherwise he would help out here for a while. The boys are the only friends he has and he is much like most of them.'

'Has he any special friends?'

'Anil and Kenneth, Inspector, sometimes they would look after my little girl at the fire shows.'

'What were those?' he said, hoping to extend the interchange and learn more about her too.

She told him of the evenings, songs and stories around the fire, plus a little magic from Ashook, the former manager who organised the shows and performed magic tricks. She and her daughter enjoyed them so much that Shamiana wanted to live here. Ashook left and the evening shows stopped.

'Why was that Mrs Jha?'

He left for personal reasons as far as she knew, yet in her answers to his remaining question, he sensed protection, not obstruction.

He recalled his tutor Professor Karmarth, under whom he studied at Delhi Criminal Institute, 'You may think you can be hard on criminals Joshi but remember, the heavy hand does not always work. You catch more flies with sugar than salt, be patient, press kindly and persevere. Criminals may be hateful or likeable but with persistence – and even kindness – you will eventually reach your objective with felons – and the same thing applies to women.'

'I'm sorry to press you Mrs Jha,' he persisted, careful not to upset her as his own resolute tenacity surfaced, 'are you aware why he left?' He sensed further protection when she hesitated and shook her head slowly, increasing his difficulty – and his admiration.

'Mrs Jha,' he said kindly, 'there is a chance he is in danger and I cannot make progress without help, I would value yours.' He looked closely into her face, again understanding her dilemma between incrimination and vindication, and waited a moment before prompting further, 'Did he leave, Mrs Jha?'

'Ashook came from a good family, Inspector, wealthy and educated, yet he took this position on probation and very low pay. He managed the boys and the camp to allow Sanjay to concentrate on construction. He was here some months and to everyone's surprise and my disappointment, he left – suddenly.'

He recognised her attempt to excuse, loyalty he supposed, and for some strange reason he felt disappointed. 'You have no idea why, Mrs Jha?'

For a moment, she seemed trapped. He pressed gently, aware now of her attempt to shield. 'Was there a particular reason?'

'Rumours inspector, I do not believe them and I should not repeat them but he is supposed to have stolen a great deal of money. It was simply not like Ashook.'

'Low pay is often an incentive to steal Mrs Jha.'

'No Inspector, Ashook was far too honest and much too pleasant.'

'Thieves are like that I'm afraid, cunning and deceptive. Good superficial behaviour and popularity is part of their trade. Was there anything else?'

'Rumours give accusations credibility but I would swear to Lord Rama that Ashook Grewall was honest,' she said, defending again.

He wanted to tell her that he was inclined to believe her and apologise – but that would be unprofessional. He also had more questions, not necessarily associated with the case, but they could wait until he shook off his trailing Sergeant.

'Thank you, I will bear your testimony in mind if I ever meet Mr Grewall,' he said, and turned to his sergeant. 'That's about all isn't it,' he asked.

The sergeant nodded and, picking up his cap from the desk, Joshi said quietly, 'Was Grewall a particular friend of Samuel?'

'Not to my knowledge Inspector, he got on well with all the boys. Ashook left over a month ago and Samuel, apparently, left on Sunday, last week.'

'Sunday? Morning, evening, Mrs Jha?'

'Night,' she laughed.

'Thank you again,' he smiled. 'I must apologise if I appear to have been persistent, we are very concerned and this matter is clearly worrying Mr Prichard.' He stood, 'I will return the file,' he said holding up the thin folder, 'and keep you informed.'

'Thank you inspector,' she said holding out her hand again.

He grasped it, holding it longer and exerting a little more pressure than necessary. 'Thank you for your time and your help and I hope I did not bully you too much. May I say that you are as charming as your letters indicate and it has been a pleasure to meet you.'

Turning to the sergeant, he said, 'There is no need to write that down.'

She was laughing when they left and that, he thought, was a good sign.

TWENTY-TWO

John pointed the Enfield towards Periyar and, twenty minutes later, rapped on a dingy door at the side of the low, whitewashed building, leading into what he assumed to be an office. He waited.

He knocked again, this time thumping heavily with clenched fist. Still no answer, he tried the handle, it was locked.

Stepping back, he looked along the unkempt wall and imagined the noise during the monsoons when rain hit the low corrugated iron roof, and when he saw the tiny, closed windows, he could almost feel the overbearing humidity. His eyes searched for another entrance, there seemed none on this side so he walked alongside for a hundred feet to the corner of the building and stopped.

Two sliding rear doors were wide open, he stood for a minute listening to the coarse whirr of machines and, stepped towards the opening, he craned his neck to look inside at the activity in a warehouse.

A lad of about ten struggled to lift a bolt of blue denim. The weight was too much for the underdeveloped boy, and he dropped the bale, breaking the string and spilling the contents over the floor. He cursed, 'Ari baab re baab!' and called a second boy. A man of about sixty, bent at the shoulders with wispy hair of grey wearing a black jacket over a soiled dhoti appeared and, reaching the boy, he delivered a sharp blow. The lad reeled away, holding his head.

John stepped forward from behind the door. 'Mr Mahmood?' he asked.

The wispy-haired man stopped dead, John wasn't sure if it was the sound of his voice or the mention of Mahmood's name that stopped him

Looking up in surprise he said, 'I am not Mr Mahmood.'

'I know that, who are you?'

'More to the point who are you?'

'I am a friend of Mr Mahmood.'

'What do you want?'

John did not like his demanding loftiness, 'I want to see Mr Mahmood's manager,' said John stubbornly.

'I am his manager, what do you want?' he said briskly.

Contrary to his appearance, he was well spoken and the displayed arrogance took John aback for a second. For no reason, he had expected to deal with someone younger but when he thought about it, this man was more Mahmood's style, scruffy, dogmatic, haughty and cheap and, like Mahmood, he too was unhealthy in appearance but not as well fed.

John summed him up quickly, and adopting an elevated stance said, 'Mahmood is the employer of an acquaintance who has been severely let down by the management of this company. If you are the manager, you must take responsibility and if, as you say Harbens is not available and you cannot help, then I will visit him at his home.'

He watched the man's jaw drop, his mouth twitched uncertainly. He seemed to chew on his tongue moving it from side to side summing up the strength of the statement. The apparent closeness of John to his employer was enough for him to say, 'Discussions concerning employees are conducted through me, if I cannot resolve the issue, then I would welcome the intervention of Mr Mahmood. What is the problem?'

'For your benefit I think we should talk inside.'

With a grumpy cough that seemed to say, 'Follow me,' he turned his sloping back and led John into the building.

The whirring and buzzing from lines of sewing machines deafened him as operators worked at a frenetic pace. He looked along the lines and recognised some of the women and waved, noting the disapproving looks from the bent man. They reached the dingy office and Jaitley seated himself behind a littered table. The syrupy voice asked if he could help?

Standing, John placed two hands on the edge of the table and leaned over, deliberately presenting an imposing and confrontational figure, swamping the man's forward vision, 'What is your name?'

'I am the manager.'

'Alright,' he said with a nod, 'then you know Mrs Chopra – Mr Manager?'

'I do.'

'You fired her. Why?'

'How I run this establishment is none of your business.'

'I have just made it my business, why was she fired?' he demanded.

Ahmed started to say, 'I said that is n ...' but in no mood for evasiveness John's voice cracked like a pistol 'Why she is starving?' he demanded, 'and what does she earn? Tell me or I will go to Harbens now!'

The mention of Mahmood's Christian name again appeared to have an effect. Ahmed sat back, leaned his elbows on the arms of the chair and placed his hands together as if in prayer. 'Let me see,' he said, trying to keep his composure while John's bulk hovered over him like a cloak. 'It depends on the hours she spends . . .'

'Five days a week, ten hours a day,' he snapped.

'It will take time to look up her record and I should refer . . .'

'I'll wait . . . and while you are about it I'll have the names of other absentees and if I find they are starving too, I will bring the police,' said John calmly, tilting forward from the waist, with his lips parted in a sardonic smile.

Ahmed looked alarmed. His hands dropped to the desk and, eyes darting about in panic, he started to chew his tongue again, intimidated by John's six feet two and a fifty-inch chest and the threatening look. 'I . . . I pay thirty rupees . . . a day,' he stammered.

'There,' said John patronisingly, 'thank you! Now, why is she starving?'

'Perhaps she cannot manage. We cannot carry people. Even your friend,' he said with a supercilious smile on his unshaven face, 'instructs me to replace absentees.'

'How cleverly put, Mr Manager,' John drawled, 'you are instructed to replace absentees? I understand from Harbens that you are instructed to temporarily replace the sick until they are able to resume full employment,' said John, guessing. Ahmed's expression told him he had struck home.

'Not in so many words . . .'

'Are you recovering a debt?'

'Well . . . no,' he said uncertainly, 'no . . . not exactly.'

'But you are recovering money?'

'She, has certain, um . . . certain obligations.'

'What obligations?'

'Mr er . . .' said Ahmed beginning to twitch, 'if I can pinpoint the problem can I take it the matter will be kept . . . confidential?'

'Of course,' said John, slightly mocking.

'Her obligations are part of her terms of employment. We deduct certain introductory fees, it is normal practice and in her case it is ten rupees per day.'

'Ten rupees a day?' shouted John screwing up his face in contempt, pulling out a chair and brushing the seat before sitting astride. 'I think you'd better tell me the story Mr Manager – and I don't want a cock and bull story either!

'Well, her obligations to me are . . .'

141

In ten minutes, with all his questions answered John left with unexpected knowledge and a smile as wide as the doors through which he'd entered. His pockets jingled and his wallet was stuffed with rupees. He mounted the Enfield and made for the police station whistling contentedly as he drove through the quiet side roads.

It's an ill wind he thought. Samuel's absence had triggered off an enlightening train of events that alarmed, worried and pleased. Had it not been for him John would never have discovered what was taking place on his own doorstep.

Well, he thought, the Good Samaritan was about to change; it was time to tighten up and as Tony had remarked once or twice, 'time to fill his boots'.

* * *

John crossed the square, towards Joshi's office, where the remnants of the election campaign lay strewn in the street, banners and posters, pristine on walls yesterday, in tatters on the ground today.

He'd been satisfied with his speech and so were the public who believed Mitra was their man for the legislature. Now though Mitra, more vulnerable in prominence than obscurity, was publicly obligated and therefore in no position to wriggle.

The disagreement that caused their differences years ago, that Mitra would take boys into his hotels no longer, was never explained and he refused any attempt at reconciliation. John was furious and until last Sunday they had not met. There were times when he had regretted the split, particularly when he saw the possibilities that Mitra held for advancement. He envied his wealth but had no illusions about how he got it, he was conniving, vicious and tight fisted, especially in his money lending operations. It was a dirty but lucrative business, threefold payment for services rendered and no mercy to defaulters through his injurious goondas who wouldn't think twice about physical harm.

Today he should be able to resolve the Samuel issue. He knew the ropes, having lost a child or two over the years, and he was confident that, as in all other cases, police enthusiasm would soon die. It had been a week now and under the old chief such matters were too insignificance to bother about.

On arrival at the police station, a young, new, self important policeman, unknown to John, lolling back on the rear legs of a chair said, 'You'll have to wait, he's busy,' and 'no idea,' when John asked when the inspector would be free.

He wanted to kick the chair from under his arse. 'Tell him that Mr Prichard is here, *for his appointment.*'

The loafing PC was transformed he sat up as stiff as a stick, buttoned his tunic and took on a look to show he was the essence of alertness.

'Ah, Mr Prichard, yes,' he said leaping from his chair, 'I'll see the Inspector right away sir.'

'Mmm,' John grunted, disappointed not to be able to give the man the rough end of his tongue.

Joshi came out, 'Good morning John,' he said shaking his hand, 'well, are you?'

'Morning Shankar, busy, tired and too old for this business, the struggle is wearing me down. Dealing with the public is never easy, is it?'

'As you Christians say John, "we all have our crosses to bear",' he laughed, 'so I will be brief. We have made no headway and have no idea why Samuel left. No witnesses, no sightings no reasons and no idea of his whereabouts. As a last resort I will need to see his two friends, let me see,' he leaned over the desk, 'Kenneth and Anil. If that fails,' he said spreading his hands, 'we will close the issue.'

'You will get nothing from them,' said John hoping that would be enough to close the matter, 'Sanjay has already asked.'

'Then I may have to see him as well, it's a matter of records John. I will see them . . . um,' he bent to look at a paper on his desk, 'at ten tomorrow.'

It was like a punch in the head. Kenneth! Jesus Christ, what if the little sod opens his mouth? The shock gave him a sudden headache 'They are very young, Shankar, children of that age make up tales. Let me speak to them again.'

'Of course John, but have them here at 10 a.m.' he said adamantly. 'And while you are here can we resolve one point. Why was Rasa not informed until Wednesday?'

'Let me think,' . . . said with a prepared reason but seemed to be seeking inspiration in the ceiling . . . 'I was in the UK until Sunday, slept most of the next day, visited Madrigali camp Tuesday. You could say I was out of commission until Wednesday and Sanjay had done as much as he could. He told me and Rasa and I looked into the matter on Thursday.'

'I see. Who is responsible in your absence, Kumar?'

'Do you know Kumar?' he asked hoping to digress.

'I met him earlier. Protective isn't he?'

'Yes,' said John intrigued by the Inspector's grin.

'However, three days' delay was excessive.'

'Sanjay was being discreet, attempting to resolve the issue without burdening you, he's that kind of man – very dependable. I'll talk to him,' he said, trying to take the initiative away from Joshi.

'Yes and I will too . . . later,' he said.

John shuddered, much like a horse bitten by a fly.

'The circumstances of your former manager's departure also concern me, John.'

'Who, Grewall? That was an internal matter Shankar, if we broke the rules I'm to blame,' he said generously. 'We try to keep those matters in the family, shy of advertising our errors I suppose. I dismissed him,' he said with a self conscious laugh, hoping to lighten the atmosphere. 'Just imagine what the public would say if they discovered my manager was a thief and a drunk? It is not good publicity.'

Making a note, Joshi nodded absently, 'Indeed, well I won't detain you any further, it was good of you to drop in, I'll see you at ten tomorrow and we also can have a chat.'

No easier in his mind when they shook hands at the door, John felt it was like trying to find a slow puncture. He'd better have another word with Sanjay, who had nasty habit of causing punctures lately.

He approached the Enfield gloomily, his visit to Mrs Chopra took on a new importance now, and Kenneth had better know where to place his loyalty.

* * *

Joshi leaned back in his chair with closed eyes thinking about John's hierarchy. He was an honest man but far too involved in administration to know what goes on at ground level. From what he knew, and had heard, Parmar was unlikely to yield much either, being too involved in construction. His intuition told him that the boys would hold any key and possibly enlighten him on the mysterious Mr Grewall. Joshi smiled. How easy would it be for his Sergeant to find a thieving drunk?

But who knows? Suddenly his face lit up, some days he faced prospects of grinding, investigative boredom, on others there were occasional benefits. Today would be one of those days, perhaps not the proper thing to do as senior officer, it's a sergeant's job, but he had good reason to indulge himself in pure enjoyment.

He tapped Samuel's file with his forefinger, in which there was nothing of any real value, thinking of Karmarth again. 'Information needs confirmation,' so confirmation it will be. Why not combine business with pleasure . . .?

He picked up the file and looked at it, 'No, perhaps not,' he muttered and laid the file back on his desk.

TWENTY-THREE

Silent fans gently drove air onto water that tinkled harmoniously down a high rockery into a lily filled pool and, despite the one hundred and ten degrees outside, Mitra, surrounded by newspapers, sat in seventy-five degrees of comfortably chilled air permeating his conservatory-like office.

He was happy, having seen off the opposition comfortably in the Amitar rally, and pouted under his still, apparently, offended nose, reading the varying accounts. He assessed and dismissed the hostile reports, read and re-read favourable ones with ego-inflated purring to his attendant.

'Sixty four per cent in favour,' said one news-sheet in large captions while another predicted defeat for this 'upstart' in the next round. 'Dhankar Mitra attacked,' 'Police arrest rioters,' sensationalist, dramatic and confusing but, reading between the lines, it seemed that the National Congress Candidate would be home and dry if he maintained his momentum.

Replete in satisfaction he looked up at the glass canopy above, recounting his words that so engaged the audience, encouraging, persuasive, influential. Re-living the experience, increasing the pleasure, like a golfer whose forty-foot putt sank repeatedly in mental playback.

Could anyone stop him now? This preliminary was the gauge and he had won over the public, easily motivating the crowd and mastering the initial hostility. With the press support he *was* home and dry. It made John's role less significant and it momentarily crossed his mind that he could save a quarter of a million rupees . . . but perhaps not – he had a causeway to a potentially huge tourist business. John played it down but he was cunning, the venture was far more profitable than he'd said, and meaningful English phrases came to mind . . . no smoke without fire, his foot was in the door, take an opportunity not a chance . . .

'Mr Prichard, sir,' his man said, nodding deferentially as John entered.

'Ah good morning my friend,' he breezed pleasantly, extending his hand, 'what a coincidence! I have just been thinking of you and the remarkable success we had. Have you read the papers?'

'Not in years, Dhankar.'

'Full of good news and wonderful things about our victory giving us the influence we need to go forward together, my friend.'

John lips turned down at the corners, he looked dubious. 'Don't get carried away with the press Dhankar, reporters are fickle not factual.'

'But having hit the headlines, as we say, press promotion will give us much wider influence, nationally too,' he enthused with a smile of supreme confidence. 'I sincerely believe we are on a winning streak, as we say.'

'Great oaks, you know Dhankar – and I'm glad to have planted the acorn. Now, I'm sorry to hurry you but I have a meeting with Sharma.'

'How interesting, we too are dealing with him. One of my companies has tendered to remove the sand from the lake this year and it would be coincidence indeed if some found its way to assist your new building project,' he breezed, and wondered why John returned an extraordinarily broad smile.

'Sorry Dhankar, I don't have time for a chat, you know why I am here.'

'Indeed but we need to discuss our future roles to build on our success.'

'I know what they are Dhankar, you deal with the politics, I talk to people at rallies and get kicked in the head for my trouble – look!' he laughed and pointed to an ugly weal on his forehead.

'Perhaps,' said Mitra ignoring the injury, 'you did not understand my inference. I said our successes, I consider that we are a team, joined in a common goal to develop the enterprise to our mutual benefit.'

'Ever the optimist.'

'Then perhaps you will enlighten me. I understand your new building is for servants, unless you intend your boys to live in luxury with en-suites. Unless it is speculative?'

'Meaning what?' said John.

'Meaning prospects in you venture are perhaps better than I have been told?'

'Prospects are only prospects and I live in hope,' he replied.

'Is that why you have reserved more land,' he said, hoping the extent of his knowledge might break John's reticence.

John didn't reply but pondered for a moment. Who had told Mitra? Did he need to ponder? He knew!

'As I have offered a gift horse, as we say, I would like to know the full extent of the potential, after all I might be in a position to help one day.'

'Mmm,' mumbled John.

'You must remember John, 'For the sake of a nail – the venture could fail.' Mitra smiled at his rhyme.

'When I know something more positive I will tell you, at the moment it is speculative. If I am right and I need help I will come to you, in the meantime I will be truly thankful for what I am about to receive?'

It was no less than Mitra expected – John had not denied the existence of another building or the reservation of land, and that did not match the uncertainty that John had conveyed in their earlier conversation. He was hiding something – unless his informant got it wrong. Mitra would have a word . . .

They said goodbye and with the money safely stowed in his panniers, John left, convinced now that Sanjay was closer to Mitra than he imagined, since Dhankar had never seen the building!

* * *

John checked that Mrs Chopra was improving, paid the neighbour from Mrs Chopra's cash recovered from Ahmed Jaitely, keeping the remainder, and assured her that her job would be waiting, cunningly banking that his actions would guarantee Kenneth's silence. Then he headed back to see Sharma.

After what he had learned today, things were beginning to slot together and he grinned all the way to town imagining the arguments between Mitra and his informant, whom he was certain was not Mr Malik. John's little friend and former lover's interweaving intrigues placed him in position as prime suspect, so if Mr bloody Parmar wants to deal with people out of his league, who better to start with than Sharma, why deprive Sanjay of a task so fraught with consequences?

Parking the bike, he received the usual multitude of greetings, paid lip service to them and by the time he reached the steps to Sharma's office sweating in the exhausting heat he was longing to be in Mitra's air-conditioned luxury. Perspiring profusely, he formed the beginnings of an aversion to motor-cycles and the embarrassing dampness they could produce as he followed a western suited girl to Sharma's office with thoughts directed at evasion and Parmar.

'Something wrong Kashi?' he said as the door closed behind him.

Sharma stopped rapping the desk-top with his pen and leaned back in his chair, he pulled a face that said if only you knew and emitted a long sigh. 'The usual, John.'

'What, short of money and not of work?' he laughed.

'Exactly,' he said shaking hands and returning a restrained laugh, 'and you would know all about that.'

'True, Kashi, but we are independent and please ourselves whom we help, financial or otherwise,' he said, hoping the inference would strike home. It seemed to.

'I'll bear that in mind John,' he said, with what John thought was a look of hopeful expectancy. 'Nadu seems to think you wanted me for something special.'

'Does he? It's Sanjay you need to see – he uses me like kindling wood, I put our case and he, being the technician, stokes it up.'

Sharma looked inquiringly at him, 'I need to see him, what for?'

'We have a problem with the approach to the Lake, it's dangerous and, as you probably heard through your clerk, it needs improving for insurance purposes. Sanjay can provide the detail and some assistance, physical or financial and the alterations will widen our income – and our generosity.'

'Bhopali said nothing to me, not that it would have made much difference. My budgets are tightening as they tend to at election time.'

'It couldn't happen at a worse time Kashi. As you know, initial approached are difficult and Sanjay is so much better than me. He speaks your language,' he said, hoping he understood the innuendo.

Sharma rested his chin on one hand and nodded judiciously, 'Tell me, what exactly is needed?'

John smiled, 'No idea Kashi, diggers, that's all. I'll arrange for Sanjay to see you, say tomorrow at ten? He has his own formulae for persuasion . . .'

Minutes later John left the building, having laid the foundations, and returned the task to its rightful owner.

'He's the bloody builder, let the little bastard build on that!' he hissed.

* * *

Reaching the land office a minute or two later, he completed the deposit formalities and left having satisfied himself that Mr Malik had said nothing. He walked briskly towards Linkers Bank, opened another new account in his name deposited the cash taken from Ahmed and Mitra and drove to the Lake, whistling.

He knew when he started out this morning that he would have an eventful day, he'd nullified the lover's approach, got his hands on Ahmed's and Mitra's money, contained Kenneth and secured for himself a profitable sideline and, with his confidence at a peak, he was finally on his way.

Nothing could stop him now.

TWENTY-FOUR

With his Sergeant occupied on plans for crowd control at the next rally, Shankar Joshi parked his car and stepped up to the door of Shamin's office. In anticipation he removed his cap and smoothed his ruffled hair before tapping lightly on the door. It was his polite tap, not the hammering he usually employed on the suspected.

She called for him to, 'Come in,' to a smile that said she was surprised and he was welcome.

'I won't keep you a moment,' she said and turned to replace a file in the cabinet. Stretching forward, her choli lifted, exposing firm skin around her waist, he found what was an insignificant movement unbelievably exciting. But then, everything about Mrs Shamin Jha was, her voice, her face, her figure and her presence.

Dressed this time in a close fitting choli with a scooped neckline and short sleeves, her upper figure and slim arms were pleasingly exposed, the full length maroon skirt trimmed with gold gave her height, emphasising an even lovelier, slimmer elegance than before. Black hair hung loosely to her partly exposed shoulders and she looked cool in the oppressive heat while he perspired profusely.

She was tall, about five feet eight and, so far as he could see, her skin was faultless. Some would say she had a large mouth, Joshi preferred generous with full lips which, when parted, showed perfect teeth that drew as much attention as the smile itself. She wore no make-up except black eyeliner, serving to highlight the whiteness of her eyes and the deep, rich brown iris.

'What can I do for you, Inspector?' she said, closing the drawer, exposing porcelain petals again. 'I hope I'm not under investigation?'

His grin was self-conscious and his normal resolute approach soft. 'Certainly not, Mrs Jha,' he hesitated, looked up and, suddenly brave said, 'I'm sorry, do I have to use your surname, it sounds so official.'

'Please, call me Shamin, everyone does.'

The sensuality of her voice fascinated him. Soft, with a slight huskiness, the effect was to make him more nervous, and that, added to the need to ask intimate questions, brought the fear of causing offence. She sat opposite to him and cleared papers to a drawer.

He stared indiscreetly, finding it difficult to take his eyes off her, beginning to doubt his ability to handle the interview professionally. He coughed nervously, looked down at the notes on his lap and fiddled.

'Some of the questions, Shamin,' he said, shuffling papers, 'might appear . . . um . . . well, er . . . presumptive,' he said, careful not to get off on the wrong foot. 'It is a necessary part of my brief I am afraid. You do not have to answer,' he added hastily, 'if they are . . . er . . . too . . . er . . . too' he could think of no other word and he was sure he sounded inane when he repeated, 'presumptive'. He looked up and caught her smiling.

'It all sounds terribly serious, Inspector,' she said lightly, 'but I am not easily shocked. I was married four years before I lost my husband.

The words shook him – she was a widow – and so young, was she passing the information for his benefit? Perhaps . . .? His heart went out to her, she must have seen such sadness already in her young life and yet, oddly and guiltily, he was encouraged and pleased.

Concealing his optimism, he said sympathetically, 'I am sorry Mrs . . . um . . . Shamin,' temporarily disorientated, 'I had no idea.'

'It was a long time ago Inspector . . .

'Shankar . . . my name is Shankar . . .'

'Thank you Shankar. We were students in Madras,' she said in an unexpected explanation. 'Economics. We married when he was twenty-four, I was two years younger. Inside a year Shamiana was born, she was three when he died.'

'I am sorry Shamin, my work sometimes lends itself to clumsiness. I hope I have not revived painful memories,' he said, not fully recovered from the surprise. Suddenly she seemed so unprotected and although the situation was to his convenience, this was not the moment to take advantage.

'Shamiana is a lovely name: that would be the little girl you took to the fire evenings?' The question wasn't very bright but the mention of her daughter lit her face.

'Of course Inspector,' she smiled, 'I only have one daughter, she is nine now.'

'I see. I am digressing, sorry. You said Samuel was solitary, was anyone close to him?'

Her hair shook forward when she nodded, partially obscuring her face, he wanted to brush it aside and . . . he was digressing again . . .

'I thought about you . . . your question I mean, I knew you would be back, you had to return his file.' She smiled

His heart gave a leap, she had been thinking about him. 'Ah, yes,' he said slowly, unable to stop his own face from creasing with pleasure, 'I am sorry Shamin, I appear to have forgotten it. I will have to return it on the next occasion.'

Her eyes twinkled when she looked into his. She knew – and he knew that she knew.

'Anil and Kenneth were his friends and so far as I know nobody else in particular.'

He held her gaze and said pointedly, 'That's sad Shamin, everybody needs someone close.'

She looked a little sad when she said slowly, 'Yes . . .' and he could feel his heart thumping in the short silence that followed.

'There is little security here Shamin, is that important?'

'No. We are more likely to have people break in than out. John says that he does not run a prison. There are checks of course, Kenneth does a head count while Sanjay is working and leaves it with me. I pass it on.'

'And when were you aware of Samuel's absence?'

'Monday, I passed it on that evening.'

So Sanjay was aware of his absence Monday while John was away, why did he not report it? He remembered John saying Sanjay was investigating, yet he took his time telling Rasa.

'What is a typical day for the boys, Shamin?'

Up at six, wash, prayers, clean and tidy the dormitories, make breakfast, off to school at seven Monday to Friday, back around four, prepare their evening meals, do the chores, gardening, cleaning, painting, Saturday workshop training with Sunday off. Routine you see, Shankar.'

He listened to every word, intent and admiring.

'And you, Shamin?' He liked to use her name, it seemed so much more intimate and her answers brought a sensuous flow of sound that he was reluctant to interrupt.

'I am a volunteer, it keeps me out of mischief.' She made a self-effacing grimace, wrinkling her nose attractively.

'Mischief? I see,' he said forging seriousness, 'then I should warn you that I may question you formally, under oath if I detect any signs of misconduct.'

She laughed, a lovely bubbling, rippling sound that made him smile broadly. It gave him the chance to look directly into her eyes again.

'I have little opportunity these days Inspector, it is difficult for widows and I am lucky that my mother adores and cares for my daughter. It allows me some freedom.'

'Yes,' he murmured, 'but back to business Miss Jha,' he said in a fictitious, official voice. 'Can we talk about Ashook . . .?'

In confirming that Grewall had been popular Joshi felt a tremor of jealousy, he wondered if there was a liaison between them, deliberately asking if she found him likeable. To his chagrin, she said she did – very much. He pulled at his collar to loosen his damp shirt, saying she had been warned of impertinent questions and hoped that she would see the implications.

'Did he socialise with anyone in particular Shamin? Women . . . er . . . men?'

His apprehension vanished with another captivating smile, 'Not to my knowledge Shankar, he was dedicated to the boys . . . a normal heterosexual male, although I know nothing of his friends. He was strong willed and sincere and I was disappointed not to see him when he left.'

Joshi nodded. 'Please forgive my bluntness Shamin but I am told that Ashook,' he liked to use his Christian name, it gave a more supportive feel, 'was dismissed for stealing and drunkenness . . .'

'I cannot believe that, Shankar,' she interrupted.

'Contradictions, Shamin, leave me in a quandary. In solving cases one becomes sceptical, sometimes cynical,' he said feeling the flush deepen, knowing she was aware of his discomfort. 'I did warn you. I have it on good authority that he drank, can you confirm that?'

'I am certain he did not. I will get his file.'

She went to the cabinet and drew out another file, her elegant movements diverted his thoughts again. She turned suddenly and caught him studying her and handed him the file.

'One final question, Shamin, how did he leave . . . on foot, cycle?'

'Motorcycle,' she said, laughing

'I see. Now, I have taken up too much of your time. May I take this,' he said holding up the file.

'Will you remember to return it?' she said, smiling.

'When I do, I promise not to discuss contentious subjects.'

'It's a pleasant change, Shankar, you can imagine the kind of conversations I have. Children are not always verbally stimulating.'

'Constant association, Shamin. Kings among children, children among Kings.'

'Inspector!' she said with a giggle, 'I hope you do not think that of me.'

'No, no,' he protested. 'No, certainly not, you are much too,' he stopped to search for the word, trying not to disclose his own feelings or upset hers, 'too sensible,' he finished weakly.

'Sensible? Yes,' she wrinkled her brow thoughtfully. 'Yes, that's accurate, there are times when I wish I was not so quite so – sensible.'

He seized his chance. 'In that case, Shamin may I be presumptuous? If ever you are in need of conversation I am at your disposal.'

She pursed her lips prettily and with knitted brows, tilted her head to one side, looking as though she was considering the proposal. 'Yes, Shankar,' she said thoughtfully. 'Yes – that would make a very pleasant change. Of course,' she laughed, 'I will have to ask my mother first . . . I take it you have no wife to ask?'

His heart gave another leap and hearing a note of hope in her voice, he shook his head. 'No Shamin,' he said, 'I have not, and if your mother becomes difficult, I will arrange for an assistant to take her, with your daughter, into custody – purely to ensure they are well cared for, you understand.' Then, in a low voice, as though in droll revenge, he said as he slowly stood, 'That will keep my inquisitive sergeant busy.'

They both laughed, and he left, knowing the bond they had both been hoping for, had been established.

* * *

That evening John leaned on the veranda rail looking at the eastern mountains, the tips lit in twilight and bases covered in blackness as the evening sun formed shadows that seemed to cover the earth in despair while lighting the heavens in rose coloured hope. He wondered if he could ever get used to living without the advantages this life offered, the freedom, the status – the boys? They had all been part of his life for so long now that he felt a sense of disloyalty when he thought about retirement.

Would it be a terrible wrench? He was getting older and they held less fascination for him than they did – and he had to face the inevitable. To be consoled by unimagined wealth of course, would soften any blow and from the tone of Colin's latest telex, things were beginning to happen. Flocking was not the word, flowing was – and if perpetuated he would soon see his pot of gold at the end of that unmade road. Before that though, he needed someone reliable to replace him.

At one time Sanjay's accession would have been automatic, but not now; he lied, had unsavoury friends and had apparently added new ones, together with new tricks.

Grewall was different. Without his weaknesses, he could have been a contender. He had every attribute until he started to display Graham's symptoms, greed and booze, but him apart, there were no prospective candidates, leaving Orphindi like a headless chicken.

There was also his relationship with Colin to consider. Switzerland would suit him far better than India. Poor boy, he had almost scratched himself to death during his short stay after they met in Geneva in the eighties, prickly heat had made his life intolerable. The cool of Switzerland would suit him much better, but they were forced into separate lives now, meeting only when their occupations allowed.

He could hear the boys chattering as they left the water and wandered back to the minibus, and looking North he again let his imagination wander, visualising his complex and developing his dream of a dozen buildings with tourists lounging in the sun with his boys providing the services, culminating in the glorious vision of millions in the bank. How he needed that lieutenant to allow him to live in the cool luxury of Switz . . .

An unpleasant, sweaty odour wafted under his nostrils. 'Did you see Rasa?' he said without turning.

'Yes.'

'Then don't stand upwind of me, see Sharma at ten tomorrow and go and shower.'

Without a word, Sanjay started to move towards John's room as the boys filed quietly past. 'Not there – at your place,' he called, and saw Sanjay's mouth tighten.

'Go on then!' he said, prompting him towards the entrance. 'If you are quick you will catch the bus. And tell Anil and Kenneth I'll collect them from school tomorrow at ten.'

Unmoved John watched the pathetic figure follow the boys into the vehicle, catching a glimpse of his misery amongst the noise and laughter that terminated on his arrival. He cut a sad figure, leaning against the open window, his lips tight and misty eyes staring into space as the bus pulled away.

With a sigh of despair, John flopped down into a chair heavily, staring contemptuously after the bus. Kumar arrived from the kitchen and placed a tray of drinks in front of him without a word. John stared after him. 'What's wrong with you?' he snapped.

Kumar ignored him and walked away.

'Evening John, you look perplexed.'

He looked up at the red head of Andrew with Tony and the girls in tow. 'Things are never what they seem Andrew.'

'Gilbert and Sullivan,' said Hillary.

'Is it?'

'Aye,' said Andrew, 'the only good thing to come out of England.'

'Don't take the Mickey, Jock – remember what Doctor Johnson said.'

'What?'

'The best thing coming out of Scotland is the M1.'

'Idiot,' said Sam.

'Had a good day?' said John.

Sam, with a grimace, complained that 'these two ghouls' had watched a fight between a mongoose and a cobra. Tony defended himself saying it was fascination, not enjoyment, like the Indian Rope Trick.

As usual, Sam struck back, 'The Indian rope trick, Anthony, misleads by cleverness and illusion, but to see a reptile killed while an audience gawks is not fascinating, it's a barbaric execution, like bull fighting. Premeditated, bloody murder.'

John blamed visitors with large wallets. 'Snakes,' he said, 'are just another source of income. What else did you get up to?' he said quickly to avoid an issue that was clearly contentious.

'Hillary got lucky,' said Sam smirking, 'she . . .'

'Samantha,' said Hillary sharply, 'John doesn't want to know about that.'

'Okay then,' she said sticking her nose in the air, 'I won't tell him you were groped by an elephant.'

John gave a chuckle, Hillary looked daggers. 'Samantha,' she scolded, 'don't!'

'Well you should have held the bananas out instead of clutching them to your bosom. He was only after the bananas.'

'He got more than he bargained for, Hill, didn't he?' grinned Tony.

'Don't show that picture, Tony.'

'Now would I do that?' he said. 'I'll leave it to Sam.'

'You should have seen her expression when the trunk went down her bra John – and the scream!' said Sam. 'Even the elephant's eyes opened, and you know how sleepy they look . . .'

'Samantha, please, you are embarrassing me . . .'

'Alright, I'll say no more,' she acquiesced and leaned towards John, whispering loud enough for all to hear, 'When we're alone I'll tell you all about it. Even Sunil and Vijay held on to the bus for support, it was a real giggle . . .'

'Samantha, can we stop this and go to dinner, I'm famished?'

'Sorry Hilly. What's for dinner John?' asked Sam.

'Fried bananas,' he replied.

TWENTY-FIVE

It had taken Kenneth most of the long night to get to sleep, he'd tossed, turned, sat up and shivered despite the unrelenting heat, occasionally calling softly to Anil, unsuccessfully.

When he woke next morning his head and eyes were heavy and he worried, the nearer it got to ten o'clock the more nervous he became. What had he done wrong, why meet Mr John, would he take him to the bungalow again and the same thing happen, should he warn Anil? And where was Kumar? He needed Kumar . . .!

'Is there something wrong Kenneth? . . . Kenneth!' he heard the annoyance in the voice.

'Miss . . .' he answered, jerked into attention.

'You seem preoccupied today. Pay attention – please.'

'Yes Miss Chatterjee.'

The door opened, a six year old entered and whispered to her. 'What for?' she complained.

'I do not know Miss.'

Her eyes turned towards him, 'Kenneth, Anil, you are wanted.'

His brain stopped working and an uncomfortable sensation crawled under his skin, he shuddered and felt suffocated, he stood in need of fresh air.

'You do not look well Kenneth, are you sure there is nothing wrong?'

His chin quivered, his hands shook and in his head he heard the voice of Kumar; 'Say nothing to Mr John, say nothing to Mr John,' alongside a dreadful buzzing. He thought of facing him again, it was all he could think of and he dreaded the moment. He didn't hear her voice until it repeated, 'Kenneth Chopra, I am speaking to you.'

Jolted, he answered by instinct, 'Yes miss', his foggy mind filled with Kumar's promises –'I will look after you, tell him nothing.' But where is Kumar now? Blind panic gripped him, what should he do? He wanted to shout, 'No,' but faintly through the clearing haze he saw Anil walk ahead of him and, petrified, he instinctively followed to the door.

Rasa's promise of an exciting motorcycle ride did not quell the fear that skulked inside him, he couldn't muster spirit enough to respond, despite Anil's nudge and beaming grin.

'Don't look so glum Kenneth,' said Rasa, 'Inspector Joshi is a nice man; he will help us find Samuel.'

It cheered him to know that a policeman would be there but his spirits dropped when he remembered the stories about police beatings. He nodded and looked at the new floor.

'Well done,' said Rasa.

John's face appeared suddenly in front of his; the cold, hard eyes had lost their friendliness, they stared; only Kenneth could see the peculiar, threatening smile at face level, he wanted to run from the menace. He shuddered again as the pale, blue eyes penetrated, intimidated and frightened. John was so close he could feel his breath on his cheek, 'Of course he'll help Rasa, Kenneth is sensible, he will tell the inspector all he can about Samuel – won't you Kenneth? He doesn't want to know about anything else.'

He remained stooping, eye to eye, 'By the way, I have seen mata, she's improving, I will look after her – provided you behave.' He laughed loudly, falsely but the warning was clear and clearer still when John stood and eased him towards the door with his hand on Kenneth's neck, squeezing and hurting until they neared the Enfield.

With his stomach churning, and the chilling reminder still ringing in his ears, he clung to Anil and Anil to John, as they sped through the school gates.

The wind seemed to clear his head a little, the panic subsided but the fear remained with the promise of unpleasant consequences if he was foolish.

They drew up outside a building, he wanted to run and as John parked the bike under trees, he stuck close to Anil recalling Kumar's words, 'Say nothing!'

A delicious smell of toffee drifted under his nostrils, he felt Anil's nudge and saw his finger point to an old lady selling fried bananas covered with toffee batter. They watched in envy as customers wandered to and from the kerbside stall.

'Behave,' said John pointedly, 'and you can have some.'

Anil's eyes opened, a wide grin split his face. He nudged Kenneth again.

Their arrival brought a policeman into the foyer who led them to a room, Kenneth kept his eyes glued to the floor while John left, moments later he heard, 'Send them in, Sergeant,' and felt John's hand on his neck, he stepped inside, looking first at Anil and then, uneasily, around the room.

Apart from the desk with telephone, four chairs and two dull, grey, metal filing cabinets, the room was sparse. A single picture of Ghandi hung on the rough, white painted wall behind the policeman's desk and another of a bearded man, under which was the word, 'Karmarth.' Two windows with shades took away the glare and as Kenneth dropped his head, he slid a second sideways glance at Anil whose unconcerned eyes were busy roaming every corner.

Joshi seemed very tall, at least as tall as Mr John – younger and thinner with a narrow nose, neat wavy hair and a kind face. His shirt and trousers were khaki and smartly pressed, Kenneth wondered, for a moment, if only policemen and teachers wore long trousers. Neither Sanjay nor Mr John did and most other men wore dhotis.

Although he did not look as formidable as Mr John, Mr Joshi was a policeman and, despite his pleasant expression, Kenneth's heart instantly started to pound when Mr John introduced them.

Shivering as the arm slid around his shoulder again he heard, 'The handsome one with the glasses is Anil, our school craftsman and this good-looking chap is Kenneth, our school Captain. Kenneth is a little upset, his mother is sick.'

The policeman sounded kind when he said,' I hope she recovers soon Kenneth, in the meantime we need to find Samuel and all I want . . .'

He listened, guardedly with Kumar's warning constant in his head, 'Say nothing to Mr John.'

'. . . and we do want to find him don't we . . . provided I can capture master Anil's attention that is,' said the policeman. 'What are you looking at Anil?'

Anil pointed at the window, 'The fish Sir,' he replied, 'I made it.'

Joshi turned looked and rose from his chair, he walked to the window took the carved wooden fish from the sill and brought it back to the table. 'This? You made it?'

'Yes Sir, two weeks ago Sir.'

'Well it's a beautiful piece of work, have you seen this John . . .'

John's face was passive as he handed it over but his mind was working overtime.

'. . . I bought it in Maroutai only last week, on the central square in the shop next to the temple, it was the best, unique I'm told. Is that so Anil?'

'Yes sir,' he said with a wide smile.

'Then congratulations,' said Joshi and placed the piece back on the ledge.

'Now,' he said, resuming his seat, 'as you were both friends of Samuel was he upset, worried?'

Kenneth's kept his eyes down to avoid eye contact, Anil too remained quiet.

Joshi looked at each in turn, 'Nothing at all? Were you his only friends?'

'Don't know sir,' they said in unison.

Kenneth dared to lift his head and caught Joshi observing him, he looked down quickly. Joshi leaned back and, with a heavy sigh he tapped the desk with his right forefinger.

It frightened Kenneth, he'd heard storied how police treat prisoners, he wanted to say something, anything to break the strain of silence but he remembered Kumar's words, 'Say nothing.'

'Let me talk to our craftsman for a moment John.'

John stood and motioned Kenneth outside, Kenneth shook again with John's hand on his shoulder. He bit his lip, sure he was going to cry, and glanced quickly at Anil who returned a cheeky, nonchalant grin.

John's arm wrapped around his shoulders in the entrance hall. Loudly, he said, for the duty officer to hear, 'I'll visit your mother again Kenneth, but please tell the Inspector all you know about Samuel, only Samuel, that's all he wants to hear. Do you understand?'

He nodded as he sat down to wait.

It seemed an eternity before the door opened and Anil strolled casually into the room, still smiling.

The officer beckoned to Kenneth, his fear deepened again as John's unblinking stare propelled him towards the open door. He wanted to talk to Anil or preferably Kumar, what should he say, had Anil said anything? He wanted to run again and looked around for reassurance, but there was none, he was alone, standing behind the chair, in front of Joshi.

'Nothing to be afraid of Kenneth,' said the friendly voice, 'sit down please and tell me about your mother, it must be a worry.'

White knuckles showed on the chair he gripped with both hands, what he'd heard about policemen had been frightening, they ordered, they never asked, sometimes they didn't bother to speak, they just used their stinging sticks. The request surprised him, important people like him order and you obey – but he had asked. It made him appear less formidable.

'She is a little better now sir.'

'Then you must be grateful to Mr John.'

The inspector paused, Kenneth looked at the floor.

159

'Now young man, Anil has been very helpful, he says you can help too. Would you like to sit and tell me about your friend?'

Anil had said he would say nothing, it was a trick, he was a policeman – but would he lie? For a second he lost his anxiety only to have it return when Joshi stood and walked around the desk towards him!

He looked huge, would he be beaten? He saw Joshi's arm reach out and looked down quickly, ducking his head between raised shoulders prepared – for what he didn't know – he heard something being dragged, he looked up to see Joshi pull a second chair towards him and straddle it.

Sitting astride the chair made him seem less frightening still, he couldn't be beaten from there. Kenneth sat.

The friendly voice, accompanied by an easy smile, said quietly, 'Confidentially Kenneth, I am having great difficulty finding a motive. Do you know what a motive is?

He nodded.

'We need to find a reason why Samuel left, he may have been taken against his will and, between ourselves, we are hopelessly lost. I know that is a terrible thing for a policeman to admit, but it's true. If only we knew why he left . . . can you think of a reason?'

Kenneth concentrated on the floor again.

'I know he was very upset, and he would want you to tell me, wouldn't he?'

Kenneth looked up. How did he know he was upset? Anil! He told him, he must have, he promised to keep quiet – but Anil could never keep quiet.

Kenneth looked at Joshi. The kind, friendly face smiled; he shrugged his shoulders and rolled his eyes comically upwards. Kenneth's lips parted in the thinnest of smiles.

Then moving closer and lowering his voice, Joshi said, 'I know too that he was frightened, but why?' Joshi looked furtively towards the door and moved his chair closer still, 'I should not be telling you this Kenneth, it is secret police business,' he whispered, 'but we believe he didn't leave – he was kidnapped!'

'No, no!' Kenneth mumbled into his chest.

'Don't you think so Kenneth? We do; in fact we think we know who kidnapped him.'

Kenneth raised his head, he was a nice man and deserved help but Kumar's words came back yet again, 'Say nothing to Mr John.' But this had nothing to do with Mr John. Kumar meant don't speak about that. Anyhow, Anil had said something, he must have. How would the Inspector know Samuel was upset?

The Inspector was sitting upright and holding the back of the chair, he let his hands drop with a slap against his thighs. 'So there you are Kenneth, we are desperate!'

He seemed kind – but so did Mr John – and still he heard Kumar's voice prevalent in his inner struggle. 'Keep quiet, say nothing.'

He thought about his mother, how could John be so kind to her and so cruel to him If he told Joshi, would he be cruel too? Would he be breaking a confidence and letting Samuel down? If only he knew what Anil had said – if only he could talk to him! Tormented, he clamped his lips together and looked again towards the floor.

Placing his arms on the back of the chair once more, Joshi said, 'We are baffled Kenneth! We need your help. You see, we believe he is in very great danger and . . .'

'No sir . . .' he mumbled.

'Not in any danger Kenneth? Good,' he sighed, 'I am very glad to hear it. Are you sure?'

'Yes sir.'

The inspector paused and let out another long sigh, 'Ari baab ri baab, as long as we know he is safe. Tell me, where is he?'

'I don't know sir but . . .'

* * *

Waiting in the lobby John rubbed his hands on bare knees, sighed nervously and blew out air in short puffs from rounded cheeks. Anil's interview had taken only five minutes; Kenneth had been inside for ten already. What was that little tyke up to and how did that bloody fish get into that store? Orphindi had never sold to them.

Anil, the empty headed craftsman, might say it was his, but would he know? Copyists make hundreds of replicas in wood, metal and ceramic and some unscrupulous rogue could have done exactly that – unless . . .? Boys were thieves, nobody knew that better than him, he had taught them – but somehow at the back of his mind he doubted it and his questions to Anil in the lobby revealed nothing except the insistence that it was his and the only one he'd ever made. John couldn't wait to get back to check the papers he had taken from the workshop – then, perhaps, that bloody Sanjay will have a few more questions to answer . . .

He looked at the clock, what was keeping him? Kenneth has been with Joshi nearly a quarter of an hour, he breathed deeply, anxiously, puffing again.

The door opened unexpectedly, he glanced up. 'Will you come inside for a moment John,' said Joshi looking surprisingly amiable.

Then, turning to a much-relaxed Kenneth, he whispered, 'Now its Mr John's turn, I will not be so easy with him.'

* * *

Not relieved at all by Kenneth's wan smile, John followed Joshi into his room, but his relief was short-lived when Joshi straddled the chair in front of him.

'I'll come straight to the point John, I know you are a busy man, but how do you monitor the boys when they leave your care?'

'I don't, Sanjay finds them work and I help with contacts. After all I can't keep lifelong tabs on them Shankar. Why?'

'It's a question of their safety John, and I must be frank. You have serious problems and I prefer to deal with delicate matters personally. If I take it through law, the law will carry me along and the outcome will be out of my control and bad for you. I don't want that and hope, that even after our short acquaintance, I may consider myself a confidant and deal with you on a personal level.'

John did not like the direction this conversation was taking. He straightened up, placed his hands on his knees and exhaled in apparent resignation. 'What have they been saying?' he said flatly.

'I must be forthright John. There have been comments, well complaints, serious complaints . . .'

He felt the blood drain from his face, his heart thumped, his neck seemed to swell, little bastard, he thought as his wet hands started to slip from his knees. He repositioned them, fidgeting as Joshi continued with an indulgent smile that furthered John's worry.

'. . . and as you rightly say it is not always easy to judge the truth with children. They can, in all innocence, mislead through spite, shame or fear and are themselves easily influenced by mature people. It's necessary to read between the lines sometimes – and that brings me to your problem.' He paused for a moment.

Sweat, running down John's forehead, ran into the corner of his eye, he took out a handkerchief and mopped.

'Actions of individuals who appear caring,' Joshi continued, 'can sometimes be misinterpreted, persuasion equals coercion, encouragement can be intimidation, sometimes caused by illness not necessarily intent . . .'

John's breathing quickened, he felt uneasy, pressure built in his neck and rivulets of sweat ran down his spine, tickling uncomfortably. His moist fingers slipped down his knees again. He gripped tighter, so tight that he winced. He mustn't panic! He knew what Joshi was driving at but he wasn't sick, he was a respected figure and that little bastard's word would not stand against his!

'. . . Without recognising it themselves,' continued Joshi, 'people can be mentally disturbed and . . .

The room became oppressively hot and airless, John's hands started to slip once more from wet knees and a painful pounding started in his temples. In the rising heat, sweat ran down his back, arms and forehead profusely . . .

'No Shankar,' he said suddenly and rather more loudly than he intended, 'I've worked with them . . . they . . . they fabricate stories, they . . . er . . . they conspire. You know what kids are like . . . they . . . lie and . . . accuse, you can't believe them,' he said, stampeded into raising his voice by Joshi's inferences as the panic took hold and blood pounded through his veins.

'Your problem is John . . .'

He couldn't hear properly, his head really hurt, it was as thought it was about to explode. His temples pumped and throbbed, his head whirled and spun, revolved and whirled and whirled and whirl . . . suddenly everything seemed calm . . . Joshi's voice faded, fainter and fainter, he was falling, groping at space, clawing at black emptiness around him in total darkness and total peace and a voice, indistinct and distant said, 'John . . . JOHN . . . SANJEEV . . .'

* * *

He felt the support under each arm, something was held to his lips, he clutched and fumbled, cold liquid spilled on to his knees, he shivered. His mouth was dry; he gulped, his head throbbed and hammered, had he been hit? What happened?

A voice from the wavy blackness said, 'Drink this.' He gulped something cold, it spilt from disobedient, bloodless lips on to his shirt. His eyes opened and, shaking hands slopped more of the contents from the glass that he, and Joshi, held. He became conscious of a door in the gyrating room closing and a serious look on Joshi's face while he waited for the shaking to stop.

John took another sip, 'You can go now Sergeant. Feeling better John?'

He'd regained some of his senses and felt a hand on his shoulder. He knew what was coming and closed his eyes managing a wincing nod. Was this the end?

'This has come as a terrible shock, John. The boys had better go back by car.'

'N . . . no, I . . .'

'You are in no condition to drive,' argued Joshi.

Drive? He felt confused.

'Don't worry, we will do nothing until we have completed our investigations, so please keep the matter quiet, we have no wish to alert him.'

In his state of insecurity, John thought he recognised the word, 'him'.

'What?' he muttered through unruly lips, 'him?'

'Yes, we will need a few days; in the meantime we think his movements should be restricted.'

There it was again, 'His,' it dawned on him. 'His?' Not . . . yours . . . Oh God! He meant someone else . . . someone else!

The release was monumental, he closed his eyes so tightly they began to hurt, replacing the pain and tension that drained downwards, rushing from his head through his chest into his stomach. Instantly, he regained the use of his mind and a degree of control of his mouth.

'I can't believe . . . it Shankar, tell me again exactly . . . what . . . you suggest, it's been something of a . . . shock . . .'

* * *

Dust obscured the receding machine as it pulled away after Joshi had satisfied himself that John was safe to drive. He waved goodbye to the boys, who clutched paper bags stuffed full of toffee bananas, and thought how lucky they were to have someone like John Prichard to care and support them.

He felt an affiliation with and an affection for John, they had a lot in common. His service, to a degree, looked after the welfare of adults, John cared for their children. Together with Dhankar Mitra they made a formidable team, despite what he had heard to the contrary. However, having heard their speeches on Monday, Joshi had been moved by their concern and was pleased that some of the unprotected were, at least, in caring hands.

About to walk back into his office he halted, as a khaki coloured police car pulled up sharply in front of him in a cloud of red dust, and Sergeant Birkram got out. Joshi fanned the air in front of his contorted face and stepped back into the shelter of the entrance.

'Good morning', said the sergeant, 'did you get anything sir?' he said intrusively.

'Yes – your dust Sergeant, you are supposed to slow not skid,' he replied with a wry grin and walked inside quickly, brushing his uniform and speaking over his shoulder to the hurrying sergeant.

'My talk with the boys has thrown up an entire new avenue, there is more to this than we believed Sergeant. And you? Have you found anything?'

'Not a whole avenue, sir, but a sighting on a route and part of a number.'

'Well done sergeant, let me see,' he said, taking the offered papers and reading. 'This is helpful. It means I will have to pay a visit to the Outpost again.'

A sardonic smile crept across the sergeant's face, 'Certainly sir,' he said, 'something of special interest there sir?'

'Yes,' retorted Joshi, 'special interest that you will hear about in due course Sergeant. For the moment though, you will concentrate on solving the motor-cycle mystery and I will pursue further enquiries!

* * *

Her smile was as bewitching as ever when she greeted him at the door, her voice so enticed him he wanted to close his eyes and just listen as she purred her greeting.

'Good morning Inspector, what a pleasant surprise. Tea?' she asked laying her head to one side and raising one eyebrow in the same attractive inquiry but with a little more familiarity.

He nodded, smiled and watched as graceful movements drew his thoughts and eyes again. Today she was wrapped in the silk cloth of a pale blue suit, the jacket stopped at the knees and trousers, fitting tightly at the ankle, exposed gold sandals and red painted toenails. Her feet flowed across the bare boards and long elegant hands, with white palms and manicured nails, caressed the cups as she carried them. How he envied those cups.

Excusing his visit with the need to return one of the files, he fraudulently slipped in questions to confirm the motorcycle number and type, although guilt nudged his conscience. That was necessary before electing not to waste a moment of her company on other unnecessary business. After subtle questioning, they enjoyed a conversation until Shamin pointed out how late it had become.

Nervousness replaced his natural confidence. Uneasy, yet determined to seize his chance, he could wait no longer. 'Shamin,' he said, seizing the moment.

'Yes, Shankar?'

'Shamin, would you like to continue this conversation over dinner? I mean, I ... er ... would not want to be, um ... be presumptuous but ...'

Her reply took a moment. The look she gave seemed warm enough and the accompanying smile gave him hope, yet for a second or two, he was uncertain. He waited anxiously, longer than he wanted, her hesitancy putting him in doubt until she said, smiling widely, 'I would Shankar, but ...'

'... But what, Shamin?' he said edgily.

'Had you forgotten, you have a problem?'

'A problem, Shamin?'

'You have to find a reason to take my mother and daughter into custody.'

'Ah . . . of course!' he laughed. 'I will put my best man on the case.'

TWENTY-SIX

They looked to Sanjay like a group of huddled conspirators when he climbed into the passenger seat, he had expected their silence and noted the austere smiles that passed between them.

Of course, he looked smart, he knew how to dress when he had important work that could reinstate his standing with John. Pressed trousers, ironed white shirt, clean shoes and well scrubbed, he was only with them because the lift was convenient and quicker than his bicycle. He didn't want their company any more than they wanted his but their attitude would change if they knew he would put right what John had failed to do properly yesterday.

He didn't want the bloody road; it meant more tourists like them, constant work and continued obscurity, but by the end of today his skills and importance would be recognised and nullify the unfair reprimands he'd received lately and if his status was recognised today, he would be back at the bungalow soon.

The minibus eased to a halt in front of the council building, Sanjay slid the door open, stepped out and strode off without bothering to close the door. Nobody spoke but, waiting until he was a little distance away, he cast a disdainful glance over his shoulder, catching their inquisitive looks. He smirked and mounted the steps.

A clerk with a supercilious sneer and a strapped headset raised his eyebrows at the mention of Sharma, plugged into a switchboard and spoke into the mouthpiece. Sanjay strolled over to a line of chairs against the wall with equal arrogance and studied the notices. Ignoring the clerk's cough forced him to call, 'Mr Parmar', and the same smart, western suited secretary, who met John, appeared alongside him.

Sharma's office was a revelation. Compared to the last incumbent his working environment was luxurious, the place had been transformed. A highly polished mahogany desk, with brass fittings, stood at one end of the room beneath two, revolving brass fans. Red leather armchairs had replaced cane seats in the dust free room and when he stepped on to the hand woven carpet, he did so apprehensively

167

wondering, rather cynically, if the modernised, lavish interior had resulted in budget cuts about which Nadu had complained. Whatever was being trimmed from the council's budget did not affect the comfort of Mr Sharma. More money was being spent inside than out.

Sanjay suspected there was a touch of Mitra about this man; he seemed to enjoy good taste well beyond his means and that could be useful.

'Mr Sharma,' he said, 'you left the meeting on Saturday, I saw Nadu but he couldn't help.'

'Apparently not, what is it you are wanting?'

'I won't waste your time,' he said without regard to finesse. 'John said it was too complicated for him.'

'Some leaders are not technically minded, Mr Parmar, he tells me we can probably talk on the same wavelength, so what seems to be the problem?'

'I want heavy equipment to rough level a road. I can supply labour but I'm short of a mechanical hammer and driver, it's purely groundwork and should take no more than a week of his time.'

'I see,' he said looking severe. 'Budgets are tightening, I cannot afford to deprive another project.'

'Perhaps over the weekend, I can help with your expenses.'

'Have you something special in mind?'

'I can usually find a way.'

'What do you propose Mr Parmar?'

'Labour, cash, it depends on you.'

Sharma placed both elbows on the desk and leaned forward, 'Would you care to clarify that – in confidence of course – just to make our relative positions clear.'

The words were music to Sanjay's ears; he smiled a smile of elevated hope as he recognised the overture. He too leaned forward, his self-assurance surging and, lowering his voice he said, 'Well . . .'

Within half an hour, Sharma, relieved of a pressing debt, could see no barrier to a start this weekend.

Sanjay left the building on a high, having achieved, again, something that was beyond John, surely it would be acknowledged, surely he had earned his transport. After all he'd provided a gateway to John's bridge and now, to complete the whole thing, he had added a road!

* * *

Negotiations are thirsty work and with time on his hands, Sanjay walked cockily towards the taxi rank, and stopped by the door of a bar he frequented with friends. It was only 11 a.m. and it would make a change to have a drink while he was smart in the cool elegance of the restaurant before returning to a scorching site and slavery. He deserved it anyway, particularly after two major successes in one week. John would never know.

Inside the doors he shivered under the draught from the air conditioning vent and looked around for a table not directly in line with the airflow. It may be pleasant to stand in the livening chill for a moment but he didn't want to freeze, no wonder people kept their coats on.

The atmosphere was different in daytime, serious and businesslike, not as exhilarating as evenings with friends. He was with his own kind not these spoilt people or those pretentious westerners that had so dominated and ruined his country. He didn't respect them and neither did John. They were just funds to him.

Rotating his head, he surveyed the tables, hoping for a window seat. He liked to watch the traffic, particularly motor-cycles, it gave him an idea of the selection.

A waiter, known to him, made towards him and raised his hands, 'Namaste, Mr Parmar.'

Nodding complacently he said, 'Window?'

The waiter shrugged and rocked his head, 'I am sorry sir, as you can see all the tables . . .'

He got no further; Sanjay's wandering eye saw an arm wave. He glanced across, Graham and Nadeen sat in a front window seat. He pointed and in a moment was following the black suit with a white towel over its arm towards them.

Apart from occasional pleasantries at meetings, they were not well known to him. Graham on his arrival a year ago had stayed at the Lake until John complained he was 'lording' it over the boys, he'd arranged work and his removal to town, where Graham met Nadeen. John's relationship with Graham deteriorated, Sanjay had no idea why and he didn't much care, for they were always pleasant to him.

Graham smiled politely, stood and offered his hand. Sanjay shook it, nodded and smiled at Nadeen.

'Whisky?' asked Graham, to an assenting nod, and ordered.

'Day of rest, Sanjay?'

'No,' he scoffed, 'I've been to see Sharma – about that road.'

'With success I would imagine?' said Nadeen.

'Mmm,' he said nodding, surprised at her confidence in him, 'they are starting this weekend.'

'Really Sanjay,' said Graham, 'how marvellous old boy, what would he do without you?'

'Yes, what would he?' he said. 'I am his fixer, fetcher, carrier and builder,' he mumbled derisively, took the glass of whisky and swallowed half the contents. 'He rubs people up the wrong way, that's his trouble, and Sharma is one,' he said, deliberately belittling John, and swallowing the remainder of his whisky.

'You know why, Sanjay,' said Nadeen. 'You are the technician.'

He turned to look at her, she was right, he *was* a technician. That's what he liked about them, they recognised his importance. 'Technician,' he repeated, it sounded like a new eminence, 'that's right,' he said smugly, 'he's no technician.'

'And,' Nadeen said whispering across the table, 'you understand the machinery of persuasion too, don't you Sanjay?'

He returned the smile, savouring her words again, they were worth remembering, 'The machinery of persuasion.' He never thought of putting it like that. She was very clever.

'How are things at Paradise Lake?'

'I was moved to a hut for those whites. I only go to dinner, if I'm invited.'

'Really? How galling Sanjay, you built the bungalow. I suppose the invitations are to show the face of equality – a native born presence?'

What a shrewd woman! He had asked himself the very same thing several times and yet she came to that conclusion after only a few minutes. How shrewd, she understood his inequality. Looking back, he suddenly realised that he had never really been equal; John was a typical Britisher, the boss, superior, lazy and condescending, the master and him the servant. He had no right to ban him from the bungalow – or the camp.

He nodded. 'I never thought of that.'

'Another whisky?' asked Graham hailing the haunting waiter. 'A double please.'

Sanjay was happy that their view coincided with his, he could never have analysed his situation as they did, he accepted things as they were, but they highlighted the very things he knew were unfair but could not put into words. How perceptive and intelligent of them to recognise those things and his significance.

'John has an ability to select the right man, Sanjay,' said Graham. 'Today's success proved it.'

Sinking most of the Scotch, he nodded. 'You're right, I just gave Sharma a little push.'

'Ah ha,' said Nadeen, evidently conversant with the format, 'it's a question of keeping people happy with what they need most. Did he have a problem that you were able to solve?'

Such a sharp, sensible woman, she knew exactly how things worked. She was not in the least as John described. It was so good to mix with intelligent company who saw his value and his point of view.

'He did,' he said incautiously as the whisky took hold.

'I see,' she said with a smile, 'a rupee in the right pocket . . .?'

He smiled, 'Mmm. Now John wants three more bases and the road done before the monsoons,' he said, looking again at the empty glass as Graham signalled the waiter to leave the bottle, 'keep it quiet though.'

'He hasn't got the money Sanjay, you'll never do it.'

'He got plenty from Mitra . . .' he said and missed their looks of concern as his head tipped back to swallow the whisky.

'I suppose now he's bullying you to get started?' Graham said casually.

'Of course he bullies. He is a bully,' he mumbled again, happy to find a kindred spirit.

'I grew up with him Sanjay, tough people he charms, helpful ones he bullies, outsiders don't see that. He offloads all his dirty work and others are soiled.'

'That's right,' said Sanjay surprised by the accurate summary. 'He's pushing harder with Mitra behind him,' he said holding the glass ready for another refill, unaware of the panic opposite.

'We thought the Mitra connection was a rumour,' said Nadeen.

'It's not,' he said, a trifle annoyed that the knowledge wasn't his exclusively, 'but who told you?'

'People . . . and we are his accountants Sanjay. Do help yourself old chap,' said Graham, seeing Sanjay's eyes fixed on the bottle.

'Yes, 'course,' he said, nodding as he filled his glass.

He then leaned forward until his chin almost touched the table-cloth, and jabbed the table with his finger. 'I fixed up Mitra too and what do I get? Nothing!' he moaned, tossing the whisky down his throat while frantic signals passed between the alarmed lovers.

'Nothing? You will get something from the sixty thousand pounds profit, surely?'

Sanjay thought he'd heard incorrectly . . . 'Sixty thousand . . .?' he said incredulously, 'sixty thousand? He told me a few thousand – you sure?'

'Sixty thousand over the two years,' Graham said.

'What?' said Sanjay, 'sixty . . . Wait till I see him, I'll . . .' he threw the whisky down his throat.

The rapid effect of the alcohol on an empty stomach had not only loosened his tongue but befuddled his mind. He found it difficult to co-ordinate word and thought, and with caution now abandoned completely, he repeated how he brought Mitra and John together and how he had paid off Sharma, believing his audience were sympathetic to his own disgruntlement, unaware of their alarm and panic.

He stopped speaking, and suddenly tired, exhaled lengthily. His eyes were heavy, more comfortably closed than open, and with his mind in alcohol-led confusion, he mumbled, 'Must get back,' and emptied the remainder of the scotch from the bottle into his glass and sank it.

He tried to place his hands on the armrests and missed one, fell to one side and pulled himself up to slump in the chair with an irritated grunt. A voice, Graham's he imagined, said something about a taxi. He tried to stand on legs that felt like foam rubber, someone touched his arm, it slipped again from the armrest and he fell awkwardly back into the seat again. He struggled to sit upright, eyes vacant, scowling, while the buzz in the restaurant grew louder.

It became overbearingly hot, he felt himself lifted and looked hazily into vaguely familiar faces as tables moved past him. His head seemed to detach and float, then suddenly it became unbearably bright, he breathed in hot air and fumes and heard a popping noise. He felt sick and bewildered. The support under his arms left, he fell onto something soft – it didn't hurt but he kept falling and spinning and bumping and swaying ...

* * *

They watched his exit with a mixture of embarrassment and anger as a noisy black and yellow taxi-bike drew up outside. In a moment they heard a series of rapid pops as the vehicle drew away with Sanjay crumpled, face down, on the back seat of the door-less vehicle and a trail of blue smoke dissipated into the already polluted street.

For a moment, they looked in stunned silence at each other, 'What has he done now, old girl?' Graham said baffled and angry. 'He has reneged!'

'So it would seem Graham, so it would seem, but all is not lost,' responded Nadeen, with a note of optimism, as they resumed their seats at the table. 'Let's not be hasty, and look at our assets. He has involved a prospective Member of the Legislature into deceiving the public, he has lied and bribed a public servant, and we have accounts to prove his dishonesty. Then there is always his past, the reason for his isolation and the sale of his house in England. He is vulnerable, Graham, very vulnerable, and so are Mitra and Sharma, it would not do for them to upset us!'

Graham smiled. 'You are absolutely right my dear. Father, as you know, hated him for his way of life and refused to have what he called, "a fairy" in his home. That is why he left the bulk of his estate to me – even though he relented a little in the end.'

'We must be careful though, Graham, he is cunning and Mitra is a powerful man, but as I indicated, "vulnerable by association", or as John would say, tarred with the same brush. What we have is enough to make life difficult so perhaps it's time to remind him of his commitment and how he suppressed our desire to present the truth to the committee?'

'True, true my dear, I'm sure you can find a reason for us to visit him.'

'I have the final accounts in my case. But wait a moment; Sanjay seems particularly well known here.'

She scanned the room and raised her arm, 'Vickram,' she called to the waiter.

* * *

They woke a taxi driver and seated themselves in the saggy, tiger print seats of an old yellow and black Morris Oxford that smelled of stale cigarettes and jasmine. Nadeen ground down the rear window and the driver, keen to return to his nap, started off at breakneck speed with Graham beside him gripping the door armrest as wandering pedestrians scattered before the flying cab.

Hooting and swearing with impatience at slow moving traffic that thwarted the driver's effort, he bullied his way to the outskirts of Amitar and onto the highway.

Opening the throttle and, brushing the sides of trucks, buses and cyclists who pedalled in contented ignorance until they were practically swept aside, he grimaced his determined way clear of the town. Puffing at his cigarette, he raced along the new road, skimming past everything in unnecessary haste, to eventually swing right on to the unmade road where, to their surprise and his frustration, they were held up by a trundling taxi-bike.

The driver swore and hooted impatiently, until he was able to peel off at the fork. Passing the slower machine, they glimpsed the horizontal figure of Sanjay still lying across the rear seat.

* * *

They were not the only people to see Sanjay in his incapable state while he was driven towards his dwelling. A blissful Inspector Joshi, driving slowly and alone along the unfamiliar path, eased to one side of the narrow track, catching sight of the prostrate Sanjay as his car and the taxi-bike passed each other.

It surprised him, only a few hours ago he had asked John Prichard to keep him under observation.

Seeing the Outpost on the first occasion, he had been full of praise for Parmar, the layout, the condition and the organisation, but from what he had learned since, he was becoming less favourably influenced. Parmar was flawed and, if what he was beginning to discover was true, then he simply did not understand how John, a man of selfless devotion, could have such implicit faith in him. He still had work to do but his instinct and experience told him that John's blind certitude was not entirely justified.

As yet he was undecided and wondered if his cynical views had been formed through constant dealings with criminals. A job such as his tended to have that effect, while John's probably encouraged faith, making him less of a sceptic and more of a saint. On the other hand, like many good men, he could be gullible?

He rarely came across the John Prichards of this world; he was more likely to meet the Sanjays, and the fascination of discovering which was which continually held an interest implanted by Professor Karmarth. The fascination of character analysis taught him to observe, sift, categorise, reject and conclude, much as a merchant would select his stock from the vast array of shelved alternatives, and he was aware that the habit might well have helped develop a callous streak. He tried to confine that tendency to his work and not allow it to spill over into his private life. After all, to be thought callous by Mrs Shamin Jha would be very upsetting indeed.

She fitted a unique category, one very new to him, sensuous, charming, dignified. How could he be heartless, callous or unfeeling with her? It bothered him enough having to resort to deceptive methods to obtain Grewall's motor cycle number and type, hating the deception that impinged on the real pleasure of dealing with her. Underhand methods were for thugs, criminals and miscellaneous anomalies like Mr Ashook Grewall.

'I wonder,' he mused, 'into which category he fits?'

TWENTY-SEVEN

The shabby seats of the ancient Morris could have done with a clean. The one on which Graham sat was sticky and partially glued him to the cloth. The smell, at first overpowering, had dissipated a little since she had whispered that the reek of stale cigarettes would never leave her sari and opened a window. The run-down machine and road to match did not make for a comfortable ride, although Graham thought himself lucky when the driver slowed to a trundle, sensibly, after hearing the thud of springs bottoming out on the hillocks.

They drew up at the bungalow; Graham looked up from the window and saw John shirtless, with the garment in his hand and an irritated expression that increased as the dust slowly enveloped him. He flapped about with his shirt as the driver ran round to open the door for Nadeen before moving to Graham who struggled with his door. Once the fare was in the driver's hand, he opened the door from the outside, grinning with teeth like nicotine-stained tusks.

'Wait here,' ordered Graham. The driver parked under shady trees, happy in the certainty of a waiting time payment, a return fare and a quiet snooze in the meantime.

'To what do I owe the pleasure?' said John, showing none and walking away.

Graham considered offering his hand but it had never been their habit. 'We brought the modified accounts and need to finalise arrangements.'

John made no reply.

'Do you think we could have a drink,' he said, undaunted by John's sour expression, 'my throat feels like a sand hill.'

He bellowed for Kumar. 'I haven't got much time,' he grumped ungraciously, 'so be quick.'

Graham pulled a cheque from his pocket and placed it on the low table, and John inclined himself forward from his seat to look as Kumar arrived with the tray.

Kumar carefully pushed the cheque aside, put the tray down and stepped back to his usual place at John's shoulder.

'Be good enough to sign these,' Graham said taking the accounts from Nadeen.

John took the sheets. 'What,' he said, 'now?'

Kumar bent forward deferentially, his face close to John's and whispered, 'Drink, Mr John?'

'Pour them will you son – leave these with me,' he said to Graham.

'Can't do that old boy, we need to lodge them in the records office.'

'Not today you don't.'

'Anything else, Mr John?' said Kumar close to his ear.

'No thanks.'

Graham gave a testy smile and Nadeen stepped in swiftly and, reaching for the papers said, 'I will have copies made by the end of the day, John.'

'No thanks,' he replied, holding them firmly and fixing her with a stare. She released them; he emptied his glass.

'Another drink, Mr John?' asked Kumar, bending at the waist.

'No, Kumar.'

'Shall I take the tray, Mr John?'

'No, leave it.'

'Shall I wait, Mr John?' he said, leaning forward again.

'For Christ's sake, Kumar, leave it and clear off.'

'Thank you, Mr John,' he said, and walked sedately away.

John tucked the papers behind his cushion, and, in the strained silence wiped his damp chest with the shirt.

Graham eased his own jacket away from his body, as embarrassment and heat combined to make him uncomfortable. He waited, sipping his drink, unsure now how to proceed. Why should he bother to be judicious, John was no foreigner to bluntness. 'Is that sufficient?' he said, pointing to the cheque.

John looked, and hesitated. 'It's not that simple Graham.'

'It is perfectly straightforward, there's the cash – as agreed.'

'Well,' he said into his chest, 'in the delay I accepted another offer.'

'Delay? What delay?' snapped Graham. 'You can hardly say we delayed, it's only four days, we kept our promise, now you keep yours.'

'I indicated, Graham, I didn't promise! Altering my arrangements now will place me in a difficult position. I've heard it all before, people make promises and that's all they do! I had to take the money while it was on the table before my backers refused their help.'

'You didn't mention backers when we offered,' said Nadeen quietly.

'Who are they?' Graham snapped.

John said nothing.

'I see, any friend of Sanjay's is a friend of yours?'

'What has Sanjay got to do with it?' John snapped back.

'He's your fixer isn't he, or should I say "one of your bedfellows", as the old man would call him. He worked the oracle again I hear,' he said, grinning slyly at Nadeen.

'Don't believe all you hear, brother, Sanjay's friends are not mine and you of all people have no right to criticise me. Still a member of the Golf club, are we?'

The question evoked the memory of Graham's indignity; he cringed with embarrassment and tried to defend his action, 'How dare you! I sold father's farm in good faith,' he growled, 'how was I to know it would fail?'

'You sold the farm and good ground separately; your golfing mates bought a flood plane, Graham. We lived next to it for thirty years. They put their money into it and you disappeared – like most of the land for most of the year – under a foot of bloody water.'

Graham face went purple, he spat through clenched teeth, 'That was unfortunate, an investment that failed, I did not cheat them deliberately, nor did I sell my house, take the money and come to India forgetting an outstanding mortgage hoping to benefit from the laissez-faire here. I didn't pass myself off as a preacher and set up a strumpet camp. Preacher,' he spat, 'the only thing you preach is self interest.'

'And you fooled the old man didn't you? He had no idea what an irresponsible little thief you were – you left your job for the high life when you got his money and frittered away your inheritance in five years pretending to be the country squire. Then you ran to me for help.'

'And your wonderful Orphindi,' Graham shouted, on the verge of losing control completely, 'only serves to satisfy your lust. From what I have seen,' he said recklessly, 'you use it as a breeding ground for young models like him,' he said, throwing his hand in the direction of the kitchen. 'Intimidation and persuasion – persecution and pimps?' he spat. 'Is it surprising your resentful ex, Sanjay, goes elsewhere? You are enough to drive a saint away!'

With a face like thunder, John opened his mouth to avenge the attack. 'I said his friends are no friends of mine,' he shouted, 'I do not take advantage of my boys, so . . .'

'Not now perhaps – age overcomes lechery but . . .'

'Stop this now,' said Nadeen loudly, standing as the brothers glared fiercely at each other. 'This is not helping. We are after the same thing, so let us pour oil on the water – there is room for compromise.'

John released the chair arms and eased himself back from the edge of his seat, glaring fiercely as she calmly adopted the role of mediator.

'We are all aware of the prospects, so let us be honest. A Member of the Legislature could open doors and John is right to seek his help and, as his public endorsement cannot be rescinded, there is no point in reprisals – unless someone,' and she looked meaningfully at John, 'fails to co-operate . . .'

She pointed out that although his reputation with the public may be admirable, there were issues that would make him vulnerable. 'For your benefit alone I recommend that you co-operate and then your friends Mitra, Sharma, Sanjay and Nadu will not be implicated. I suggest . . .'

Graham watched; there was no need to intervene, John was being butchered, each word cut deep and John seemed to pale, his confidence in shreds. He remembered that as a child, when John was seriously shaken he collapsed, and he looked on the verge of that now. Her intimidation made it impossible for him to refuse their involvement.

'The point is, old boy,' said Graham confidently, calmly now, 'if you accommodate us none of this need be disclosed, provided we receive an equitable return.'

Speaking now with dictatorial authority, Nadeen insisted that John talked to Mitra and introduced them into the equation. 'We will run the organisation for our mutual benefit, John, otherwise . . .?'

The threat of consequences hung in the air and in the silence that followed, John seemed to acknowledge their victory. He did not respond; he merely looked down at the cheque, lips clamped. On a high in the moment of victory, Graham looked him squarely in the eyes, unable to resist a final dig.

'In your speech, brother, you made a very moving reference to the needy and how well they should be looked after. Well, now is your chance!'

'That will do, Graham!' snapped Nadeen, and stood, ready to leave.

Graham followed suit and shortly they were rumbling off towards town in the old Morris.

* * *

John didn't move from the chair. Distraught and outwitted by an idle brother and a smart-arse woman, he considered the implications, assimilating the damage in prospect. It did not take him long to decide where they had acquired their information, but he had no idea how to counter the threat.

His anger obliterated all sensible thought, but conscious that anger was the wrong approach, he calmed quickly, seeking a way out. They believed he was in their hands, obstruct them and the consequences would be dire yet they forgot he was in league with a vicious, more powerful, ally.

He didn't understand the reference to pimps, but if anyone would, Sanjay would!

Only a few hours ago he had preened himself on having achieved safety; now his problems had multiplied. Pulled in one direction by a manipulative pair, forced into an alliance of convenience with Mitra, destabilised by a dim-witted builder and under scrutiny by the police, he was besieged, surrounded by animosity. He felt like a fugitive, trapped and ready to murder his way out.

He reached for the glass and sipped the tepid lime-juice, pulled a face and threw it over the veranda on to the garden, watching the liquid being absorbed into the dry earth. Unlike the liquid his anger did not dissipate, it brought his problems more sharply into focus, and in a moment of sudden clarity, he saw that his future lay only with Mitra. In opposing him, they all opposed Mitra, how dangerous was that?

Slowly he began to see his way forward: vulnerable maybe, but blackmail would infuriate Mitra and citing the cause would direct his anger at others. Then his spiteful ally would use all his resources to protect his ambitions.

He reached for the jug to refill his glass and his glance fell on the cheque. He stared at it, put the jug down and touched it for the first time. When he looked closely it had Graham's signature on it.

'Well, well,' he muttered, 'five grand, I wonder?' He flicked the Linkers International Bank cheque with his finger and placed it back on the table as the faintest of smiles crept across his face. 'Another bank visit, I think.'

Then, taking the accounts from under the cushion he slowly started to read and slowly, unknowingly, accepted the blissful entry into the nothingness of sleep, liberated, temporarily, from his worries.

*   *   *

Kumar caught a glimpse of the visitors as they passed the kitchen door where he had been listening and heard the taxi start and rumble off. Wary of John's activities now and still smarting at his sharp retort, he pursued his kitchen duties quietly then, poking his head from the door occasionally, he noticed John's head had fallen to his chest in a deep sleep.

Papers lay in disorder in front of him and, leaving the kitchen, he walked cautiously forward, reached the table and saw that other papers were beginning to slip from John's grasp. He reached out and caught them before they fell.

'Mr J . . .' he started, but stopped when he saw the heading:

Travel Account
J. Prichard. Proprietor.
Year ending March 1996.

Removing them gently, he crept silently away to the kitchen where he sat and spread the accounts out before him.

TWENTY-EIGHT

John felt a movement, something was shaking him and a voice, vague and distant called, 'Mr John.'

Slowly he opened his eyes, grunted and closed them again, unable to keep his eyelids apart in the startling brightness – not even wanting to. He rubbed his face, pressing his hands hard onto the skin encouraging blood into his cheeks and life into his brain, and peering through half-closed, bewildered eyes.

'Sanjay is coming.'

His hand went to his head, it felt very hot and the face before him was a vague blur in the confusing brilliance. He screwed up his face and stretched his arms upwards causing his chest muscles to hurt as they pulled taut with the expansion of his cramped frame. The action simultaneously released perspiration that rolled on to his belly. He smacked the dry lips of a foul tasting mouth.

'What?' he grumbled, yawning and looked at his watch. The indistinct dial made him screw up his eyes and extend his arm. Four thirty, I must get some glasses, he thought, and looked again, FOUR THIRTY.

'Sanjay is coming, Mr J . . .'

'Bloody hell Kumar!' he tried to say. Instead he croaked something unintelligible and flopped back into the seat. God he felt hot, his forehead was fiery and when he rubbed his shoulders, they were sore.

'Why didn't you wake me?' he complained, easing himself from the seat. 'You let me sleep in the sun you silly sod – get me a drink.'

He felt shaky, his head spun, and in no condition to confront Sanjay he said hoarsely, 'Tell him to wait, I'll . . . I'll be . . . in the shower.'

Grabbing the papers that lay tidily on the empty table before him he groped his way along the veranda rail to his room. The shower would drive the sluggishness from his system and bring some strength to his tottering legs.

* * *

Sanjay, for different reasons, didn't feel too steady either when he dragged himself up the rear steps with an acid-full stomach and a head like the conclusion of a fairground ride. He ignored Kumar, who stepped back into the kitchen shadow, and made for the veranda rail.

Leaning over, he looked towards the lake. The view from this elevated point came as something of a surprise; he rarely looked out since he found the spot, twelve years ago. The surroundings had changed, the lake, formed when the dam was built, looked vast and the alterations had transformed a, once natural, river valley. Having lived with the changes he'd hardly noticed their fragmented arrival and it was only now, when he had a moment to stand and look, that he realised how different it all was.

He walked down the steps and turned to face the house. The lines were imposing, it looked important. When he built it he intended it to be shared – until John had taken it over completely. 'Build one of your own Sanjay,' he'd said a couple of years ago, 'a small place, we can't afford much but you'll be comfortable and private there.' He meant he'd be private with his new selection.

Everything else had changed too, daily routine, tourists, inspections, an interfering committee. If a kid ran off before, no one bothered, now it's police business. He had a better chance of finding them than the police, he knew the kids, or did until John became difficult and prevented him from entering the huts, but he understood them better and knew who experimented and who enjoyed his help with practical adult education. It was part of his, and their, pleasure. Now, since Kumar came, John objected. 'Keep away from the boys,' he said, 'I don't want you teaching them your tricks!' He could do nothing right and yet he was expected to turn a blind eye towards Kumar. That, argued John, was private.

Sunil should have left the little rat when his parents died in the crash, someone would have looked after him, but once John saw him he was a target, and weaned. From school he became gardener, house-boy, helper and groomed for years until installed. He was a cunning, conniving, deceitful snake, yet John didn't see it. Still, after his achievement today, it could be the start of that reptile's slither into a hole.

The sound of a shower drew his attention. He left the view and his belligerent thoughts behind, ambled up the steps and along the veranda to John's room, drawn by splashing, grunting noises from the shower, he stood in the doorway to watch.

His naked body glistened and shone, retaining the attractive suggestion of power and excitement – even at sixty odd. Sanjay, in voiceless admiration, peered longingly, stimulated by his nakedness. Would the time come again for him to share the pleasure of a mutual appetite?

John turned off the shower and slowly rotated towards him, shaking his head and rubbing water from his eyes. Sanjay thrust a towel into his hands and smiled warmly. 'You look as good ... do you remember the old times?' he asked cheerfully certain that his coup today would aid John's humour.

'I try not to,' replied John rudely, snatching at the cloth and showing no surprise at his presence.

Disappointed, undaunted and anticipating a change of attitude when he broke the news, he said in preparation, 'I used to do that, do you miss it?'

Ducking his head into the towel John ducked the question. 'Where have you been?' he demanded.

With another success under his belt, the implied disapproval did not shake Sanjay's confidence; he sauntered across to sit on the chair by the dressing table. 'I saw Sharma,' he said casually.

'And that took all day did it?' retorted John, talking to the floor.

He shrugged unconcerned, waiting for his attention, determined to make him fully aware of his accomplishment.

The head appeared from under the towel. John took a few paces forward. "Well? I said, that ... took ... all ... day ... did ... it?' he insisted, stopping after each staccato word.

Sanjay had seen the face of intimidation too much recently, this time he drew confidence from the fact that John's hostility was wholly unjustified. He had concluded something significant today and was determined it would be appreciated. If there was ever a right time to make him take notice, it was now.

Summoning every ounce of courage, he looked up contemptuously, 'Who are you talking to?' he said calmly, copying John's own tactics, 'you never stop complaining, go and see him yourself!' He stood abruptly and stepped towards the door but John was too quick for him.

He leapt aside to bar his access, his white, podgy, body filling the entrance, looking ridiculous naked with arms stretched wide like Christ on the cross. 'No you don't,' he roared, stopping Sanjay in his tracks, 'who else did you see?'

'Nobody.'

'Not those two sodding accountants then?'

'No ...' he said in a customary lying reaction when he was too slow to find a reason, '... well I had a drink with them, what's wrong with that?'

'You told them about frigging Sharma – and Mitra!'

'I did not, they knew.'

'Knew,' he shouted, 'knew? How did they know, got second sight have they? With you while you fixed Sharma's remuneration were they? You gormless, bloody idiot!'

'It doesn't matter . . . they are friends.' . . . and realised he'd said the wrong thing . . .

'Friends . . . whose bloody friends?' John yelled, 'yours, because they are no friends of mine! You had a nice friendly chat, implicating us, and now those bastards are blackmailing us!'

'Blackmail? No . . . they'll be alright . . .'

'Alright? Alright? Of course they won't be alright you bloody thick head, they pretended they knew and you fell for it, they took you for the fool you are and strung you along, then you have the temerity to turn up here, lie your eye-teeth out and try to tempt me with, "I used to do that!" When Mitra finds out he'll murder you – and I know he's capable – but this time I'll help the bastard.'

Sanjay, shaken and baffled simply didn't understand John's over-reaction, they were the accountants, one was a relative, they were bound to know everything, and John's dislike of them was no excuse to round on him. 'They won't say anything, they are reasonable . . .'

'Reasonable? Reasonable?' John practically screamed. 'Don't be so bloody stupid! They are a pair of greedy, manipulative blackmailing bastards and your slack mouth and dormant brain has put us in trouble again – or is that too complicated for a berk like you to understand . . .?'

Sanjay's hopeful thoughts of a new beginning receded, he listened without response to the ranting and without wit, or grounds, for defence his confidence seeped away while John berated him about that bitch and his brother jerking them about like frigging puppets.

'You frigging idiot, fancy telling that brother of mine! He was good for sod all in England, sacked from every post for drinking like a fish and womanising, and now he's been given more frigging ammunition than the Indian Army. Put it right, I want them off the planet, dead preferably, do you hear me, or they'll mangle us!'

Dim-witted, uncertain and unaware of the complications, Sanjay frowned and rubbed his lips, 'I'll speak to them . . .' He stopped dead when he saw the look on John's face . . . Or I can tell Mitra – he'll listen . . .'

John's look stopped him in mid sentence, 'Yes . . . so he will,' he said slowly, 'so he bloody will and as he is . . .'

A knock brought a halt, John opened the door and Sanjay heard, 'Mr John . . .'

'Not now Kumar,' John yelled, 'clear off.' He slammed the door.

'. . . as he is your mate, tell him. Perhaps he will ask them nicely, "Please don't blackmail me, it makes me ever so cross,"' he mimicked. 'Or perhaps, with a bit of luck, his goondas will creep up behind them and tap them on the head with an iron bloody bar!'

Sanjay stood immobile, his indignation rising rapidly. He'd worked his guts out for this man; he had no right to treat him this way. 'No!' he snarled fiercely, screwing his face into a deformed, determined sneer, 'you sarcastic bullying bastard, you deal with him. I take all the chances and I do all the work. If it wasn't for me you'd still be in a bus shelter abusing the kids and living off what I stole!'

John stepped so close that Sanjay felt tiny pieces of spit hit his forehead through teeth that seemed to grind out words, a finger rammed repeatedly into his chest, 'And – you – don't – see – it – you – bloody – thick – head. We are being held to ransom, our troubles stem from you, they are after my business and they've got Mitra, Sharma, Nadu, you and me over a frigging barrel!'

With his defence overpowered by the argument and his ability to reply harnessed by ignorance, John's confident, accusing word crushed his ill thought out mutiny. His resentment dwindled; his breathing slowed and, although he did not believe his actions were that severe, he now had a spark of understanding. Were they genuine, surely they would not mislead him? Were they really his friends? If not, perhaps John was right, they were cunning.

He searched for a way back and after a lengthy silence said, 'Alright, I'll see someone, he will know what to do. Last month he . . .'

John listened, open mouthed and shook his head in disbelief when Sanjay finished, 'I don't believe you Sanjay! I-do-not-believe-you! You have an in-built ability to suggest the extreme because you are too bloody thick to be subtle. Do what you like but don't involve me – do you hear? LEAVE ME OUT!'

John moved away from the door and took some clothes from a drawer, Sanjay stood impassive, uncertain of his next move when John suddenly turned to face him, 'That lot will be going soon so when you've seen whoever this mate is, get your gear and move back into the spare room, but keep away from town! Do you hear, keep away from town!'

He stood as if struck, had his stand made such a difference that he was being invited back? He may have lost the argument but he'd shown he would not be intimidated. His stand had worked! Now he could tell him the good news, perhaps that would improve his humour . . .

'The machine will be here Saturday,' he said brightly.

'I know,' snapped John.

'How do you . . .?'

'They told me, they took the ground from under me you silly bastard!'

There he goes again, he thought, he has no idea what I achieved, 'You don't seem to realise,' he said, 'I kept the screamers away from Sharma's door. He was in debt and . . .'

'Jesus Christ man you've completely missed the bloody point. It's not a question of Sharma's gratitude it's a question of confidentiality. You still don't realise . . . oh, never mind. For God's sake see your mate and come straight back, I want a chat, about your sidelines. Now, sod off!'

Panic took hold – sidelines? What did he know about those, what had he heard?

Sanjay felt suddenly shaky again and looked up in time to see Kumar cross the window. Had he been listening? Not that it mattered now, he had an invitation to return and he could keep an eye on that reptile.

Maybe today had not turned out quite so badly after all he thought as he passed the kitchen, completely unaware that Kumar had exactly the same thought.

*　*　*

John lay on his bed with a slight headache from a touch of sunstroke that had not improved after the contretemps. The bloody man's indiscretions were too repetitive, round and round – like that bloody fan. There would be a hell of a backlash from Mitra but John would make sure to lay the blame firmly at Sanjay's door.

It had made perfect sense to align with money, strength and power than be exposed to his violent antagonism. The partnership might leave him with less of a business but with Mitra's millions, he would become ten times richer ten times as quick. He smiled, 'half a loaf my friend . . . as we say.' In this case half a loaf would be worth a bakery.

If things went wrong – and there was every chance of that with Sanjay involved – it was a racing certainty that Mitra would retaliate. He'd soon see that madam had stamped her kite mark on the arrangement and that she, having caught the aroma of a replacement for Graham's squandered half-million, had sucked Simple bloody Simon in too, and John Prichard would be free of blame.

Gullible Sanjay caused trouble through stupidity and carelessness, Graham and that bitch did it by calculation. Graham's half a million quid had gone in only five years, now the bastard wanted more and now between them, they would bleed his business dry. The new road would begin this weekend, he mused, and gave serious thought to the possibility of burying that pair beneath it!

He gave a wry smile. No, animosity would only alienate them. Maybe Sanjay had it partly right – appear to be friendly?

With his hands behind his head, he rummaged through his thoughts for ten minutes seeking a solution, finally giving up. He accepted the inevitable, they would be a pain in the arse and he was primed for that, but he was unprepared for a bigger pain that lurked only yards from where he lay.

Sitting up in bed he bellowed, 'Kumar,' and waited until he saw his shape cross the window. 'Get me some tea – and an Aspirin.'

TWENTY-NINE

When Joshi arrived back at the station, Birkram was cheerful, 'Were you successful in your trip, sir? 'he asked, with a supercilious smile – as though sharing a secret.

'Wipe that silly grin from your face Sergeant,' said Joshi tetchily, 'there's a good chap, unless you enjoy traffic duties.'

The sergeant swiftly lost his smirk.

'Come inside and tell me what you found. Did you solve the motor cycle challenge, or does that expression denote an attempt to cover up a failure?'

The sarcasm brought a cough to the Sergeant's throat; he looked down at the papers he held, shuffled through them, and selected one. 'The sighting I mentioned earlier, sir, has given us more information on the make of machine but not the number.'

'I am relieved to hear that you have not wasted your time Sergeant, so carry on. No doubt you will inform me if it proves to be the person we want and, on arrival, perhaps you will allow me to participate in his interview – if you have thought that far ahead.'

Looking abashed, the sergeant nodded. 'Yes sir.'

'Now let us look at what we have after my visit to Miss Jha at the camp and my interview with the two boys. Indications are that our Mr Parmar is not all he is supposed to be. He is not popular with the boys, his reputation in town is sullied and he is not, as Prichard believes, dependable and diligent. The questions are obvious, why should a likeable sober man like Grewall be accused of thieving and drunkenness and be dismissed on flimsy evidence, while an unpopular, known inebriate remains for his reliance in the face of verification to the contrary? It seems odd. Are we looking at faith, falsehoods or foolishness?'

'I see what you mean sir.'

'Indeed Sergeant. Grewall is supposed to be intelligent, yet his attempt to hide stolen money was crude and naive, that does not sound like the Grewall I have heard about. My informant tells me that he was not an habitual drinker yet he has been branded a drunk; that he was fully heterosexual yet there is a suggestion of impropriety with children, his family has wealth and yet he stole cash. None of those observations fit; in fact they are diametrically opposite to what I have learned. Perhaps we should bear that in mind when we meet the illusive Mr Grewall, who, according to the work completed while you were out, could be the manager of the Star of India Hotel in Maroutai – whom you will arrest on Thursday.'

'Yes sir,' said the surprised sergeant.

'Conflicting views and personalities Sergeant; now there is an interesting aspect. I understand certain differences erupted in a row in front of witnesses and I have good cause to believe them. So today I want you to continue your enquiries using the motor cycle details you acquired and, from the acquaintances we identified yesterday, avail yourself of their views on Sanjay Parmar and his friends, written here,' he handed the sergeant some papers, 'if I may be allowed to advise you.'

The sergeant said nothing; he had learned that when Joshi was in facetious mood, it was better to listen until he got it out of his system.

'I have also, conversely and confusingly, a very believable verbal affidavit of the integrity of Mr Parmar. When you were out yesterday, his boss was so upset by my accusations that he fainted in my office, as Sanjeev witnessed, and I can hardly believe that after thirty years Mr Prichard got it wrong – although we must never discount the possibility.'

'So, you have work to do and, as we have been partly successful with the driving case you may be equally triumphant with this case of drink, if you see my pun? There is also the question of theft; you might want to unlock that case too. Mrs Jha may hold the key but I will deal with her simply because I have her confidence Sergeant – and for no other reason. But from others you may recover the evidence that turns that key in that particular lock.'

Joshi looked up from his notes and grinned at the widening smile of the sergeant who now looked relaxed after the minor reprimand.

'So what do we gather from my synopsis Sergeant, and what would your next step be, bearing in mind that your boss has indicated the course?'

'Well sir, since you ask,' said Birkram, grinning now, 'having summed up the situation with your usual astuteness, I would follow up your suggestions, collect Grewall and check Mr Parmar's acquaintances. Based on that information, we will, hopefully, link the answers to those we already have and find the truth. Then sir, you will reap the benefit for solving yet another case.'

'Well done Sergeant, there's hope for you yet,' grinned Joshi, gently clapping his hands. 'We do not sit around the office watching while idle policemen rock on the rear legs of chairs, or make wild guesses; we go forth and find out . . . Namaste.'

* * *

Sanjay opened the throttle of the Enfield, kicking the machine into top gear as soon as he hit the new highway. The cool, rushing air cleared his head like magic. This was the way to travel, quickly, coolly and without the hindrance of a complicated gear-box. Just a pull and a press, lean here and there and the machine did the rest.

The exhaust sang, contentedly cruising while he weaved in and out of heavy traffic, squeezing into gaps, between elaborately decorated buses crammed with travellers or hanging on outside hand rails. At the turn off he slowed, turned right and picked up the mountain road to Mitra's residence.

Traffic was sparse, apart from a bullock cart and a cyclist on their way down, one restraining his team the other enjoying the speed and freedom of the ride, both careful not to venture too near the exposed edge.

John's Enfield made easy work of the journey, five hundred cc didn't stutter or hesitate like the minibus, but thrust its way up the steepest gradients with ease, taking the many hairpins easily and racing up the occasional straight at a touch of the throttle. He kept well to the left, ensuring ample room between him and the edge in his dash to the summit.

Near the top, he shut down and tilted the machine over acutely on the final hairpin, keeping as flush to the wall of rock as he could. Then opening up again, he pushed the machine up the steepest, final gradient, over the brow and coasted the half mile down another steep gradient to Mitra's home.

He parked the bike and headed for the garage to see his mechanic friend, who shared similar interests and frequented the same hotel in Amitar, before he saw Mitra.

The welcome from him sounded, as always, genuine. A sharper intellect would have spotted the illusion when Mitra said, without looking up as Sanjay followed his goonda in:

'And to what do I owe the pleasure of this visit, my friend? I hope you have not come to tell me that my delivery will not take place, my manager will be annoyed.'

Sanjay stopped in momentary panic. The deliveries! In the turmoil of the last few days, he'd forgotten. 'No,' he lied, 'I'll bring them later,' nervously trying to cover up, 'it's something more serious than that!'

'Delayed deliveries are serious enough my friend, I hope you are not having difficulties.'

'No, I'm picking them up later,' he repeated, realising he could do so, now he had the bike.

'I am glad to hear it. Now what have you found out, the last piece of information you brought appears to be dubious, have you brought me, tidings of great joy, as we say?' he said looking up, smiling and preening himself at his wit.

In a series of staccato statements, Sanjay, nervous and confused, tried explaining the complex mission. Nadine and Graham were making his position precarious, it concerned John, involved Mitra and indicted Sharma and Nadu too.

Mitra's raised eyebrows and questions increased Sanjay's anxiety leading to a disjointed and baffling explanation until Mitra 'tut tutted,' gave out a long drawn-out bored, 'Y-e-e-s', or, 'I se-e-e-e,' without looking up from his paperwork, adding to Sanjay's dismay. Sanjay dried up.

Mitra casually placed the pen on its tray and sat back. He raised one hand to his forehead and rubbed, indicating that the whole thing was really too tiresome and said with some irritability, 'Do get down to the nitty gritty dear boy, how exactly am I implicated?'

Blunt and caution-less, Sanjay blurted out another series of dis-jointed statements that neither explained nor resolved anything, ending in desperation with, 'you have got to do something or they'll tell!'

Mitra remained calm, indifferent almost. 'Let them tell, Sanjay,' he said, 'more to the point what will they tell, and to whom? But wait, be calm my friend, take some refreshment. I will attempt to sum up.'

'Asif,' he called, without taking his eyes from his nervy visitor, 'bring Mr Parmar some refreshment.'

'Now my friend, what you say indicates that I am connected with a fraudulent business that persons are threatening to expose if we do not conform to their wishes?' he said, as Sanjay fidgeted on the edge of the seat and gulped the juice.

Mitra raised his head to look down his nose at the unsure figure in front of him, placed his fingers to form an arch and said calmly, 'The inference is that I am implicated in an illegal matter, is that so?' He leaned his chin on the arch.

'Yes', replied Sanjay, 'that's what I said.'

'It is possibly that you tried to say so but it is not what you said, Sanjay,' he said hardening his tone. 'If you cannot elucidate, I do not understand why you bother seeing me. Now, I have no involvement,

I merely helped an acquaintance. However, with what do these people intend to coerce my friend?'

'They know about everything, they are our accountants. They say you bribed him to lie about Orphindi at the rally and bought into his business to get on the committee, they wanted it and gave him the money . . .'

Mitra raised a hand, 'Wait my friend, I bought into his business and contributed to Orphindi, that is all.'

'But they know all about the money he used from Orphindi, he said you gave it and you didn't, and they are going to tell, and you being an ML . . .!

'A prospective ML,' Mitra corrected modestly.

'Well . . . yes . . . it's bad.'

'Really Sanjay you have a most annoying technique of explaining yourself! What other money and what is so bad?'

'I just told you, they know about the sixty thousand and . . .'

'Sixty thousand rupees?' he interrupted. 'Huh, that's nothing my dear boy.'

'Not rupees – pounds!'

Mitra shook his head, 'No dear boy, rupees.'

'No, pounds, and he can't have it until October that's the trouble and . . .'

'Stop there dear boy. Are you telling me that John's business produced sixty thousand pounds sterling?'

'Yes. Colin says we've got to get more up, they're booked and . . .'

'Colin? Get what up? What are you talking about? What has Colin to do with it? No . . . wait just one moment,' he said raising his hand as his confusion mounted, 'let us start again, from the very beginning. Just answer my questions, there's a good chap, now . . .'

Probing, searching and sporting his prissy smile, Mitra fixed his attention rigidly on Sanjay's mouth and every answer that tumbled from it. Minutes later, having compiled the picture, he leaned back in the chair, nodding. 'How very interesting dear boy . . . every cloud has a silver lining, as we say.'

Although Mitra had been slow to grasp the situation, Sanjay congratulated himself on his ability to communicate. Mitra looked pleased, as pleased as if he had discovered a gold mine.

'My friend,' said Mitra, 'you have put matters into perspective very well, thank you, I am deeply grateful but I see no need for you to concern yourself. I must say it is good to have a friend such as you who keeps his ear to the ground, as we say, and I will show my gratitude when you next deliver the clothing . . . will that be soon, by the way?'

'Tomorrow,' he said delighted to have received more acclaim from Mitra in an hour than from John in a year. With his self-esteem enhanced further, Mitra offered a whisky but, acutely aware of the deliveries, he refused, needing to be away quickly, his supplier would be anxious to off load after the wait.

He stood, ready to leave. Mitra stopped him, 'Do me one small favour Sanjay, there's a good chap, tell my friend I would like to see him – right away.'

* * *

Mitra leaned on the chair arm with one hand on his lips and a frown on his face. He had not foreseen other involvements or complications when he had planned his association and neither had he seen such an opportunity. At the outset he wanted help with his campaign but now, handled correctly, he could gain a large portion of, what appeared to be, a hugely profitable business. Sixty thousand pounds in only eighteen months, now that was a return worth pursuing, no wonder John had been evasive. With such sums at stake who could blame him? If their liaison was to continue, and it must now, Mr Prichard really must desist from deceitfulness.

Graham and his paramour were unknown quantities but, having created this eddying disaster alongside that dimwit Sanjay, their threat would help contribute to their own downfall. It was an affront to undermine the credibility of Dhankar Mitra, nobody would thwart his ambition and for anyone to believe they had the upper hand was a big mistake!

Prichard too must bear some of the blame; he seemed to have no control of his own people – that needs correction – even extreme solutions. Deeds are encouraged by rewards, and the rewards, in this case, are large.

He moved his hands away from his lips as his man entered the room. 'Master,' he said, 'your mechanic has just received a proposition from Sanjay Parmar . . .'

Listening carefully to the explanation he said, 'I will place the solution in his hands. I will not participate but he will be well rewarded if it becomes necessary.'

* * *

Ahmed was jittery, irked at having to pay his workers without deductions, annoyed at having to sideline bundles without payment and worried further that Mahmood might arrive and ask him to explain the pile of surplus stock in the warehouse. His business acquaintance had not arrived yesterday nor the day before and he sweated on him arriving today. He had news of an unpleasant nature to impart – and the cessation of profit pleased no one.

He paced the floor, nervous of possible exposure, and stopped to stare from the doorway, knowing it was unnecessary. Noise was his herald and when he heard a machine cough to a stop, he greeted it, and Sanjay, with trepidation. He strolled back through the door and planted himself in his chair.

With a quizzical look at the nervy, wizened man Sanjay said, 'Trouble in town, Ahmed?'

'No, that is ... no, nothing to do with town ... I have something important to tell you.'

'Not now, I'm in a hurry, get the packages.'

'No,' he gushed, 'our arrangement must end forthwith, there will be no more supplies. I have been threatened with exposure, you must leave ... right away.'

Sanjay, ever slow to respond, stared. 'Leave ... why?'

'I had a visitor, a very threatening man, guardian of one of my employee's children,' he said raising his voice above his usual whisper. 'He has threatened to call the police and as you know I am in no position to face them. I am sorry.'

'What? What do you mean?'

'No more business ... I'm sorry!'

'You can't do this, my client is desperate,' he said standing. 'Let me take what you've got.'

'No,' he said, 'you must go.' He indicated the door, the movement emphasising his desperation.

'What about our arrangement in town ...?'

'That too is finished. I'm sorry.'

Sanjay had a sudden thought. 'What was he like – this man?' he asked.

'He did not give his name, a big man, white, and drove a motor cycle similar to yours and ...'

Sanjay heard no more; he felt as though a horse had kicked his abdomen, his shoulders collapsed. 'No,' he breathed with eyed closed, 'oh, no, for the sake of Krishna.'

Certain that if his heart did not restart soon he would die, he slunk from the building.

* * *

Dusk saw John anxiously waiting at the rear steps looking for signs of the bus, conscious now of insurance problems. He'd had enough trouble for one day and this being the last evening he wanted no upsets. Besides, he needed to see Andrew.

Turning away to leave he heard it, the faint hum of a protesting engine as it traversed the craggy plain. Swivelling his head, he caught sight of headlights rising over a mound, it brought similar beams of relief to his chubby, face and, instructing Kumar to make sure the drinks were cold, he went to change.

In no time the travel weary group had showered and returned to the pergola, refreshed and ready for their pre-dinner routine around the rattan table.

'Late today Tony.'

'Yeah, some berk took a corner too fast in an overloaded hay lorry, old Sunil's brain was in gear even if the other bloke's wasn't. He held back and the load fell on a passing car. We stopped to help. Nobody was hurt; in fact, we had a giggle. The lorry driver, his mates and the car driver all mucked in to clear the mess and then sat sharing their food at the side of the road waiting for the breakdown wagon. I can't see that happening at home.'

'Not with you,' groaned Sam. 'You would be out of your precious car hanging on to the other driver's throat!'

'It comes back to religion,' said Hillary. 'Hindu's are fatalists of course, quite prepared for death and a better life when they return to the world.'

'Sort of recycling?' laughed Sam.

In a relaxed atmosphere John enjoyed the banter and turned the chat to India. How had they enjoyed their stay – despite the heat?

Their response was unanimous – the beauty, the excitement and the simplicity had intrigued and delighted them. 'It'll be Balance Sheets and accounts next week,' said Andrew.

'Me too Andrew, I get so confused with ours. I'm doing them now.'

'Can I give you a hand?'

Feigning surprised, John said, 'I couldn't ask you to do that Andrew, you are on holiday.'

'Ach, I don't mind at all, I'll have a peek now if you wish.'

'It'll save me hours,' he said standing immediately, 'Sorry about this folks, but it will be a weight off my mind.'

They left for his room.

Andrew bent his head to the Orphindi papers spread out on John's table. Slowly and meticulously he read each sheet, placing them aside, and after fifteen minutes he knocked the papers square.

'Everything appears to be in order John but, to use an accountant's standard excuse; I would need to see the books and paperwork to support the entries.'

'My brother prepares them so I think we must assume it is accurate. He is very fussy.'

'Aye,' he laughed, 'we all are. They've been prepared in the standard manner and so long as the statements from your bank and bills tally, you should be OK. Just make sure that cheques are written to J. Prichard or Orphindi,' he laughed, 'or else your brother may find himself a rich man.'

'I imagine it's very difficult to play games with accounts these days, I mean, not a lot could go wrong surely.'

'That depends on the controls, with a brother involved fraud controls should not be necessary.'

'Fraud controls?'

'Yes, proper audits, regular checks by outsiders. Simple things like cheques made out correctly and genuine expenses. You have an advantage that it is difficult to separate between guests and the camp services.'

'Really?' said John.

There are ways and tricks, unlikely with you brother involved of course, Teeming and Lading is a technical term for withdrawing money from an account and replacing it with new income. The perpetrator merely mortgages existing money against future income, it's simple to operate and, carried out effectively, it's untraceable for years. Another method, and a charity would be susceptible to this, is to include false bills or bogus receipts. You can take benefits in kind of course, the consumption of food and drink, the use of facilities and transport is difficult to allocate, so it is essential to control all bills. From what you say, if your brother has done his job you should be safe.'

'That's fine Andrew, thank you. You have saved me a great deal of time and worry,' he said as they retraced their steps. 'Just think, if I had known about those swindles I could have been a rich man!'

He was still laughing when they rejoined the others.

'You were asking before you left John,' said Hillary, 'would we come back? Yes, this is a never to be forgotten place, I hope it never changes. It would be such a pity to loose that rudimentary exoticism of being part of real India. It feels like India is supposed to feel, and not like the Goan coast which is becoming like Spain, English bars, English food and discos. If India goes that way it too will loose its attraction. Why come at all if India is anglicised, go to Spain, its closer to the UK and just as warm. India is unique, keep it like that.'

'I will pass on the gospel Hillary.'

'The kids help,' said Sam. 'That reminds me, have you any news of the boy?'

'Oh yes,' he said easily, 'he's been found, he'd gone back to his village.'

'That's been worrying you John, hasn't it?'

'You can say that again,' he said as his stomach churned. 'However, time for dinner and an early night for an early departure.'

* * *

Despite the relief of his reinstatement, Sanjay delayed his return for as long as possible, staying in town to eat and delaying the moment to face the inevitable backlash from John.

Assuaged by a moderate amount of whisky, he returned to his dwelling at ten to pack and shower in the hope that his freshness would pacify John's assault. It would come, and his future depended on the answers he gave about his sidelines? He'd made nothing, he'd made very little? No, he would not accept that, from what Ahmed said John knew everything.

How could he counter the threat? What if he said he had saved the money for John – a surprise gift? Yes that might work, it was worth a try. Marginally easier in his mind, he stuffed most of the cash into his bag and, softened by a mixture of booze and optimism he left at ten, allowing the Enfield to drift quietly the last hundred yards or so to the bungalow with the engine off.

The place was in darkness except for the pergola lights and there was no laughter either from those contemptible Westerners who were usually on the roof enjoying the kind of attendance they never got in their own country.

He stood and listened intently at the foot of the stairs and heard nothing, were they keeping their conversation deliberately low as they had in the minibus?

With a swift look towards John's room he saw no sign of life and, taking advantage, he switched on the kitchen light, grabbed a glass and a bottle of whisky from the cupboard and walked cautiously back to the end of the pergola and sat.

Loosened and relaxed he filled the glass and swallowed the spirit slowly, and, after thirty minutes, over sweetened by several glasses, he stood, and sauntered unsteadily towards the room next to John's, where he threw his gear on the bed. He stood still for a moment, listening. Was everything normal, no Kumar, no John no visitors? It was too quiet!

Curious, he stepped uncertain of his footing from his room to listen at John's door, just in case Kumar was with him. Hearing nothing he gently pushed the door and peeked into the gloom.

The big man breathed heavily, making sounds like those he had once known, it gave him sensual stimulation like the uncoiling of a spring in the pit of his stomach. He pushed the door open the final few inches and crept quietly to where John lay to stand beside the bed to stare down at the big man, lying peacefully, lit by the moon.

Moved by the recollection of him naked in the shower, slicked down hair, skin glistening and muscles rippling with movement, his senses heightened, his breathing shortened and with shaking hands he reached out to lift the sheet . . .

THIRTY

Dawn was breaking, when Kumar rose, it was hot and humid signifying the threat of monsoons. He washed quietly not to disturb the others and, used to John's habits, cleared the whisky-bottle and glass from the rattan table before busying himself preparing the last breakfast of the season for the final, departing group.

In the hot, clammy air the slightest effort made him perspire, glasses misted as soon as they were polished and plates felt damp to the touch. Frustrated after repeated wiping, he placed them on the table. It was always like this with approaching rains.

He made tea, hot and black, picked up his books and took his early morning position at the end of the pergola to learn as always in a morning ritual. He peeked into the communal bedroom and as he passed heard a snort from either Chef and Vijay who were still asleep. He smiled as he placed his books on the rattan table at the end of the patio with the passing thought that as Vijay joked about him snoring, today it would be his turn.

They were good friends. Quiet and thoughtful, easy going and intelligent, Vijay was so unlike Sunil, both in appearance and personality. Five years younger, six inches shorter at five feet eight and neatly built, he was good looking and his neat wavy hair was always tidy. He amused them with stories of the Westerners but liked most of them.

Sunil never did, he was the serious one, quiet and composed – and he could become belligerent. Kumar remembered how formidable he looked arguing with John over the nice Englishman with blond hair, who had played with him, Vijay and some of the other boys in his house on the hill when they were very young. Sunil had stood his ground so defiantly that even John backed down, promising he would never take the boys to the house again. They were disappointed; the blond man had been showing them the garden and playing with them on the bed until Sunil became angry and herded them back to the bus shouting at Mr John. They'd never been back – neither had Sunil spoken of it.

After that they spent two years at Maroutai College and Kumar missed them. It was about that time Kumar started in the garden for Mr John, sometimes staying overnight. Mr John had been kind, he soothed him when he became upset over the deaths of his mother and father and explained that the blond man was just being kind. He liked to teach young people about life and Sunil should not have taken offence, after all he was only introducing them to facts needed in later life. It was then that Mr John showed him – not crudely like the boys in the camp but properly, tenderly. He'd never known such kindness and understanding, nor such excitement, and shared the only love he ever knew in their all-male environment.

Sunil became angry when he returned from college, Kumar heard him arguing again with Mr John and, instead of finding work outside, he insisted on staying to help on the farm and to eventually drive the bus.

Kumar had had little to do with him but, after seeing the white woman naked, he felt the need for someone older and more experienced to explain his confusion, particularly since sensations arrived when he thought of her. She was so soft and round, smooth white and so different, she provoked thoughts and emotions like those he experienced with Mr John, yet more fascinating. She intrigued him and yet, guiltily, he was hesitant to talk to John. What made him so reluctant? Was there another kind of love, was it different from that which John had taught him, did he really want what he'd learned from John? Kenneth didn't!

There were so many questions and his doubts troubled him, John's recent behaviour too had driven a wedge between them, it filled him with disgust and heightened his curiosity. John may have seen the change in him; perhaps that's why he'd asked Sanjay back to Paradise Lake.

Sanjay's lies and John's new passion for money would lead to trouble, the atmosphere was already edgy and Sanjay's unconcealed resentment of tourists didn't help. He was stupid not to see that tourism and Mitra's money went hand in hand, it would be good for them; Kumar could see it and had begun to use his stealth to confirm it. As God Shiva used his third eye, to discover, reveal and store, he did the same, he found the telex from Colin in John's pocket and he wondered what would happen when Graham discovered that that all revenue to the Bank of India had stopped and gone to Linkers Bank?

He'd heard their threats and seen their cheque; they'd manoeuvred like wrestlers to get the best hold over John and Mr Mitra, they were spiteful and treacherous and, seeing that, Kumar decided to follow God Shiva's other objective, use his intelligence, demolish the obstructions and pave the way for re-creation.

To do so he set about reducing his own limitations, spending more time at the camp, learning how to organise the boys, finding out what the workshop produced, how to run the farm, who sells to whom and who supports Orphindi and where their income came from?

His encounter with Joshi had confirmed his inexperience, he needed to know more, he knew nothing about a great deal and a great deal about nothing, but he could learn. He had time now, with two boys covering his work, which John had not even noticed.

He looked up from his books at the early sky, brilliantly lit with silken clouds brushed with vermilion and watched the vast shadow retreat from the western valley towards the east, hiding among the folds of the eastern hills. In the emerging light he smiled – how appropriate for his emerging future.

Undisturbed in the solitude of the empty pergola and able to see discreetly but be unseen, he concentrated on expanding his English vocabulary but, disturbed by a faint scraping to his left, he lifted his head stealthily and leaned forward, barely beyond the corner of the building.

He froze. In his shorts, carrying the remainder of his clothes, sneaking from John's room into his own, was Sanjay!

* * *

John woke early, showered quickly and prepared for the ritual sadness of goodbyes and promised returns, the first was not genuine and the second rarely kept. He saw Kumar through the door slats moments before he knocked.

'Breakfast Mr John.'

'Thanks son, come in. I . . .?' he said but Kumar was gone in a trice. John pulled a face, shrugged and moments later Sanjay sauntered in.

With barely a glance John snapped, 'Where were you last night?'

'I had to eat and then sort my stuff,' he replied belligerently, 'I got here at ten, you were in bed, Mitra wanted to see you.'

'Did he now?'

Sanjay ignored him, 'They're ready,' he said, flicking his head towards the front of the building.

'Right, hang about, I want a word after I've seen them,' John said and pushed past him.

The guests said goodbye while the luggage was loaded. 'I have so enjoyed the stay,' said Hillary putting out her hand.

'It's been marvellous,' said Sam throwing her arms around his neck and placing a kiss on his cheek. 'Thanks for everything. Can I take Kumar home?'

He smiled and watched them climb into the bus, pulling away with voices calling and arms waving.

Standing for a second or two, he walked to the breakfast table, relieved but otherwise unaffected by their departure. They may be his bread and butter but they were transient and he didn't want to see another guest until ensconced in his new complex. And now he could concentrate on all that beckoning wealth.

'Kumar!' he called impatiently, and jumped when a reply came from just behind his ear.

'Can I help?'

'Bloody hell Sanjay, don't creep about! Where is he?'

Sanjay shrugged and John glared, 'Never mind him then, what did Mitra say?'

'He wants to see you quickly. You'd better get up there.'

John turned sharply, about to make a rebuke but checked himself and, in a voice more appealing than commanding, having decided on appeasement, he said, 'Don't tell me what to do Sanjay, there's a good lad, first things first, I'll see him later. Stay here this morning and draw up the roster for the weekend, then go to the camp and sort out the groups to start on that road, I want them working the moment that digger starts ... alright? Kumar!' he called without drawing breath.

'Kumar!' he shouted again ...

'For Christ's sake where has he got to?' he fumed, 'go and see if he's in the kitchen.'

Sanjay ambled to the kitchen and then into the boy's quarters, he raised his arms in a signal of failure.

'Sod,' he said, 'I bet that bloody woman took him after all!'

THIRTY-ONE

John, with Andrew's advice in mind, waited inside the office of Linkers Bank. A smartly dressed, western suited, turbaned man stood behind the counter, 'Good morning Mr John.'

'Mr Singh,' he said politely, 'I wonder if you could help? The clerk at the Bank of India told me that cheques might have been mistakenly credited to the account of Mr G. Prichard, my brother. He is away at the moment and as a matter of urgency, asked me to identify any that have gone astray. Will it be possible to check?'

'I would need his direct authority Mr John, perhaps he will call on me.'

'That's why I am here Mr Singh, he is visiting another camp and the auditors are pressing.' He leaned forward and looked about him. 'I do not need to tell you how difficult they can be.'

The clerk looked sympathetic, 'I cannot allow you access Mr John, I am sorry.'

'I don't need access, all I want is a list of names on cheques to confirm they have been posted to the correct account. There is no need to remove or alter anything, just confirm that the cheques were made out to G. Prichard. Graham will amend any errors.'

'Are there any in particular, Mr John?'

'That is the problem Mr Singh. My memory is not what it was; there are hundreds of contributors as you will become aware when you are familiar with our account, but if you will be good enough . . .'

'It is highly irregular Mr John, but I understand the urgency and as you have been good enough to transfer your accounts, I will see what I can do.'

'That is very kind of you Mr Singh . . .

* * *

As it had with Mr Singh, John hoped the vein of good fortune would continue with Mitra, his catalyst for a healthy financial future. He pointed the Enfield up the hill, it would mean coming clean of course but if Mitra bit, and that would take finesse, they would get back on level terms. But just in case he got the bit too firmly between his teeth, John had something else up his sleeve.

Yes, he thought, as the machine climbed the hill, diplomacy; small arms not big guns, secure the partnership, dispose of the garbage and it will be a Mercedes and not a second-hand Enfield.

Bringing his machine round the final hairpin, he pushed it up and over the steep summit, shut off the engine and cruised downhill to the gates that, expectedly, slid inwards. He dismounted and followed one of Mitra's goondas looking, as usual, splendid, but thugs are thugs and they could inflict serious damage. That was OK so long as it was on others. He followed the flowing turban into Mitra's study.

The extended hand in front of a stern face showed that the occupant was not in the best of moods; a fact made more evident by a reprimand for lateness, before waving him into a chair opposite.

John restrained a retort, intent on reaching his objective, and was again tempted when Mitra complained that he was not aware of the implications so clumsily explained by Sanjay, pompously declaring that it was a reflection of John's security.

Offended but still refusing to retaliate, John asked if Sanjay had explained how the conspiring two had obtained the information.

'I am not a detective my friend,' he said curtly, with a smirk.

'Then let me enlighten you. You believe Sanjay to be your man, Dhankar ...'

'I most certainly do not, I ...'

'Well let me tell you we are both wrong! He is anybody's man for a drink, a pervert, a thief and a liar whose indiscretion caused this situation and ...'

By the time John had finished his story with the inclusion of Graham and Nadeen's involvement, Mitra had lost his smirk.

'Tell me my friend, how serious are they?'

'Like cobras Dhankar, they'll strike when they choose. If we agree they can, if we disagree, they will. We are cornered and our friend Sanjay is the source of our trouble. One day Dhankar, as sure as God made little apples, they will expose us.'

'Then we must act with all speed and correct the situation. My man advises me that Sanjay has made approaches, preposterous though they may be, and I have told him he must deal with the matter as he sees fit, so retribution is at hand, as we say. In view of what you now say, I will ask him to modify his action to allow Sanjay to play a starring role.'

'Now, let us lay our cards on the table, face up this time my friend. Tell me, why did you press for money when you have sixty thousand pounds?'

'Sanjay?'

Mitra nodded, John smiled, 'In the pipeline Dhankar, but not available until October, and a delay in building will be disastrous in view of the bookings. With your backup we can be up and running by then. I hoped to maintain control but the situation has changed and I am offering a full partnership.'

'A partnership, my friend, fifty percent . . . agreed?'

'Agreed,' said John, they shook hands.

'Now, with those bungalows up we can treble our profit next year.'

'Then we must push forward with all speed to turn up trumps, as we say. My company will undertake the construction immediately.'

'One other matter,' John said, allowing a smile to light up his features. 'I will ensure continuous supplies from Mahmood's factory from now on, but that must be a separate arrangement. It is my pocket money, to coin a phrase.'

Mitra gave a knowing smile, 'Ahh . . . I see, you have discovered my arrangement, anything else?'

'Yes I would like you to start taking some of our boys, I know it was the cause of our disagreement a while ago but . . .'

John stopped . . . he saw Mitra's jaw compress in repugnance, his knuckles showed white through his clenched fists, he half stood in his chair and his voice rose uncharacteristically.

'I will have nothing to do with that filthy business, I told Sanjay before and if that is part of our deal I refuse, I did so before and do so again and . . .!

'Just a minute Dhankar!'

'No,' he shouted, on his feet now. 'I will not use boys in my hotels for immoral purposes!'

'What?' John stared in disbelief. 'No, no Dhankar, hold on . . . Ah I see,' he said as the realisation hit, 'I see . . . Sanjay, he offered the boys, is that what caused our disagreement? I was not aware Dhankar, honestly,' he said shaking his head, 'and you thought it was my doing all those years ago? My God!'

Mitra resumed his seat and colour came back into his cheeks. 'I am so I relieved to hear it my friend, I was surprised at the time.'

He sat back in the seat, calmer and smiling, and ruminated for a moment. 'Then my friend, it is essential that we arrange a starring role for Mr Parmar. If you agree, perhaps you had better stay to dinner.'

* * *

John returned to the illuminated bungalow at midnight, letting the machine drift back the last few hundred yards on momentum, with a switched off engine.

He quietly pushed his head into the boy's room looking for Kumar. He wasn't there. He checked his own room, he was not there either. He went next door and poked his head cautiously around the door of Sanjay's room. It was empty!

Kumar missing was one thing but Sanjay was different. Where was he, not in town with his mates for God's sake! Panic gripped, his stomach churned – what if Joshi knew? He felt sick and raced outside opening doors and crashing into each room, finally into the boy's quarters to switch on the light.

Shocked and bleary eyed, Vijay and Chef screwed up their faces and raised their arms to deflect the glare.

'Where are they?' he bellowed.

Vijay croaked and grimaced, 'Who?'

'Who?' he yelled, 'for Christ's sake. Who do you think, Sanjay and Kumar?'

They looked at each other in confusion and shook their heads.

'Well keep your bloody eyes open in future!' he shouted leaving the light on and charging out of the room, terrified what Joshi might say. Sanjay was supposed to be under scrutiny and this was the very thing he wanted to avoid.

For a moment, he considered jumping on the Enfield to search the town but he would be conspicuous at this hour and if one of Joshi's men saw him it might raise questions. 'Sod,' he snarled and made for the kitchen, rummaging angrily through the shelves. 'Where the hell does he keep the bloody bottle, and where's a bloody glass?' he yelled, petulantly flinging open cupboards in his search, before finding what he wanted and stalking back to the rattan table to threw himself into a chair.

'God all bloody mighty,' he said in frustration, 'what now?'

Sweating with nerves and worry he tipped the contents of the first glass down his taut throat and refilled it.

THIRTY-TWO

Ashook Grewall sat uncomfortably on the metal wheel arch in the rear of the noisy police van as it roared along the road from Maroutai. The booming of the empty shell made his head ache, despite intermittently covering his ears with his hands in the hope of some relief, and dust, sucked in through the open windows of the cab, eddied around the interior, irritating his throat and blocking his nose. His eyes were sore, partly from being woken so early and partly from the powdery red grime swirling in the confines of the rear. The pungent smell of cigarette smoke wafting through the grill made him feel sick, and three policemen, laughing at their success, swigged from bottles of water, adding to his depression.

After fresh air motorcycle travel, the noises and atmosphere inside the van felt intolerable. It was hot, airless and claustrophobic. He hated it and wiped his eyes again, leaving ludicrous, muddy-red streaks like war paint on his brown skin. In the oppressive heat, he needed a drink to ease his parched throat and tried to generate saliva by squeezing his cheeks and wriggling his tongue, it failed and his throat remained rasp-like. It would be futile to ask for water from them, the rude awakening at 6 a.m. and the subsequent treatment showed they were not well disposed.

With no time to put on his watch before being arrested and dragged from the hotel, he guessed he had been travelling an hour. He'd not washed and he needed the toilet – a discomfort brought about more by the shock of three policemen crashing into his room than a normal call of nature. The resultant turmoil too, did little for his physical comfort, he was frightened and worried but by extreme luck, they had found him alone – he was grateful for that. And he now had the chance to think.

Despite a throbbing head and an alien environment, he recalled events. How naive of him to believe he'd get away with it. He had to accept arrest as the result of mediocre planning and ignorance, learning in the process that desperation is not a good companion to common sense. Being caught so quickly was the real disappointment, he'd had no chance to finalise plans with those he had left behind and they would worry too.

It was only a matter of time before they found Samuel and he could only hope to delay the moment and use Samuel's absence as a bargaining base. If, in the meantime, Samuel took it into his head to run off Ashook would be in real trouble.

Occasional glances from those in the front told him they were keeping an eye on him, only Lord Rama knew why! Handcuffed, with no windows in the back and no way out of the door secured from the outside he had no chance of escape.

A cloak of dust enveloped the van as it drew to a sliding halt in front of Amitar Police Department. Thrown forward, his head struck the metal grill; he felt the sticky warmth of blood begin seeping down his forehead into the corner of his eye to mingle with sweat. The rear door was thrown open and someone dragged him along the floor and on to his feet out of the dust, grime and dimness into dazzling sunlight. He closed his eyes trying to blink away the blood and shield his eyes from the blazing sun. The gruelling heat dried the fluid and stiffened the corner of his eye where the rivulets had run.

Prodded unnecessarily and shoved forward towards the steps of a building, the tight handcuffs scuffed and pulled at his wrists, two officers grabbed his arms, wrenching them, causing agonising pains to shoot through his shoulder. He'd heard that policemen stood no nonsense and wouldn't think twice before they cuffed his ear or swipe at him with sticks. He believed the rumours when, in front of their colleagues they gleefully prodded him in the back, pushing him towards a doorway marked in bold letters, 'Inspector Joshi.'

'Grewall, sir,' said one with two stripes on his arm as he dragged the bedraggled man into the Inspector's office.

'Thank you,' said Joshi, without looking up, apparently absorbed with something more important.

Grewall waited, expecting he did not know what. Joshi paid no interest.

After a few minutes Joshi said politely with his head down, 'You are a difficult man to find, Mr Grewall. Have you been hiding?'

Ashook found that he was trembling, more from shock and fear than the blow on the head. The vibrations shook his black hair forward where it dangled on to his perspiring forehead and stuck to the blood. The clean room intimidated him as much as the van, and the power of thought seemed to have deserted his muddled mind after his treatment at the hands of those bullies. He felt queasy inside and scruffy outside, particularly now in front of Joshi, who looked the essence of smartness in his ironed khaki shirt and trousers.

He did not fancy his prospects at all, he knew, and they knew, why they had brought him here. There was little point in making excuses. His intelligence told him that the only route to leniency was to justify the steps he had taken. What was the point of lying, they had traced him easily and a follow up operation among the hotel staff was bound to result in Samuel's eventual discovery! His only chance was to tell the truth, hope for clemency, create a delay and a base from which to bargain.

'Not exactly in hiding, sir, I would have preferred not to be found. I misjudged your efficiency.'

'How very complimentary of you to say so Mr Grewall,' said Joshi facetiously, still taking a greater interest in his paperwork than in him, 'but why would you prefer anonymity? Have you something to hide?'

'I know what you want sir but I will say nothing unless I have an assurance there will be no forced return.'

'No forced return? Thank you Mr Grewall, you have just confirmed that you know why you are here,' said Joshi sharply. 'So, what should I do with a man who thinks he has the right to take the law into his own hands?'

Ashook looked perplexed but said nothing.

'You kidnapped a boy from a secure home Mr Grewall, forced the police and his guardians to spend countless hours in fruitless searches, and . . .'

'. . . It was not kidnapping sir, it was a rescue . . .'

'. . . Don't interrupt!' snapped Joshi raising his voice and lifting his head simultaneously. 'A rescue! You removed a child from a secure home, concealed him, broke the law and claim it was a rescue! And then you have the effrontery to praise my staff on their efficiency! You must think we are fools Mr Grewall!'

Ashook's eyes reflected the worries of a trapped man, completely dispirited he felt a trembling, unwashed wreck with clothes and hair dishevelled and a gash that still seeped blood.

'What happened to your head?' said Joshi in sudden, surprising, concern.

'An accident sir.'

'Sergeant,' called Joshi to an immediate response. 'Remove those hand-cuffs, clean him up – and get something to cover that cut.'

He was led out. In five minutes, he returned refreshed, surprised what cold water could do. He rubbed his wrists pleased with the freedom and his senses sharpened immediately, his ability to think improved too.

'Do you need a drink?'

'I was given one sir, thank you.'

'A moment sergeant', said Joshi, 'outside!' He stood and left the room with the officer in tow, in a minute he was back. 'Well! What have you got to say?'

'It was not a kidnap sir, it was a rescue, I took him because he was distressed. It was my intention to report the matter but events moved against me, and if I am punished, don't punish him by sending him back.'

'Leave that to me Mr Grewall I will decide what to do without your help! Why not come to the police?'

'You would not have believed me – there were circumstances.'

'You mean accusations! I suppose you will tell me they were mistakes and you were misunderstood?'

'Well I er . . .'

'It's strange how often we hear that excuse in this profession Mr Grewall, always *after* someone has been caught and never before.'

A knock on the door stopped him, 'Come in.'

The sergeant entered and whispered something, Joshi nodded and the officer left. 'I am sorry about the cut, my man confirms it was an accident. Now,' said Joshi indicating a chair, 'sit down.' He leaned across the desk; 'You will answer my questions and tell me what happened – and no tiresome lies please.'

Ashook saw that Joshi was no fool. Shrewd, straightforward and seemingly fair, despite the toughness and sarcasm, he would have to remember not to make fragile excuses.

'You stole some money, Mr Grewall?'

'No sir. Money was found under my pillow.'

'Someone put it there?'

'Yes sir, five hundred rupees from the workshop cash box.'

'How do you know where it came from Mr Grewall?'

'I was told sir – after it was found.'

'Had someone reported it missing?'

'No sir, it was found to be missing after it was discovered under my pillow, if you see what I mean, the box was checked after the money was recovered. It was under the pillow sir, but I didn't steal it. I have some intelligence Inspector and an idiot could have found a better hiding place.'

'But not enough to realise you would be caught absconding with one of the boys, Mr Grewall,' said Joshi tapping on the desk with the end of a pencil. 'The cash . . . that was a misunderstanding?'

'Not a misunderstanding, sir.'

'Who found it?'

'Mr Prichard said he discovered it.'

'Said? Don't you believe him?'

'I don't know sir.'

Joshi eyed him coldly, 'I see,' he said after a minute. 'What did you do?'

'I was more upset than angry, Mr Prichard is usually a fair man. He said he would consider his actions and talk to me the next day.'

'Did you mention it to anyone?'

'No sir, there was nobody to talk to except the young lady in the office. That evening I went out.'

'You are referring to Mrs Jha? What kind of relationship did you have with her?'

Ashook thought it was a curious, irrelevant question to ask. 'We were colleagues sir, we worked together. Shamin was a good friend, she appeared to understand, but I left suddenly and had no chance to discuss the matter.'

Joshi seemed relieved, 'Just colleagues?' he asked and Ashook saw the first sign of malleability in him. 'I see. You went out, where?'

'To a restaurant, I needed a meal.'

'And . . .?'

'I came back and checked the huts. It was past nine sir, Samuel was terribly upset, crying, sobbing and accusing. My appearance was fortuitous, apparently, so I sat and listened to him, comforted him, and after half an hour calmed him and left. Parmar saw me and asked me what I was doing. I told him, he made an accusation, we argued and then I went to bed. Next day Mr Prichard dismissed me for inappropriate behaviour, stealing and drunkenness! I didn't understand; none of those things are true.'

'Did you ask for a hearing?'

'Yes sir.'

'And he refused?'

'Yes sir.'

'So out of spite you arranged to abscond with a minor!'

'No sir,' he said fiercely.

'Yes sir!' declared Joshi; 'Did you or did you not make arrangements with a thirteen year old to abscond for your own shameful purposes . . .?'

'No sir . . .'

'. . . and you now pretend there were valid reasons. You are a thief, a liar and a pervert Mr Grewall . . .' said Joshi raising his voice thunderously.

'No sir, I am not . . .'

'. . . and you imply that Mr Prichard, together with Mr Parmar, were involved in a conspiracy, yet soften your accusation by saying he is a fair man. Whom are you accusing, him, his helpers?'

'Whoever concealed the money . . . I don't know . . . he trusts his helpers, they have reason to be loyal sir . . .'

'So they conspired?'

'Well I . . .'

'Never mind!' he said sharply. 'Now, let us turn to Samuel. Where is he?'

'I am sorry sir I need your assurance,' he said bravely.

The irritation in Joshi's eyes told Ashook he had met yet another difficulty, he had not made an ally of the man, and he wondered if he would behave like the other brutes – but to reveal Samuel's whereabouts would defeat his object.

He waited while Joshi checked his paperwork, and when he looked up, his approach had changed. 'Young man,' he said, in a fatherly manner, 'you do not appear to see the seriousness of this situation. With the evidence before me I could charge you now.'

'Before you do sir,' said Ashook with a spark of defiance, 'had you better check some information?'

'I have made my enquiries Mr Grewall and it is not necessary for you to divert attention from your own wrong doings or,' he raised his voice again, 'tell me how to do my job!'

He paused and fixed Ashook with his eyes, 'Remember you have committed a criminal offence!'

'Yes sir, but I can help, and I need your assurance.'

'And I need to see Samuel and hear a sound reason for kidnapping other than merely saying you witnessed a child in distress. If you do not comply then I will charge you with abduction, I could even consider murder, if you fail to co-operate – and make no mistake, you will be charged! I do not bargain with criminals!'

'I am sorry Inspector, but I must have your word.'

'No, Mr Grewall, I want sight of Samuel, at home, in Orphindi preferably.'

'Home, inspector? That is not his home, it is a place of defilement, and from what I have seen Samuel is not the only one to suffer. No sir, I would rather go to prison.'

'Who suffers? What do you mean? You have given me no proof of mistreatment or is this another fantasy to divert attention from the real reason for his abduction?'

'That is the reason sir, if you do not believe me let me tell you about the night I left, perhaps that will convince you.'

Joshi's pencil tapped the desk again, 'You may try.'

'I collected all my things about 10 a.m. and stayed overnight in Amitar. That evening . . .'

During the narrative Joshi placed his elbows on the desk and watched Grewall's face intently, he placed the tips of his forefingers on his lips and listened without interruption. At the end he seemed better disposed, as though in belief that the man was genuine.

'Is that proof enough sir?' asked Grewall wondering if what he had said had the desired impact.

Joshi appeared to be letting the implications sink in before committing himself, still with his hands pressed hard against his mouth.

Ashook found himself shuffling in the chair impatiently and, after a few minutes, Joshi called in his sergeant.

'Make Mr Grewall comfortable and bring my car round, we have things to do.'

He stood and pushed his hand across the desk, 'Thank you Mr Grewall, you have been a great help,' he said pleasantly to a bewildered Ashook.

Then, looking as though he was about to open another line of enquiry, he hesitated, and with a twinkle in his eyes said, 'When you have eaten and rested, one of my men will drive you to your friend's house to collect Samuel.'

* * *

John woke that morning, sweating in unremitting heat after a long uncomfortable sleep in a pergola armchair. The steamy air and forty degrees of heat seemed to burn his lungs and sap his energy. Moisture ran like tributaries from his hair, dampened his face and dripped on to his belly. The humidity would remain until the monsoons broke and only then would the temperature start to fall. The discomfort though, would stay alongside the constant dampness.

Sitting upright, he looked sleepily towards the lake. It was his barometer, nothing moved except heat haze that shimmered, oscillating the scene like a mirage – another sign that it would get even hotter and more humid. It was then he realised he smelt unpleasantly of stale whisky and perspiration – a shower would remove the offensive odour and the stiffness in his joints. He looked at his watch. The figures would not quite converge and it crossed his mind, once again, that he needed spectacles. He screwed up his eyes and stretched out his arm.

RON GOODMAN

It was 6 a.m., and, as his morning mind came slowly to life, he saw a movement, someone walking towards the front steps. He squinted, peered, and still with unsettled vision finally recognised Kumar.

'Where have you been?' he called.

The disrespectful reply accompanied a glare, 'Out,' he replied, showing insolence that questioned John's right to ask.

'I know that, where's Sanjay?'

'Don't you know?' said Kumar disappearing into the kitchen to re-appear carrying a tray that he banged impertinently down on the table before pointedly lifting the nearly empty whisky bottle.

'Have you finished with this?' he said contemptuously.

'Don't be so bloody cheeky! This place is like the Marie bloody Celeste. Get my breakfast. Where's Sanjay?'

Kumar looked again at the whisky bottle, 'Can't you remember?' he said with a supercilious smile.

'That's enough my son! Go and find him.'

Kumar marched off with the whisky bottle in one hand, insolently slapping the empty tray with the other against his thigh in time with his steps, slap – slap – slap.

'Hey!' he yelled, 'he's not in the bloody kitchen, he's probably in bed.'

Kumar, with unconcealed arrogance, said calmly over his shoulder, 'Yours or his?'

In that half turn, John saw a sneer, as though he had achieved an objective. 'Cheeky bastard, do as you are told,' he grumbled loudly and called for Vijay, who appeared from the boys' quarters, still half asleep. 'Where's Sanjay?' he snapped, hoping to regain authority in the wake of Kumar's insolence. Vijay merely rocked his head.

'When did you last see him?'

'Yesterday afternoon, when I arranged the roster . . .'

'You arranged the roster?'

'Ye-e-e-s,' he said in a tone that conveyed he too was talking to an idiot, 'I am capable, I did learn something at college.'

John glared at him, he sounded as disdainful as Kumar. What the bloody hell is going on here?

'Don't you start, Vijay! Go and find him, then get yourself up to Mahmood after breakfast and tell him I want to meet him in his factory at two this afternoon. Take the minibus – and be quick,' he said rising and making for the shower.

Passing Sanjay's room, he looked in. His bed was tidy, that was a worry – he would never make his own bed with Kumar about. Could he have left? He'd threatened to and just to be sure John opened his wardrobe to check but nothing seemed to be missing.

He worried while he showered and, while waiting for breakfast, he shuffled impatiently in the chair, nervous that Joshi might turn up. With Sanjay absent it could be a problem.

Where is Kumar with my breakfast, more important where *is* that bloody Sanjay? If Joshi turns up and finds him missing, he'll have me for bloody breakfast!

Sick of waiting he stood and walked towards the rear steps, he stopped at the kitchen and looked in. Kumar was sitting at the table, wiping cutlery.

'What's your bloody game, Kumar?'

Nonchalant and disinterested, his head shook slowly from side to side.

'Did you hear me?'

It nodded this time.

'Jesus wept! Don't say I'm going to have trouble with you, I've got enough on my plate!'

'Then you won't need breakfast,' snapped Kumar.

'Oi! Lay off you cheeky sod! Did you look for Sanjay?'

Kumar, still focusing on his work, shook his head.

'For heaven's sake Kumar,' he said changing tactics to an appeal. 'Look son, I've had a hard week, don't sod about, take your eyes off that for a minute . . . look at me. Who has upset you, come on, talk to me!' he persuaded, knowing that a few chosen words usually overcame this temporary impasse.

It was a kind of role-play. Kumar would appear angry, John would appeal and manoeuvre with soft, deceptive words and always accomplished what he wanted. He tried this time to coax and moving closer he slide his arm across the bare shoulders, feeling the thrill of touching him for the first time in days.

'Have you missed me?' he whispered, 'I know I haven't had time for you lately, I'm sorry. Let's have breakfast together, come on son.'

'And Sanjay?'

'What about him?'

'I saw him yesterday,' Kumar said with cool belligerence as John's arm, strong and caressing, wrapped around his young shoulders and large soft hands stroked his neck. For a moment Kumar seemed to weaken, John felt him shiver, evidently aroused. His breathing quickened, his eyes closed briefly as if thrilled with the stimulation of John's caress.

John moved closer still, his smile of self-assurance returned, he bent forward, his face close to Kumar's ear, 'Look son I . . .'

'No,' he shouted and leapt to his feet rocking the table violently, sending the chair sprawling, 'have you looked in your bed?' he yelled defiantly as John stepped backward, shocked with the ferocity of his reaction, staring into a face twisted into ugly hostility.

'My bed?' he said looking aghast, 'I have nothing to do with him!'

'Liar!' he spat and moved around the table towards the door.

Was this Kumar, gentle, submissive Kumar who never raised his voice?

'I am not a liar!'

'You are!' Kumar shouted. 'You lie to everyone, your wife died in childbirth,' he scorned, 'what wife? You had no wife, only boys, it's why you came here, hoping to share us with Colin until he left, you took to Sanjay and then me. Now you change back again . . .'

'What are you saying? Use your imagination in our liaisons if you like son, but don't talk stupid . . .'

'Sanjay is stupid . . .' he wanted to say depraved, 'and so are you!'

Unlike Sanjay, he'd been innocent and vulnerable and fallen victim to John's charm. He wanted to tell him that like Sunil, he might believe in John's ability to run Orphindi, but not in him, and now he considered himself a security shield alongside Sunil. He wanted to tell him that seeing the woman had made him realise he was not what John believed him to be but something moulded from innocence and ignorance. He wanted to say, 'don't lie to me, lie with him as you did yesterday!'

Astutely though, even in temper, he saw no advantage in burning bridges. As his aunt had taught him, he reserved his words and pushed past John hissing, 'Go back to Sanjay,' and stalked from the kitchen.

John, in complete confusion, stood motionless, numbed by aggressive charges and bewildered as regards their origins.

He stared at Kumar's back and opened his mouth to call but said nothing as his words echoed, 'Go back to Sanjay . . .'

Where the bloody hell did that come from?

* * *

With his head down on his chest, kicking at the ground, Kumar seethed and calculated the consequences of his argument as he stepped out smartly towards the camp.

He did not expect to forfeit anything and neither did he expect John to take retribution, he would treat it as a tantrum, expect his return and make amends. Well, things had changed, he would return and hopefully he would discover the depth of Sanjay's renewed friendship. Not that it mattered any more, he believed he had found himself and he knew now exactly what and who he was.

John's second betrayal was the final straw, it showed him up for what *he* was, a deceiver, a liar and a seducer, and Kumar felt not only justified but relieved in concluding their liaison. He wondered how Lord Shiva would deal with the situation, would he be vengeful, would he be forgiving or would he be careful to check, seek out opportunities and then capitalise? The latter he thought ... so the latter it would be.

Since working with the boys he had discovered his own abilities, he had influence, ability, aptitude and popularity, he had organisational skills, a natural interaction and an inborn understanding of machinery that, until now, in his cosseted life, he never realised, but then, he'd never been tested. His findings had increased his confidence, he may not be ready for everything but he was ready to try anything, he would follow Lord Shiva's advice, 'Do not rely, check, make sure and make use.'

The conclusions diffused his gloom and, satisfied, he increased his pace towards the camp through the tall brush. He would talk to Mrs Jha, she would show him the administration system and teach him more about the organisation and ...

He stopped, dead, a movement caught his eye. Intrigued, he ducked behind some tall burdock and, concealed by the undergrowth, watched Sanjay, fifty yards from him, trudging wearily towards the bungalow, his tired feet dragging tiny puffs of red dust. His sodden flowered shirt outside grimy shorts clung to him and matted hair dangled over a sweating forehead in the sweltering, exhausting heat.

He looked tired, as though he had been working, yet it was too early to finish. He came nearer and passed only ten yards from his hiding place, head down, eyes firmly fixed on the earth, tired feet tramping the track.

Amazingly, he was humming!

Stock still, Kumar waited until he had moved a respectable distance away then, dodging behind cover from bush to bush, he carefully tracked him back to the bungalow.

* * *

Prompted by Ahmed's warning and forced now to re-ingratiate himself with John, Sanjay had worked all night to finish the new building as part of his plan of appeasement.

Incited by worry, he had actually thought ahead for once and finished the outstanding tasks, leaving the building ready for habitation. It was inevitable that John would ask about Ahmed, his secondary sideline, but he might have to postpone those activities for a while but he could leave the way open for a resumption in trade later.

Never the less it was with a mixture of high hopes and trepidation that he made his way back to Paradise Lake.

The work had drained him, he tramped along the dusty footpath mentally checking the list, drains connected, generator working, lights and water on, anything else? No, even the rubble had been cleared. He stopped humming when he climbed the steps of what appeared to be an empty bungalow, apart from a gardener poking about at the rear. He entered the vacant kitchen, desperate for a beer, and took three cans from the fridge. He drank one down thirstily where he stood, left the empty can and picked up the other two.

As he emerged, he almost collided with John.

'Sanjay,' he said pleasantly, surprised and remarkably cheerful, 'I've been looking for you everywhere. Where have you been?'

He clutched the cans so tightly he thought they would burst, 'Working,' he said.

John laughed, 'Been on the nightshift have we? If I had known, I'd have sent a torch!'

'The generator was on, I had light,' he said humourlessly. 'I'm surprised you didn't hear it.'

John cast him a disdainful glance, 'Sit down and drink your beer,' he said, 'I'll make some tea, I want a chat.'

* * *

Perched on the edge of his chair Sanjay opened a can of beer that squirted over him before he nervously poured the remainder into his parched mouth. He heard John rattle china in the kitchen, and, expecting the worst, sure that Ahmed would be on the agenda, he watched John come out of the kitchen carrying a tray, smiling agreeably. He sat opposite.

'Working,' he said cheerfully, 'all night eh? You'll tell me it's finished next?' he joked as he poured tea.

It was another of John's soft lead-ins, like the words of a priest to a dying man. Sanjay felt constrained. If he spoke, he would most likely open the door to biting criticism and a blasting censure on the very subject he was trying to avoid. He remained silent; John watched him over the rim of his teacup.

He pulled nervously at the ring on the third can and, trying to look casual, he moved the can towards his mouth. Just before it reached his lips, he mumbled, 'It is finished.'

In the middle of swallowing tea, John choked, coughed and dribbled liquid on his chin. The indignity caused a sneaked grin from Sanjay. John wiped his mouth on the back of his hand. 'It's what?'

'I hired some help, it's OK I paid them out of my own pocket,' he said quickly.

John shook his head and stared, 'Finished?' he said in disbelief and, with a look of suspicion that heightened Sanjay's belief that he was thinking up something sarcastic to goad, irritated and berate him about, he said again, 'Finished ... are you serious?'

Sanjay nodded.

'What – all of it?'

'Isn't that what finished means?' he said, chancing his arm.

John shook his head, 'I don't believe it ... nice one,' he said appearing to congratulate him. 'Finished eh? I'll have to look at that ... Well, well, well. In that case, I expect you are hungry. Chef will make something special when he comes back, I'd ask Kumar to do it now but he's out, God only knows where he gets to lately.'

'I can look after myself,' replied Sanjay selflessly.

'That's right Sanjay,' said John, 'you most certainly can!'

That was it! The tone told him something was brewing. Sanjay held tight to his can as John's meaningful look lingered a fraction too long ... was he about to mention Ahmed?

He didn't, and hoping he wouldn't he sipped, trying to fathom John's, long silent scrutinising gaze. Where would he pounce? He could stand it no longer, 'What,' he said, 'what's wrong?'

'Well my son,' John drawled, 'since you ask, things haven't been right between us lately have they, and that upsets me Sanjay.'

He tipped the can down his throat, trying to figure where the attack would come from, his eyes now fixed on John's face. Is that the tone of truce or cunning? John often waited before striking, like a hangman tensioning the noose before opening the trap door.

John gazed at the tea cup. 'To be honest Sanjay, you have been neglected, ignored and, I'm ashamed to say, wronged sometimes ... it's my fault.'

An apology – was it a trap? It had to be a trap. He waited again without speaking ... any second now ...

'I'm uncomfortable, I have harassed you relentlessly, and what have you been doing without my knowledge eh? What have you been doing ...?'

Sanjay was on the verge of panic, he'd heard this preamble before, he lifted the can and closed his eyes as though part of his drinking habit.

219

'Without one word, you have finished my building ... brilliant! Frankly, I am embarrassed.'

The empty beer can fell with a hollow clatter on the floor; he left it, he couldn't believe it, words of praise, and yet ...

'Frankly Sanjay, my son, I feel guilty and ...'

Unable to comprehend the about turn and knowing John's unpredictability Sanjay remained cautiously quiet, John's apparent repentance would not fool him, he'd seen it all before. Yet, with an expression that Sanjay interpreted as apologetic and a tone that was conciliatory, he said he had seen Mitra who had considered Sanjay's idea. He had decided to negotiate with the lovers.

'Now, confidentially my son; we are forming a new limited company, you will be a partner ...'

It was a dream, praise not complaints, offers not rebukes, it did not ring true, and yet ...

'Mitra is particularly keen. He is grateful for all the business that you brought him, he thinks a lot of your abilities. I know it's a bit cheeky, selling our trinkets behind my back, but he says it's creative and I agree – but I'll come to that in a minute. Graham and Nadeen will join us at Mitra's for dinner on Saturday. You know how high and bloody mighty he likes to be, everything has to be formal, so get yourself dolled up.'

Still held in the wrap of surprise Sanjay said weakly, 'A partnership ...?'

John nodded, 'You'll learn about it at dinner.'

Sanjay shook his head in stunned disbelief, it did not seem like a trick but he hadn't mentioned Ahmed yet.

'Keep it quiet mind – do you hear me? One word, especially to Kumar, and you are out, I know what you are for showing off in front of him. In the meantime, take a rest, run the boys ragged but stay away from town, do you hear? And one more thing,' he grinned, 'no restoration of privileges – keep out of my room.'

'I slept in the chair, I came to tell you about Mitra but fell asleep.'

'I know that but Kumar thought ... never mind. Now, let's come to Ahmed ... all right son,' he said quickly, tolerantly, seeing his instant discomfort, 'I know all about Ahmed and your arrangements,' he said patting his knee. 'Very imaginative Sanjay, I have straightened that out and, as of now, all the proceeds all go into one pot.'

Was it tiredness or perhaps the beer, he felt light-headed. The moment he had been dreading had come and gone and without a murmur, John had accepted, and applauded his dealings. Did he need any more proof of his sincerity? His grin widened and, with his head in buoyant euphoria, he couldn't quite grasp the significance of it all, he only heard an occasional word, 'Reconsidered . . . enough for all . . . new start . . . partners, new transport for you . . .'

He flopped back in the chair stunned, giddy and overwhelmed by good fortune.

'Partners . . . transport?' he said as though anaesthetised and opened his mouth to say more but nothing came. His throat had tightened and his eyes filled, having lost all doubts. John had shown no malice but saw him, not just as a street thief, but also a resourceful, intelligent partner.

'You should have told me about your businesses Sanjay, we could have combined and expanded, I mean, just look at your sources.' He looked skywards, raised his hands, and, pressed a finger back. 'Workshop sales, carvings, pottery, jewellery, that sort of thing, jeans, from our friend Ahmed, he pressed a second finger. 'Nadu, you retain part of the payments I give him and receive a steady income from women's service charges, in cash too! but I'll come to that in a minute. He's leaving by the way,' he said casually.

The euphoria began to fade at the mention of the women. He feared he may have been lulled out of caution, was the crunch coming after all?! It usually did, his face reflected his worry.

John smiled, 'Don't look so concerned Sanjay, Ahmed told me everything. You don't seem to realise you have created a base for a Personnel Agency, we can now provide workers to industry. It's another winner. Clever my son, very, very, clever.'

The words cheered him, he felt euphoric again, 'I suppose so,' he said modestly, more surprised than ever at John's elation.

'One more thing Sanjay, did you do Mahmood's factory floor?'

'Nadu, not me . . . it's not paid for yet.'

'Then it must be,' he said, 'I'll see him myself, it will be a rare pleasure.' He paused for a moment, to empty his cup.

'Do you know my son, Mitra is a shrewd bugger, no wonder he wanted you with us. You have a natural aptitude for business and I've know it for a long time. Now, getting back to the women, how did you keep them quiet?'

'While they work for Ahmed and I am in charge of their kids, they all do as they are told.'

'Clever Sanjay, very clever and what a bloody good income too,' he said approvingly, 'you control the kids and their mums by obligation. No wonder the lads wouldn't say anything to Joshi.'

'Joshi?' he said feeling a, now familiar, grip in his stomach, 'Which lads?'

'Anil and Kenneth, no need to worry though,' he said putting Sanjay's mind at rest right away, 'it's all over.'

He relaxed again and with all doubt removed Sanjay hid nothing.

Relieved by John's support he explained not only his sidelines but his connections in town. John concealed his shock in silence and purred encouragement, 'Good work, very clever Sanjay,' his apparent authorisation increasing the flowing frankness, justifying and rationalising his grubby sidelines under the asylum of endorsement.

Still aware of a potential ambush, Sanjay used his final escape route, 'I saved the money for you.'

'I knew it!' said John triumphantly, slapping his knee, 'I told Mitra you would do exactly that.'

Sanjay grinned and with his vanity roused to an incautious peak, he stood, 'Wait a minute,' he said and went to his room to return grinning and waving a wad of rupees.

John laughed and flicked the edges, I knew you were the best thief in the business. How much?'

'About fifty thousand.'

'Fifty thousand . . .? Is that . . .' about to remonstrate at the paltry amount he stopped himself, appeasement was the order of the day. 'Why didn't you buy transport, there's enough here?'

'Now who's being stupid? You would know.'   .

'Ah yes, of course.' he said, continuous in his approval. 'You see Sanjay, that's clever thinking. We'll have to get one thing straight though, no more hotel business and drop your friends in town. That has to stop.'

Sanjay looked peeved but nodded.

'Well, that's about everything, I'll see Mahmood and . . .' he stopped suddenly, 'No . . . one more question. That trouble with Grewall, what happened?'

'He interfered, I nearly had him trained.'

'Who Samuel . . . on the verge was he? I see, let's hope Joshi doesn't find Grewall then, not that there's any likelihood of that, by the way, did you hide that money?'

Sanjay laughed, 'No, I told one of the boys it was a joke. As you said, control by obligation.'

'You haven't lost your ability have you my son?' said John. 'Inventive, resourceful, artful, I simply can't think like you. Now then 'he said, 'you must be tired, get yourself to bed, I'll wake you when Chef's got something ready. Off you go . . .'

Confident and safe, Sanjay stood. John's tolerant acquiescence proved without doubt that he had made the right impact and the right decision. He was admired, not vilified, praised not rebuked and there had been no need to worry at all.

* * *

Kumar, furious with what he had heard, waited before he crept away from concealment and resumed his walk towards the camp, wiser in some respects, more confused in others.

With Sanjay reinstated he was about to be discarded, that was obvious, the conspiratorial remarks proved it, 'Don't tell Kumar' indeed! How could John accept what Sanjay had done without censure, it was disgraceful and immoral – and the change of plan was intriguing too. Would John and Mitra really hand part control to the opposition placing themselves in the very position they sought to avoid? It was bizarre and worse for him if they joined in partnership, he saw a swift erosion of his own future.

Yet something did not ring true. Was John trying to fool witless Sanjay again? He knew John's mercenary ambitions were paramount now and he was far too selfish to share the spoils with gullible Sanjay. No, something was not right.

He lifted his head from his deliberations and looked ahead. A dust cloud approached. He recognised Joshi's car at the front of it and stepped quickly aside from the track again to duck behind a bush. It passed him slowing down and, for a second time that morning, he turned on his heels and raced back to his listening post.

* * *

While Sanjay slept, John congratulated himself on the ease with which he'd acquired the incriminating information, appalled at Sanjay's involvement in such depraved businesses. If Joshi got wind of it he could be considered guilty by association: Sanjay had outlived his usefulness. His sidelines were a waste of effort, fifty thousand rupees from a year of stealing? It was hardly worth the bloody petrol. But then, he was always a shallow thinker. Petty thieving was his game and his excitement, it was in his blood and, no matter what, he would remain a petty thief! His mate Ahmed had the right idea, his hundred thousand was more like it.

With Mr Singh's information, Graham's bank balance of five grand would eventually help. The bloody crook had not only indulged himself at Orphindi's expense, misdirecting and drip-feeding contributions, but, according to Colin's enquiries, he had stuck to the ten thousand left to John in his will by a repentant father.

Keeping Joshi at bay until Sanjay reached his sell by date was a dilemma with which he had to deal, and as for Kumar – teenagers! His strange fits of pique were baffling lately but it was to be expected, he supposed. All the same, his long absences were curious and John couldn't resist random checks. Without a word, he would poke his head round the kitchen door – to the surprise of Chef and Vijay – say nothing, and retreat to his favourite chair, where he now sat, in the rising humidity.

He wiped the sweat from his forehead with the back of his hand and looked at his watch. Ten thirty a.m. He re-filled his glass with lime-juice as the sound of an engine reached him. That would be Vijay back from his errand. He stood and walked to the steps just as Joshi's khaki police car pulled up.

His heart sank; he closed his eyes as if in prayer and said in despair, 'Oh Christ!'

'Namaste, Shankar,' he said pleasantly.

Joshi leaned from the rear window. 'Some developments John,' he replied. 'Is Parmar still in your care?'

'Asleep in his room,' he said.

'Good, keep him here, I will see you next week. In the meantime would you ask, discreetly, if he knows a man named Jaitley?'

His heart skipped a beat. 'Jaitley,' he said looking puzzled, 'certainly – why?'

'I have an interest, who is he, where is he, anything – keep it low key.'

'Jaitley,' repeated John. 'OK, Shankar.' His mind was working like mad. 'By the way, I'm taking Sanjay to dinner with Dhankar Mitra tomorrow, is that alright?'

'That's fine John. Don't forget Jaitely. I'll see you next week. Namaste.'

The sergeant put the car in gear and pulled away, John stood watching the receding cloud.

'Jaitley,' he said, 'Ahmed bloody Jaitley – now there's a thing. No time to lose, I'll kill two birds.'

THIRTY-THREE

His finger raced up familiar columns in a familiar Friday ritual, the whiskered face creased in concentration, spectacles slid down his sweaty nose causing him to lift his head to focus. Having checked once, Ahmed checked again – slower this time – yes, the figures were correct. He leaned back to a series of creaks from his ancient chair and his ancient frame, nervous and apprehensive, waiting for twelve o'clock when Mahmood, the messenger said, would arrive.

Before Prichard's visit, he had been content with his progress, now he would have to start again. It wasn't only the hundred thousand that had disappeared with the motorbike, but the prospects of an early retirement. He was irked too; something exciting had gone together with his hard-earned cash, leaving a vacuum filled with boredom and mounting disgruntlement. It was not only the money – it was the thrill, the illegality of it all and the pleasure of getting something for nothing. He had paid the price once but this, he thought, had been an untraceable certainty until Prichard's intervention.

His apprehension increased as the time passed. Mahmood might be a sloth of a man but he was astute and Ahmed had made sure, before his arrival, through shuffling forays into the workshop, that it buzzed, cuffing the boys and berating the cutters with a rule of fear, tactics that were perceived by him to be good management. It had always paid dividends, yet strangely, and he could not understand why, output was higher than ever. Had it not been for Prichard resolving the issue by offering to dispose of the surplus, he would have a problem explaining to Mahmood a sudden increase in warehouse stock.

Satisfied the modifications tallied, he swept all the other papers into a pile, pushed them to one corner of the table and placed his new sheet in the centre. He drew from his jacket pocket a soiled piece of cloth resembling a grey handkerchief to wipe his forehead. The dampness served to clear the smuts on his glasses as he held them high, peering critically through the lenses into the mote-filled sunlight. Satisfied, he adjusted them on his bony nose then, opening the drawer, took out a pile of old and limp rupee notes.

He stopped to listen for a moment, turning his head in the direction of the door. Was that a motorcycle engine? He hoped not, not with Mahmood due.

It was, and the machine stopped with a h-rrr-ump.

Ahmed stood as quickly as his painful back would allow, dragged himself to the unlocked door and peered through the crack with no intention of allowing entry.

A sinking feeling hit his stomach, his face drained of blood. 'No!' he whispered looking up in dismay. His instinct told him this would not be enjoyable.

Backed by bright sunshine the figure totally filled the doorway when the door was pushed open. There was only one person of that size. Ahmed stepped backwards, out of the way, as John strode into the room.

Hoping to preserve some status, he said politely, 'Good afternoon Mr Prichard.'

'Pack your things Mr Jaitley!'

'How dare you! Pack . . . what?' he stammered, his inert face pallid under the stubble. 'I have done all you asked Mr Prichard and . . .'

'There's been a new development. You are leaving, unless you want to join your business partner now being investigated by the police.'

If John's appearance worried him, the announcement sent shock waves from his head to his feet. 'The police,' he spluttered '. . . leave . . . Police?' he whispered, the words choking in his throat, 'It has taken me ages to recover from . . . I mean, I'll never get . . . work is hard to find.'

'You should have thought of that before you stole from my women and started your nasty little enterprise in town. Now, clear off, unless you want to join your pal in jail.'

He opened his mouth to say something but John's look struck terror into him. Caught between an unpalatable decision and a meeting with Joshi, Ahmed's courage failed. He moved surprisingly quickly for someone who creaked and, collecting his belongings; he placed them on his mat and rolled it into a sausage. Opening the cupboard, he started to remove a black ledger.

'Leave that, take what is owed from that cash!'

The slam of a car door heralding the appearance of Mahmood galvanised him further. He hastened to count his dues as Mahmood's frame filled the lower half of the doorway, accompanied as usual by the smell of stale cigars.

With oily pleasantness he said, 'You are early John . . .' stopping in mid sentence. 'What are you doing Jaitely?'

'I cannot continue working with Periyar Fashions, something has arisen, a personal matter,' he said in a sudden breathless surge. 'I must leave immediately. If you will be good enough to allow me to take what is due . . .'

He turned back to the pile of cash.

'Just a minute . . .' started Mahmood.

'. . . I am sorry, I will not be moved,' he gushed, 'I must leave immediately,' and dipped his head to finish the task. He was soon done, and in a moment he picked up his things and shambled past them without a word.

Mahmood's mouth opened, 'What, in the name of Shiva . . .?'

'Bad news apparently, he was packing when I arrived.'

'What am I to do with no manager? I have no time to run this place,' said Mahmood, fretful and apprehensive.

Towering over him, John looked at the troubled, waxy face puffing the cigar. 'Well,' he said slowly, as though thinking his way through, 'I might have someone you can use temporarily.'

'It's not that simple, factories are not easy to organise.'

John laughed, 'Huh! Have you forgotten, Harbens, that I run an organisation of hundreds? I'll talk to the women now and in the morning I'll be here with a man or two. If you are not happy inside a week I'll take them out.'

Mahmood looked desperate. 'A week's trial, free of charge?'

'Free. But if they are successful you pay double.'

Mahmood looked doubtful, but trapped and in no position to argue, he agreed.

'While you are here,' said John, 'there is another matter – I am only the messenger you understand,' he said quickly. 'Now, how can I put this?' He held his chin for a moment, 'I know . . . let me show you something.' He stepped forward a few paces and opened the door to the factory, 'Come out here.'

'What?'

'You're standing on it!' he said pointing down. 'Handling debts Harbens is, as you know, a matter of delicacy.'

Despite the noisy factory, John could hear his wheezy breathing quicken. Mahmood's look of surprised anger gave John a moment of pure enjoyment; he had Mahmood in a corner. He'd never liked the greasy man, his appearance alone created an aversion. A great hard balloon-like belly rose and fell under his unbuttoned buff jacket and his blue cotton shirt, wet around the chest, hung over shapeless trousers. Receding hair on a skull, shining with sweat, completed the unsavoury picture. John watched him pull a handkerchief from his pocket and wipe his bulky face and thought if he did an honest day's work he might loose weight. He grinned wickedly, he'll be relieved of some in a minute.

'I see,' said Mahmood.

'Your friend asked me to keep his proceeds safe until he returns,' he said lightly, 'a sort of guarantee of confidentiality, Harbens. As I said, this is a delicate matter and we need to keep it confidential, particularly since there may be an enforced absence.'

Mahmood's jowls drooped like a bloodhound, enhancing his sour expression. His forehead creased in distinct lines and he dribbled sweat, 'Enforced, you said?'

'I did, our new Police Inspector has an interest.'

'I see.'

John stooped low. He couldn't resist whispering, 'I thought you would!' and recoiled from the smell of stale, smoky breath. 'I have a receipt for the cash, signed on his behalf. It will secure your exclusion from any proceedings,' he said feeling like Mitra with the flowery language. 'I am only the errand boy but your friend, who can be quite vindictive, tells me he is prepared to look after your interests if he is indisposed provided the payment is in his hands.'

Mahmood closed his eyes for a moment and nodded, 'I see. Where is my guarantee?'

'Here, it's all perfectly normal, I will confirm that he did the work if I am asked, without involving our friend Nadu.'

Mahmood gave another assenting sigh and took a chequebook from his pocket.

'No thank-you my friend, rupees please! Our acquaintance needs to see the cash!'

THIRTY-FOUR

Sunil stood outside the office door surveying the outside of the dilapidated building, while John unlocked the factory. It was prison-like with dirty white paint peeling from walls and a line of tiny closed windows covered in dust and grime high up in the wall.

His gaze took him to the employees gathered outside the rear doors; he recognised several and thought it odd that so many Orphindi mothers worked here.

John opened the door and, stepped inside the dingy office, Sunil followed and looked around at the squalid interior. 'What's this, a store room? Am I expected to work here?'

'Don't complain son, clean it up while I am at the bank,' said John quickly, sensing a complaint. 'Open up and get that lot working, see what you can make of the place before I come back.'

After setting the girls to work, Sunil stood in the middle of the dingy office and watched John depart. He looked around at the sordid mess and shook his head, not sure where to start. First, he opened the street door to improve the miserly light and now that he could see the labels clearly, he tried all the cabinets and drawers.

His teeth clenched at the screeching drawer when he took out a file marked, 'Production Returns.' He cast a scrutinising eye over the contents and put it aside. He tried the 'Staff' file and placed it on the table.

After pulling hard at the window, which would not budge, he gave up and turned his attention to the factory and, opening the door, the overpowering humidity and odour of confined bodies mixed with the sound of whirring machines hit him. He waited a moment while the draught cleared the air before stepping into the factory proper.

For a moment, he stood in the doorway watching the activity, to his left the cutter and his assistant kept their eyes down while the women, in uniform rows, did likewise. He walked slowly along the central aisle looking left and right observing the working pace, and, recognising a young widow he stopped.

'Namaste, Sangeeta?' he said above the din.

229

'Mr Sunil, namaste,' she said returning his smile, 'Why are you here?'

'Helping, that's all Sangeeta, how are your two girls?'

'Much better now.'

'Have they been ill?'

'No,' she said smiling. 'Hasn't Mr John told you?'

'Told me what?'

He listened while she explained, 'Mr John is a good man Mr Sunil.'

'He is Sangeeta. Your son is well, I will tell him I saw you.'

He continued his walk conversing, learning, making mental notes and forming pictures. He reached the warehouse. Two boys scurried at his request to clean the office and while they were occupied, he examined the cloth and finished goods. Half an hour later the boys returned, he left the warehouse and stopped at the cutter's bench.

'Namaste, I am Sunil, what is your name and who is in charge here?'

'I am sir, I am Raju.'

'When you have finished that batch Raju, please come into the office.' He caught the cutter's look of alarm and said reassuringly, 'I need your help.'

The office looked cleaner and felt fresher and with both doors open. He turned his attention to the cabinets again, removing a file marked, 'Purchases,' and another marked 'Production Returns'. A black ledger drew his attention, partly hidden, in a corner. He took all the books, cleared the table and laid them side by side, leaned over them and compared purchases, sales, quantities and prices. Checking the seat of the creaky chair, he sat down and took up a pencil; sales of goods, deliveries, stock, production. He looked at specifications, two point five metres per pair multiplied by . . .

Sensing a presence, he looked up. The cutter stood nervously to one side of the doorway, his hands clasped in front of him.

'Come in Raju, fetch a chair and sit with me.'

With Raju apprehensive and sweat dampening his turban, Sunil laid before him a page showing production returns. 'Is this Mr Ahmed's writing?'

Raju's eyes darted from the sheets to Sunil's face and back. 'I do not know, I collect the slips only sir.'

'Which slips?'

'Output sir, daily returns, they are kept there, one for each of us.' He pointed to a box on top of the cupboard.

Sunil lifted the box down, checked and found the batches he wanted.

'How many employees Ragu?'

'Thirty sir.'

He counted several wads, 'Are you sure?' he said holding the batch towards him, 'there are only twenty eight in some. I suppose we have absentees?'

'No sir, never less than thirty, sir, we replace absentees.'

Sunil pondered for a moment, 'I see,' he said and asked Raju to call out the quantities. Half an hour, and a dozen questions later, Sunil sat back, content that he had solved some of the ambiguity in mismatched figures. 'That's fine Raju, thank-you, you may go.'

Raju started to close the office door, 'Leave that please, it will help keep the factory cool – and get someone to open and then clean those windows.'

'Yes sir, certainly sir,' he said, grinning.

Sunil settled in the chair, took out the slips and checked again, then on a note pad he began to compare, opening stock, closing stock, purchases, sales, output . . .

* * *

He knew it was John. The distinct thump of the single cylinder Enfield gave it away and, looking through the open door, he saw him dismount. Dropping his pencil, he leaned back in the chair to wait, fixing him with an inflexible look as soon as he entered.

'That's a lot better, son,' he said cheerily, looking around. 'Move over, I'll get this pay ready and I can be off.' He laid the bag of coins and notes on the table.

'Sit down!' said Sunil firmly, 'Look at this.'

'Not now I haven't got time . . .'

'Then make time,' said Sunil resolutely, fixing him with a commanding glare.

John sat.

'This,' said Sunil, pointing to a sheet, 'is an analysis of production, wages and costs per unit, and this,' he pointed to another, 'is a record of sales. Each girl produces twenty pairs; thirty girls produce six hundred pairs per day yet only five hundred and eighty pairs are recorded . . . why the discrepancy?'

John pulled a face, 'How do I know? It's not our worry and we don't want to rock the boat. Just carry on.'

'Am I expected to run this factory?' said Sunil fixing him with an insistent stare.

'Temporarily.'

'Then it will be run properly. Twenty pairs, and sometimes forty, are missing and . . .'

231

'Forget it,' snapped John. 'I will look after that.'

'I see,' he mused. 'Well let me tell you! In unit costing it is a fact that with stable labour higher output reduces costs, yet here costs are constant as output increases.' He paused and looked into John's eyes. 'Someone has been doctoring these returns – and not very cleverly.

'I said I'll look after it.'

Sunil laughed. 'You said that before, but *you* only look after *you*!'

'I look after you too!' he patronised.

Sunil shook his head, 'When will you realise I will not be your accomplice?'

'And when will you realise that you cannot hold a past transgression over me forever? I didn't know what he was up to and none of the boys were harmed!'

'No! I prevented it, apart from Kumar! Your proficiency and fatherly love coerced that child while I was at college, you had your lecherous claws into him before I could do anything about it. Now he doesn't know who or what he is! Thank Lord Shiva that your blond friend decamped when he did! I hope he didn't leave his legacy with you.' he said vehemently. 'I told you before, stop these games or I will stop you! I have been hearing things recently.'

'That's nothing to do with me,' retorted John.

'I hope not! I live in town and see something of what goes on!' he snapped, showing none of the tolerance known to visitors.

'I said those days are over! I stuck to my word, I have always looked after you and Vijay.'

Sunil gave a repetitive, knowing, nod, 'You were compelled to,' and stayed silent, staring at John, long and hard. 'You knew about this didn't you?'

'It's not my concern.'

'But you knew about the stealing and hoped I wouldn't notice. What were you hoping, that I would perpetuate it . . . what are you doing with the surplus?'

'If, as you say, there is a surplus, someone will take it, a shop, a store or a . . .'

'A thief?'

'What are you implying?'

'Nothing, I am telling you. I will run this business my way and I will run it honestly!'

'Just you hold on! I got rid of the last manager because he was robbing the mothers of money and Mahmood of goods and . . .'

'*So you did know*!' Sunil said triumphantly and paused to watch

John's embarrassment. 'And what do you mean by, 'the mother's money?' he asked quietly.

'Ahmed was taking a commission from them and . . .'

'And you reinstated their earnings,' said Sunil finishing the sentence. 'I heard. Did you return the money to Kenneth's mother?'

'It wasn't much . . .'

'Liar!' he interrupted again. 'You took it didn't you? Ready to take over where he left off were you?'

John wouldn't meet his gaze; he looked glumly down at the table.

'Ahmed himself paid for two girls and kept their output, he stored it in the warehouse for you to pick up didn't he? How do you dispose of it?'

'Ahmed was taking food from their mouths,' countered John, 'I saved them and deserve recompense. Anyway, Mahmood never knew then, and there is no reason for him to know now!'

'And neither did the women. They think you are wonderful because you stopped the service charges, they don't know you put the residue into your own pocket!'

Sunil rested one elbow on the desk and leaned towards John. 'I have learned a lot this morning. I know you helped them and they are grateful, but because you did them a service on one hand you have no right to rob them with the other. They can believe you are a fairy godfather if they like, but you a mercenary deceiver and you will pay those women back their money. So do it and keep out of my way and away from those boys – I said I've been hearing things.'

'That business in town is nothing to do with me.'

'Perhaps, but that remains to be seen,' said Sunil continuing his hard line. 'Vijay and me will run this place and any extra production will benefit the women, not you, so return that money – and tell Sanjay to stop whatever dirty little game he is playing in Amitar or I will intervene.'

John looked ready to erupt, he bit his lip and slapped his knees as he stood. 'Alright, alright,' he retorted in a fit of petulance, 'it's all yours.' He pointed to the wages on the table, 'and you can sort that out too – make sure you do it right, we wouldn't want your precious ladies to be short changed would we?'

Sunil grinned, 'Good to see that you understand. Now, tomorrow Vijay will work out what you owe the women and collect it, namaste.'

John stood up, his face a picture of thwarted fury. 'You nasty bastard, make your own way back to Amitar,' he snarled and stomped out.

Sunil laughed, 'I'll take a taxi . . . I'll give you the bill.'

THIRTY-FIVE

Saturday morning

The rat-tat-tat of the heavy mechanical chisel shook the ground as it split the rock with its unstoppable power. The red volcanic base yielded easily to the constant assault by the powerful device, operated inside a closed window of a vibrating cab filled with a mixture of smoke, from a soggy cigarette, and swirling dust. Sweat shook from the driver's forehead and nose soaking both the cigarette and his lunghi.

Knowing his stuff, he selected peaks severe enough to damage the underside of vehicles and moved his machine slowly along the track, attacking one after the other, easily removing the peaks, leaving a trail of melon sized pieces for the boys to break down as they followed in his wake. With no time for rest, the driver worked steadily and continuously. He spat out the old cigarette, pulled a dry one from a battered packet, lit it and pulled again at levers, hammering the ground and rattling his teeth.

The lone operator smiled as he watched the vigour of the inexperienced from his sweaty, stinking cab, 'All effort and no effect' he grinned without sympathy, used to seeing whole families, from father to toddler, grapple with the heavy rocks. It was common practice and a game to children, who diligently helped their father reach his work target, keep his job and survive.

The group at first gazed in wonder as the huge noisy beast carved great lumps from the ground giving rise to clouds of dust that hung in the humid air and stuck to damp bodies. No part escaped. Heads, arms, legs and torsos were coated as if painted with red mud, through which tracks of sweat coursed like rivers on a map. In just one day, the machine could produce enough rubble to occupy fifty men for weeks; in their place were twenty-five boys between six and twelve years old, stripped to the waist. The driver had shown them how to crack the volcanic rock into segments with a sledge hammer, too big and too dangerous for skinny, underdeveloped arms, yet they

234

performed the backbreaking, tedious work, severe even for full grown men, at the order of their benefactor.

Left to supervise, an unhappy Vijay took on the heavy work. He swung the sledge, breaking the larger pieces. When there were sufficient, he squatted on his haunches with the boys and chipped the material into fragments with a hammer, raked, tamped and levelled it to form a crude but flat, road.

Some of the bigger boys shared the heavy labour while the youngsters chipped. Rock flew randomly and incessantly, smacking into bodies with painful pricks as the volcanic material struck. Small bodies and thin arms took punishment, exhausted in unrelenting, withering heat. Assailed by the machine clanking and beating the devil's tattoo, their brains shook in unison with the pounding apparatus.

Under the scorching sun there was no respite and, at the end of only an hour, backs ached, arms were leaden and shins sore, bodies were so covered in red rivulets that they looked as though they were bleeding to death.

Vijay surveyed the activity, the process was brutal, the demands cruel, age no consideration and the outcome, John's personal gain. It was unjust and dangerous, rousing him to uncharacteristic anger. It had to stop. The boys, now red from head to foot, began to slow and then collapse under the severity of the task.

He stood, surveying the spectacle, considered his options and called a halt.

He walked to the bungalow.

* * *

Kumar could hear the hammering from inside the kitchen, he stood at the top of the rear steps and looked across the terrain towards Amitar. A low cloud of red ochre dust rose behind the weary, bedraggled figure of Vijay as he approached. He had no need to ask what was wrong.

'How long will they last Vijay?'

'One English hour,' Vijay replied through clenched teeth with ironic humour, 'They can handle the light chipping but they not the sledges, there will be accidents. Sanjay ordered a change every four hours, it's too much, then expects them to prepare their own meals and cover the camp chores. We want labourers.'

'John is out,' said Kumar, 'but wait.' Turning to Chef he said, 'fill that container with lime juice, slice a dozen mangoes and come with me.'

Chef started to protest, 'I have to prepare Mr John's . . .'

'Do as I say,' snapped Kumar, 'he can wait!' Minutes later all three, handed out refreshments to the exhausted boys. Kumar picked up a hammer, sat and chipped, watching points as the chisel drove into the rock, noting a head turned in one direction was often the recipient of someone else's chip.

He stood, for a moment, 'From now Vijay, they work half an hour and rest for ten minutes. After two hours they return to camp, they will not use the sledges, push the large pieces aside. Sort the boys into groups of four, well apart with their backs to each other to lessen the danger, in the meantime, stay here and help with the heavy work until I return.

'Chef, go to the Outpost, prepare the next group, arrange meals and refreshments for these, find some oils, they will need a massage, then come back and take over from Vijay, I will need him after I see Mr John.'

He collected the empty containers and hurried off, angry. He concentrated on how he could influence John and, hurrying back, he heard the distinctive reverberation as the Enfield, approached from behind. It drew level and stopped.

Despite his unsuccessful handling of Sunil, John showed no signs of hostility when he told Kumar to jump on. 'Giving the boys a drink are we, good idea, I gave them a wave, they're happy enough,' he said cheerfully.

Kumar shook his head. There were times that his greed made him inhuman, and his absence of compassion was upsetting, it placed him in the same mental category as Sanjay. Kumar though could ignore that for the present, he had an objective and John was in an affable mood.

'You left early Mr John, where have you been?'

'The telex office and Periyar with Sunil. Why?'

'What is he doing at Periyar?'

'Helping to run a factory. I will need Vijay this afternoon.'

'Take him and work stops, Mr John, he is breaking the large rock. We need some labourers.'

'Why, they'll manage.' he said as they drew up to the bungalow.

Kumar slipped from the pillion, incensed, and thought of his aunt again, 'Discretion, diplomacy!'

'But you are their guardian Mr John, you should take care of them.'

'I do,' said John, swinging his leg over the saddle and smiling. 'You seem to be getting back to normal son, feeling better are we?' he asked placing an arm round Kumar's shoulders. 'By the way, I wanted a word about the other night. You got hold of the wrong end of the stick you know? Sanjay slept in my chair.'

Kumar knew, but appeared to acquiesce. 'Then I will have to make it up to you Mr John, but first I must take care of the injuries,' he lied. 'Can Vijay use the bus to take them to hospital?' he said, looking at John with an expression of childish innocence.

John stopped dead. 'No he bloody well won't! How bad are they?'

'One could loose an eye!'

'Don't be melodramatic Kumar! No one will loose an eye!'

'Some have been hurt with chips and one damaged his hand,' he said perpetuating the lie. 'I sent four back to camp for treatment in the first hour Mr John, and we have run out of first aid equipment. Shall I ask Vijay to buy a box when he takes them to hospital?' he said insistently.

'No.'

'Then can I get them some goggles . . . and some labourers? You must take care of them . . .'

'. . . I do take care bloody of them,' he said angrily, 'so leave off. You are beginning to sound like that bloody Samantha, she was always on about the poor little sods! It will do them good to learn how difficult it is in the world outside. They are tough enough . . . you don't seem to realise how . . . how important this is . . .'

'At the cost of an eye?' he said, noting John's hesitation.

'Well . . . alright get the box.'

'Thank you Mr John, I will take charge if you like.'

'You?' he said, 'where's Sanjay?'

'Probably sleeping Mr John – I shall take charge?'

'If you think you can,' he relented, worn down by arguing. 'You'll be no worse than him, he wouldn't see a tree until it fell on him – but keep away from that hospital.'

Kumar's face lit, 'I shall see you tonight then,' he said cunningly, aware of the answer.

'No, not tonight son, I am going to dinner.'

Kumar looked disappointed, 'I was hoping you would be here for me Mr John.'

The hint of a smile ghosted across his face, 'So that's what's been troubling you my son?' he said gently running his hand through Kumar's hair, 'there's always tomorrow Kumar . . . Look,' he said, reaching into his shorts pocket, 'what is it you want?'

'First Aid box and eye protectors – twenty five pairs.'

'OK, twenty five,' he agreed, fanning out the wad of rupee notes and selecting three, 'Here, take this, get Vijay to drive you to Amitar, Sunil can manage without him for a day, it might teach him a bloody lesson.'

'Thank you, Mr John, shall I get some labourers too?' he said grinning and pulling at the notes.

John smiled again, 'Cheeky sod,' he said smiling and released his grip.

* * *

Kumar, leaned against the inside door, watching Vijay steer and manipulate the gears.

'We have been together a long time Vijay,' he said casually.

Vijay nodded, 'Things are changing Kumar, we are becoming commercial and John is becoming greedy and unpredictable,' he said, reading Kumar's thoughts. 'Aren't you curious why he brought Sanjay back and why he checks up on you?'

'I know why. He is anxious about everything now.'

'Sunil said there need to be changes, things are returning to what they were ten years ago. When I told him about Samuel, he said he has been watching hotels in town and has suspicions. What John and Mitra argued about before seems to be happening again and that is why Sunil will not leave Orphindi. He doesn't trust John. Do you remember when Sunil argued at the big house?'

'Yes, before you went to college.'

'Well I was reminded of that when I went to the big house on Sunday. Do you remember John's blond friend, Colin? You were about ten; he had his eye on me – apparently. That's why Sunil raged.'

'They are still in touch Vijay, he has a tourist agency in England and when the changes come, he will be involved.'

'What changes?'

'I'm not sure but I will find out, tell Sunil too but no one else.'

Kumar stared from the window saying nothing and after a while, he turned in his seat towards Vijay. 'Will you tell me something Vijay; have you ever been with a woman?'

'No, why?'

'The dark one cornered me in her room, she was naked . . .'

'Really? What was she like?'

Kumar laughed, 'She made me think, about me and John. I wonder if I am what I am or what I have been trained to be. I never thought this way before, she was . . . well . . . lovely, and gave me feelings . . . I never thought about John until I saw her.'

'Yes, but what was she like?' he asked excitedly, 'did you see the other one? She is my favourite, so pretty, pale and neat . . .'

'That's not the point Vijay. I can't stop thinking about her, not just her body and her shape, that is not what I mean. Seeing her and thinking about her has made me unsure and confused about me. When I looked, I was surprised, pleased, afraid and very confused. She is very attractive and so different, I want to know more, I see women in another way now. I'd want to learn about them Vijay.'

'Talk to Sunil then, Kumar.'

'Yes,' he said thoughtfully. 'How long to Periyar?'

'Half Indin hour,' he laughed.

Kumar laughed too. 'Shall we see him now Vijay? John won't know. Then on the way back you will teach me how to drive!'

THIRTY-SIX

The mistrust she felt prior to the deliver of the letter from Mitra disappeared when she opened the envelope and saw an invitation that bore Mitra's signature. Nadeen's doubts reduced further when she read the contents.

Her demands had worked, John had communicated everything to Mitra and his authority added a degree of protection, it also removed the unpleasant obstacle of dealing entirely with John!

A note with the invitation, indicated an intention to discuss arrangements in a, 'New to be formed company,' and, with doubts dwindling, she spent time deciding on an equitable target before tackling Graham.

A twenty five percent share would suffice but as a starting point, she would ask for one third to net them a satisfactory starting level of control. Her intention was not to allow their portion to stay at that level but to increase their holding, and their power, without falling back on the knowledge they held.

Graham hardly looked at the invitation, so far as he was concerned they were about to receive a freebee, something for nothing, a gift. In his shallow, apathetic way he said, 'Take what you can get my girl, if you press and overdo it you will find them resentful and you know how spiteful dear brother can be.'

They argued a little – her resolutely ... 'You saw the way he crumbled in the face of our determination,' and Graham with lethargy ... 'Don't upset him my dear. Antagonise him and we might loose everything.'

She won, remembering they had evidence against both should they choose to use it.

'We must insist on a written agreement within a week, without that, we could be left with nothing but a nasty taste, Graham.'

'Indeed old girl,' he said, 'but be careful. They are cunning and Mitra is rich and, from what I have heard he will stop at nothing.'

His lethargy worried and frustrated her, he should not be content with something other than excellence, drive for more than they want and receive more than they expect, and, acting as devil's advocate, she primed and drilled him to counter his passivity.

Still doubtful when she stepped into the Mercedes on Saturday evening, she believed she would probably be negotiating on her own and sat stoic, determined and thoughtful in the rear.

They swished along in style. Her white, gold trimmed sari struck a stark contrast with her dark features. Her hair, peeping from under the gossamer cloth, pulled back tightly in a bun that allowed the gold edge to wrap, like a nuns habit, close to her face.

'This is the life old girl,' said cream-suited Graham. 'It could be worth conceding a little to ensure such extravagance, don't you think?'

She looked straight ahead, expressionless and nervous, ignoring his calm weakness, while the vehicle, insinuating luxury, swept through villages and up the mountain road towards Heavens Aspect. Even the sleek machine pulled hard as they approached the summit and braked constantly to control the swift downhill into the drive, stopping at the foot of the marble steps.

From the rear seats, they viewed the grandeur, unable to prevent self-satisfied smiles slipping across their faces. The oozing luxury caused her to lose any wish to war with her opponents, instead she envied the opulence, this was copious wealth beyond her wildest dreams and tonight, provided she could secure what she wanted, something similar could be theirs.

The Chauffeur slid from the driver's seat to open the doors and, for the first time, she saw Mitra at the top of the steps, wearing a Neru cap. Tight fitting white trousers clung to his ankles beneath a matching knee length white coat, closely clipped at the collar. She looked at his puckered grimace and raised eyebrows, sensing insincerity, as he showed his small teeth in a shallow, welcoming smile.

With hands raised, he said to Graham between pleated lips, 'Namaste, how very pleasing to meet you at last Mr Prichard, and you dear lady, how kind of you to accept the invitation to my humble home.'

She recognised his words as the conceit of understatement and followed him in. Graham gazed blatantly at the extravagance, she hinted at his indiscretion by tugging his sleeve.

John was already seated when they entered the room, casually but smartly dressed in a white open necked shirt and long dark trousers. She had never seen him without shorts, he was quite good looking when he was tidy, yet so unlike his brother. He stood to greet them.

'Good evening', he said pleasantly with a handshake and an unexpected smile to her and a nod to Graham, politely directing them towards a seat where, to her surprise, Sanjay, smartly dressed in slacks and shirt, stood and raised his hands.

'Namaste,' he said.

The evening got under way casually with small talk and drinks. Nadeen, like Sanjay, took only water and, she observed, that although John was far more affable in this company, Mitra took the lead. Parmar, completely out of place, was subservient, appearing in awe of what was happening. He said nothing, his assured conversation heard in the restaurant, missing.

Nadeen, having steeled herself for expected disagreements when the conversation turned to business, was surprised when Mitra gave way to her proposals. 'We must consider John, the extent to which our partners will contribute to the task. It is only right and proper, as we say, that they receive a one third share.'

No arguments, no intimidation and no need for her to use prepared justification. She breathed easily at the lack of dissension, knowing probably, that they could not fight against her resolute statements, particularly when she realised that her ally Sanjay's ten percent helped her and Graham.

She found the atmosphere sedate and composed over dinner, even Sanjay smiled and Graham, aided by the wine, became quickly amiable as business was forgotten. He congratulated Mitra on his rally success. It was a mistake.

With hands clasped, Mitra looked towards the ceiling. 'I was perfectly pleased, my dear friend. You may have read that the opposition was routed, a resounding defeat as the more observant newspapers noted. Those opposed were proved totally incorrect and their comments on the ineffectiveness of my campaign were shown as inaccuracies. In the coming weeks, with John at my side . . .'

What she had heard of Mitra was beginning to show, he was a conceited man, egotistical, carried away with self-importance and displaying a self-perceived popularity. Very soon, she found his crowing tiresome and looked about her. It was evident that others felt the same, John fidgeted, Sanjay was simply bewildered and stunned into silence by his elevation as she was by Mitra, while Graham became more affable, even with John, under the influence of wine.

It became late, she looked about her several times, hoping to catch Graham's eye, hoping he would see her discomfort and help with an excuse to leave. He looked as though he was listening but he was good at that, she worried that he might reach incapability, and caught

John's eye. He too looked dulled, contributing little except for a readiness to accommodate her. For one brief, weak moment, Nadeen felt a preference for his company to Mitra's. She actually smiled at him, without parting her lips of course, and in his nodded acknowledgement, she felt a first touch of unity.

Yet did she imagine it, there was something artificial, the easy agreement, the politeness, the conviviality? Was she being over suspicious? Somehow she could not purge the feeling.

It was nearly eleven when Mitra suggested, to her relief, 'Moving into the Drawing Room for coffee, in celebration of our new found partnership,' and by eleven thirty, she and Graham were standing in the porch ready to leave, pleased at the prospect of being beyond the sound of Mitra's voice.

As they said their goodbyes on the porch, a combination of the warm air and the dull evening began to affect even her alertness and she felt suddenly tired, the longing to return to her flat, overwhelming.

A manservant appeared from the direction of the garage, whispered an exchange of words with Mitra and left. A few minutes later, he was back, shaking his head.

Mitra's arms flapped with embarrassment, 'I fear we have met with a minor inconvenience my dear sir. We have, it seems, a fault with my vehicle.' He paused and looked towards John. 'It may have been damaged from a journey over rough terrain a few days ago. I am sure it will be dealt with in just a moment or two.'

Although irritated, her dignity would not allow her to protest; instead, she was amused at the effect on his and gave an understanding smile – even the mighty are vulnerable.

Minutes passed, Mitra's man returned, his body language announced a lack of success. She heard his impatient whisper, '. . . take the runabout,' before turning to them and saying, 'I'm sorry, will you be happy to use the spare vehicle? It is not a Mercedes of course but serviceable. Unfortunately it is not an automatic and my driver is unfamiliar.' He looked at Sanjay. 'I believe you are an accomplished driver Sanjay, would you do me a great service?'

Sanjay turned towards John, who nodded. 'Collect me later,' he said, 'I'll wait.'

'I can, of course', said Mitra quickly, trying to cover his embarrassment, 'ring for a taxi, if you are prepared to wait. Unfortunately it will take half an hour to reach us and I have grave doubts that a taxi will be in better condition than my man's vehicle.'

'Whichever you choose,' she said, holding Graham's arm tightly and pulling him closer as he began to sway.

A moment later a weather beaten, grey, Morris Oxford approached across the courtyard and rolled quietly to the steps. Sanjay climbed in the driver's seat and familiarised himself with the instruments, aided by Mitra's man who helpfully leaned forward with a smile. Thrusting his body deep inside pointing out switches and features, he gave laboured instructions.

Nadeen looked at Graham, his eyes were beginning to close, she pulled him closer, Mitra said goodnight and waved, the car began to roll into the black coolness.

Her eyes felt dry and sandy and, with a long thankful sigh she let them close, squeezing them tightly for a moment to remove the grittiness as the vehicle moved forward. Taking a final look at the mansion, she closed her eyes and relaxed completely in the modest comfort of a jasmine scented interior and slid her arm around Graham, letting his head sink to her breasts. His weight pressed her against the door; she smiled and looked at him as the road ahead blackened when the moon hid shyly behind the mountains.

The car moved swiftly forward, climbing towards the peak. With windows closed and a blower circulating cooling air, Nadeen sighed again, pleased to be clear of the contrived atmosphere and an egotistical, overbearing little man. She had shown, early on, without being too assertive, that she would not be intimidated but could, with reason, be persuaded. Now, having met the man, she sincerely hoped that the periods spent in his company would be limited.

'He has a very high opinion of himself, hasn't he,' she whispered, but the boredom, the alcohol and the comfort of her arms had overcome Graham's resistance. She pulled him to cradle his head against her and, yielding to the romance of the moment, stroked his hair.

Graham had been clever to inveigle the money meant for John from his father's estate; the old man finally relented to his wife's demand and left John ten thousand. He didn't deserve it so Graham had put most of it to better use buying their flat and providing for their future, releasing her into independence free from a domineering, conventional father. Now she had freedom to enlist in the modern world with new exciting opportunities, rescued from the tedium of life in an arranged marriage with someone she had never met.

The last few months had been heaven. Living, loving, devoted to each other. She forgave Graham's occasional lapse and now they were on the verge of an advance into comfort and a future about which they had only dreamed. It was in that moment she realised just how much he meant to her and how deeply she had grown to love him.

The journey would take an hour and, tired in the aftermath of her concentration, the din of the engine became a hum and the hum a murmur. In only a few minutes the seclusion and gently vibrating security felt like a reward for suffering an evening in Mitra's company.

She relaxed completely, listening to Graham breathing, heavily and steadily. Smiling, she closed her eyes and before the car had reached the crest of the steep hill, she too had fallen fast asleep.

* * *

Viewing the pair in the rear mirror, Sanjay saw him leaning against her and her against the rear door. They did not realise how lucky they were. Had it not been for John's clemency and Mitra's change of plan, they would have concluded their final deal in Mitra's house and be spending their last moments in the company of one of Mitra's trained goondas. Instead, they were being driven safely towards their home with the peaceful hum of a vehicle working a particular magic that had sent them into a secure, tranquil sleep.

Sanjay may have been a little hasty in his effort to provide the ultimate end but it was all he could think of at the time, his friend in Mitra's employ had dealt with more than one defaulting merchant in a similar manner. Arranged falls from windows, accidents at work were stock in trade to him and part of the employment conditions in the money lending business, this though was a more satisfactory ending. On amiable terms with nice people like those now sleeping in the back he was ready for a leap forward towards great riches with them as partners.

After frequent trips to Mitra's home to deliver his goods, this was familiar territory, he sat snug and assured against the seat-back as they quickly topped the rise. The gears were surprisingly smooth and the car powerful but then, even if the vehicle was old, Mitra would have good equipment.

He slipped from third gear into top and drove quickly up and over the steep incline watching the familiar verges in the headlights. Despite the darkness beyond their glow, he knew every rock and turn on the winding road. The Morris was not at all like the minibus; it climbed the crest smoothly, swept rapidly over and straight and down the steep descent.

He flicked on the main beams and increased the draught from the blower thinking how much better this was than a motorcycle, and it suddenly occurred to him that, as a partner, he might even be able to afford a car of his own as he slipped the vehicle back into third again.

The racing engine protested at the sudden change of gear without a change of pace, and whined. He sensed he was travelling a little too fast and lifted his foot from the accelerator relying on the constraint of the gears to slow them. The whine increased with the steepness of the slope and the vehicle still gathered pace. He saw the hairpin, it was OK he could make the turn comfortably, just apply the footbrake and well before reaching it he pressed – nothing happened! He pressed harder, still nothing, he pumped the pedal vigorously and watched the edge of the cliff approach rapidly, too rapidly. Pressing his foot fully down and simultaneously grabbing the handbrake he yanked it upwards with all his strength, forcing the footbrake to the floor in desperation and a futile attempt to stop.

Desperate and in total panic he tugged the handbrake double handed and felt it bite – he was too late. He felt the wheels begin to grip as the brake feebly took hold, but the velocity of the vehicle was too much to hold. He locked the brake and grabbed the wheel in a final desperate effort to veer away from the edge, unsure if it was too late.

With the unstoppable vehicle approaching the thousand feet drop and the sleepers unaware in the rear, he snatched frantically at the door handle in a despairing attempt to wrench it open and free himself from the speeding car, it would not budge. The door release, where, where is it? He searched frantically, snatching at knobs and levers, searching the door, working the handle . . . Where was it? He didn't tell me, he didn't say, he'd done it . . . he'd leaned inside, he'd locked it – deliberately but where, where, WHERE?

It was too late; he felt a sudden release of traction and in his dying moments he knew who, and understood why, as the car leapt over the edge in a death plunge.

His loud, wailing cry woke up the passengers in the rear to face their last moments of terror.

'Baaastaaaards . . .' he screamed as the Morris turned in mid air on its way to the rocks and pretty silver streams below.

THIRTY-SEVEN

John, content to witness the charade played during the evening as the plan, not fully known to him, but initiated between Mitra's goondas, took shape. There had been no need to watch Sanjay to ensure his sobriety, having been offered only water.

Since their departure, John sat with Mitra, who seemed, as usual, able to smell something unpleasant. His man poured brandy and Mitra glanced at his Rolex, his finger tapped the chair but stopped when his man came in the room, having tracked the car at a distance. He whispered in his ear and John saw Mitra's face crack into a series of lines, not exactly a smile but close to. He cast John a look of contented confirmation and John assumed that all the obstacles to impair their future had been removed.

Grateful though he was, it also confirmed his belief, at this moment of release, that Mitra was a savage bastard – but he was a winner, a winner with money who would deliver his prospects.

The subtle plan change had eliminated leakage and what had happened was an accident with little evidence remaining for investigators. The catastrophe was all the more acceptable in that Sanjay was known for poor driving skills.

'Will you join me my friend,' asked Mitra beckoning to his man, 'another?'

'Should I indulge?' said John raising a bushy brow.

'I assure you that our troubles are over.'

He took the offered glass and sipped silently, immersed in the immediate release of tension.

John was the first to speak.

'So,' he said slowly, 'that concludes most of our business.'

'All, I believe, my friend.'

'Not quite Dhankar,' he said, placing the glass on the side table.

Mitra looked puzzled. 'Is there something more? We are surely in a position to forge ahead, as we say.'

'Possibly,' John said through tight lips, 'but as this is the day of reckoning, we should clear up one final point and clear the decks –

as we say. Enlighten me Dhankar, our friend was an entrepreneur but no businessman – but you knew that.'

'Your man Sanjay, he was indeed. He supplied, I paid – and you knew that!'

'You can hardly call him *my* man, especially since he disposed of articles worth more than fifty thousand rupees from our workshops and set up arrangements in your hotels. I am surprised you, during our heart to heart, didn't bring it to my attention. After your protest the other day I am surprised to find that he uses your hotels to deal in the same commodities.'

Mitra was upright in his chair in a flash, 'Commodities? My hotels? How dare you implicate my hotels in that vile business,' he shrieked. 'I have already told you I will have no truck with that contemptible trade nor have myself or my hotels tainted with an immoral business. I used your boys in service positions, not in that repulsive trade. They are safer working with me than staying with you, it would appear!'

The fierce response stunned John, he couldn't speak for surprise and when he found his voice his reply was weak, 'But Sanjay did his business with you, are you saying he lied?'

'Are you saying he told the truth? If disbelief and deception is going to be part of our relationship,' said Mitra with his face set rigid in anger, 'then we may as well conclude our partnership now and this whole exercise has been a dangerous waste of time. You had better look in another direction, and when you find the truth, you can apologise!'

John, stunned by the rebuff and locked in embarrassment, did not move, but and from the corner of his eye he saw Mitra's man take a pace forward and stand on the balls of his feet.

John retreated, 'Are you saying they were not your hotels?' he said half-disbelieving.

'Do you take me for a fool? As a prospective ML I accept your way of life but as a bachelor – and inclined in no other direction, I will not allow my hotels to be used for that purpose.'

John put his hand to his open mouth and chewed the edge of his finger; he shook his head in disbelief. 'I can only apologise Dhankar, I am sincerely sorry. I remember how vehemently you reacted before but Sanjay told me he relied on hotels for his business and with your connection . . . I am so sorry.'

'I accept your apology for an understandable mistake but I am not the only hotelier in the area.' He acquiesced. 'Now, tell me my friend, how did you find out about the trinkets? You have never been in my establishments.'

'Our visitors saw a chess set, unique to us, in your hotel shop, then – and this struck me as amusing – a piece unique to Anil was displayed in Joshi's office! Can you imagine Sanjay's face if confronted in a police station with a piece he stole from his own workshop?'

'What do you mean, what has Sanjay to do with the chief of police?'

'Didn't I tell you? He and his associates are being investigated by Joshi.'

'Indeed,' he said, 'then it is fortuitous for us both that he is not available, and I thank God Shiva that my hotels are *not* the only ones in Tamil Nadu.'

* * *

At 8 a.m. the following morning John left for his drive back to the Lake. He drove very slowly through the gates and, a hundred yards on, before reaching the steep rise, he pulled hard at the front brake and pressed the foot brake, repeating the process three times before reaching the hairpin and drive cheerfully, and securely, downhill.

On reaching an area of newly laid chips on the partly smoothed out approach to the bungalow, he slowed the Enfield to a crawl and, passed through the centre of a group of boys working.

With hardly a glance at Kumar, Vijay or the new labourers, he drove on blithely as pieces smacked the mudguards. 'Bloody dangerous those bits flying about,' he muttered.

THIRTY-EIGHT

'Inspector Joshi sends his condolences sir, he will call on you later.'

'Thank you Sergeant Birkram, I didn't realise he was back.'

'Did the Mareth Area officer give you details this morning when he called sir?'

'No sergeant, only that there was an accident and all the three were killed. Is there any more information?'

'They were travelling too fast sir, hardly any skid at all, who was driving?'

'Mr Parmar.'

'Mareth said the car was smashed and scattered, no possibility of finding the cause. As I said sir, they believe it was a speed accident. It's a sad business.'

'Thank you Sergeant,' said John briefly to avoid conversation. 'Namaste.'

'Namaste.'

Aware that his company was superfluous the sergeant diplomatically left, leaving John in his chair, a look of misery on his countenance but with muted joy in his heart.

There would be no repercussions, a serious, but simple accident with only one witness on a bicycle confirming the sight of a fast, uncontrolled vehicle late at night.

Mareth Police had arrived at eight thirty that morning. 'Yes, he had been with them all evening, why? Yes, all three left before him, yes, he had driven himself home on the Enfield this morning, no, he did not notice his unused bed. No, Sanjay had not been drinking! For goodness sake why all these questions?'

Then they told him.

Gloomy and in apparent sorrow, he moped about the bungalow in front of Chef and ate lunch alone. Knowing the signs, Chef gave him a wide berth.

It had been a good day for him, for the first time in weeks he experienced the sensation of complete release from worries, on the patio listening to the silence, he imagined the period of stability and advancement that lay ahead. No more was he besieged, no more would he be ambushed by avaricious bastards, he was free to concentrate on developing the business alongside his friend, Dhankar Mitra. No more would he be burdened with Sanjay's deviations or have to cover his digressions, no more would he be at the mercy of a blackmailing accountant and his manipulative girlfriend who had robbed him of ten thousand pounds of his inheritance and retarded progress that would have benefited him.

He was free of restraints, henceforth it would be plain sailing and he, ironically, would become the owner of a flat and the proceeds from the bank account of his only kin.

Sanjay's building skills would be missed of course but no one is indispensable – even bloody Kumar, who had done a disappearing act again. Never mind, he could let the dust settle and then think about sorting everything out, ready for a new start.

* * *

The only occupant in the police car appeared to be the sergeant when Kumar saw it; he heard the horn warning the youngsters; had the half-expected event occurred?

'Look after things Kenneth,' he said and ran like the wind towards the bungalow, only to reach his hiding place midway through their conversation, '. . . travelling too fast sir, hardly any skid at all, who was driving?'

'Mr Parmar.'

'Mareth said the car was smashed and scattered . . .'

'Thank you Sergeant,' he heard, 'Namaste.'

He heard the police car start and leave while he sat in concealment below the veranda. Was this his moment, had he heard enough? He leaned back contemplating; timing was important, should he gather more evidence or strike now?

While he was deciding he heard the hum of another engine, two cars in one morning; he sensed more enlightenment coming his way.

'Over here Rashid,' he heard, and gained the impression that John was drawing the messenger away from the kitchen and towards his hiding place.

'What happened?'

In a low, secret voice he heard, 'Master has been seen by Mareth Police, he wishes me to tell you that he could not help and that he knew no reason for the unhappy accident. He indicated there could have been some recklessness on the part of the driver resulting in the three unfortunate deaths. The officers spent less than an hour and left, satisfied.'

'Fine Rashid. Thank you, Namaste.'

Kumar heard the slap of sandals as John followed the messenger back to the steps. He waited a few minutes until the car disappeared, before stealing back toward the pathway, wearing a broad grin when he emerged from the brush.

Instead of turning towards the boys, he retraced his steps to the bungalow using the main route, satisfied that he had the final piece of the puzzle.

'Now,' he said, 'it's my turn!'

* * *

John retreated to his chair, happy that he had established parity with Mitra; a bond of secrecy inextricably linked them with interdependence. Without his conspiratorial adviser Mitra was weaker, while John was, at last, in total control of his own affairs.

Spreading his arms wide and cheered into whistling a tuneless song, he leaned on the veranda rail looking out over the parched earth at the shimmering heat haze. He saw little of it, he visualised the new complex instead, spread out to the lake's edge, brimming with people and him brimming with wealth. He stood there a while and then turned to walk down the steps out of the shade into the burning sunshine.

'Symbolic that', he thought, 'out of the shadows.' He stopped whistling as his face broke into a wide self-congratulatory grin. 'Fireproof!' he said aloud, 'at last, fireproof!'

'What does that mean Mr John?'

He whirled around at the sound, 'Kumar – you bloody fool, what the hell are you doing creeping about? I told you about that the other day, *don't creep about!*'

'What does fireproof mean Mr John?' he asked ignoring the reprimand.

'It means don't sneak up on me.'

'I am not thinking so Mr John.'

'It's just an English expression – you wouldn't understand . . . Wait a minute! How long have you been speaking English?'

'I have had learning for two years, as you hear my English ver' good?' he paused. 'What is fireproof? Is it simile or cliché?'

'You kept that bloody quiet – where did you learn English? Why didn't you tell me?'

'I am tell you now Mr John, but you tell me nothing. What is fireproof?'

'It means safe, Kumar.'

'Ah,' he said appearing to understand, 'you now are safe Mr John?'

'I think so Kumar, things are looking better,' he said continuing in English. 'Now then, rustle up some lunch. If there is one thing to put a man right it's a good lunch.'

'I have learn it is a good English breakfast that put a man right. I have learn much lately Mr John.'

'Have you now? Like what?'

'Much, Mr John – I get you good lunch Mr John, like English breakfast.'

Kumar walked towards the kitchen leaving John mystified, watching his retreat. He moved back into the shade and threw himself into his chair. There was something about Kumar's self-assurance he didn't like, something reminiscent of Sanjay on one of his good days, cocky, that's the word!

Fifteen minutes later, returning from the kitchen, Kumar stepped up to the table and placed the tray before him. John looked at it and reached for the knife and fork. 'Look at that,' he enthused, 'now that's what we call "brunch" Kumar, scrambled eggs on toast, bacon, tomatoes, bread with butter – brunch.'

Kumar stood over him for a moment, facing, observing and silent.

John looked up; Kumar's eyes seemed to follow every movement, as though he was about to ask a question. John felt examined in the uncomfortable silence.

'Look son, don't ruin my meal staring at me like that, smile, or bugger off unless you have something to say!'

Aware of John's discomfort Kumar persisted in his tease. He pulled out a chair and sat opposite.

'Why are you safe Mr John?' he said with childish innocence.

John looked uneasy, 'I told you, it's an expression.'

Kumar placed his elbows on the table and looked directly at him as if prepared to wait. His attitude was confident and probing. 'An expression?' he said. 'Of what Mr John?'

'Relief.'

'From what, Mr John?'

'Kumar, don't be so bloody inquisitive – you are giving me indigestion. Are you worried about something?'

'No, Mr John,' he said, continuing to stare, the corners of his mouth showing an outline of a smile, and with continued self-assurance he said, 'Are *you* worried about something Mr John? One must not keep worries a secret Mr John. Flee your worries Mr John, is that what Englishmen say?'

'You mean escape from your worries Kumar.'

'Yes, like boys Mr John, he escape too. Sanjay not tells you, not tells police so you not knows, it make big worry.'

John stopped eating and looked up from his plate into a broadening smile, raised brows and eyes that he knew so well. In them, he saw triumph – Kumar had something up his bloody dhoti.

'Know,' John corrected, diverting and hoping to avoid a follow on.

'Yes Mr John, my English not yet good. Know – I know, you know, he and she *knows*, everybody knows!' He waited a moment, his confidence mocking the pseudo simplicity he cunningly conveyed. 'That is conjugation, Mr John — everybody knows!'

He said it with such an edge that John slapped down his knife and fork beside the plate. He placed his hands on the edge of the table, aware now that Kumar's was a calculated performance; he had something to say. Somewhere, there was a sting.

'And what exactly is it that you *knows* Kumar?' he said with a touch of ridicule.

'Nothing Mr John, perhaps Sanjay know – knows' he corrected himself. 'Where is he – by the way – that is what the English say isn't it Mr John, "by the way"? He is not in room.'

The fake surprise together with the suggestion of victory beneath the smile, told John he knew. How, he had no idea, but there was no doubt that Kumar had stumbled on something. He saw it; Kumar was teasing.

'Alright Kumar, I am upset, Sanjay was killed in a terrible accident last night.'

'Yes', said Kumar without a change of expression, 'I know – yesterday.'

'Yesterday? But the accident didn't happen until midnight and . . .?'

'I know that too Mr John! And how is your brother and lady Nadeen – by the way?'

John felt paralysed, his heart stopped and started pumping and racing, pulsating and paining his chest, his breathing increased to a pant, he gasped, bringing a flush to his face at the fear of discovery! Faint and about to buckle, he knew he'd been caught, and sat with eyes closed, shaking from head to foot; his stomach aching, as though it had taken a heavy beating. He felt sick and pushed the food away.

He knows! After all my caution, the little bastard knows! He has known all along, he has been watching and waiting, what a bastard, Sanjay was right!

In whispered abdication, he said, 'What is it you think you know Kumar?'

'I know all Mr John . . .'

With his mind in a whirl and his thoughts vague, panicky and disordered, tripping over each other, he had no idea what to do. What could he do . . .? God in heaven, Mitra! What will he say? He held his head in his hands and exhaled slowly in final defeat. 'Jesus,' he breathed and bit his lip. What next he wondered, what bloody next?

Hoping to salvage something, he tried to cover. 'It was an accident Kumar, the car was old, the brakes failed and . . .' He stopped speaking suddenly, seeing Kumar smile, his mixture of disbelief and jubilation accompanied by a rocking head. John had said the wrong thing!

'How you know? Police not knows!'

He tried to cover his tracks, 'I was guessing Kumar, I mean it was a steep hill and . . . and, well there can be only one explana . . .' His words faded. 'Look son, it could be to your advantage,' he said, 'there's no reason for anything to change. Sanjay has been a barrier to our relationship; you know that. We can start over again, the accident could be a blessing in disguise . . .'

'Accident, Mr John? Aahh!' he said in a long drawn out wail, 'It was accident?' He shook his head and frowned, stopping John in his tracks again. 'I think not so.'

'I do not think so, Kumar,' corrected John.

'You think not so either Mr John? I know not so.'

Kumar's positive offence was too strong for John and, forced to acquiesce, he nodded in response, 'I see! What is it you want Kumar?' he said in capitulation.

'What is the word in English Mr John? I want anvancemet?'

'You mean advancement.'

'Yes Mr John, I will go to Maroutai College to learn laws and numbers. I will manage camp and join committee with Mr Mitra and . . .'

'Camp manager, committee, lawyer, huh,' he laughed, 'that's a bit ambitious. What the hell makes you think you could handle that Kumar? You have no experience and . . .!'

He never finished the sentence, Kumar leaned across the table, pinned him with a steely, inflexible stare and reached underneath to place a hand firmly on John's knee saying, patronisingly, 'Look – my son, I have told only two friends – two ver' good friends!'

THIRTY-NINE

'Let me call Kumar, Shankar. I've had to make some emergency changes; he needs to know what's going on now he has more responsibility.'

Joshi saw him make for Kumar's room while he took a seat on the patio and heard him ask if Kumar could spare a minute, Kumar appeared smartly dressed in a white, short sleeved shirt and blue jeans. He raised his hands, 'Namaste Inspector Joshi, I hope you are well.'

Taken aback by the transformation, Joshi perceived a sudden commanding maturity. He placed himself opposite the two men and started to speak, oddly addressing the younger man. The purpose of his visit; to clarify the events leading up to the death of Parmar based on the Mareth police report.

Joshi did not dwell on it, Prichard had been through enough; he just wanted to tell him the facts about Parmar and his friends of which they seemed to know so little.

Parmar, Joshi said, was weak and gullible, he had been tempted by friends to supply inmates for work in hotels on leaving Orphindi, he took a commission. Covert arrangements were made and co-ordinated between certain hotel owners around the district to use the boys for immoral purposes. Sanjay had primed some school leavers and, tempted by high earnings, some boys succumbed, 'He was a pimp, to put it bluntly, exploiting Orphindi children ...'

He stopped to look at the disbelief on the open mouths of the faces opposite, 'Clearly you were unaware,' he said,

'Totally, Shankar.'

'He picked the wrong one in Samuel, who was easily led but quite close to Grewall. Grewall was suspicious and argued but without evidence, he had no case and having been dismissed in adverse circumstances he could do nothing – I must speak to you about that John, by the way. Eventually he was able to pass some evidence to me. He then, foolishly, took Samuel to, as he said, rescue him.

We will never know if Parmar was coerced, volunteered or bullied into the business. He was a weak man and a superficial thinker who became involved in a depraved business.'

'Never, Shankar,' protested John shaking his head, 'I can't believe that.'

Joshi gave a shallow smile, 'Evidence John. We interviewed Grewall; he was suspicious of Sanjay's behaviour when Samuel became his target, afterwards Kenneth and Anil provided confirmation too, they knew but were under an obligation.'

Kumar and John looked at each other in astonishment.

'Yes,' said Joshi, 'I thought you would be surprised. We have now made a number of arrests,' he said reading from his notes without noticing John had turned quite pale. 'We originally thought his accomplice was a man named Jaitley . . .'

He saw John look up sharply, 'Yes John?'

'Er . . . nothing, it's just that . . . it's terrible . . . Shankar . . .' his voice tailed off, his face the colour of putty.

'. . . It turns out not to be so, he was a participant, a client . . . Are you sure you are alright John?'

'It's the shame, inspector,' said Kumar stepping in, 'Mr John feels ver' bad.'

'I understand Kumar, but you, John, do not escape entirely,' he laughed. 'Had you given Grewall a proper hearing instead of depending entirely on Parmar we might have found out earlier. Grewall is not a thief nor a drunkard, he undermined Parmar and Parmar became frightened when Samuel pinpointed him. Parmar crudely, almost naively, arranged Grewall's departure and, in a way, you seconded that.'

'I trusted him implicitly, Shankar, that's why,' he muttered.

'You did indeed John, so in future we need closer co-operation, a monitoring system perhaps, a sort of after sales service. One of my officers will act as liaison officer with the committee and your man, whoever is selected will join him . . .'

'It will be me, Inspector,' said Kumar swiftly.

'Fine, Kumar. It's a pity that our prospective ML Dhankar Mitra was forced to drop out of the race, he could have been a big help.'

John said nothing.

'In another sense – probably inno-cence,' Joshi chuckled at his own pun, 'you helped by sending Grewall off that particular day. He witnessed a transaction with a former Orphindi inmate that provided a vital piece in our puzzle.'

'Will Grewall come back inspector?' said Kumar. 'John will retire and I will be studying part time in Maroutai and we need him, don't we John?'

'Um, yes Kumar,' he replied to a winning smile.

Kumar went on, 'Sunil and Vijay will train boys at Periyar . . . and we are forming a company called, Graham Prichard Fashions to enter the fashion industry. Sunil and Vijay are running Periyar fashions temporarily to add fashion income to . . .

'Periyar Fashions?' interrupted Joshi.

'Yes . . ..'

'Then you may be there for life.'

'Why Shankar?'

'Didn't I say? Mahmood was arrested, he was the instigator and it was his hotels that were being used.'

'Mahmood, arrested? Good God, it's as well that we are running his factory then inspector.'

'It is indeed John. It's an ill wind . . .'

He stood, 'I think that concludes everything,' he said and offered his hand. 'Thank you John,' he said, and turned to Kumar. 'I am sure we will work well together.'

'Thank you inspector, it will be a pleasure to have you and Mrs Jha to dinner . . . yes Mr John?'

'Yes, we would enjoy that,' said John surprised, 'indeed we would.'

'Thank you and goodbye John – you seem to have a very able deputy there.'

'Yes . . .' he grumbled with a sickly smile, 'He never lets me forget it.'

Joshi laughed at his joke.

FORTY

One year later

Kumar, Sunil and Vijay accepted the luxury, attention and service showered on them at the prestigious Cochin hotel in their new status as company directors. Leaving the hotel early each morning they returned in the evening to meet John, Shankar and Mrs Joshi who spent their time visiting the sights or relaxing in the luxury of the surroundings and pool.

Before dinner of the third day, the three sought John out and found him alone, lounging in the cool of the conservatory. Vijay and Sunil sat beside him, Kumar paced the floor in front of them.

'What's up?' asked John, 'you been up to something?'

Kumar stopped pacing and stood in front of him. 'Finalising arrangements to expand the Mitraphindi Hotel Group on the Kovalum coast John, in Southern India. It's a very popular resort.'

'Oh yes,' he said, peeved, 'and when was that decided?'

'It's no worry of yours.'

'Well you might have told me!'

'I'm telling you now,' he said allowing no room for manoeuvre.

'Don't treat me like an also ran, you forget you were garbage before I picked you up.'

Kumar froze and looked at him disdainfully. 'And if I had allowed you to continue on your course that's what I would be now, we can't be grateful forever!' he snapped, daring John to respond.

'Now, since Dhankar's paralysing stroke we negotiate, we expand, we run the company and you enjoy the benefits. With that in mind, I have arranged an interview with the press – you are to retire . . . officially.'

He paused a moment to let the realism sink in, John said nothing, he sat obediently – with teeth gritted.

'You will tell the press of our expansion plans and here,' he said handing him a crib sheet, 'is a run down on the content.'

Without looking at the paper John said, 'Who the frigging hell do you think you are Kumar?'

Kumar bent down, his face a foot away and waited, watching the tension build in John's eyes. After a lengthy silence he said slowly, 'I know exactly who I am and I could expose you as a cynical spider enticing ill informed flies like me into your rotten web. Thanks to your guest Samantha, I was lucky; I discovered what I am and not what you tried to make me. So, understand this, you are retiring to rooms in Dhankar's home where you will help look after him, a place where you will do no harm, live in luxury and we can keep an eye on you while we use the place as the head office. You may invite Colin if you wish, we bought his agency and it will be relocated to London. Sunil and I will leave for the UK to set up a new Mitraphindi Office.'

'He said nothing to me.'

'You are not affected. Now, since Dhankar is incurable we have disposed of his Goondas and made his business a user friendly finance company, so, when you speak to the press you will mention that, and that Vijay is off to Delhi to purchase new transport for our guests who are expected to number over two hundred this year and double that next.'

'And who is running the shop while all this activity is going on?' snapped John, annoyed and baffled.

'Ashook of course, we all have mobiles and we are in touch with each other.'

John's mouth dropped open, his shoulders slumped, he whispered into his chest, 'You are a right bastard Kumar, you set this all up behind my back.'

He stopped and looked slowly in turn at the three stern faces around him. 'You are all bastards, I'm not going anywhere!' he said stubbornly.

Kumar bent close again and looked closely into John's eyes. John might sound defiant but the fire had gone, his face was pinched and pale in defeat. He stared back and whispering vehemently, 'You underhand, cunning bastard, you can't get away with this, I was the frigging founder, it's my life and you won't take it away.'

'You will do exactly as we say John and so long as you do, you are free to enjoy what you have always wanted, the cool hills and the use of a Mercedes. Now, your audience is waiting.'

Unbalanced by Kumar's fearless certainty John looked shattered, he scrutinised the three faces around him with a look of bewilderment and closed his eyes. His lips fastened in utter dismay, he had nothing to say except to repeat, 'You cunning bastard!'

Kumar with a look of satisfaction in his eyes saw the look of guilty comprehension in John's. He put his mouth close to his ear.

'I had a good teacher,' he whispered, 'and a better reason. Remember Kenneth?' he asked, looking into John's distraught face.

Seeing the recognition he said, 'I thought you would – and that makes *me* fireproof!'